Dear Reader,

I am a hopeless romantic who believes that any man—heartbreaker, womanizer or die-hard philanderer—can be tamed. I knew the moment Redford St. James appeared in my book *What He Wants for Christmas*, as Sloan Outlaw's best friend, that Redford was my man.

There was no doubt in my mind that Redford would be a challenge, since I was well aware of the reason he was guarded. But I believed there was a woman out there who could heal his broken heart. A woman who could tame the heartbreaker. A woman by the name of Carmen Golan, who decided Redford was her soulmate. He was the man she intended to marry one day. Redford's response to that was "When hell freezes over."

The question is, will she or won't he?

I am honored to be part of Harlequin's 75th Anniversary celebration, and I hope you enjoy Redford and Carmen's story as much as I enjoyed writing it. Happy anniversary, Harlequin, and may you have seventy-five more years of providing love stories to the romantics out there, those of us who believe in happy-ever-after.

Brenda Jackson

Brenda Jackson is a *New York Times* bestselling author of more than one hundred romance titles. Brenda lives in Jacksonville, Florida, and divides her time between family, writing and traveling. Email Brenda at authorbrendajackson@gmail.com or visit her on her website at brendajackson.net.

Synithia Williams has loved romance novels since reading her first one at the age of thirteen. It was only natural that she would one day write her own romance. When she isn't writing, Synithia works on water quality issues in the Midlands of South Carolina while taking care of her supportive husband and two sons. You can learn more about Synithia by visiting her website, synithiawilliams.com.

TAMING A HEARTBREAKER

NEW YORK TIMES BESTSELLING AUTHOR
BRENDA JACKSON

FREE STORY BY
SYNITHIA WILLIAMS

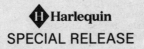

SPECIAL RELEASE

Recycling programs
for this product may
not exist in your area.

H Harlequin®
SPECIAL RELEASE

ISBN-13: 978-1-335-00730-8

Taming a Heartbreaker
First published in 2024. This edition published in 2024.
Copyright © 2024 by Brenda Streater Jackson

A Little Bit of Love
First published in 2024. This edition published in 2024.
Copyright © 2024 by Synithia R. Williams

Harlequin Enterprises ULC
22 Adelaide St. West, 41st Floor
Toronto, Ontario M5H 4E3, Canada
www.Harlequin.com

Printed in U.S.A.

CONTENTS

TAMING A HEARTBREAKER   7
Brenda Jackson

A LITTLE BIT OF LOVE   213
Synithia Williams

TAMING A HEARTBREAKER

Brenda Jackson

Prologue

Sloan and Leslie Outlaw's wedding...

"Sloan definitely likes kissing you, girlfriend."

Leslie Outlaw couldn't help but smile at her best friend's whispered words. "And I love kissing him."

She'd married the man she loved, and she'd had her best friend Carmen Golan at her side. Leslie followed her friend's gaze now and saw just where it had landed—right on Redford St. James, who was being corralled by the photographer as Sloan took pictures with his best man and groomsmen.

Unease stirred Leslie's insides at her friend's obvious interest.

Leslie had known Redford for as long as she'd known Sloan, since she'd met both guys the same day on the university's campus over ten years ago. Redford had been known then as a heartbreaker. According to Sloan, Redford hadn't changed. If anything, he'd gotten worse.

"Carmen, I need to warn you about Redford," Leslie

said, hoping it wasn't too late. She'd noted last night at the rehearsal how taken her best friend had been with Redford. She'd hoped she was mistaken.

"I know all about him, Leslie, so you don't need to warn me. However, you might want to put a bug in Sloan's ear to warn Redford about me."

Leslie lifted a brow. "Why?"

A wide smile covered Carmen's face. "Because Redford St. James is the man I intend to marry. Your hubby is on his way over here. I will see you at the reception."

Leslie watched Carmen walk toward Redford. Marry? Redford? She had a feeling her best friend was biting off more than she could chew. Redford was not the marrying kind. He'd made that clear when he'd said no woman would ever tame him.

Chapter One

Two years later...

Redford St. James froze, with his wineglass midway to his lips, when he saw the woman walk into the wedding reception for Jaxon and Nadia Ravnell. Frowning, he immediately turned to the man by his side, Sloan Outlaw. During their college days at the University of Alaska at Anchorage, Sloan, Redford, and another close friend, Tyler Underwood, had been thick as thieves, and still were.

Redford had been known as the "king of quickies." He would make out with women any place or any time. Storage rooms, empty classrooms or closets, beneath the stairs, dressing rooms …he'd used them all. He had the uncanny ability to scope out a room and figure out just where a couple could spend time for pleasure. He still had that skill and used it every chance he got.

Although he, Sloan and Tyler now lived in different

cities in Alaska, they still found the time to get together a couple of times a year. Doing so wasn't as easy as it used to be since both Tyler and Sloan were married with a child each. Tyler had a son and Sloan a daughter.

"Why didn't you tell me Carmen Golan was invited to this wedding?"

Sloan glanced over at Redford and rolled his eyes. "Just like you didn't tell me Leslie had been invited to Tyler and Keosha's wedding three years ago?"

Redford frowned. "Don't play with me, Sloan. You should have known Leslie would be invited, since she and Keosha were friends in college. In this case, I wasn't aware Carmen knew Jaxon or Nadia."

Sloan took a sip of his wine before saying, "The Outlaws and Westmorelands consider themselves one big happy family, and that includes outside cousins, in-laws and close friends. Since Carmen is Leslie's best friend, of course she would know them." Sloan then studied his friend closely. "Why does Carmen being here bother you, Redford? If I recall, when I put that bug in your ear after my wedding, that she'd said she intended to one day become your wife, you laughed it off. Has that changed?"

"Of course, that hasn't changed."

"You're sure?" Sloan asked. "It seems to me that over the past two years, whenever the two of you cross paths, you try like hell to avoid her. Most recently, at Cassidy's christening a few months ago." Cassidy was Sloan and Leslie's daughter. Redford was one of her godfathers, and Carmen was her godmother.

"No woman can change my ways. I don't ever in-tend to marry. Who does she think she is, anyway? She doesn't even know me like that. If she did, then she would know my only interest in her at your wedding was getting her to the nearest empty coat closet. The nerve of her, thinking she can change me."

"And since you know she can't change you, why worry about it?"

"I'm not worrying."

"If you say so," Sloan countered.

Redford's frown deepened. "I do say so. You of all people should know that I'll never fall in love again."

Before Sloan could respond, his sister Charm walked up and said the photographer wanted to take a photo of Jaxon with his Outlaw cousins.

When Sloan walked off, leaving Redford alone, he took a sip of his wine as he looked across the room at Carmen again. Sloan's words had hit a nerve. He *wasn't* worried. Then why had he been avoiding her for the past two years? Doing so hadn't been easy since he was one of Sloan's best friends and she was Leslie's, and both were godparents to Cassidy. Whenever they were in the same space, he made it a point to not be in her presence for long.

He could clearly recall the day he'd first seen Carmen at Sloan and Leslie's wedding rehearsal two years ago. He would admit that he'd been intensely attracted to her from the first. It was a deep-in-the-gut awareness. Something he had never experienced before. He hadn't wasted any time adding her to his "must do" list. He'd even flirted shamelessly after they'd been introduced, with every intention of making out with her before the weekend ended.

Then he'd gotten wind of her bold claim that he was the man she intended to marry. Like hell! That had wiped out all his plans. He was unapologetically a womanizer, and no woman alive would change that.

Carmen wasn't the first woman to try, nor would she be the first to fail. Granted she was beautiful. Hell, he'd even say she was "knock-you-in-the-balls" gorgeous, but he'd dated beautiful women before. If he'd seen one, he'd seen them all, and in the bedroom they were all the same.

Then why was he letting Carmen Golan get to him? Why would heat flood his insides whenever he saw her, making him aware of every single thing about her? Why was there this strong kinetic pull between them? It was sexual chemistry so powerful that, at times, it took his breath away.

Over the years, he'd tried convincing himself his lust for her would fade. So far it hadn't. And rather recently, whenever he saw her, it had gotten so bad he had to fight like hell to retain his common sense.

Although Sloan had given him that warning two years ago, Carmen hadn't acted on anything. Was she waiting for what she thought would be the right time to catch him at a weak moment? If that was her strategy then he had news for her. It wouldn't happen. If anything, he would catch *her* unawares first, just to prove he was way out of her league…thanks to Candy Porter.

Contrary to her first name, he'd discovered there hadn't been anything sweet about Candy. At seventeen, she had taught him a hard lesson. Mainly, to never give your heart to a woman. Candy and her parents had moved to Skagway the summer before their last year of high school. By the end of the summer, she had been his steady girlfriend, the one he planned to marry after he finished college. Those plans ended the night of their high school senior prom.

Less than an hour after they'd arrived, she told him she needed to go to the ladies' room. When she hadn't returned in a timely manner, he had gotten worried since she hadn't been feeling well. He had gone looking for her, and when a couple of girls said she wasn't in the ladies' room, he and the two concerned girls had walked outside and around the building to find her, hoping she was alright.

Not only had they found her, they'd found her with the town's bad boy, Sherman Sharpe. Both of them in the backseat of Sherman's car making out like horny rabbits. The pair hadn't even had the decency to roll up the car's window so their moans, grunts and screams couldn't be heard.

Needless to say, news of Candy and Sherman's backseat romp quickly got around. By the following morning, every household in Skagway, Alaska, had heard about it. She had tried to explain, offer an excuse, but as far as he'd been concerned, there was nothing a woman could say when caught with another man between her legs.

Heartbroken and hurt, Redford hadn't wasted any time leaving Skagway for Anchorage to begin college that summer, instead of waiting for fall. That's when he vowed to never give his heart to another woman ever again.

That had been nearly nineteen years ago, and he'd kept the promise he'd made to himself. At thirty-six, he guarded his heart like it was made of solid gold and refused to let any woman get close. He kept all his hookups impersonal. One-and-done was the name of his game. No woman slept in his bed, and he never spent the entire night in theirs. He refused to wake up with any woman in his arms.

Redford knew Carmen was his total opposite. He'd heard she was one of those people who saw the bright side of everything, always positive and agreeable. On top of that, she was a hopeless romantic. A woman who truly believed in love, marriage and all that bull crap. According to Sloan, she'd honestly gotten it in her head that she and Redford were actual soulmates. Well, he had news for her, he was no woman's soulmate.

When his wineglass was empty, he snagged another from the tray of a passing waiter. When he glanced back over at Carmen, he saw she was staring at him, and dammit to hell, like a deer caught in headlights, he stared back. Why was he feeling this degree of lust that she stirred within him so effortlessly?

There wasn't a time when she didn't look stunning. Today was no exception. There was just something alluring about her. Something that made his breath wobble whenever he stared at her for too long.

He blamed it on the beauty of her cocoa-colored skin, her almond-shaped light brown eyes, the gracefulness of her high cheekbones, her tempting pair of lips, and the mass of dark brown hair that fell past her shoulders.

Every muscle in his body tightened as he continued to look at her, checking her out in full detail. His gaze scanned over her curvaceous and statuesque body. The shimmering blue dress she wore hugged her curves and complemented a gorgeous pair of legs. The bodice pushed up her breasts in a way that made his mouth water.

"Now you were saying," Sloan said, returning and immediately snagging Redford's attention.

"I was saying that maybe I should accommodate Carmen."

That sounded like a pretty damn good idea, considering the current fix his body was in.

"Meaning what?" Sloan asked.

A smile widened across Redford's lips. "Meaning, I think I will add her back to my 'must do' list. Maybe it's time she discovers I am a man who can't be tamed."

Sloan frowned. "Do I need to warn you that Carmen is Leslie's best friend?"

"No, but I would assume, given my reputation, that Leslie has warned Carmen about me. It's not my fault if she didn't take the warning. Now, if you will excuse me, I think I'll head over to the buffet table."

He then walked off. At least for now, he would take care of one appetite, and he intended to take care of the other before the night was over.

"I wish you and Redford would stop trying to out-stare each other, Carmen," Leslie Outlaw leaned over to whisper to her best friend.

Carmen Golan broke eye contact with Redford to glance at Leslie and couldn't help the smile that spread across her lips. "Hey, what can I say? He looks so darn good in a suit."

Leslie rolled her eyes. "Need I remind you that you've seen him in a suit before. Numerous times."

"Redford wore a tux at your wedding, Leslie, and he looked good then, too. Better than good. He looked scrumptious." Carmen watched him again. He definitely looked delicious now.

She knew he was in his late thirties. He often projected a keen sense of professionalism, as well as a high degree of intelligence far beyond his years. But then there were other times when it seemed the main thing on his agenda was a conquest. Namely, seducing a woman.

Carmen knew all about his reputation as a heartbreaker of the worst kind. She'd witnessed how he would check out women at various events, seeking out his next victim. He had checked her out the same way, the first time they'd met.

She'd also seen the way women checked him out, too and definitely understood why they fell for him when he was so darn handsome. His dark eyes, coffee-colored skin, chiseled and bearded chin, hawkish nose, and close-to-the-scalp haircut, were certainly a draw.

Then there was his height. Carmen was convinced he was at least six foot three with a masculine build of broad shoulders, muscular arms and a rock-hard chest. Whenever he walked, feminine eyes followed. According to Leslie, although he made Anchorage his home, his family lived in Skagway and were part of the Tlingits, the largest Native Alaskan tribe.

Since their initial meeting two years ago, he'd kept his distance and she knew the reason why. She'd deliberately let it be known that she planned to marry him one day, making sure he heard about her plans well in advance. And upon hearing them, he'd begun avoiding her.

"Granted, it's obvious there's strong sexual chemistry between you and Redford," Leslie said, interrupting Carmen's thoughts. "Sexual chemistry isn't everything. At least you've given up the notion of trying to tame him. I'm glad about that. You had me worried there for a while."

Carmen broke eye contact with Redford and looked at Leslie. "Nothing has changed, Leslie. I'm convinced that for me it was love at first sight. Redford is still the man I intend to marry."

Leslie looked surprised. "But you haven't mentioned him in months. And at Cassidy's christening you didn't appear to pay him any attention."

Carmen grinned. "I've taken the position with Redford that I refuse to be like those other women who are always fawning over him. Women he sees as nothing more than sex mates. Redford St. James has to earn his right to my bed. When he does, it will be because he's ready to accept what I have to give."

"Which is?"

"Love in its truest form."

Leslie rolled her eyes. "I've known Redford a lot longer than you have, and I know how he operates. I love him like a brother, but get real, Carmen. He has plenty of experience when it comes to seducing women. You, on the other hand, have no experience when it comes to taming a man. Zilch."

"I believe in love, Leslie, and I have more than enough to give," Carmen said softly.

"I believe you, but the person you're trying to give it to has to want it in return. I don't know Redford's story, but there is one. And it's one neither Redford, Sloan nor Tyler ever talks about. I believe it has to do with a woman who hurt him in the past, and it's a pain he hasn't gotten over."

"Then I can help him get over it," Carmen replied.

Leslie released a deep sigh. "Not sure that you can, Carmen. Redford may not ever be ready to accept love from you or any woman. You have a good heart and see the good in everyone. You give everyone the benefit of the doubt, even those who don't deserve it. I think you're making a mistake in thinking Redford will change for you."

Carmen heard what Leslie was saying and could see the worried look in her eyes. It was the same look she'd given her two years ago when Carmen had declared that one day she would marry Redford. She understood Leslie's concern, but for some reason, Carmen believed that even with Redford's reputation as a heartbreaker, he would one day see her as more than a sex mate. He would realize she was his soulmate.

"I'm thirty-two and can take care of myself, Leslie."

"When it comes to a man like Redford, I'm not sure you can, Carmen."

Carmen shrugged. "I've dated men like Redford before. Men who only want one thing from a woman. I intend to be the exception and not the norm." Determined to change the subject, she said, "I love June weddings, don't you?"

The look in Leslie's eyes let Carmen know she knew what she'd deliberately done and would go along with her. "Yes, and Denver's weather was perfect today," Leslie said.

"Nadia looked beautiful. This is the first wedding I've ever attended where the bride wore a black wedding dress."

"Same for me, and she looked simply gorgeous. It was Jaxon's mom's wedding dress, and she offered it to Nadia for her special day."

Nadia not only looked beautiful but radiant walking down that aisle on her brother-in-law Dillon Westmoreland's arm. Both the wedding and reception had been

held at Westmoreland House, the massive multipur-
pose family center that Dillon, the oldest of the Denver
Westmorelands, had built on his three-hundred-acre
property. The building could hold up to five hundred
people easily and was used for special occasions, family events and get-togethers.

Carmen glanced around the huge, beautifully decorated room and noticed the man she had been introduced
to earlier that day, Matthew Caulder. He'd discovered
just last year that he was related to the Westmoreland
triplets, Casey, Cole and Clint. It seemed the biological
father Matthew hadn't known was the triplets' uncle,
the legendary rodeo star and horse trainer, Sid Roberts.

It seemed that she and Redford weren't the only ones
exchanging intense glances today. "You've been so busy
watching me and Redford stare each other down, have
you missed how Matthew Caulder keeps staring at Iris
Michaels?" Carmen leaned in to whisper to Leslie.

Leslie followed her gaze to where Matthew stood
talking to a bunch of the Westmoreland men. Iris was
Pam Westmoreland's best friend. Pam was Nadia's sister and was married to Dillon. "No, I hadn't noticed,
but I do now. Matthew is divorced, and Iris, who owns
a PR firm in Los Angeles, is a widow. I understand her
husband was a stuntman in Hollywood and was killed
while working on a major film a number of years ago. I
hope she reciprocates Matthew's interest. She deserves
happiness."

Carmen frowned. "What about me? Don't I deserve
happiness, too?"

"Yes, but like I told you, I'm not sure you'll find it
with Redford, Carmen, and I don't want to see you get
hurt."

"And like I told you, I can take care of myself."

At that moment, the party planner announced the father-daughter dance, and Dillon stood in again for Nadia's deceased father. While all eyes were on them, Carmen glanced back over at Redford. As if he'd felt her gaze, he tilted his head to look at her, his eyes unwavering and deeply penetrating.

Like she'd told Leslie, she didn't intend to be just another notch on Redford's bedpost. Their sexual chemistry had been there from the first. It was there now, simmering between them. He couldn't avoid her forever, and no matter what he thought, she truly believed they were meant to be together. She had time, patience and a belief in what was meant to be.

She would not pursue him. When the time was right, he would pursue her. She totally understood Leslie's concern but Carmen believed people could change. Even Redford. His two best friends were married with families. She had to believe that eventually he would want the same thing for himself.

Was he starting to want it now? Was that why he'd been staring tonight after two years of ignoring her? Her heart beat wildly at the thought.

When everyone began clapping, she broke eye contact with Redford and saw that the dance between Nadia and Dillon had ended. Now the first dance between Jaxon and Nadia would start. As tempted as she was, she refused to look back at Redford, although she felt his eyes on her. The heat from his gaze stirred all parts of her.

When the dance ended, Jaxon leaned into Nadia for a kiss, which elicited claps, cheers, and whistles. As the wedding planner invited others to the dance floor and the live band began to perform, Jaxon and Nadia were still kissing.

Carmen smiled, feeling the love between the couple. She wanted the same thing for herself. A man who would love her, respect her, be by her side and share his life with her. He would have no problem kissing her in front of everyone, proclaiming she was his and his only. He would be someone who would never break her heart or trample her pride.

How could she think Redford St. James capable of giving her all those things when he was unable to keep his pants zipped? Was she wrong in thinking he could change? She wanted to believe that the same love and happiness her sister Chandra shared with her husband Rutledge, the same love Leslie shared with Sloan, and Nadia shared with Jaxon, could be hers. Even her parents, retired college professors now living in Cape Town, were still in love.

People teased her about wearing rose-colored glasses, but when you were surrounded by so much love, affection and togetherness, you couldn't help but believe in happily ever after. She was convinced that everyone had a soulmate. That special person meant for them.

Unable to fight temptation any longer, she glanced back at Redford. His eyes were still on her and that stirring returned. He smiled and her heart missed a beat.

Then her breath caught in her throat as he began walking toward her.

Chapter Two

Easy-breezy. That thought ran through Redford's mind as he moved toward Carmen. He felt her response all the way across the room. He saw it in her light brown eyes and noted it in the way she stared back at him. Granted, he doubted she would agree to a quickie in one of the closets somewhere in Westmoreland House, but as far as he was concerned, she was ripe for the picking.

She'd had two years to change her mind about that marriage foolishness. Other than acknowledging her presence whenever he saw her, he had not given her any reason to think he supported that nonsense. If the meaning behind him avoiding her for two years hadn't been clear, then that was her problem, not his.

Sloan had reminded him that Carmen was Leslie's best friend. He loved Leslie like a sister, but like he'd told Sloan, Leslie should have talked her best friend out of her foolishness long ago. According to Sloan, Leslie had tried, so as far as Redford was concerned, Carmen had been dutifully warned. There was nothing left for Leslie to do but stay out of his and Carmen's business. They were both adults and old enough to do what they wanted to do.

The people Carmen had been standing with earlier were out on the dance floor and she'd been left alone. Coming to a stop in front of her, he extended his hand. "May I have this dance, Carmen?"

He wondered if she was aware that her smile contained a spark of sexual energy. She placed her hand in his. "Yes."

The moment their hands touched that energy increased, and a ball of need burst to life inside his stomach. He wasn't surprised by the reaction, just by the magnitude of it. Blood pounded at his temples and for the life of him, he couldn't stop staring at her face... especially that smile. It was as if her beauty was hitting him up close and personal, and had him spellbound. How was that possible when he'd never let a woman get to him?

They reached the dance floor where others were moving to a slow song. Drawing her into his arms, he said, "I think us dancing together is long overdue." From the look he saw in her eyes, it was obvious she agreed. Her next words confirmed it.

"You're the one who's been avoiding me, Redford."

There was no need to deny it when she was right. "I had my reasons for putting distance between us."

She lifted a brow. "You *had* your reasons? Does that mean they aren't there anymore?"

"It means I've abolished any misgivings I had in the past." She could take that to mean he'd surrendered to her foolishness, if that's what she chose to believe. However, that's not what he'd said. What he meant was any misgivings about sharing her bed were gone.

"I'm glad you're open to change, Redford."

Open to change? Did she honestly think that one dance with him meant that? If she did then she was totally wrong. Just like he didn't expect her to change her optimistic, cheerful attitude, she shouldn't expect him to change his "bed as many women as you can" frame of mind.

"When it comes to change, Carmen, I've heard it's the one constant." No need to tell her that's why he'd changed his mind and added her back to his "must do" list. Life was too short not to do those things you enjoy. His pleasure was bedding women.

"I understand you're a college professor," he said, starting a different line of conversation.

She smiled proudly. "Yes, I am. I come from a long line of them. My grandparents on both sides, my parents and my sister. I guess you could say education is in our blood."

He also knew from Sloan that she and Leslie had met when Leslie had left the University of Alaska Anchorage to attend Howard University in Washington, DC, where the two had become roommates. Carmen was an economics professor at Georgetown University. "You like teaching?"

The way her smile brightened gave him her answer, but he wanted to hear it anyway. He liked the sound of her voice. "Yes. I love teaching. I started out being an elementary school teacher while working on my PhD. Once that was done, it took me two years before I was hired as part of Georgetown's faculty. That was four years ago. I love it there and hope to get tenured in a few years. My home is right in the neighborhood. That makes it convenient, and I don't need a car."

"Tell me about your family." He knew from Sloan that she had a sister and her parents were alive.

"My parents are retired college professors who moved to Cape Town five years ago. My sister Chandra is also a college professor. So is her husband, Rutledge. They both teach at Georgia State University in Atlanta." She paused and then added, "Then there's Elan, my twelve-year-old nephew. He's adorable."

Redford lifted a brow. "Adorable at twelve?"

She threw her head back and laughed. "I know, right? That's the age when they begin getting beside themselves. So far, Elan is still as lovable as ever. However, he has informed us he intends to break family tradition since he has no intention of being a college professor. His love of trains overrules such a notion."

Redford smiled, recalling the days when he loved trains. Like his father and grandfather, he'd wanted to become an engineer for the Skagway Railway System.

"Both my father and grandfather retired as engineers for the Alaska Railways. Dad was one of their best. Even now he occasionally works as an engineer for the train tours in Skagway. It's such a scenic route through the mountains, glaciers and waterfalls."

He watched her eyes light up. "I can't wait for Elan to meet you. He will be thrilled to know the son of a train engineer."

Redford was just about to ask her what made her think he and her nephew would ever have a reason to meet, when the dance came to an end. "Want something to drink before we dance again?"

"Yes, and will we be dancing again, Redford?"

He smiled down at her as he led her off the dance floor. "Yes."

No need to tell her he intended to keep her in his arms on the dance floor—and later tonight in his bed.

Carmen couldn't believe that instead of avoiding her like he normally did, Redford had stuck by her side the rest of the night. He was being very attentive, dancing with her for every dance, whether fast or slow. Even after the newlyweds left to start their honeymoon, the party continued well into the night.

The Westmorelands had been gracious enough to make sure all the attendees at the wedding had a place to spend the night on the grounds of Westmoreland Country. Some of the traveling family members would be guests in several individual homes, and others would be staying at Bella's Retreat.

Bella was the wife of Dillon's brother, Jason. Years ago, Bella inherited land connected to the Westmoreland property from her grandfather. When the ranch house burned down, she rebuilt it into a beautiful fifteen bedroom guest house for family, friends and associates of the Westmorelands. Over the years, as the Westmoreland family continued to grow, Jason and Bella added numerous guest cottages on the property. Carmen had been invited to stay in one of them.

"Well, it's certainly been a wonderful day," Carmen said, glancing up at Redford. "The newlyweds are on their way to their honeymoon in the Maldives."

Redford chuckled as they danced to what the DJ had announced would be the last song. "Not quite. When they left, unknown to Nadia, they headed straight to

Jaxon's ranch in Virginia to stay the night. He has a special surprise for her there."

Carmen couldn't help but smile, wondering what the surprise could be. She started to ask Redford but changed her mind. According to Leslie, the Outlaw and Westmoreland men and their friends often exchanged confidences they didn't share with anyone when asked not to. At times, not even with their wives. She figured it was no different from when women kept each other's secrets. "That's wonderful."

When the dance came to an end, Redford asked, "So how long are you staying here?"

"I fly out tomorrow evening after dinner. What about you?"

"I plan to hang around for a few days. There are several card games happening, and I plan to participate."

Carmen often heard how the Westmoreland and Outlaw men, along with their friends, enjoyed playing poker whenever they got together. "I wish you the best of luck."

"Thanks."

At the sound of a baby crying, Carmen glanced over to where Bane and Crystal Westmoreland were surrounded by six kids. Two sets of triplets. One set, around six years old, and the other set, all three in diapers, were boys they'd named Raphel, Ruark and Rance. All six of Bane and Crystal's kids had their father's hazel eyes and were adorable.

"Sounds like someone isn't happy," Redford said, removing his tie and unbuttoning the top button of his shirt but keeping his jacket on as they reached the elegant hallway that led outside. Why at that moment did he have to look so sexy?

"Yes, sounds like it," she said, trying to concentrate on what he was saying and not on how sexy he looked. "Do you like kids, Redford?"

"Yes, I like kids. However, I don't plan to ever have any of my own."

His words surprised her. "Why?" she asked like she had every right to know. In a way she did. When they married, she wanted at least four.

"Because I just don't want any."

He'd spoken with such finality that Carmen couldn't help wondering why he would feel so strongly. She knew from Leslie that he was an only child, but she hadn't heard anything about him not having a good family life to the point where he wouldn't want a family of his own one day. In fact, she could hear the love in his voice when he'd spoken of his father.

His not wanting kids would definitely be a subject they would need to address again. She suspected there was a reason he didn't want any children, just like she knew there was a reason he never wanted to share a serious relationship with a woman.

When they headed out of the building, which was decorated with greenery and lanterns, she asked, "Is there a card game tonight?"

He glanced down at her. "Yes, but it won't start until after midnight. I understand Nadia's sisters, Pam, Jillian and Paige, will be hosting a wedding after-party for the ladies and expect the men to make an appearance for at least an hour."

"Are you going to the after-party?"

"No. I've had enough partying for one day."

She nodded. "Like you, I've partied enough today, too."

"So, what are your plans for tonight?" he asked her.

"I don't have any."

He slowed his pace. "I have a suggestion."

"What?"

She wondered if this was where he would suggest that they go to her cottage or his. If that was his plan, she had news for him. It wouldn't happen. Although she would admit that just being near him had desire like she'd never felt before twisting inside her. This was all new to her, but regardless, she wouldn't lose her common sense over it.

"A wine and cheese moonlight picnic by the lake," he said.

She stared at him. Why had he suggested something so romantic? The smart response would be to decline. Now that he seemed to be showing interest in her, she should set a pace that wasn't too fast.

"Carmen?"

She was about to say she wasn't interested in such a picnic, when instead she said, "A moonlight picnic sounds wonderful." He smiled and she wished that smile didn't stir her insides the way it was.

"Good. How about we meet at the gazebo in about thirty minutes? I need to get everything."

She lifted a brow. "Get everything?"

"Yes, the food, wine and blanket."

Blanket? Right. They would need one to sit on. "Okay. I need to change out of this dress anyway."

His gaze roamed over her. "No, don't change. I like seeing you in that dress. It looks nice on you."

Why did his compliment make her heart skip a beat? "Thanks. I'll see you in half an hour."

"And I'll be waiting."

Chapter Three

Redford watched Carmen walk away while thinking he wanted to be the one to take that dress off her tonight. There was something about her that brought out the primitive male in him. It had been nearly too much for his heart to take, while they'd been dancing, to focus on her face and not her cleavage.

And whatever perfume she wore was also doing a number on him. The scent made him want to growl at the moon instead of sitting on a blanket beneath it. Why in the hell had he suggested a picnic instead of proposing they go to her cottage and have their own party?

When Carmen was no longer in sight, Redford released a deep breath, stunned by the degree of desire he felt for her. They'd danced to every single song, and he had loved it. Seeing how she'd moved her body during the fast songs, and then the way she felt in his arms during the slow ones, had fired up his libido even more. There had been something about holding her in his arms while their bodies were close that made him think of sharing even more intimacies.

He glanced at his watch again. Carmen would be back soon, and he didn't want her waiting. Leaving the area, he went back inside Westmoreland House and approached Alpha, who was married to Riley Westmoreland, and who'd been the wedding planner. She assured Redford there was more than enough food left for a picnic. After telling her he only wanted a bottle of wine and an assortment of cheeses, she left and returned within minutes with a basket for him. She'd even brought a blanket.

Redford was glad he hadn't run into Sloan or Leslie. Leslie had watched him like a hawk when he and Carmen had been on the dance floor, and he'd deliberately ignored her stare.

With the picnic basket in hand, Redford rounded a corner and saw a crowd standing around Bailey Westmoreland Rafferty. She and her husband Walker were the proud parents of a newborn son they'd named Thomas, after Bailey's father.

Before reaching the exit door, he ran into Maverick and Phire who were pushing their son, Legend, in a stroller. Following not far behind the couple were Cash and Brianna Outlaw with the newest member of their family, a son they'd named Brian.

Babies seemed to be everywhere. He recalled the look on Carmen's face when he'd stated he didn't want kids. Like he told her, he liked kids. After all, he was godfather to Sloan and Leslie's daughter, who he adored. However, that ordeal with Candy had shattered his life in so many ways. Her betrayal had cut deep, right into his heart. After that, nothing else mattered in his life other than succeeding in college and career.

It was then that he'd vowed to remain a bachelor for life and dismiss all the things that went with loving a woman. Such as marriage, children and a house with a white picket fence.

Tucking the blanket firmly under his arm while he carried the picnic basket, Redford continued walking to where he and Carmen were to meet. So far none of those he'd passed had asked about the basket and blanket. They seemed in a hurry to get to the after-party.

He rounded the corner of Westmoreland House. The surrounding area was lit by beautiful torches, but the yard was empty. He figured most people were inside attending the party. From the sound of things, it had already started. Those Westmorelands and Outlaws were definitely in a festive mood. Well, he was in one hell of a horny one.

"It's kind of late for a picnic, isn't it?"

He rolled his eyes, figuring it had been too much to hope he could avoid seeing Sloan again tonight before the midnight card game. Smiling humorlessly, he said, "It's never too late to do anything you've set your mind to doing."

Sloan frowned. "I hope you know *what* you're doing, Redford."

"I always know what I'm doing when it concerns a woman, Sloan."

Shaking his head, Sloan walked off and Redford was glad that he had. Carmen was an adult. As long as he kept things honest and didn't make promises he didn't intend to keep, there was no reason for him to feel guilty about anything.

Redford looked at his watch when he reached the gazebo, and when he glanced back up at the yard, he saw

Carmen walking toward him. Like he'd requested, she kept on that dress, although she'd replaced her stilettos with more comfortable shoes.

He was intensely aware of everything about her, especially the way she was looking at him. Suddenly, feeling somewhat weak in the knees, he propped against one of the gazebo posts. Why did seeing her do that to him?

"I hope I didn't keep you waiting, Redford," she said, cheerfully, when she came to a stop in front of him.

"No, you didn't keep me waiting," he said, fighting to regain control of his senses and his body. "Ready for our picnic?"

"Yes. Since you got the basket, I can carry the blanket," she offered.

"That will work," he said, handing the blanket to her. Their hands touched in the process and he heard her sharp intake of breath. As they walked toward Gemma Lake, he thought about what Sloan had said earlier... *"I hope you know what you're doing, Redford."*

At that moment Redford hoped like hell that he knew what he was doing as well.

As they walked the length of the yard that led to the lake, Carmen tried switching her thoughts away from the man beside her. That wasn't an easy thing to do. In fact, she doubted there was anything about Redford St. James that was easy. Except for falling in love with him. Even with his less than desirable reputation, she truly believed he was the man she'd been waiting for.

When she'd gone back to her cottage to change shoes and freshen up, she'd given herself a serious pep talk. If she could feel the strong sexual vibes between her and Redford, then she was certain he could, too.

The last thing she wanted was for him to think that was a cue for sex since it wouldn't be happening. Granted, she was curious to find out if all those wild and passionate stories she'd heard about, read about in romance novels, and even dreamed about a time or two, were anything close to the real thing. But she refused to be a notch on any man's bedpost, even the man she intended to marry one day. There was more to a relationship than the physical. If no other woman had gotten that point across to him, then she didn't mind being the first.

Deciding to kick-start conversation between them, she said, "I understand you own a number of successful resorts." According to Leslie, his business was a multibillion-dollar enterprise consisting of fishing, hunting and ski resorts spread out from the Gulf of Alaska to the Yukon.

He glanced down at her. From his expression she could tell she'd caught him during a moment of deep thought, and it took him a second to process what she'd said. "Yes, that's right. People would be surprised at the number of tourists that visit Alaska each year. And that number is increasing tremendously."

Why did the sound of his voice caress her skin? Every part of it. "I can believe it. Although I'm not a fan of cold weather, I'm glad I get to visit Alaska to see Sloan, Leslie and Cassidy. It's amazing how much land there is in Alaska. Developed and undeveloped."

"I heard your first time to Alaska was when you attended Tyler and Keosha's wedding with Leslie as her plus-one."

It happened again, his voice and her skin's reaction to it. She had controlled it while they danced together but was having a hard time doing so now. "Yes, it was. When Leslie lived in DC, her father would come spend most of the holidays with her and her aunt, so she wouldn't have to return to Alaska."

"And run the risk of her path crossing with Sloan's," he said.

Since it was a statement and not a question, she figured he knew firsthand about Sloan and Leslie's breakup in college that had sent her from the University of Alaska at Anchorage to finish college at Howard in DC. For years, Sloan hadn't known where she'd gone. It had taken ten years for their paths to cross again and for Sloan and Leslie to discover their breakup had been based on a lie, one deliberately orchestrated by her ex-roommate. Now Sloan and Leslie were back together and happily married.

"I understand that you, Sloan and Tyler were roommates in college."

"Yes, we were. Those were the good old days. Tyler and Sloan had steady girls, namely Keosha and Leslie. I was the odd man out—their fun-loving, nonserious, won't commit to any woman friend."

Was he telling her that for a reason? Had she read the signs he was putting out tonight all wrong? Although a leopard couldn't change his spots, she wanted to believe the right woman in Redford's life could make a difference, and she intended to be that woman.

"I think this is a good spot, don't you, Carmen?"

Instead of looking at him, she glanced around. The last thing she needed was to get caught up in the beauty of his dark eyes again. "Yes, it's perfect."

Carmen spread out the blanket and then eased down onto it and stared out at the beauty of the lake. Like she'd told Redford, this spot was perfect. It was far away from Westmoreland House where the noise from the after-party could not be heard, but the lights from all those torches around the property, as well as the full moon in the sky, were a shimmering glow across the waters.

Out of the corner of her eye, she watched as Redford placed aside the basket and eased down onto the blanket beside her. When she had left her cottage to meet him at the gazebo, she debated the idea of going through with sharing a moonlight picnic with him. However, in the end she had pushed her misgivings aside. What harm would being alone with him cause?

When it came to staying in control of any situation, she was an ace. No amount of desire, passion or attraction could change that. Her family often said she was the most in-control person they knew. She didn't try to control others, but when it came to herself, she had the ability to maintain a level head. Being a thirty-two-year-old virgin was proof of that.

"Anything else in the basket besides wine and cheese?" she asked him.

"You sound hungry."

"No, just curious," she said, grinning.

"Alpha prepared it for me, and I told her just cheese and wine. However, I didn't look to see what was inside." He pulled the basket toward them. "Let's take a look, shall we?"

In addition to the bottle of wine, wineglasses, a container of assorted cheeses, and the necessary eating utensils, Alpha had included slices of wedding cake. Carmen glanced over at Redford. "I guess we won't go to bed hungry tonight."

He chuckled. "No, I don't think we will."

Chapter Four

The night was perfect. While pouring their glasses of wine, Redford realized he'd never had a moonlight picnic before and he rather liked it. There was something about being alone with Carmen on this lake at night, sharing a blanket and wine, that had sexual energy hitting him low in the gut.

So far everything about it spelled seduction in big bold letters and being here with her aroused him in a way he hadn't expected. Anticipation for what he hoped would take place later had his pulse beating way too fast to be normal. On top of that, his brain was filled with salacious ideas for making love to her.

In an attempt to get his mind and body under control, he forced his thoughts from Carmen to his surroundings. Gemma Lake, which sat smack in the middle of Westmoreland Country, was beautiful and even more so at night. The lighted, colorful water fountains in the middle of the lake were a spectacular sight.

There was a full moon in the sky and the stars dotted around it like a majestic court. The night's temperature was perfect, and as far as he was concerned, so was the woman with him. He rarely thought of any woman as perfect. What he wanted from all women was the same. There could never be any exceptions.

He doubted she'd known what he'd been thinking when she'd mentioned them not going to bed hungry tonight. There was a totally different type of hunger invading his body. One that had nothing to do with food.

"I thought I was full after eating that dinner at the reception, but there's nothing like wine and cheese. And I can't wait to get into the cake since I passed on it earlier," she said.

He took a sip of his wine. "Why did you pass on it?"

"I was full from eating and didn't have room for dessert. Now I do."

He grinned. "I had room for dessert then and I do so again now. I love cake."

She nodded. "What's your favorite?"

Redford chuckled. "Cake."

She threw her head back and laughed. He liked the sound of it.

He chuckled too. "I've never encountered a cake I didn't like. I inherited a love for cooking from my mom. But not for baking. Mom made the best cakes. For a while she ran a bakery out of our home since Dad preferred she didn't work outside the home until I was in junior high school."

Redford wondered why he'd told her that. Usually, he didn't share any personal information about himself or his family with any woman. His only excuse for doing so now was that he was trying to make sure Carmen felt relaxed with him.

"I rarely cook. Leslie says I need to buy stock in every fast-food place in the city. However, I do enjoy baking cakes and even took a cake-baking class in college. My specialty is carrot cake."

"That's one my mom never made."

"Well, one day I intend to bake a carrot cake just for you."

He didn't say anything. Instead, he took another sip of his wine. This was the second time tonight that she'd hinted at them seeing each other again. Of course, that wouldn't be happening unless their paths crossed because of their friendships with Sloan and Leslie.

Wanting to change the subject, he asked, "Have you lived in DC long?"

"Close to fifteen years now. I moved there for college from Atlanta."

"That's where you're from? Atlanta?"

"Yes, born and raised. My father attended Morehouse and my mom attended Spelman College. They liked Atlanta and thought it would be a great place to live, marry and raise a family."

Redford took another sip of his wine and began eating some of the various cheeses. He was easing Carmen into a steady stream of conversation to get her relaxed. Experience had shown him that a relaxed woman, especially one who was trying to fight an intense attraction, was more open to seduction. He had it down to an art form. His approach was so smooth, usually the woman didn't know what was happening until she was captivated to the point of no return.

"Do you ever star watch?" he asked her, easing to lie flat on his back on the blanket to stare up into the sky.

His question made her switch her gaze from the lake to the sky. "All the time. I've got a good view from my bedroom window. I enjoy ending my days by lying in bed and staring at them before drifting off to sleep. However, I don't claim to have my own personal star up there like Canyon."

Canyon Westmoreland was one of Dillon's brothers. Canyon said he recognized one particular star from childhood that he still claimed as his. "I guess you heard about Flash," Redford said.

He liked the sound of her chuckle. "Yes, I heard about Flash. I understand Canyon and Keisha had a nighttime wedding just so Flash could attend, and that Canyon wouldn't let the wedding begin until he saw it in the sky," she said.

"I heard that as well." When things got silent between them, he said, "Make a wish upon one of those stars up there, Carmen."

"A wish?" she asked, looking down at him.

Redford felt heated lust the moment their gazes connected. "Yes, a wish. I heard whenever you make a wish upon a star there's a chance it might come true."

She glanced back into the sky and closed her eyes. When she reopened them she looked at him. "Now it's your turn."

He nodded and did the same thing. He wished she would be an easy conquest tonight. And more than anything, he wished for a night of intense pleasure in her bed.

Glancing back at her, he said, "I hope both of our wishes come true, Carmen."

She stared at him. "So, what did you wish for?"

He could say their wishes could not be shared. But then he thought, what the hell, why not tell her? In doing so, she would know just what he wanted.

Easing into a sitting position, he reached out and took her hand in his. Trying to ignore the intense sexual hunger stirring inside him, he said, "My wish was for you, Carmen."

He watched her blink before asking in a soft voice, "For me?"

Redford nodded, holding her gaze steadily. "Yes. My wish is for you to be mine."

Carmen forced back a gasp of surprise at such an admission from Redford. Her heart swelled with love for him. Were his words his way of letting her know she had somehow eased her way into his heart? The mere thought of such a thing had joy flowing all through her.

"What did you wish for, Carmen?"

She had wished for a couple of things. For him to accept that he was her soulmate, like she'd accepted that he was hers. For them to live a long and happy life together. Instead of breaking down every single detail, she summed it up by saying, "My wish was for you to be mine, too, Redford."

From the smile that spread across his lips, he obviously liked her answer. "Then let me grant your wish." He reached out and pulled her into his arms.

Carmen was convinced her body went into a pleasurable shock the minute Redford took possession of her mouth. She hadn't been given time to think and already her tongue surrendered to his. She'd been kissed before by men who thought they were experts. She'd thought so, too.

Until now.

Redford's mouth mated with hers in a way she'd never experienced before. She'd always enjoyed the art of kissing as long as it didn't go any further. She could handle even the most passionate of kisses. However, when Redford deepened the kiss, she moaned. No man's kiss had ever made her moan before.

Then he wrapped his arms around her and his fingers stroked the length of her spine. She felt them through the material of her dress. It took everything in her to retain control of her senses. When she heard herself moan again, she knew she was about to lose them.

When her mouth could barely take any more bold strokes of his tongue, she eased her hands up to his shoulders. Instead of pushing him away, though, like she should do, her fingers traced his upper arms, loving how powerfully male they felt. Then her breasts pressed firmly to his chest. She could actually feel the hardened tips of her nipples poking into him.

Suddenly, he released her mouth, but just long enough for them to inhale and exhale. Then his mouth reclaimed hers again, deepening the pressure. He was giving her something she'd never had before—full contact, wet tongue, unapologetic, raw. This was the kind of kiss she'd read about. She always thought she could tell fantasy from reality. Now she wasn't sure.

Presently, she wasn't certain of anything other than how his kiss was making her feel. Redford was not holding himself in check. He was going at her mouth with toe-curling determination and hot abandonment.

Needing to breathe, she was the one who ended the

kiss this time. Heat stirred in her stomach, and before she could say they were moving too fast, he began feathering kisses around her mouth, corner to corner. His hands were no longer at her back. Now his fingers tunneled into her hair, and she loved the feel of it. His fingers' magic touch steadily broke down her defenses and zapped her control.

"Redford…"

He captured her mouth again, with even more intensity. He was creating a physical need within her that she hadn't known could exist. One she hadn't known she could feel.

Breaking off the kiss, he cupped her face in his hands. Carmen noted he was breathing just as hard as she was. Staring into her eyes, his gaze seemed to melt into hers. Then he claimed her mouth yet again, his tongue taking hers in long, hard, and devouring strokes.

When she felt herself ease down on the blanket, she relished the feel of his strong thighs when he placed his body over hers. He had slid his hand beneath her dress—and then suddenly, he broke off the kiss and sat up. Droplets of rain sprinkled down her face.

"Come on, let's go before it starts raining harder," he said, standing.

When he extended his hand to her, she took it and stood to her feet, trying to ignore the sensations still rushing through her. They quickly gathered the blanket and put the wine bottle and glasses in the basket. With her hand held firmly in his, they quickly moved toward the guest cottages.

Carmen knew she should appreciate the rain coming down when it had. She didn't want to imagine what they would be doing if it hadn't. His hand had been under her dress just inches from the waistband of her panties. How had she allowed him to get that far? To take liberties she hadn't ever given any other man?

"Which one of these cottages is yours?" he asked.

"That one." They moved in that direction. Moments later they stood in front of the door.

"Sorry our picnic got interrupted, Redford." With that, she knew she should thank him for a nice picnic and go inside.

"Carmen?"

Redford saying her name held her still. "Yes?"

"May I come in so we can finish off the wine?"

For some reason she couldn't discard from her mind what he'd told her about looking into the stars and wishing for her. Whether he knew it or not, that meant everything to her. His wish had been for her to be his.

Her mouth still reeled from the effects of his kisses. She still felt the intensity of them through her entire body. Even now, while they stood facing each other, the sparks were still flying between them. It was raining harder now. She couldn't send him away to get totally drenched, could she?

If he came inside, would the storm brewing between them, turbulent and tempestuous, get out of control? No. She would admit his kisses had almost done her in while on that blanket, but now she was in full control of her faculties.

"Carmen?"

She drew in a deep breath and said, "Yes. Come in so we can finish off the wine."

Chapter Five

As Redford poured the remainder of the wine into the glasses, out of the corner of his eye he could see Carmen move around the cottage. It was identical to the one he was using, with a spacious living room, bedroom and bathroom.

Redford tried forcing his concentration back to what he was doing. That was hard, especially when thoughts of the kisses they'd shared ran rampant through his mind. The kisses had been expected. Gone according to plan. What had not been expected was the impact her taste had on him.

It was as if the moment their tongues tangled, something had come over him that was deeper and stronger than mere desire. It was something that had caught him off guard. A rational part of him wanted to believe there was a first time for everything, but the irrational part could not accept he'd let go of his smooth moves with this particular woman.

For a short while, all the legendary exploits he was known for had been eradicated from his brain. His focus had been only on her. Mainly, how she made him feel, the way she tasted and his desire to connect their bodies in the most primitive way. He ached to get inside her, and even now he could feel her heat.

Turning with both wineglasses in his hand, he saw Carmen now stood at the window, peering out. It was raining even harder and the sound of it beating on the cottage's roof was almost deafening. He wondered if she knew that the weather could affect a person's sex drive, especially when it was raining like it was now.

He could feel it. And seeing her in that dress wasn't helping matters. He almost regretted having asked her to keep it on.

"Here you are," he said, moving toward her.

She turned and smiled. "It seems Denver's weather is so unpredictable. There was no sign of rain when we were watching the stars."

"Yes, I would say it surprised us," he said, handing her the wineglass. Not only had the rain surprised him, but it had angered him. His hands had made it under her dress, and he'd been about to slide his fingers under the waistband of her panties, when he had felt the first droplets.

"Thanks."

Meeting her gaze, he said, "You're welcome."

After taking a sip of wine, he moved to stand beside her and look out the window. "It's coming down pretty hard." That meant even if he finished his wine, she wouldn't send him out in the storm. At least, he hoped she wouldn't.

"Do you want to sit on the sofa and talk?" he suggested, turning from the window to look at her.

She arched a brow. "Talk about what?"

"Anything." Conversation was part of his strategy for tonight. Sexual chemistry crackled in the air. Some due to the rain, and some due to the lust flowing between them. He had no problem with all the arousal consuming them both.

"Okay, we can sit and talk," she said. "Hopefully the rain will stop soon."

Redford watched as she moved to sit on the sofa. She'd made sure the side split in her dress didn't show too much thigh. He was tempted to tell her not to bother because he intended to see her naked by morning.

He moved to sit down as well. However, he didn't take the wing-back chair across from the sofa, but eased his body down beside her. Other than the lifting of her brow in surprise, she said nothing. Instead, she took another sip of wine like she really needed it.

"Tell me about your classes, Carmen."

"What classes?"

"The ones you teach at Georgetown." Redford figured talking about something she was passionate about would relax her, and he wanted her as relaxed as she'd been by the lake.

Leaning back against the sofa, he slowly sipped his wine while listening. He had honestly thought he would find the subject of economics boring, but quite the contrary. The way she broke it down made it relatable to his business model regarding his resorts.

Talking made the shape of her mouth even more alluring, and the sound of her words was like a soft caress. Suddenly she chuckled about something. Whatever had been amusing, he regretted missing the punchline. When she asked about his resorts, and how he determined when to buy or build, he knew it was his time to talk.

The last thing he wanted to do was discuss business, so he decided to make it quick. He'd gotten comfortable enough to remove the jacket he had slid back on when it had begun raining. And she'd relaxed to the point where she'd kicked off her shoes to sit with her legs tucked beneath her. It was such a sexy pose. She was obviously listening to what he was saying.

He wondered how long it would take for her to notice that he'd shifted positions and now they were sitting closer than they had been before. When she leaned over to place her empty wineglass beside his on the coffee table, he took her hand in his and entwined their fingers.

"I enjoyed listening to you, Carmen."

"And I enjoyed listening to you as well. I find your work fascinating, Redford."

He glanced down at their empty wineglasses and then over at the window. "We finished the wine, but it's still raining."

"So I hear."

"Do you plan to send me out in it?" he asked, tempted to bring her hand, the one he was still holding, to his lips to kiss it.

"Surely a little water won't hurt you," she said. At that moment he knew she'd realized how intimate their positions were.

"It might."

"Do you think you're made of sugar, Redford St. James?"

He tightened his hold on her hand and eased closer to her. "You've tasted me, Carmen. What do you think?"

When she unconsciously licked her lips with the tip of her tongue as if remembering his taste, he got hard. He doubted she knew that seeing her do such a thing made him want her with a vengeance. He'd never wanted any woman with a vengeance before.

"Well, what do you think, Carmen?" he asked again when she'd yet to answer.

Their gazes locked. When he heard the sound of a moan, he wasn't sure if it had come from him or her. What was there about her that convulsed his body with such sexual need? His body was on fire. Dazed to the point that just being this close to her was pure torture.

"I think you tasted kind of sweet," she finally said.

He inched his mouth closer to hers. "You know what that means, Carmen?"

She shook her head. "No, what does that mean?"

"It means," he said, inching even closer to her. "I need to share my taste with you again so you can be certain."

And then he captured her mouth.

Redford took Carmen's mouth with a ferociousness that made everything inside of her feel his possessiveness. This kiss was even more torrid than the others. She could actually feel her veins throb.

At present, her veins were the least of her worries. This kiss was making it hard for her to think…at least logically. All she could concentrate on was his delicious, all-consuming taste. And it *was* sweet. The sweetest flavor she'd ever consumed. However, she couldn't say it had anything to do with sugar. It had everything to do with the man himself.

He tightened his arms around her as his mouth continued to devour hers in a way she wasn't used to. Everything about Redford was seductive and intense. Just the thought that she was the one he'd wished for, the one he wanted to make his, had her falling in love with him even more.

Something else was increasing as well. Need. And it was creating a sexual longing within her, making her think things, do things and want things. Her brain, which she could usually count on to be logical, dependable and reliable, was letting her down in the most salacious way.

Without breaking contact with her mouth, he stood, drawing her up off the sofa in a pair of strong, powerful arms. That's when she felt him. He was aroused. Totally and fully. He wanted her. A man's erection couldn't lie. She'd felt an aroused male body pressed against her before, but at the time she'd known it was a waste of time and effort on the guy's part.

Why wasn't she thinking that way now? Instead, she wanted to do something that she'd never done before in her life—touch it. How illogical was that? But at that moment, under the onslaught of his tongue, logic was being tossed out the window and getting rained on.

Lightning crackled the sky, followed by a boom of thunder that shook the earth. As far as Carmen was concerned, neither could compare to the tempestuous desire that was taking her over.

Redford suddenly broke off with a half-strangled moan. The lamp light behind him flickered when thunder and lightning fought for dominance of the storm outside. Inside, there should be another fight going on, but there wasn't one. How could she fight this? Feelings and sensations so new and unique, they had her craving them instead of rebuffing them.

"I think we have on too many clothes, Carmen."

Redford's words should have knocked some sense into her. Instead, she felt the erection pressing against her middle get harder. It was as if that part of him was calling out to her. Pleading for release from its confinement. Was that why she agreed they had on too many clothes?

Expelling a breath, not of frustration but of need, she tipped her head back to stare up at him. This was the man she loved, had loved from the moment she'd laid eyes on him. And tonight, after two years of avoiding her, he had admitted to wishing for her on a star and saying he wanted to make her his. No man had ever said such a thing to her. She believed deep in her heart that he had meant it; his words hadn't been just a line. It had taken two years for him to finally accept her place in his life.

"What are you thinking, Carmen?"

His voice was low, husky and unmistakably masculine. It was a voice that would not only get a woman's full attention but also send sensuous shivers through her body. Maybe she should tell him what she was thinking. Specifically, how happy she was that he'd come around. But the need that had been building inside her had reached its peak. They would talk about their future later.

"I was thinking that you're right, and we do have too many clothes on, Redford. How do you think we should remedy that?"

The smile that touched his lips sent even more shivers rushing through her. The man wasn't just sexuality on legs, he was that all over, especially in his smile. "Trust me. I have plenty of ideas."

Redford leaned down and took her mouth again in a very demanding, deeply hungry kiss. He even gripped his fingers in her hair to hold her mouth in place while he plundered it.

Energy crackled in the air. Not from the storm outside but from the one raging inside. She placed her arms around his neck. His kiss was raw, inflamed and unapologetic. When he exerted even more provocative pressure on her mouth, she got weak in the knees.

His hands were at her back, hunting for the zipper to her dress. When he found it, he eased it down the length of her spine. Sliding his hands inside the opening, he gently stroked her back. The feel of his hands on her skin had desire lacerating her insides. Never before had she felt such primal want for a man. Now she fully understood why. He was meant to be hers like she was meant to be his.

Suddenly he broke off the kiss and she went to work on removing his shirt, trying not to pop any buttons in her haste. He must have felt her urgency because he began helping her. Easing the shirt from his shoulders, she ran her hands over his muscular upper torso, using her index finger to sign her name onto his skin.

Then she felt compelled to do something she'd never done before—she leaned in and kissed his chest. A chest she now thought of as hers. One kiss wouldn't do. She planted them nearly everywhere on his broad chest, determined not to miss a single spot.

Suddenly, he tipped her chin up to meet his gaze. The

look in the dark depths of his eyes was filled with a degree of need that stunned her. "I think we should finish this in the bedroom. What do you think?" he asked.

At that moment, she couldn't think. All she could do was feel the need to be with him, to seal a commitment, to begin their relationship in the most elemental way. Later tonight they would talk about their future. The thought made her happy. Deliriously so. Smiling up at him, she said, "I think you are right."

Chapter Six

Redford swept Carmen into his arms, barely able to hold it together. It had to be the stormy weather sending them both over the edge. Also, for him it was her beauty and her scent. Just knowing that in mere minutes, he would take her sexy dress completely off had him quickly moving to the bedroom. The anticipation was killing him. He had one intent only and that was to make her his.

His...?

He nearly stumbled at that thought, but quickly recovered when he mentally clarified what he meant. She would be his only for tonight. One and done. That was the only thing he *could* mean because he considered no woman his.

The moment he reached her bed, he stood her beside it and quickly dispensed of her dress. His breath caught in his throat when he saw her. He had figured she wasn't wearing a bra, but the sheer, barely-there scrap of satin covering her femininity enticed more than it shielded.

His tongue felt thick in his mouth just imagining her taste. If it was anything like the deliciousness he'd discovered in her mouth then he was in deep trouble.

Lowering to his knees, he slowly slid the pair of thong panties down her gorgeous legs, while inhaling her arousing scent. When she stepped out of them, he tossed them aside and leaned back as his gaze trailed over her entire body, not missing anything.

"Now it's my turn to remove the rest of your clothes, Redford."

"Not yet."

She lifted a brow. "Not yet?"

"No. There's something I need to…"

"To what?" she asked when it was apparent that he'd lost his train of thought.

He needed to taste her as much as he needed to breathe.

"Redford?"

He met her gaze. The heat sizzling between them totally consumed him. Instead of answering her, he leaned forward, clutched her hips. Like a greedy man wholly ravenous for his next meal, he began kissing her all over her belly and lavishing licks around her navel. When she grabbed hold of his shoulders, the touch sent him spiraling over the edge.

His mouth inched downward from her belly to the juncture of her thighs. His target was the core of her femininity, and unadulterated desire ripped through him. Unable to hold back or keep himself in check any longer, he planted his mouth right at her center.

His tongue slid through the hot wetness of her feminine folds. Unable to help himself, he tightened his hold on her hips and drove his tongue deeper, stroking his tongue inside of her.

From the way her fingers dug into his shoulder blades and her deep moans, she was already there. But he wanted her totally consumed, like he was. With a greed he didn't know he possessed, his tongue delved even deeper. He stroked her clit faster. She was so hot he could taste her heat.

Driven by a need to make her even hotter, he began using circular motions with his tongue. This was only the beginning.

Carmen was convinced Redford was trying to kill her. She had lost the little control she'd had the moment he removed her dress and slid her panties down her legs. But nothing compared to the moment he'd slid his tongue inside her and began making love to her with his mouth.

She had read about it and heard about it, but to experience the real thing was sending her up in flames. First it was kisses and now this. She was convinced his tongue was a weapon of mass gratification. When torrid sensations ripped through her, she screamed, unable to hold back any longer. Her body exploded into what she knew was her very first orgasm.

It was everything she'd dreamed it would be with the man giving it to her. The intensity was so great she tried pushing him away one instant and then digging hard into his shoulders to keep his mouth latched to her the next. It was only when her screams ended, and her shivers subsided, that he got off his knees and swept her into his arms. She was glad because her knees were about to give out on her.

He placed her on the bed, and she gazed at him through glazed eyes, watching him unzip his pants and slide them down a pair of masculine thighs. His briefs followed and when he stood there naked her gaze automatically went to his middle.

The sight of his large, thick shaft nearly overwhelmed her, and she felt her satisfied body become needy again. What on earth was wrong with her? She needed to focus but the only thing her mind wanted to concentrate on was him. When he'd sheathed himself in a condom and moved toward the bed, she leaned up, ready for him.

He joined her and pulled her into his arms. The only thing that mattered was that the man she loved was about to make her his. When he positioned his body over hers, she gazed up at him, awed by the look in his eyes. Tonight would be the beginning of what she knew would be a wonderful relationship. She would heal whatever pain he'd endured, whatever had driven him to act the part of a heartbreaker. He would see that all women weren't the same.

When she felt him sliding his hard erection into her, she adjusted her body as it became difficult for him to continue. She knew the moment he realized why. Before he could say anything, she wrapped her arms around his neck and brought his mouth down on hers.

She began kissing him the way he'd been kissing her. The tension she felt within him eased away under the onslaught of her mouth. He took over the kiss and their mouths mated with the frenzy of earlier. It wasn't long before he pushed through the barrier and began thrusting inside of her. Slowly at first but then her inner muscles began clenching him tight, harder and faster.

She felt no pain. The two years waiting for him had been worth it. Hopefully, he felt the same. Over the coming years she would show him that a soulmate was far better than a sex mate could ever be.

She stopped thinking when he began licking around her mouth, corner to corner, while he continued to thrust hard inside of her. "I can't get enough of you, Carmen."

That admission further thrilled her heart and then, simultaneously, their bodies exploded together. She screamed, and he threw his head back and hollered out her name. It was like an orgasmic volcano had erupted and they were caught up in the aftermath. She felt submerged in pleasure so profound that after her screams ended, she chanted his name over and over again.

Their bodies were still shuddering, and the magnitude triggered another orgasm, then another. Outside the cottage, Denver, Colorado, steadfastly felt the impact of the storm. Inside the cottage, Carmen experienced the impact of profound, unadulterated pleasure in Redford's arms.

Chapter Seven

It was no longer storming outside. The storm inside had ended as well. Redford glanced down at the woman sleeping peacefully beside him and, even now, heat spread low in his belly, indicating he was getting aroused all over again.

Carmen Golan was unlike any other woman he'd ever known, any other woman he'd made love to. Never in his life had he experienced multiple orgasms. Yet with Carmen, by the time one earth-shattering, apocalyptic climax had ended, another was right there, slamming into his body so powerfully he was still experiencing aftershocks.

When had he become such a greedy ass where a woman was concerned? Each orgasm had simmered in his balls, quivered in his stomach and thrilled at the base of his spine. Even now pleasure was washing over him, seeming to be absorbed in his skin along with her scent.

And she had been a virgin.

The reminder of that had him sitting straight up in bed. The movement so sudden, he'd nearly awakened Carmen, whose legs were entwined with his. Other than shifting in her sleep, she continued to doze peacefully.

The thought of her virginal state assaulted his senses. Never in his life had he made love to a virgin…other than Candy. At least Candy had claimed to be one. However, after her stunt with Sherman Sharpe, he'd been convinced he'd been played.

There was no doubt in his mind it had been the real deal with Carmen. He had felt the barrier, had pushed through it even when his mind warned him not to do so. He'd seen that flash of pain in her eyes before it was replaced by pleasure—a pleasure that kept coming and coming and nearly consumed them both.

He wanted to wake her up to make sure she was alright since it had been her first time. He was a womanizer, but he wasn't a thoughtless ass. At the end of their lovemaking, he'd gotten out of bed to run bath water to ease the soreness he was certain she would be feeling. However, when he returned to bed, she had fallen asleep and he'd decided not to wake her up. Feeling quite exhausted himself, he had gotten back in bed, taken her into his arms and joined her in sleep.

Even now he was tempted to snuggle her closer and doze off. Later, when they awakened, he would give her the hot bath he'd imagined last night. Then they would enjoy breakfast together before returning to the cottage to make love again…

What the hell!

Suddenly, he felt a panic attack coming on. Emotional overload. This was another first for him. He didn't cuddle with a woman after sex. They went their way, and he went his. And had he actually referred to what they'd done as lovemaking? Then there was the fact that he never, ever, repeated the process, regardless of how enjoyable it might have been. His number one rule was to never have sex with the same woman twice.

Trying to regain control of his senses, he slowly untangled their naked limbs and eased out of bed. He rubbed his hand down his face. He needed to get the hell out of there. He breathed in deeply then wished he hadn't when he inhaled Carmen's scent. His erection throbbed, an indication of just how badly he wanted her again.

Redford backed away from the bed. Picking up items of clothing off the floor, he quickly slipped into his briefs and pants. Glancing around for his shirt, he recalled she had taken it off him in the living room. He was about to leave the bedroom when he stopped and turned around.

He had a feeling that thoughts of this night would remain with him for the rest of the day, whereas with other women, memories were forgotten the moment he left.

Tonight, Carmen had given him something she'd obviously kept sacred for over thirty years. He hoped like hell she hadn't assumed doing so meant the start of a relationship between them because that was definitely not the case. Not understanding why he was doing so, he walked back to the bed and placed a kiss on her lips. A part of him wanted to believe there was a man out there who would make her happy. She deserved it.

Redford finally walked out of the room, retrieved his shirt and put it on. Glancing at his watch he saw that it was nearly four in the morning. There was no doubt in his mind—regardless of the weather, the Westmorelands, Outlaws and their friends had started a poker game at midnight and it was still going strong.

If he were to show up now, the guys would know why he was late. Hell, they might even suspect Carmen was the woman he'd been with, since he'd practically stayed by her side all night. He had even danced every dance with her. Sloan would definitely know what he'd been doing and with whom. Normally, Redford wouldn't give a damn if the name of his conquest was known, but for some reason he didn't want that for Carmen.

Fully dressed, he grabbed his jacket off the sofa and headed for the door, then something stopped him. It was a yearning that stirred deep within him. What was wrong with him? Why did the need to see Carmen again take over his senses? Unable to fight the craving, he headed toward where she slept.

Making sure the sound of his shoes was as noiseless as possible, he opened the door to the bedroom and looked at her still sleeping soundly. His breath caught at how beautiful she appeared. He wasn't sure how long he stood there before he closed the door.

Nothing about this made sense. Tonight he had intentionally ignored red flags, and there had been a lot of them. Allowing a woman to push him over the edge the way she had was not acceptable.

As Redford walked out of the cottage, locking the door behind him, he knew he needed to put as much distance between him and Carmen as possible. That meant changing his plans to remain in Westmoreland Country. He needed to leave now.

His company had a corporate jet, which was how he'd gotten here. He would call a private car to take him to the airport, spend the night at the hotel and then have his pilot return him to Anchorage first thing in the morning. He would leave a message for Sloan that he'd left because something had come up that needed his attention. That wasn't far from the truth.

What needed his attention was his common sense. For a short while tonight, he had lost it with Carmen.

Carmen came awake the next morning with a huge smile on her face. When she glanced around, it was apparent Redford had left. She was disappointed until she remembered the poker game. Evidently, he'd had the energy for other things after their lovemaking, but she had not. Multiple orgasms had worn her out completely. She'd heard about them but never in a million years had she thought her first experience would give her so much pleasure in rapid succession. Redford had definitely been worth the wait.

The last thing she remembered was drifting off to sleep in his arms. She couldn't wait to see him today, hopefully this morning. Even dedicated, card-playing men had to eat sometime.

Easing up in bed she grabbed the pillow where she knew his head had lain the night before and squeezed it to her chest feeling over-the-top happy. By no means did she think last night would produce a marriage proposal, but at least they'd established a relationship.

A long-distance romance wouldn't be easy with him living in Alaska and she in DC, but together they could do anything. Wishing on a star for each other had been the first move and uniting their bodies had been the second.

Getting out of bed, she felt sore, but she couldn't expect not to feel that way since it had been her first time and it had been an explosive lovemaking session. Blushing profusely, she thought about her four orgasms with him. Five if you counted what he'd done to her while on his knees. Just thinking about it made even more color come into her cheeks.

She had showered and finished dressing when she heard a knock on the cottage door. She smiled as she quickly walked toward it, hoping it was Redford. More than anything she wanted a good morning kiss. The smile eased from her face when she opened the door and saw it was Leslie.

"Oh, it's you," Carmen said, taking a step back to let Leslie enter.

Leslie raised a brow. "Yes, it's me. Who did you think it was?"

Carmen found no reason not to tell her. Besides, she was bubbling with so much happiness it was about to spill out. "Redford."

"Redford?" Leslie stared at her curiously. "Why would you think it was Redford?"

Carmen couldn't help the huge smile that covered her face. "Because Redford and I have forged a relationship."

"What sort of relationship?"

"One where we agreed it was meant for us to be together."

Leslie didn't say anything. Instead, she stared at Carmen like she wasn't sure she had heard it right. "Are you saying Redford committed himself to you?" Leslie asked in a disbelieving voice.

"Among other things," Carmen said, grinning widely. "And just so you know, he spent the night. That means

I'm not a virgin anymore, Leslie. I feel great. He was great. It was the best night of my life. First, we had a picnic by Gemma Lake, and when it began raining, we came here to finish the wine and then—"

"Wait, hold up, you're going too fast and my head is spinning. Let's go back to when Redford committed himself to you. How did he do it?"

Carmen was trying not to let it annoy her that Leslie wasn't sharing her excitement. A part of her understood. Leslie honestly believed a man like Redford couldn't change.

"It was at the picnic. Everything about it was beautiful. The lake, the cheese and wine, and our conversation. The stars in the sky were beautiful, big and bright. It was like you could reach out and touch one. He suggested I make a wish upon a star. He did, too. Afterward, I asked what his wish was, and he said he had wished for me. He even said he wanted to make me his."

Leslie nodded and then said softly, "And of course, your wish was for him."

"Of course. And I told him I wanted to make him mine, too."

Leslie didn't say anything for a moment as she stared at her. "We need to talk, Carmen."

"What about?" she asked, allowing Leslie to lead her over to the sofa where they sat down.

"Just because Redford told you his wish was for you and that he wanted to make you his, that doesn't constitute a commitment."

Carmen rolled her eyes. "Of course, I know that, Leslie. However, for me it was his way of letting me know he's ready to settle down. Surely you think that as well."

When Leslie didn't say anything, Carmen patted her

best friend's hand. "I understand why you're skeptical. You truly didn't think Redford was capable of changing and forging a solid relationship with a woman. I know it will be a process, and I'm fine with that. At least last night was a beginning."

Standing, she wrapped her arms around herself and twirled around the room. "I'm so happy this morning I can't stand it. A long-distance romance won't be easy but together we can make it work. We *will* make it work. I can't wait to meet his family and for him to meet mine. Be happy for me, Leslie."

She then checked her watch. "I can't wait to see Redford, hopefully at breakfast, so we can make plans. I told him I'd be leaving later today. After dinner."

Leslie stood. "You won't be seeing Redford at breakfast, Carmen."

Carmen lifted a brow. "Why? Did the guys decide to play cards through breakfast?"

"No, that's not the reason. Redford left Westmoreland Country to return to Alaska."

Shock appeared on Carmen's face. "He left?"

Leslie nodded. "Yes."

"But I don't understand. He'd planned to be here for a couple of days to participate in the card game. I figured that's why he wasn't here this morning when I woke up."

Leslie shook her head. "According to Sloan, Redford never made it to the card game. He sent Sloan a text around four this morning and said he was returning to Alaska."

Carmen was quiet before she asked, "Did he say why he left?"

Leslie nodded again. "Yes. He said something came up that needed his immediate attention in Anchorage."

A semblance of a smile touched Carmen's lips. "I'm sure whatever it was had to have been important, and the reason Redford didn't wake me up to say goodbye was because he figured I needed my rest. There's no doubt in my mind that I'll hear from him sometime today, and he'll explain everything."

Leslie just stared at her and said nothing. Seeing the doubt in her best friend's eyes, Carmen captured Leslie's hand in hers. "I know what you're thinking, but I refuse to believe I was a 'one and done' like all those other women. Last night was too special between us for me to think such a thing. Redford will contact me, Leslie. He will. You'll see."

Chapter Eight

A month later...

"Will there by anything else, Mr. St. James?"

Redford glanced up at Maurice, the man who usually waited on him whenever he dined at Toni's, one of the most exclusive restaurants in downtown Anchorage. He'd been caught in deep thought, which was how things had been for the past month, and those thoughts were always on one person. Carmen Golan.

"No, Maurice, that will be all."

The man nodded and walked off. Redford figured Maurice noticed he wasn't his usual fun-loving self. Another thing the waiter probably noticed was that he'd been alone again. Usually whenever he dined here to enjoy a great meal and the live entertainment, he would do so with a woman. A woman he usually intended to sleep with before the night was over. Not this time, and not the other few times he'd come here since returning to Anchorage, and all because of Carmen.

How had one woman obliterated his desire for others? He hadn't known such a thing was possible. Especially for him. But four weeks later, he had to admit a night spent with Carmen had been a mind-blowing experience. What had knocked the hell out of him more than anything was discovering she'd been a virgin. That meant her experience level hadn't had a thing to do with her ability to infiltrate his mind and body the way she'd done. Other women with a lot more skill hadn't affected him this way. Even now, just thinking about her made sexual need curl in his stomach.

How could she still evoke such a strong sexual reaction from him a month later? What kind of passion had they shared that propelled him to break all his rules? Hell, he'd even slept through the night with her cradled in his arms. Something he'd never done with anyone else.

Dammit. What was even stranger was that he'd rushed back to Anchorage to reclaim his senses, but that hadn't helped one iota. Memories of their one night together were so strong they were damn unforgettable.

Never had a night with a woman left such a profound mark on him. He'd tried everything. Not even throwing himself into his work had helped. Her hold on him had him unsettled, agitated and downright troubled.

Why was he torturing himself this way? The sex with Carmen had been good. It had been great, off the charts, the best he ever had…but it was time to move on to the next conquest. So why couldn't he? He was certain whatever he was going through was just a phase he would eventually get over. Dammit, he had to.

After bidding Maurice goodnight, Redford walked to his car. It was windy tonight with a bit of chill in the air. That bite of cold reminded him that regardless of the fact it was July, he was in Alaska. Chilly summers were normal here. In the distance, he heard the sound of jazz music and knew an outdoor summer musical festival was happening somewhere beneath a late-night sunset.

When he'd arrived in Anchorage for college, he'd known he would make this city his home. Having the largest population of college students in the entire state of Alaska, there were always things to do, places to go and festivals to attend. Energy and adventure always seemed to flow in the air. He loved everything about Anchorage, and it was here that he'd built an empire he was proud of.

Less than an hour later, he arrived home with Carmen still on his mind. He had no regrets about that night. Even though he'd been tempted to break his own rule of not doing the same woman twice by calling Leslie for Carmen's phone number. At least that had been his thoughts before his conversation with Sloan a few days ago. Sloan had informed Redford that Leslie was royally pissed with him and had warned him not to call her about anything concerning Carmen.

From what Sloan had said, apparently Carmen had assumed that night had been a game-changer for them. A kickoff to what she thought would be their great love affair. Instead, she'd discovered she had been nothing more than a "one-and-done" like all the others.

He had racked his brain to recall what he might have said for her to make her think such a thing. Granted, he had told her he wanted to make her his…he'd meant just for that night.

Now more than ever he wished he would have clearly reiterated just how things were between them. Especially after discovering she was a virgin. However, by then, he was too much of a goner. It had to have been the novelty of making out with a virgin that had gotten to him. And regardless of Candy's claims, he'd never had sex with a virgin before.

Redford tossed his keys on the table before heading to his bedroom. He would take a shower and go to sleep. Tonight, the memories would not siege his mind like they had all those other nights.

He hoped.

"You're in the hospital?"

Carmen heard alarm in her best friend's voice. She had waited until now to call Leslie for that very reason. "Yes, but I'm okay," she said in what she hoped was a reassuring voice.

"What happened?"

Carmen swallowed to fight back her tears and hoped Leslie didn't hear the sadness in her voice. "I've been sick for the past week and couldn't hold down any food. Things got worse and I got dehydrated. My doctor sent me straight from her office to the hospital."

"Was it food poisoning? A virus? Covid? An allergic reaction to something?"

"It wasn't any of those things, Leslie."

"Then what was it?"

Carmen paused and then said, "The doctor believes it might be a severe case of morning sickness that she's hoping won't turn into hyperemesis gravidarum."

"Morning sickness? Hyperemesis gravidarum?"

"Yes."

Of course, it didn't take long for Leslie to know what that meant. "You're pregnant?"

"You don't have to scream in my ear," Carmen said, holding the phone away from her face. "And to answer your question, yes, I'm pregnant. When I began suffering from bouts of nausea, I assumed it was a virus because I was throwing up all day and not just in the mornings. When I was late, I just assumed the virus had thrown my body off schedule. After my lab work, the doctor told me otherwise." Carmen paused again and then said, "I guess I don't have to tell you who's my baby's father."

It seemed to take a while for Leslie to recover. "Of course, you don't. When are you going to tell Redford?"

Carmen drew in a deep breath. "I'm not. At least not yet. Dr. Richardson has explained that at present my pregnancy is considered high risk," she said, still fighting back tears. "I'm at risk of losing the baby."

"Oh no, Carmen."

Wiping tears from her eyes that she was glad Leslie wasn't there to see, Carmen added, "Taking care of myself and my baby is more important than telling a man who doesn't want kids that he's going to be a father."

"I hear you, Carmen, but regardless of whether Redford wants kids or not, he has a right to know about your condition."

"I'm not saying I won't tell him. I just won't tell him yet."

When Leslie didn't say anything, Carmen added, "And I prefer that you not mention anything to Sloan. He and Redford are thick as thieves, and Sloan might not feel comfortable keeping news of my pregnancy from him."

"You're right, he wouldn't feel comfortable keeping it from Redford. It's your decision as to when you tell him, so I won't say anything to Sloan."

"Thanks, Leslie."

"What does the doctor recommend, Carmen?"

"For now, six weeks of bed rest. I'll be on a strict diet geared to reducing nausea and dehydration. Unfortunately, the doctor won't release me to go home unless she knows someone will be there to assist me for the first week. After that she's arranged a nursing service to visit me twice a week to make sure I'm doing okay." Carmen paused and then said, "As you know, Chandra and her family are out of the country for the summer visiting the folks in Cape Town."

At first Carmen had planned to join them until she'd decided to begin writing her academic papers to be published next year. It would have taken her the entire summer to get started. Now it looked like she would be confined to bed rest most of the summer instead.

"I know this is a lot to ask, Leslie, but could you fly here so the doctor will release me from the hospital tomorrow? Then I can get one of my neighbors to check on me during the day for a week."

"Of course, I'll come there, and don't bother your neighbors, Carmen. I will fly out first thing in the morning and stay for a week. Longer if you need me. I'll need a reason to tell Sloan as to why I need to take an unexpected trip to DC for a while, but I'll think of something."

"I hate putting you in this predicament, Leslie. I know it's a lot asking you to keep anything from him."

"Let me worry about that. All I want is for you to take care of yourself and my future godchild."

Her future godchild… That made Carmen smile. "Thanks, Leslie. You're the best. And like I told you, I'll eventually tell Redford, but he's the least of my worries right now."

"I'm going to kill him," Leslie said, through what sounded like gritted teeth.

"You will do no such thing. Once I got over being angry and hurt, I was able to accept the fact that Redford never lied to me. The only lie was the one I told myself. I knew his type. Had known it from the very beginning. However, on that night I'd gotten it into my head that he had accepted his place in my life as my soulmate. It wasn't anything he'd said but what I had wanted to believe. For that reason, I lowered my guard, thinking he'd finally realized I was different from all those other women."

She paused a moment and then added, "I lost more than my virginity that night, Leslie. I lost my common sense to a man who was a master at seduction. A heartbreaker. A womanizer. In the end, he treated me just like he did the others. He slept with me with no intention of there being anything beyond that. I was wrong to think there would be more. That was my fault and not his. You tried to tell me. Now I wish I had listened."

Fighting back tears, she continued, "I now accept that Redford was never my soulmate and I was never his. There are no soulmates in my future. It was just an illusion I allowed my mind to concoct. For some people, true love does exist, but I've accepted that I'm not one of them."

"Carmen…"

"I'm fine, Leslie. I remember when one of my fellow professors came to school heartbroken because her boyfriend had lost interest in her. I can now top that. Redford didn't lose interest since there was never any interest on his part anyway. Just on mine."

Wiping away tears, she added, "Accepting my mistake about Redford is the least of my worries now. It's up to me to make sure I give my baby a fighting chance by doing what the doctor says needs to be done. Once the shock that I was pregnant wore off, and the doctor explained I could miscarry if I didn't take care of myself, I knew I wanted this baby even if Redford didn't."

"I believe Redford will want the baby, too, Carmen."

She shrugged. "I know what he told me, Leslie. That he didn't ever want kids. But it doesn't matter. Like you said, he has a right to know, and I will eventually tell him. But I don't plan to hold my breath that he will change his mind about fatherhood." She sighed deeply and then said in a soft voice, "I honestly don't know how this pregnancy happened when I know for certain he used protection. I saw him put it on. Of course, I wasn't using anything because I wasn't sexually active and hadn't planned to be. But it doesn't matter how I got pregnant, the fact is that I am."

"The most important thing right now is getting you released from the hospital and home to be taken care of," Leslie said. "I'll be there tomorrow. Don't worry about a thing, Carmen."

Chapter Nine

The buzzer on Redford's desk sounded. "Yes, Irene?"

"Mr. Sloan Outlaw is here to see you, Mr. St. James."

Redford raised a brow. The last time he'd talked to Sloan was when his friend had told him Leslie wasn't happy with him. That had been two weeks ago. He knew the last thing he should be contemplating was contacting Leslie for Carmen's contact information anyway.

He had awakened just that morning and decided enough was enough. It was going on another month, and he couldn't explain why the woman was still on his mind. No one could convince him such a thing was normal. There had to be a reason why thoughts of having sex with other women were a turnoff instead of a turn-on; and why thoughts of making love again to Carmen constantly dominated his mind.

If Leslie refused to give him Carmen's contact information, then he would hire a private investigator to get it. He had come up with a solution to this madness, one he believed would work. However, that meant seeing Carmen again.

"Mr. St. James?"

He'd forgotten his secretary had been waiting for his response. "Please send Mr. Outlaw in, Irene." He stood and came around his desk to sit on the edge of it. Obviously, Sloan had business in the city for him to be in Anchorage since he and Leslie had dual homes in Wasilla and Fairbanks.

Redford barely gave Sloan a chance to enter his office and close the door behind him before he said, "Funny you showed up here today. I had planned to call you later. I need Carmen Golan's contact information, Sloan. If you refuse to give it to me because of Leslie, then I'll hire a private investigator."

Sloan lifted a brow before dropping down into the chair across from Redford's desk. Frowning, he said, "You sound desperate. Didn't you seduce and drop her like you do all the others? So why do you want to contact her? Follow-ups aren't your thing, Redford. Besides, you claim it wasn't your fault if she assumed your night with her was the beginning of something more."

"Yes, but..."

"But what?"

Deciding to place all the BS aside and answer truthfully, Redford replied, "I honestly don't know what is happening to me, man. I refuse to believe I've been p-whipped, but I feel like I have. All I know is that I can't get Carmen Golan off my mind. I'm convinced her scent is embedded into my skin and the taste of her is a flavor I can't forget. I haven't thought about sleeping with another woman since spending that night with her, and I can't seem to desire anyone else."

"You're kidding, right?" Sloan asked in a disbelieving voice.

"I wish I was kidding, but I'm not. And it's mind-boggling as hell. I've never been in a state of sex deprivation before. I need to see Carmen again and bad."

Sloan frowned. "Why? So you can seduce her into sleeping with you again?"

Redford heard the disapproving hardness in Sloan's voice. Seducing Carmen again sounded pretty damn nice, considering his present sexually deprived state. However, he knew doing such a thing would only add to his troubles.

"No. I refuse to be that weak and break my rule of not having sex with the same woman twice. Besides, I've never bought into that asinine premise that in order to work a woman out of your system you need to sleep with her again. It's conjectural and unproven."

"So why do you want to see her again?"

"I did research on the matter," Redford said.

"Now why doesn't that surprise me?" Sloan responded, sarcastically.

Redford took Sloan's taunt in stride. During their days in college, not only was Redford known as the king of quickies, he was also regarded as an OCR. An obsessive-compulsive researcher. He loved gathering and analyzing data. Sometimes just to prove his point about something, and at other times just for the enthusiasm of acquiring knowledge.

"I'm going to ignore you, Sloan, since over the years a number of your companies have benefited from my skill at data crunching."

Sloan chuckled. "Touché. So why do you want to see her if not to seduce her again?"

Redford leaned closer to Sloan as if he was about to share some secret formula. "Some of the top relationship experts all suggest the same thing. It's all about the power of controlling your own body and mind, and not believing someone else has the ability to do so. That means I need to take Carmen out on a date."

"A date?"

"Yes. A date where we spend a nice evening together and where we won't end up in bed. I need to control my urges and desires and not let them control me. I have to prove my ability to do that with her."

"Do you honestly believe Carmen would go out on a date with you?"

"I don't see why not."

"Well, I do. Carmen slept with you that night believing the two of you were soulmates. She was hurt to find out that wasn't the case."

"I don't believe there is such a thing as soulmates, Sloan."

"You've done research on the subject?"

"I didn't have to. I see a date with Carmen benefiting both of us. It will help me move on and it will also clear the air about a few things. Especially all her misconceptions of that soulmates thing. Over time, I hope we can become friends. After all, we're godparents to your daughter, so it's time we build a platonic relationship based on that, and for her to stop thinking there will ever be anything more between us."

Sloan didn't say anything for a long moment and then he said, "All that research you collected might have worked if there wasn't the issue of fatherhood."

Redford lifted a confused brow. "Fatherhood?"

"Yes, fatherhood. Carmen is pregnant."

Redford jumped to his feet. "Pregnant!"

"Yes, pregnant. So I can only assume you got sloppy that night, which is so unlike you, St. James."

"I used birth control." However, Redford could certainly see how a pregnancy could happen. A condom wasn't equipped to handle the overload from multiple orgasms. Why hadn't he thought about that? "Why didn't she tell me she was pregnant?"

"I understand Carmen isn't going to tell you anything about her pregnancy until she and the baby are out of danger."

Sloan's words broke into Redford's thoughts and he all but toppled over. "Danger? What kind of danger?" Suddenly, a panic he'd never felt before took control of him. Being told he was going to be a father one minute, and then being told he might not be the next, caused him to feel disoriented.

Reaching into his jacket pocket, Sloan retrieved a piece of paper. "She's experiencing a severe case of morning sickness that's putting the baby's and Carmen's health at risk. The doctor is requiring up to six weeks of bed rest."

"Six weeks?"

"Yes. There's even a chance her condition might lead to something more serious. I wrote down the name of the condition on this paper. I read up on it and suggest you do the same. It's pretty damn serious."

Redford glanced over at Sloan after reading the information on the paper he'd been given. "I should have been told, Sloan."

"It's my understanding that you mentioned to Carmen you didn't want kids. That probably has a lot to do with her not telling you right away. And again, she wanted to make sure she and the baby were out of danger."

He met Sloan's gaze. "Regardless of the relationship, or lack of one, I would never turn my back on my child, Sloan."

"I know you wouldn't, which is why I'm telling you. Leslie has no idea that I overheard her conversation with Carmen last night, and she won't be happy with me for telling you about it when Carmen swore her to secrecy. However, I know if the roles were reversed, you would do the same for me."

"Of course, I would."

Sloan nodded. "Leslie flew out this morning for DC. All she said was that Carmen's family is out of the country for the summer, and that Carmen caught something and isn't doing well. And she needed to go check on her. What Leslie didn't say, but what I overheard, was that Carmen was in the hospital and the doctors wouldn't release her to go home unless she had someone to be there with her for a few days."

Redford rubbed his hand down his face. "Thanks for telling me, Sloan, and I appreciate that you've included Carmen's address on this note as well."

"Don't mention it," Sloan said, standing. "Your research might have told you how to rid yourself of being p-whipped, but aren't you even curious as to how a staunch womanizer, a man who is dead set against a serious involvement with a woman, was able to get p-whipped in the first place?"

Redford didn't say anything because he honestly couldn't answer Sloan's question. "Maybe that's what you really need to research, Redford," Sloan said as he turned to leave. Before opening the door, Sloan added,

"I'm in town until tomorrow, Redford. I'll call later to see if you're available to do dinner." And then he was gone.

Less than an hour later, Redford had read up on Carmen's condition. He'd even talked with the wife of a man on his executive team who had a gynecological practice. She'd explained that although severe nausea denoted a high-risk pregnancy, with the proper care the risks were lowered. Such care included bed rest, drinking plenty of liquids to stay hydrated, and avoiding foods that would aggravate the condition and make it worse. That's when the possibility of hyperemesis gravidarum would become a concern.

Redford paced his office. He would make sure Carmen got everything she needed. Even if it meant hiring a maid, butler and cook to be at her beck and call for six weeks. Yes, that's what he would do. He had reached for the phone to call someone who could arrange such services when suddenly he stopped and drew in a deep breath.

Carmen was having his baby. *His baby.* She was required to be off her feet for about six weeks while fighting for their child's life. At that moment something came alive inside of him. She was doing this for their child. He knew at that moment he didn't want anyone but him taking care of her and their baby.

Sloan was right. Control over mind and body might have been a fix, but it hadn't told him how and why he'd gotten in that position in the first place. Hopefully, spending time with Carmen would shed some light on it. Moving to his desk, he picked up his cell phone to call Sloan.

"Yes, Redford?"

"I'm flying out to DC in the morning. I want to be the one taking care of Carmen and our baby."

"Good luck with that. Leslie is there. Need I remind

you that you aren't her favorite person right now? She won't let you in the door."

He knew Sloan was probably right. Leslie was a fierce protector of those she loved. "I'll just have to convince her I'm not there to cause Carmen stress, but to give her my support."

"Leslie still won't buy it, so I better go with you."

Redford wondered if the real reason Sloan wanted to tag along was because he was missing his wife already. "Fine."

After talking with Sloan, Redford called his company pilot to have the jet ready to fly out by noon tomorrow. Carmen's pregnancy was definitely a game changer.

"Are you sure you don't want anything else before settling in for the night, Carmen?"

Carmen glanced over at Leslie, who had arrived yesterday to discharge her from the hospital. The doctor had explained everything to Leslie, and she was taking her role of caretaker seriously.

"Honestly, Leslie, the only time I feel bad is when I can't keep anything down."

"Which seems to be all the time," Leslie responded with a worried expression on her face.

The last thing she needed was for Leslie to remind her how many times she'd thrown up already today. Following the doctor's instructions, she was to eat smaller amounts of food and get as much liquid into her system as she could to stay hydrated. She had been sleeping a lot today, which helped curb the nausea.

"You never did say what you told Sloan about being gone a few days."

Leslie glanced over at her as she adjusted the covers

on her bed. "I told him your sister and her family were out of the country, and you weren't feeling well, and that I needed to come check on you. I gave him the impression you caught a virus or something. Thank God we have Nadine."

Nadine Boykins was Sloan and Leslie's live-in nanny. The fifty-something-year-old woman had been with them since Cassidy had been six months old, and Leslie had returned to work.

"I'm glad you have Nadine, too."

"Well, I'll let you get some rest now. I'll be downstairs in the living room watching a movie if you need anything," Leslie said, placing Carmen's cell phone within easy reach. "Just code me." They had established a special code on their phones if Carmen was in distress.

"Okay and thanks, Leslie, for being here."

"No need to thank me for anything, Carmen. That's what best friends are for. You would do the same for me."

Yes, she would have, but Leslie's pregnancy had been easy. She hadn't had a single day of morning sickness and had only gained baby weight. Not a pound more. She'd looked beautiful and radiant while carrying Cassidy.

Carmen switched her glance from Leslie to the view out the window. Night had settled, and she hoped the heat was departing. From what the weatherman had said, today had been one of those DC scorchers. She loved her townhouse. Especially, the side of the house where her bedroom was located. Since her bedroom window didn't face her neighbor's house, there were nights when she slept with the blinds open without worrying about anyone seeing inside.

Those were the nights she would stare up into the sky and see the stars. Now, whenever she looked at them, she was reminded of that night Redford had told her to make a wish upon a star. Nothing she had wished for had come true.

Feeling a thickness in her throat, she fought back a sob. It no longer mattered to her if she ever gained the love of her baby's father. She would have his baby. She gently caressed her stomach, amazed that a little human being was growing inside of her. A little boy or girl she would love and protect. Not being a part of his baby's life would be Redford's loss.

Another sob she couldn't hold back escaped. Suddenly, Leslie was there. Giving her the hug she needed. "Don't cry, Carmen. Everything will be alright."

Carmen wiped her eyes. "I didn't know you were still in the room. I thought you had left to go downstairs to watch a movie."

"No, I hadn't left yet. I'm not used to you being sad. You're usually the upbeat, happy-go-lucky, optimistic one. If you recall, it was your optimism that helped me get through some rough times when I broke up with Sloan. I want that Carmen back."

Carmen shrugged. "That Carmen doesn't exist anymore. She got knocked up by a man who doesn't want her or their baby."

"You don't know that, Carmen."

"Yes, I do. I know how he feels about a serious involvement with a woman, and I got it from his own mouth that he didn't want kids. So, there's no reason to think he'll want this one."

Pulling back, Carmen swiped what she was determined to be the last of her tears regarding Redford. "I'm fine now. Go on and watch your movie. I just needed to get the last of my crying out. Now I'm feeling sleepy. Before leaving, could you close the curtains for me?"

She no longer wanted to look out the window and see the stars.

Leslie heard a knock on the door. Using the remote to pause the movie, she quickly stood, not wanting the sound to wake Carmen. It was close to ten at night. Who would be visiting at this hour?

Carmen had told her about Abigail Peters, her new neighbor who worked as a foreign service diplomat for the State Department. Carmen had said the woman would be traveling out of the country for the entire summer. Had those plans changed, and Abigail was letting Carmen know about it?

She moved to the door, leaned against it and asked, "Who is it?"

"It's me, baby. Sloan."

Sloan? What on earth was he doing here? He was to fly to LA today to take care of business with his film and production company. Had he gotten concerned about Carmen and come to check on her, too? If he stayed around for any length of time, there was no way he wouldn't figure out Carmen's condition. Maybe she could convince him to go hang out with his brother, Senator Jess Outlaw, who only lived a few miles away.

"Leslie?"

Sloan had to be wondering why she hadn't opened the door. "Just a minute."

After taking a deep breath, she undid the lock to open the door. She frowned. Not only was her husband standing there, but of all people, so was Redford St. James.

Chapter Ten

Redford saw how the look of surprise on Leslie's face quickly turned to a frown. "What are you guys doing here?" she asked, crossing her arms over her chest and not moving from the doorway.

He could tell by the harshness in her voice that she wasn't happy to see him. "I'm here to see Carmen," Redford said.

Leslie's eyes narrowed at him. "Why?"

It was Sloan who answered. "I told him about Carmen's condition. I felt he had a right to know."

Leslie turned sharp eyes on her husband. "And just how did you know about it?"

"I overheard your conversation. You thought I was still in the shower and your voice carried."

She glared at him. "It was a private conversation, and you had no right to tell Redford anything."

"I disagree. I had every right. That's how Redford and I roll. You of all people know that. Need I remind you that if it hadn't been for him telling me about that asshole Martin Longshire trying to take away your company, I would not have been able to help you keep it?"

Sloan's reminder worked somewhat. Leslie dropped her arms to her side, and she took a step back to let them in. The moment Redford walked inside, he took note that the two-story townhouse had a spiral staircase off the living room. He liked the design of the modern furnishings and the bright colors of several large throw rugs on the polished wood floors. Several art pieces hung on the wall and bestowed a cheerful and sophisticated air to the room.

Redford thought the decor suited Carmen. He then wondered why he would think that when he didn't know her that well. He was basing his assumption on what he did know. Whenever he saw her, she was prone to wear bright colors that blended well with her cocoa-colored skin. He would even say the colors also blended well with her cheerful disposition.

"In the kitchen, guys. We need to talk."

From the curtness in Leslie's voice, maybe the reminder of how he'd helped her hadn't worked to the extent that Sloan and Redford had hoped. However, he would let Sloan handle his wife since his best friend didn't seem the least bit bothered by her tone and glare.

They followed her through the dining room into a spacious kitchen that appeared just as modern as the rest of the house. Shiny stainless steel appliances and granite countertops. They all sat down at the table.

"So what do you want to talk to us about, sweetheart?" Sloan asked, leaning back in his chair and giving his wife a charming smile.

Her frown deepened and so did her glare. "I will

deal with you later, Sloan. Right now, my issue is with Redford."

She then gave Redford her full attention. "As far as I'm concerned, you've done enough. You've turned one of the most cheerful and optimistic people I know into someone who now believes she's been living a lie all her life. That she doesn't deserve her happily-ever-after. That she will never have a soulmate. You did that to her, Redford."

Redford took offense to what she'd said. "How? By being me? I've never pretended to want anything from a woman other than sex, Leslie. I am a one-and-done guy, a womanizer to the third degree and a man who never intends to get married. You of all people know that."

"You're also a heartbreaker, Redford," she retorted. "You broke Carmen's heart."

He frowned. "That's not fair. I would never deliberately break someone's heart because I know how it feels. I've been there myself. That's the main reason I make sure any woman I sleep with knows the score. Carmen knew. There's no way I'll believe you didn't warn her about me."

Leslie lifted her chin. "I did warn her."

"Then it's not my fault or yours that she didn't heed the warnings. She took it upon herself to believe anything different about me." Redford rubbed his hands down his face. "But now there's a bigger concern than what Carmen assumed. She's having my baby, and I understand that she isn't well. I want to be the one to take care of her and our baby."

Leslie glared across the table at him. "There's no way Carmen will let you do such a thing."

"Why? Is she angry about that night?"

Leslie shook her head. "No. She knows it's not your fault she assumed you had accepted her as your soulmate."

Redford didn't say anything for a minute, then he asked, "In that case, why wouldn't she let me stay here and take care of her and our baby?"

"Mainly because she doesn't think you want the baby. She heard it directly from you that you never wanted kids."

Yes, he had told her that. "I might have felt like that before, but I don't now." He then shared with her the reason he'd never wanted children. From her expression, he knew Sloan had never told her about Candy, but he wasn't surprised. He, Sloan and Tyler had a bond; what they shared was between them.

Leslie met his gaze for a long moment; her glare was gone. "I regret what that Candy woman did to you all those years ago, Redford, which led to you not wanting anything permanent in your life such as marriage and kids. But even if you shared that same reason with Carmen, you're still going to have a hard time convincing her you feel differently about her pregnancy."

"There's no way I can leave without trying, Leslie."

Her glare was back. "Then what? What happens if you convince Carmen you want the baby? What about her?" Leslie asked.

Redford released a deep sigh. He should have been expecting that question from Leslie since he'd been asked the same thing by Sloan on the flight here. He met her gaze and provided the same response he'd given Sloan. "I honestly can't answer that. For me, it will be one day at a time with Carmen. I had planned to come here to see her again even before I found out she was pregnant."

Leslie's glare deepened. "Why? Did you expect her to sleep with you again after treating her like other women? And when did you begin sleeping with the same woman twice?"

"The reason I wanted to see Carmen again was to prove to myself that I could control the chemistry between us, that we wouldn't sleep together again."

He could tell from the look on Leslie's face she was confused, so he tried to explain. "I was attracted to Carmen the first time I saw her at your wedding rehearsal. But I dismissed it as nothing more than an intense sexual attraction. Then after hearing about her outlandish claim that we would one day marry, I decided to keep my distance and that's when I deliberately began avoiding her. I will now even admit I did so because deep down I knew she could do something no other woman had ever done."

"What?" Leslie asked.

"Get under my skin. I knew the warning signs, yet two years later, I slept with her anyway."

"And?"

In deference to Leslie's delicate ears, he changed the terminology from what he'd told Sloan and said, "And I became bewitched. Since spending that night with Carmen, I haven't been able to get her off my mind. Nor have I desired any other woman."

Leslie blinked. "You're kidding, right?"

There was no doubt in his mind why Leslie was surprised by what he'd said. She knew him, and she knew his mode of operation with women. "No, I'm not kidding. That's the reason I wanted to call you for Carmen's contact information."

"I would not have given it to you."

"Then I would have hired a PI. I did research and figured all I had to do to cure myself of her bewitchment was take her out on a nonsexual date where I could prove I had control over my mind and body."

"And then Sloan told you she was pregnant."

"Yes. And the moment he told me, Carmen became an exception because one of my rules was to never get a woman pregnant."

"And now?"

He released a deep breath. "And now the most important thing is her well-being and that of our child. More than anything, I want to take care of both of them."

Just like every morning upon waking, Carmen immediately felt nauseated. Quickly easing out of bed she went into the bathroom. Leslie had placed everything there within reach. The washcloths, her toothbrush and toothpaste, mouthwash, bottles of water that were kept on ice and a jar of her favorite candy—peppermints. She'd even placed a cushy mat in front of the commode for those times Carmen had to be on her knees over it.

One of the first things Leslie had done once she'd gotten Carmen home from the hospital and settled in her bedroom was wash and then braid Carmen's hair. All her strands had been pulled back from her face and a huge single braid hung down her back.

"I'm going to have a lot to tell you one day, my little bun," Carmen said a short while later as she dampened her face with a cool washcloth. After brushing her teeth and rinsing out her mouth, she decided to take a shower and change into a new gown while her stomach was somewhat settled.

She had insisted that Leslie not be at her beck and call. Carmen had accepted she was in this for the long haul. For as long as it took her body to adjust to her pregnancy. She would do whatever it took because, more than anything, she wanted her baby.

After her shower she felt refreshed. Just because she felt sick most of the time, she refused to look sick. When she'd come home from the hospital yesterday and glanced in the mirror, she had almost scared herself. Her hair had looked a mess and bags were forming beneath her eyes.

She was determined to be PWP, "pretty while pregnant," to boost her morale. She was happy about her pregnancy even if Redford wouldn't be. After her shower she walked out of the bathroom to find Leslie sitting in the chair her best friend had placed next to the bed, a tray of food on the nightstand.

"Aren't you looking pretty and refreshed. How do you feel?" Leslie asked, smiling.

"Thanks. My little bun is still kicking my butt as usual. I stayed over the commode longer than usual this morning, but I feel better now," she said, sitting on the side of the bed.

Leslie placed a tray of food in Carmen's lap. After she had eaten a piece of cinnamon toast and a boiled egg, Leslie handed her the prenatal vitamins and medication the doctor had prescribed, along with a huge glass of water.

Carmen watched Leslie walk over to the window and look out. She'd known her best friend long enough to know when something was bothering her. Before she could ask what was wrong, Leslie turned and said, "There is something I need to talk to you about, Carmen."

Carmen heard the strain in Leslie's voice. "Okay, but I already have an idea what it's about."

Leslie came back over to sit in the chair. "You do?"

"Yes, and I owe you an apology."

Leslie lifted a brow. "What for?"

"I asked something of you that I should not have."

"And what was that?"

"I asked you not to tell Sloan why you're here with me. I had no right to do that. He's your husband and you lied to him for me. Now I feel responsible for your deceit. Married couples shouldn't keep secrets."

Leslie leaned across the bed and captured Carmen's hand in hers. "I didn't consider it keeping a secret, Carmen. I considered it keeping my word to my best friend. Besides, it doesn't matter now because Sloan knows the real reason I'm here. That's what I want to talk to you about. He overheard our conversation when I thought he was in the shower."

"Well, you were talking loud that night," Carmen said, smiling. "If you want to tell me that he'll tell Redford, that's fine. I know how Redford feels about kids, so he won't contact me. When my sickness passes, I will contact him and assure him I don't expect anything from him. In fact, I don't plan for his name to be on my child's birth certificate."

Surprise shown on Leslie's features. "Why?"

"Because as long as I don't recognize Redford as my baby's father, he doesn't have to worry about having legal obligations. The last thing I want is for him to assume me or my child will stake claim to his wealth. I am giving him an out."

"You're serious, aren't you?"

"Yes, and I've made up my mind about it, Leslie. I want this baby, and Redford doesn't. So my decision to omit his name from my little bun's birth certificate makes perfect sense to me."

"And what if Redford has changed his mind about being a father?"

Carmen rolled her eyes. "Why do you keep suggesting such a thing when we both know he won't? I know what he told me."

"People can change their minds about things, Carmen."

"Yes, but I doubt he will."

"But what if he does?"

Carmen rolled her eyes again. "In that case, he'll have a hard time convincing me, Leslie. Even then I'll think his reason for changing his mind is suspect."

"Suspect how?"

She shrugged. "Like there's an ulterior motive. Namely, that he feels obligated, and that's the last thing I want or will accept. I have a good job and can take care of my baby on my own. And once I tell my family about my pregnancy, they will be overjoyed and will give my baby all the love my little bun will ever need."

Leslie didn't say anything for a while. Then, "Sloan did tell Redford, Carmen, so be prepared."

"Prepared for what? Redford doesn't want to be a father and I accept that."

"Okay," Leslie said, standing and taking the tray now that she'd finished eating.

Carmen knew by the way Leslie said "okay" that she didn't necessarily agree. When Leslie didn't add anything else, Carmen knew that meant Leslie was putting off the subject of Redford for later. Honestly, she preferred that his name didn't come up at all.

"Get some rest, Carmen. I'll be back later," Leslie said, taking the tray away.

"Okay."

An hour later, Carmen was coming out of the bathroom after dealing with another bout of morning sickness when there was a knock on her bedroom door. She wondered why Leslie was knocking. "Come on in, Leslie."

She had made it to the bed and was sitting on the side of it when a husky male voice pounded through her ears. It was a voice she recognized immediately. "It's not Leslie, Carmen."

She jerked her head around to stare into a pair of dark, penetrating eyes. She was too shocked to do anything but stare back. Then somehow, she found her voice to ask, "Redford, what are you doing here?"

Crossing the room to stand in front of her, Redford said, "Good morning, Carmen. What's this I hear about you not putting my name on our baby's birth certificate?"

Chapter Eleven

The moment Redford's gaze met Carmen's something fired to life inside of him. Had it been a month? How could she look so damn beautiful while ill? Granted he could see the circles under her eyes, but her skin looked radiant, her eyes bright and those lips he had kissed so many times looked ready to be kissed again.

He knew at that moment it would not have been as easy as he'd assumed to take her out on a date and have the willpower to not make love to her again. Even now, intense desire flowed through his veins, making him aware of everything about her. Even that cute baby-doll gown she had on.

"What are you doing here, Redford?" she asked again, quickly placing the bed covers across her thighs, which had been exposed by her short nightgown. Evidently, she'd noticed his gaze.

"I arrived last night after finding out you were pregnant and having a difficult time."

"And this affects you how?"

He couldn't believe she had the audacity to ask him that. "If you're pregnant, the baby is mine."

"You're sure of that? You used a condom."

He knew her words, spoken sharply, were meant to get a rise out of him. They didn't. "Yes, I used a condom, but I'm also aware that we shared multiple orgasms that night. A condom can only hold so much, Carmen."

The blush on her cheeks was priceless. She recovered quickly and lifted her chin even higher. "I admit your sperm might have contributed, but my baby isn't yours nor is it ours. It's mine. I got it from your own lips that you don't want kids."

"Yes, but that's a moot point now since you are pregnant. I'm not the type of man to walk away from fatherhood."

"Tell that to the next woman you impregnate. At the time we slept together you didn't want kids, so there's no reason for me to think you'd want mine."

"I'm telling you I do."

"Well, I don't believe you."

He crossed his arms over his chest. She was being difficult. Leslie had warned him that she would be. "Then I guess I need to prove it to you."

"You can't prove it to me."

"I believe that I can."

"You can certainly try."

She'd said just the words he had wanted her to. "Thanks for allowing me the opportunity to do so, Carmen. I will make sure you don't regret it."

He saw the confused look on her face. "What are you talking about, Redford?"

"You've just told me I can prove to you that I want our child."

"And?"

"And I intend to do so."

He thought she looked cute rolling her eyes when she replied, "Whatever."

"Don't you want to know how I intend to do so?" he asked.

"No, because such a thing can't be done."

"We'll see. Now I'll let you rest." When he reached the door, he turned and asked, "Is there anything you need before I go?"

"Not a thing."

Redford gave her a smile before leaving. He doubted she knew just what she had agreed to. However, she would find out soon enough.

Carmen watched Redford leave, confused as all heck. Where had he come from? When had he gotten here? More importantly, why on earth would he claim to want her baby when he'd told her he didn't want kids? And what was that nonsense about him proving something to her?

She was about to pick up her phone to summon Leslie when her bedroom door opened, and Leslie walked in. "I was just about to call you," Carmen said. "When did Redford get here?"

"Last night with Sloan. I told you Sloan had told him about your pregnancy. I didn't tell you about him being here because we got sidetracked when you said his name wouldn't go on your baby's birth certificate. I knew that wouldn't fly with Redford and felt he was the one who should tell you that. I gather he did."

"Yes, but like I told you, I don't believe him."

"But I understand you agreed to let him prove otherwise."

"Yes, but he will be wasting his time."

"I guess he feels he can prove it while he's here taking care of you."

A dumbfounded look appeared on Carmen's face. "What are you talking about? Redford will not be taking care of me."

"Did you not tell him he had to prove he wants the baby?"

"Yes, but I didn't say anything about him staying here to take care of me."

"You told him to prove he wants the baby and staying here to take care of you is his way of doing so."

"That's utter nonsense."

Leslie crossed her arms over her chest. "Redford said he asked you if you wanted to know how he intended to go about proving it and you said that you didn't want to know."

Yes, she had said that. "But I had no idea what he was planning."

"Well, he did offer to tell you."

Carmen frowned. "Whose side are you on, Leslie?"

"I will tell you what you would tell me if our roles were reversed. I am on the side of what's fair. You would take any opportunity to right a wrong, Carmen. You and I both know it. We also know you don't go back on your word and you all but gave Redford your word that he could prove he wanted the baby the two of you made together."

Carmen's frown deepened. "We might have made it together, but this is my baby and my baby alone."

"Redford thinks otherwise."

Carmen didn't say anything for a moment, and then asked, "Where is he?"

"He left to go to the hotel to gather his stuff to move in here."

"That won't be happening. When he returns, let him know that I want to see him immediately."

"Okay, I will do that. But I want to give you something to think about."

"What?"

"There are some men who would run away from their responsibility, whether they wanted to be a father or not. You should appreciate a man who wants your baby and is willing to prove that he does."

Carmen was quiet and then she said softly, "That's something I did notice during my conversation with Redford."

"What?"

"He never referred to my baby as mine, although I always do. During our discussion, he always referred to it as *ours*."

"I think that's a good mindset for Redford to have. No matter what kind of relationship you and he might share, the bottom line is that the two of you created a life together. Now…are you ready for lunch?"

She saw how easily Leslie changed the subject and knew her best friend well enough to know the move had been intentional. She'd wanted to leave her with something to think about. "Yes. I'm hoping I keep it down."

When Leslie left her alone, her thoughts shifted back to Redford and just what she would say to him when she saw him. One thing was for certain, he would not be staying here to take care of her and that was final.

* * *

Redford tapped lightly on the door before entering to find Carmen sleeping. Leslie had told him Carmen wanted to see him as soon as he returned. He figured she now knew his plan of action and wasn't happy with it. Too bad. He refused to let her renege on her word that he could prove her wrong.

Glancing around the room, he saw the colors in here were even brighter than those in her living room. The bright yellow walls were almost blinding. However, the mint green curtains managed to tone the effect down a bit. Huge throw pillows, a good half dozen or so, were lined against one wall and he figured they would have a place on her bed when it was empty.

Laying on top of the bed covers was the most beautiful woman he'd ever seen. She was slumped with her back against a pillow while sleeping in what he assumed was a comfortable position. Her hair was combed back in a single braid situated across her shoulder. He had noticed the hair style earlier; it looked rather cute on her. Sleeping made her long lashes more pronounced and her lips appeared even more kissable than he remembered.

He slid into the chair across from the bed with his gaze still trained on her. She wore a robe over her short gown, and his gaze lingered on her tummy. It was hard to imagine a child growing inside her at this moment and giving its mother a hard time while doing so.

He recalled his mother telling him how sick she'd been in the early months of her pregnancy with him. His father had told him one time, or two, maybe three, what a difficult pregnancy she'd had. He had been tempted to call his mother and ask her about it, but then she would question his inquiry.

Right now, he was reluctant to let anyone know. Especially Lorelei St. James. She would catch the next plane out of Skagway—although she hated flying—to help take care of the woman who would be giving birth to her first grandchild.

His parents would demand he do the right thing, and to them that meant a wedding. Redford would have to reiterate to his parents how he felt about marrying any woman, baby or no baby. Although he could accept becoming a father, there was no way he could accept the role of husband to anyone. Ever.

More than once, his father had questioned why he hadn't gotten over what Candy had done and moved on after all this time. It was hard to explain to a man who'd married the woman he loved at twenty and who'd been faithful to her through high school and a nearly forty-year marriage that a deceitful Candy had broken his heart in a way that could never be repaired.

Carmen shifted in bed and so did his gaze on her. It moved from her stomach to her face. She still had that peaceful look, and he was glad for that. When he'd returned with his luggage, Leslie told him Carmen had thrown up for the third time that day. He could tell Leslie was concerned. According to Leslie, the doctor had warned Carmen that things might get worse before they got better. More than anything, he wanted her to know he would be here for her and their child. No matter how long it took, he would remain right here.

Last night from his hotel room, confident of his executive team's ability to handle things in his absence, he had told them he would be taking an official leave of absence for the next six weeks, possibly longer. Although he was certain they were curious as to the reason, he hadn't told them any more than that.

Redford moved the chair sideways, closer to the bed.

Then, leaning back, he stretched out his legs in front of him. He might as well grab some sleep. He had a feeling when she woke up and he laid out his plans for the next few weeks, she would not be happy about them. That meant he needed to come up with a counter-plan.

Not only was he an obsessive researcher, but he had the art of persuasion and negotiation down pat. He intended to use those skills because he refused to leave her. She was having his baby, and he was determined to take care of them both.

Carmen's eyes felt heavy, but she lifted them open when she picked up the scent of a man. Not just any man but that of Redford St. James. There was no way she could not recognize his cologne when the fragrance had been entrenched in her skin after they'd made love. Was that the reason she had dreamed about him practically every night since? Replaying in her mind everything they'd done? Their actions in the cottage were what had gotten her in this condition. But still, she couldn't wipe from her mind all those images of a naked Redford, his dark eyes heated with desire and a certain body part fully erect.

Now he was here, clothed, with his head tilted back, sleeping. And she couldn't take her eyes off him. For now, she wouldn't question why. Her gaze moved over his gorgeous facial features. She couldn't help wondering which of them he would pass on to her son or daughter. Maybe the shape of his nose, or maybe the hypnotic curve of his lips, or possibly his noble yet angular jaw. She was certain her child would be beautiful because of him. Carmen shifted her gaze back to his eyes.

She was certain she hadn't made a sound, but suddenly his eyes opened and she fought back a gasp when his intense gaze held hers. She felt a tingling sensation that began in her breasts and slowly moved down her body to stop right there in the apex of her thighs.

Surely this wasn't supposed to be happening to her when she was a sick woman. A woman who couldn't keep anything in her stomach. Evidently, that had nothing to do with desire. Well, it should. Did she need to remind herself again that desiring Redford St. James was the reason she was in this condition?

"You're awake."

His voice was deep, husky and too sexy for this time of day. "Did you expect me to sleep the entire day?"

"It wouldn't be uncommon for a pregnant woman."

She wondered how he would know such a thing and decided to ask him.

"Research. You wouldn't believe all the information I've read on pregnancy since finding out about yours."

She'd heard about his obsession with research. More than once she'd heard Sloan call him Einstein. "We need to talk, Redford," she said, deciding not to put it off any longer.

"Okay," he said, straightening up in his chair and looking at her intently with a sensual smile on his face.

Carmen refused to let his smile get to her. There was no way she would let him stay here to take care of her, no matter what he wanted to prove. She was about to tell him that when nauseousness swept over her, and she recognized what it was. Ignoring the dizziness, she quickly got out of bed to rush into the bathroom. Before her feet could touch the floor, she was swept into strong arms—arms whose strength she remembered—as he quickly carried her to the bathroom.

Chapter Twelve

The moment Redford had placed Carmen on her feet, she dropped to her knees in front of the commode. He stood there feeling useless because there was nothing he could do. Then he felt a degree of guilt because he had brought this on her by getting her pregnant. He wasn't an amateur when it came to having sex with a woman and he had taken precautions. However, he hadn't known being inside her body would drive him over the edge four times.

He hadn't expected it and definitely hadn't prepared for it. When it had happened, all he could do was let things rip. He'd been too gripped in the throes of ecstasy to do anything other than maintain a frantic rhythm while thrusting deeper inside of her.

The sound of her throwing up caught his attention and he dropped down on the floor beside her to gently rub her back, while wishing there was more he could do. At that moment she and the baby were the center of his thoughts, and the sound of her emptying her stomach like this tore at his heart.

He wasn't sure just how long the two of them remained on that floor, but he'd known she'd finished when he felt her back flinch beneath his hand. That's when she must have realized he was down there with her. He hadn't been around a pregnant woman who'd had a difficult pregnancy before. Leslie had had an easy pregnancy, and according to Tyler, Keosha had had morning sickness but had only thrown up a few times. He could definitely see why Leslie was worried about Carmen.

"Thanks for bringing me in here. Not sure I would have made it in time."

When she stood and flushed the toilet, he stood as well. His hand moving from her back to gently stroke her braid. "You don't have to thank me, Carmen. I'm glad I was here."

She didn't say anything as she moved to the vanity. He watched as she uncapped a bottle of water on ice to drench a face cloth before using it to pat her face. Then she brushed her teeth and thoroughly rinsed out her mouth with mouthwash. She met his gaze in the mirror.

"You look beautiful, Carmen."

"Thanks."

"You're welcome."

"We still need to talk, Redford."

"Right now, I need to get you back in bed. Do you need to change your gown?"

She shook her head. "No, but I'll need another robe. Could you have Leslie come in here, please? She'll know where they are."

"Leslie isn't here."

He saw the surprised look on her face. "She's not here? Where is she?"

"Since Sloan is leaving in the morning, she went with him to visit his brother and his wife."

"Oh. I'd forgotten Jess and Paige live here in DC, too."

"Leslie told me to let you know she'd only be gone for a few hours. Tell me where a fresh robe is and I'll get it for you."

She hesitated and then said, "There's one in my closet, hanging up on the left side."

He nodded and went to get it. He wasn't surprised to see how neat and orderly her closet was compared to his. It was also a lot smaller, although she definitely had a lot more clothes. One of the first dresses he saw was the shimmering blue one she'd been wearing at Jaxon and Nadia's wedding. The one he had taken off her. He pulled a robe off the hanger while potent memories flooded him.

He made his way back to the bathroom and handed her the robe. "Thanks," she said, taking it from his hand and then looking at him expectantly.

When he didn't move, she said, "You can leave now. I need to change."

He lifted a brow. She was just changing robes, not gowns. Even if she had been changing gowns, he had seen her naked before.

Instead of reminding her of that, he said, "I'll be outside the door if you need me."

She frowned. "I'm not incapable, Redford."

Leslie had warned him she would say that. She didn't want anyone to do for her what she could still do for herself, and he admired her for that. He studied her for a moment before gently caressing her cheek. "I know you're not, Carmen. I just want you to know I'm here if needed."

He smiled before turning to leave, closing the door behind him.

Carmen released a deep whoosh of air from her lungs. Why had he given her one of his notorious smiles before walking out the door? And why did he have to play the part of the gallant hero by sweeping her into his arms and carrying her into the bathroom, where she'd performed the most unromantic act? She recalled the exact moment she'd felt his hand stroking her back and realized he was down on the floor beside her. His care had sent shivers of desire racing through her.

Desire?

Desire should be the last thing on her mind, especially with Redford St. James, she thought, removing her robe to put on another. Just knowing he was outside the door unnerved her because whether she wanted to admit it or not, she still desired him.

And then he'd told her she was beautiful. *Beautiful?* He had to be kidding. However, her parents had raised her to accept a compliment, even if it was an outright lie. Anyone looking at her could see she was a mess. Like she'd been rung through a wringer a few times.

Why was he being so nice? And why did he want to claim her child? Doing so had to benefit him somehow. What other reason could there be? And because she was convinced he had some kind of ulterior motive, she wasn't having any part of it.

There was a soft knock on the bathroom door. "Yes?"

"Are you okay?"

She frowned. What had Redford thought? She'd drowned in the commode? She bit back the retort and instead said, "Yes, I'm fine. I'll be out in a minute."

After tying the sash around her waist, she opened the door and he was right there. Before she could say anything, he swept her into his arms. "I can walk, Redford," she snapped.

"I know that. Just humor me."

She didn't want to humor him. She honestly didn't want him there. Instead of placing her in the bed like she thought he would do, he sat down on the love seat with her in his lap.

"What are you doing?"

"Holding you so we can talk."

Yes, they definitely needed to talk, but did she have to be in his lap to do so? "We could have talked while I was in the bed."

"I prefer this way. You're closer to me. I need to hold you and feel the connection to our baby."

Now why would he say something like that? The last thing she wanted was her thoughts to soften where he was concerned. "Okay, let's talk. I want to know— what's your hidden agenda?"

He honestly looked confused. "My hidden agenda?"

"Yes. There has to be a reason why a man who's always said he never wanted kids suddenly wants them. I figure there has to be a hidden agenda. What is it?"

"You honestly believe that?"

"Why shouldn't I?"

He stared at her for a long moment. "I see what I told you about not wanting kids has put you into a super protective mode where our child is concerned."

She nodded. "Of course I'm protective when it comes to *my* child."

He nodded. "I think I should tell you why I said I never wanted children, Carmen."

She wished she could ignore the fact that his voice was not only soft and husky, it was also intimate. It was as if there was more between them than a baby that she wanted but he didn't.

She studied him and saw the intense look in his penetrating gaze. "Yes, maybe you should."

He didn't say anything for several moments and then he began. "Years ago, at the age of seventeen, I met this girl. She moved to town when her father's job with the railroad transferred him to Skagway. We saw a lot of each other over the summer and at some point in our senior year of high school we decided to make a go at things. I had planned to attend college in Anchorage and her plan was to attend school in Juneau."

"What was her name?"

"Candy. Candy Porter. She and I talked about marriage after college and things seemed great. We also talked about the children we would have together one day. We wanted four."

A knot formed in Carmen's chest. She could hear the pain in his words, which made her ask, "Did she die? Is that why you can't envision yourself falling for someone else and sharing a child with them?"

His chuckle was derisive enough to send a shiver through her. She immediately knew her assumption was wrong. "Yes, in a manner of speaking, she did die, but not the way you think. She died in my heart."

Carmen swallowed deeply and didn't say anything. Instead, she waited for him to explain. "At the end of our senior year of high school, I felt something was off-kilter but didn't know what. I figured we were busy trying to make good grades and get into the colleges of our choice. I never guessed that she was sneaking around behind my back with another guy."

"What! She was cheating on you with a guy who attended your school?"

"No, he was an older guy who'd graduated two years earlier and worked on the docks."

Carmen nodded. "How did you find out about them?"

"They kept their affair secret until prom night. I took her there and found her in the parking lot, in the back seat of the guy's car, making out. From the sounds of her orgasmic screams, she seemed to be enjoying herself. Unfortunately, others were with me and saw what happened. By the next day, the entire town knew what she'd done and with whom. I felt betrayed and humiliated. She had taken advantage of my love and my entire life was left in shambles. I knew then that I could never fall in love with anyone again. As for kids, I'd always connected any kids of mine as hers. I honestly believed I would never want to be any woman's husband or any kid's father."

He held her gaze as if what he was about to say was important, something he needed her to hear and understand. "Nothing has changed about me never falling in love again, Carmen. Candy Porter's betrayal destroyed my heart, as well as my desire for marriage and a family. However, the moment Sloan told me you were pregnant, something happened I hadn't expected."

"What?"

"A father's love. I hadn't known such a thing could exist until then. But the more I thought about it, the more it makes sense. There's no reason I wouldn't make a good father since I had a great role model. My dad was the best. And my two closest friends are great dads. I am a responsible person, and don't mind taking on commitments. The only reason I had decided against kids was because I knew I would never get married."

Carmen didn't respond for a moment and then she said, "Thanks for sharing that with me, Redford."

"The reason I told you, Carmen, is for you to know why I've felt that way over the years. And why it's important to me to be here with you during this difficult time. This baby isn't just yours, it's ours. We're not married, and I can't see myself marrying someone I don't love just for the sake of a child. However, there are some things I hold sacred. Fatherhood is one of them. I have moral and ethical standards. Marriage or no marriage, I will always be there for our child and for you as the mother of our child. There is no hidden agenda for wanting to claim my child. And it's important to me to be here to take care of you."

"What about your job?"

"I'm taking a leave of absence. I have a good executive team in place. If an emergency comes up that needs my attention, they know how to reach me."

She didn't say anything at first, and then, "You've given me a lot to think about, Redford. I'm not sure, even after what you've told me, that my thoughts will change. Earlier you said I'm in a super protective mode when it comes to my child, and I am. I'm not sure you're there."

"I wouldn't be here wanting to take care of the two of you if I wasn't there, Carmen."

"Is Candy still living in Skagway?"

"No. The guy she betrayed me with dumped her. Then she left for college and met and married a military guy. I understand they have two kids."

She wondered how he knew that. Did he keep up with her? As if he'd known her thoughts, he said, "Her parents still live in Skagway, and she often comes to visit them. At some point, she apologized to my parents. The whole thing was one hell of a scandal, and for years her reputation was in shambles."

"Did she ever apologize to you?" Carmen asked.

"No, but not for lack of trying. I refused to accept her calls and letters, and I made sure our paths didn't cross whenever I returned to Skagway."

Deciding to change the subject, she asked, "I'm feeling a little hungry. Did Leslie leave the soup out for dinner?"

"Yes. I'll prepare you a bowl," he said, standing with her in his arms and then placing her on the sofa. "Do you prefer getting back in bed?"

"No, sitting here is fine."

He nodded. "It won't take me long to warm up the soup. I hope you'll be able to keep it down."

"I hope so, too."

She watched him leave, thinking about what he'd shared with her. Candy had broken his heart and that was the reason he would never love anyone else. It was sad that after all this time Candy hadn't died in his heart like he thought, but that she still had a hold on it.

Chapter Thirteen

Redford noted the lifting of Carmen's brow the moment she tasted the soup. Before returning to her home, he had gone to the grocery store and purchased ingredients for a soup he'd wanted to make for her. He'd also made a stop at a retail store to purchase one of those over-the-bed eating tables versatile enough to be used when she was out of bed and sitting on the loveseat like she was doing now. He sat in the chair across from her bed and was surprised she hadn't asked him to leave so she could eat in private.

She glanced over at him. "This isn't the soup I had yesterday."

"No, it isn't. It's a recipe I discovered that's rich in nutrients. I thought it would be good for you and our baby."

"And you discovered this how?"

He smiled at her. "During my research."

She must have been amused by what he said because

she returned his smile and began eating again. He had wanted to make her a sandwich to go along with the soup, but before leaving Leslie had warned him the only solid foods she could consume were the ones on the list the doctor had given them. He had studied the list and already his mind had conjured up several recipes he could put together for her. That is, if she decided to let him stay.

Although he had wanted to use his powers of persuasion and negotiation, after she had accused him of having an ulterior motive for wanting to claim their child, he knew the only thing that would work would be the truth.

It had been hard reliving that part of his life, which he'd done twice now in the past twenty-four hours. First to Leslie and then to Carmen. He hoped that would be the last time he'd have to bring it up to anyone. He had moved on. It was in his past and he wanted it kept there.

"This is really delicious, Redford."

"Thanks. I recall telling you that I liked to cook but not bake."

"Yes, that was one of the things you did tell me."

Had her comment been meant to remind him of what he'd said about not wanting kids? Leslie had warned him that even after telling her about Candy, it might not matter. A part of him wanted to believe that it would.

"Tell me about your childhood, Redford."

Her request caught him off guard. He glanced over at her. "Any particular part you want to know?"

"Yes, your younger years, like before you started school."

"Whoa. Not sure if I remember that far back. I would

say I was a good child; however, my parents might beg to differ."

She nodded. "They only wanted one child?"

"Nope. I understand they wanted a house full but didn't get that. It wasn't for lack of trying. However, pregnancy doesn't always come easy. They'd been married close to eight years when Mom finally got pregnant with me. They declared if she got pregnant again that would be great. If not, then I would be their only little blessing. Their words, not mine."

He hadn't told that to anyone else before. But then no one had ever asked him about his early childhood. "Any reason you wanted to know?"

She stopped eating and looked at him. "I was just wondering what I'd be in for…if my child's temperament mirrors yours."

Did that mean she was no longer considering their child as just hers? "What kind of child were you growing up?" he decided to ask.

A smile touched her lips. "I'm told I let it be known very early on that since I was the baby in the family, I wanted all the attention. And they all gave it to me. My sister Chandra was just as bad as my parents. There is a five-year difference in our ages, and she claims the only reason she helped them spoil me rotten was because she was tired of playing with her dolls alone. She had warned my parents that if they had a boy, she would order that he be sent back."

Redford couldn't help but find that amusing. "I don't think that's the way it works."

"You couldn't convince Chandra of that, so I'm glad I was born a girl. Mom and Dad tried having another child. She got pregnant but lost it. It was a boy." She stopped eating again and met his gaze. "I've been thinking about that a lot. Comparing my pregnancy with hers. But she lost the baby due to a car accident that almost killed her. A man ran the traffic light."

"Wow, that's sad. How far along was she?"

"Six months. I remember Dad sneaking me and Chandra into the hospital to see her. I was five at the time and didn't fully know what was going on. All I knew was that my mom was inside that big building in a little bed with all those big machines connected to her, instead of being home with us and sleeping in her own bed. She stayed in the hospital for almost a month."

She paused. "Dad took care of Mom, refusing to accept assistance from his mother or Mom's. He said he wanted to be the one to take care of her, and that they needed that time together to heal after losing their child."

He nodded and wondered if she saw the similarities. In case she didn't, he said, "I understand your father's position. I want to be the one to take care of you. Although we might not love each other, I honestly believe we need time together to bond, Carmen."

"To bond?" she asked, looking at him curiously. He also noted the cautious look in her eyes.

"Yes, for the sake of our child. You, as the baby's mother and me, as their father. We'll need that bond for the rest of our child's life. It will be unbreakable. Regardless of the fact that we won't be getting married, we need our child to know that above all else, we put them first and always will."

An unbreakable bond…

Could such a thing exist between them? Carmen wondered, shifting in bed. She had been thinking about

Redford's words most of the night when she should have been sleeping. It didn't help matters that when Leslie returned and came in to check on her last night, she had forgotten to ask her to close the blinds. That meant whenever Carmen woke during the night, she saw the stars, forcing her to remember a night when she and Redford had gazed up at them together.

Carmen had told Leslie just how good Redford's soup had been and that she hadn't thrown up after eating it. She had taken a nap and had slept until Leslie returned to check on her. She hadn't seen Redford anymore that night.

"Good morning."

She glanced over at Leslie and raised up in bed. "Good morning."

She should be glad it wasn't Redford greeting her, but for some reason she wasn't. Had he changed his mind about the bonding thing because he thought she was being too difficult, too wishy-washy? Or had he thought about it overnight, and after seeing her empty her stomach yesterday, decided taking care of her was too much?

"Did Sloan get off okay, Leslie?"

"Yes. Since he flew here in Redford's jet, Maverick volunteered to fly in and pick him up."

Maverick was Sloan's youngest brother. Leslie had once told her that due to Alaska's very limited road system, one of the most common ways of getting around was by aircraft. It seemed that more Alaskans owned personal planes than cars. "That was nice of him."

Leslie smiled. "The one thing I discovered upon meeting Sloan's siblings years ago was that they were close. Although they give each other a hard time once in a while, they look out for each other." A concerned look etched into her features. "Did you sleep well, Carmen?"

"Not really." There was no need to say more.

Leslie gave her one of those looks. "What bothered you enough to interfere with your rest? Rest that you need?"

She didn't say anything for a minute and then she said, "Redford and I had a deep discussion yesterday. He told me why he'd never wanted kids."

"And how do you feel about that?"

"After what that girl did, I can only imagine his pain and heartbreak at seventeen."

"Yes, but he's thirty-six now. Shouldn't he have moved on?"

Those had been her feelings yesterday, too. However, she had thought about it during the night and now she kind of understood Redford's position. "Moving on isn't always easy for people, Leslie. You of all people should know that. Need I remind you what you went through when you thought Sloan had wronged you?"

"No, you don't have to remind me so withdraw the claws," Leslie said, chuckling. "I thought I'd play devil's advocate and remind you."

Carmen frowned. "Why did you feel the need to do that?"

"Because I recall, during that time when I thought Sloan had betrayed me, you were very insistent that I be fair with him. Just like you wanted me to be fair to Sloan and give him the benefit of doubt, I think you should do the same for Redford."

Carmen didn't say anything as she considered Leslie's words. "He wants to develop a bond between us for our child's sake."

"I think you should. Remember when you taught public school before getting into the college system? One of your pet peeves was the absence of fathers in their kids' lives. You felt they should be there, whether they were married to the mother or not."

"Yes, I recall that."

"That's all Redford is asking for, Carmen. He not only wants to claim your child as his, he wants to be a part of his or her life. But the bigger question is how do you feel about that, knowing the three of you will never be a real family? How do you feel knowing that although he wants to be a father to your child, he doesn't want to be a husband to you?"

Carmen released a deep sigh. "Redford has made it very clear that although he wants us to bond for our child, he has no plans to give up his single status, and I'm fine with that. I won't marry a man who does not love me, and Redford doesn't love me. I was wrong to assume he did. Nor is he my soulmate. Redford and I are alike in one way now. He never intends to fall in love again and neither do I."

"I think you and Redford are both making a mistake by giving up on love, Carmen. Especially you. I also remember something else you would constantly preach to me when I was going through my troubles with Sloan."

"What?"

"To see the good in everyone and not the bad. I would think that even includes Redford."

"I tried doing that, Leslie. That's the reason I fell in love with him in the first place. Although I admit I had false assumptions about that night we spent together, it doesn't negate the fact that he broke my heart."

"Then tame the heartbreaker. Specifically, tame your heartbreaker."

Carmen rolled her eyes. "I recall you once warning me that Redford couldn't be tamed."

"I might have been wrong. He never wanted fatherhood, yet because of you he is embracing it now. All I'm saying is that Redford feels he has no reason to trust his heart to another woman. He might see things differently after spending time here with you. God knows you are the most positive person I know."

Carmen shook her head. "I used to be. I can't risk getting my heart broken again, Leslie."

"Then maybe this time you should approach things differently than just announcing to the world that you intend to marry Redford, like he didn't have a say in the matter. Let him get to know you, Carmen. Now is the perfect time."

"Honestly? While I'm in this condition? Sick most of the time while fighting to give our child a chance at life?"

"Yes, because both of you are fighting for the same thing. Already I can see where the two of you have made some progress."

Carmen lifted a brow. "What kind of progress?"

"Redford wants to prove your child's the most important thing in his life, and it seems he's already proved it."

"What makes you think that?"

"Because you referred to the baby as 'our baby' and not 'my baby.' That's a good start, Carmen."

Carmen was about to say the jury was still out as to whether it was a good start or not when she quickly got out of bed to rush to the bathroom.

* * *

"Come in."

Redford entered Carmen's room to find her sitting on the love seat. The same place she'd been sitting when he'd last seen her yesterday.

"Good morning, Carmen."

The moment their gazes connected, a shiver shook him. He was getting used to her beauty overwhelming him, but now their baby was growing inside her. And the sexual vibes between them were just as strong as always.

"I understand you had a rough morning," he said, taking the chair across from her.

She shrugged. "No more than usual." After downing the last of her apple juice, she glanced over at him. "I have another question for you."

"Regarding what?" he asked, extending his legs out in front of him. He rather enjoyed his conversations with her.

"Your family."

He lifted a brow. "What about my family?"

"I want to know their history."

Did she think there was something in his family's history she should be concerned about? "Why?"

"So I can one day share it with…our child."

He could see the emotional struggle in her gaze. She had referred to the baby as *theirs*. Did she not think he would be around to share that history with their child?

Pushing such thoughts from his mind, since he knew there was no way he would not be around, he asked, "How far back do you want me to go?"

"I understand your family are Native Alaskans. Did they come from Russia?"

He shook his head. "No. My father's ancestors are part of the Tlingits tribe. They were known as the Southeast Coastal Indians, and began inhabiting Alaska over ten thousand years before Russia sold it to the United States. They, along with several other Native Alaskan tribes, were living on the land together peacefully."

"How did they get there if not through Russia?" she asked, tucking back a loose tendril of hair. Why did seeing her do something so insignificant increase his desire for her?

"In school we were taught our history, which I've always been proud of," he said. "It is believed all the Native Alaskan tribes came to North America by way of the Bering Strait Land Bridge."

Over the next hour, while she nibbled on dry cereal, he told her of his heritage. The legacy that would be their child's. She seemed to enjoy listening and he definitely enjoyed telling it. It was history not only told to him in school, but relayed to him by his parents and grandparents. He told her how even after the sale of Alaskan land to the United States, very little changed. Any Russians living in Alaska at the time of the sale vacated the land, leaving it completely to the Alaska Natives. It was only close to thirty years later that the land became more inhabited due to the Klondike Gold Rush. During that period, over one hundred thousand prospectors migrated to Yukon in search of gold.

He could tell by the drooping of her eyes that she was getting sleepy. When he got tired of seeing her fight back sleep, he stood. Crossing the room, he swept her into his arms.

"What are you doing?" she asked. He figured she

was exhausted since she wasn't putting up much of a fight.

"I'm putting you in the bed. Time for your nap."

She cuddled her face in his chest. "You smell good."

He chuckled. "Thanks."

When he reached the bed, he placed her on it and watched as her body automatically shifted into what he perceived as her favorite sleeping position. He drew in a deep breath that held her tantalizing scent and fought like hell to ignore the tightening in his groin as he watched her. For the first time since arriving on her doorstep, he wondered if he was making a mistake by being here. How would he give her the proper care she needed when her beauty and desirability were playing havoc on his senses?

She hadn't demanded that he leave. But she also hadn't said if she would agree to put his name on their child's birth certificate. They had a lot to work out.

Yet even while she slept, Carmen had a calming effect on him. Redford had to believe everything would work out between them in the end. He had to believe that.

Chapter Fourteen

Carmen opened her eyes to the sound of music. She slowly eased up in bed and wondered how long she'd slept. It was daylight outside her window so hopefully it hadn't been long. A glance at the clock on the nightstand showed she'd slept for several hours.

Where was the music, a classical number by Mozart, coming from? She then saw the cell phone in the chair beside her bed and knew Redford had left it there. Had he been sitting there while she slept?

When she suddenly felt nausea coming on, she quickly got out of bed to rush into the bathroom. It was a full half hour later before she came out and almost collided with the hard figure standing there. "Are you okay, Carmen?"

Where had he come from? Had he been outside the bathroom the entire time? Now she was glad she'd closed the bathroom door. She was about to answer and say she was fine when he traced his fingertips across her cheek. She went still beneath his touch. The look on his face displayed both tenderness and concern.

"Carmen?"

He was looking at her with intense dark eyes—eyes a woman could drown in. "Yes?"

"Are you okay?"

Quickly reclaiming her common sense, she said, "I'm fine. Just the regular. I'm going to have a lot to tell my little bun one day."

He stroked her braid. "Your little bun?"

"Yes," she said, using that opportunity to scoot around him and sit on the edge of the bed. Each time he touched her, she wanted more of the same. And that wasn't good. "My little bun."

He nodded. "Is that your pet name for our baby?"

"Yes, for now. I might change it when the doctor tells me the sex."

He nodded. "Would you want to know the sex of the baby before it's born?"

"Don't know. Sloan and Leslie couldn't wait to find out."

"You and I both know, as well as a thousand others, why they wanted a girl. However, I'm sure they would have welcomed a son if Leslie had had a boy."

Carmen nodded, knowing that was true. Sloan had been obsessed with having the first Outlaw granddaughter, and he had. "Do you have a preference?" she asked him.

"No. Just a healthy baby, which means I need to make sure there's a healthy mom. That leads me to ask, are you ready for dinner?"

Carmen couldn't help but grin. The man was as

smooth as he was handsome. "I guess I slept through lunch."

"Yes, you did. For a minute I thought you would sleep through dinner, too, but then I heard the pitter-patter of feet above my head."

That meant he'd been in the guest bedroom down-stairs. The thought that he was sleeping in the bed directly beneath her sent sensuous chills through her body. "Are you cold?"

He must have seen her tremble. "No, I'm fine, and yes, I'm ready for dinner."

He smiled. "I made you another soup. This one has bits of chicken in it. That way you'll be getting some protein."

She didn't have a problem eating anything, even protein, the problem was keeping it in. "Sounds good, but before you go, we need to talk."

"Okay."

He sat in the chair and looked at her expectantly. After taking a deep breath, she said, "First, I want to say I liked the music. It was soothing and nice to wake up to."

He smiled and her tummy tingled. "I'm glad you liked it. I researched what type of music might relieve nauseousness. I guess it didn't work because you threw up anyway."

She couldn't help the smile that touched her lips. "I think it's going to take more than music to help me with that, Redford. However, I appreciate the effort. When the baby grows up and becomes a teenager, I will tell them what I went through to bring them into this world." She paused. "I want you to know, Redford, that I've decided to put your name as the father on our baby's birth certificate."

She could tell by his smile that he was happy about it. "Thanks, Carmen."

She nodded. "Since you don't have to prove anything to me about wanting the baby, you can leave."

"Leave?"

"Yes."

"Isn't Leslie leaving at the end of the week?" he asked.

"Sooner if I can convince her. Although I'm still having bouts of nausea throughout the day, I know what to expect now and I can take care of myself."

"Who will cook meals for you?"

"I can hire someone to bring food to me, Redford."

"Leslie said you have a doctor's appointment next week."

"Yes, but it will be virtual, and the doctor has arranged for a nurse to start coming here to check on me at least twice a week."

He leaned forward in his chair. "Regardless, that's not going to work, Carmen."

She lifted a brow. "What isn't going to work?"

"You taking care of yourself."

"It will work, Redford." Now that she had agreed to legally acknowledge him as the baby's father, did he assume that meant he could boss her around or have a say in her affairs? She was about to ask him that when his next words stopped her.

"I think I should stay here with you."

She tilted her head to look at him. "Why?"

"Because of that other issue you and I discussed."

Carmen arched a brow. "What issue is that?"

"Our bonding of friendship for our child. Have you forgotten about that?"

Yes, she had. "We can do that after the baby is born."

"I prefer starting the process now." He captured her hand in his, pausing as if he was trying to collect his thoughts. "It's important for me to see you through this period of your pregnancy, Carmen."

"Why?" she asked, trying to ignore the sensations flooding her being while he held her hand.

He looked down at their joined hands before glancing back up at her. "Just like you said, there are things about your pregnancy you intend to tell our baby when he or she gets older. There are things I'd want to tell them as well. More than anything, I want him or her to know I was here with you during that rough time. I want them to know I'm a father who cared and loved them from the very beginning. Since we won't be getting married, that's important to me. Will you give me the chance to do that, Carmen?"

Redford stared at her, taking in the way she nibbled on her bottom lip as she thought about his request. Although she was the one who'd suggested they talk, he figured she hadn't counted on the turn their discussion would take. More than likely she'd assumed that the moment he was told he could leave, he would do so and that would be the end of it. He could tell by the look in her eyes that she'd been surprised he wanted to stay. There was no way he could leave her like this.

He had stood outside the bathroom door and heard her. She might be getting used to all that throwing up, but he wasn't. He had done his research and knew if it continued or worsened, her condition could escalate into hyperemesis gravidarum. He didn't want that and figured she didn't either.

While waiting for an answer, he knew the one thing he should do was stop looking at her mouth. Otherwise, he would recall how it had tasted each time he'd kissed her that night, and the shape of her lips beneath his and how they were a perfect fit.

Redford forced his gaze to the bright yellow gown she was wearing. It was sleeveless and showed a pair of beautiful shoulders. He also noted the way the tops of her breasts were visible beneath the V-neckline. That's one thing he'd taken notice of since being here, her sexy gowns. Although they weren't anything too revealing, they looked sexy on her nonetheless.

Thinking it was best to tame the lust he felt humming through his veins, he lowered his gaze to her hand, which he was still holding. He suddenly noticed how it felt—smooth yet tense. He sensed vulnerability and had a feeling he was responsible for it. That night they'd spent together had been nothing but a one-night stand for him, but it had meant a lot more than that for her.

He raised his gaze from their hands to look into her eyes. That's when he saw a multitude of emotions in their depths. He saw the vulnerability he had suspected, as well as uncertainty and fear. *Fear?* What was she afraid of? He stared deeper and saw what she was trying to hide. Desire.

He now understood her apprehension. She was concerned that if he hung around, she would let her guard down and something would develop between them. He had to assure her that wouldn't be happening. He broke the silence between them by saying, "Just so you know,

Carmen, I made a decision to come here to see you even before I knew about the baby."

"Why?" Her voice conveyed her surprise.

"Because after that night I spent with you, I wasn't myself."

Her forehead bunched. "You weren't yourself how?"

He could feel the tension slowly easing from her hand. Satisfied with that, he released it to stand up. He paced, gathering his thoughts. It was important that she understood why the last thing she should do is fear him. If anything, he should fear her.

He stopped pacing and stood in front of her. "A lot happened between us that night that I hadn't counted on."

"I bet my pregnancy was one of them," she said.

He knew her statement was meant to shake off the awkwardness between them, to lighten the mood. "You're right. Your pregnancy was one of them because I honestly thought we'd used sufficient birth control."

He didn't say anything for a minute and then spoke again. "What I hadn't counted on, Carmen, was still thinking about you days and weeks later. Reliving that night in my mind and thinking it was the most perfect night I'd ever shared with a woman. So perfect that…"

She lifted a brow when he paused. "That what?"

"I haven't desired another woman since then."

Carmen stared at him. "You're kidding, right?"

He frowned upon hearing amusement in her voice and seeing her smile. He stared at her, his expression serious. She stared back and then the smile vanished. "You aren't kidding."

"No, I'm not kidding, and I don't appreciate it worth a damn." There was no reason to tell her he had dissected every second, minute, hour of their time together in order to determine what the hell had happened to him. Making love to her had literally blown his mind. He could truly say sex had never been that good with any other woman. On a scale of one to ten, with ten being totally great, he would give it a damn twenty for being undeniably exceptional. In the end, he figured it had to have been those multiple orgasms. He refused to believe such a thing was common. Okay…maybe doubles, but quadruples had to be outside the norm.

"Are you saying you haven't slept with another woman since me, Redford? And that you haven't desired one?" Although there was a blush tinting her cheeks, he didn't miss the sly smile around the corners of her lips that she was trying to keep from showing. Did knowing she was the last woman whose bed he had been in please her for some reason?

"That's exactly what I'm saying. However, I did research on the matter and discovered a way to cure my problem."

"Research?"

"Yes."

"And just what were the findings of your research?"

He was glad she asked. "Some of the top relationship experts all suggest we have the power of controlling our body and mind. I have to believe no one else has that control. That would be giving in to a weakness. Being strong and not vulnerable is the key. In order to accomplish that, I would have needed to take you out on a date."

"A date?"

"Yes. A date where we would have spent a nice evening together without ending up in bed again. I would have used my willpower to control my body's urges and not let them control me. I believe I could have done that."

She didn't say anything for a minute. "There's no way I would have gone out on a date with you, Redford."

Sloan and Leslie had said the same thing.

"Not even if you were the last man on earth," she added. "In fact, it had been my fondest desire to never see you again."

They'd said that, too. He shoved his hands into the pockets of his jeans. "The reason I told you all that, Carmen, is to clear the air between us. There's still a strong physical attraction between us, and we both know it. However, I want to assure you that you don't have to worry about me acting on it because I will never again let lust control me. I now have power over it."

She didn't say anything, and Redford hoped he'd reassured her. He wouldn't seduce her no matter how hot things got between them. What she might not realize was that even while she was under the weather, she was still sexy as hell and beautiful as sin. Lust was a powerful thing, but he intended to prove that his control was even more so.

"Okay."

He lifted a brow and stared at her. "Okay?"

"Yes, okay. Because when it comes to you, you don't have to worry about me acting on anything either. I've regained control of all my senses since that night, and I didn't have to research anything to come to a certain conclusion."

"What?" he asked.

"I was wrong. We were never soulmates and it was never meant for us to be together. I accept that." She was quiet and then when she spoke again, she said, "I understand you wanting our child to know you were a part of its life in the early stages, Redford, and I appreciate you for wanting that. Some men wouldn't. As long as you believe you'll be able to control your lust, like I know I will control mine, then I have no problem letting you stay. However, I don't think we should think about anything long term. I suggest we take it a week at a time to see how things work out."

He intended to be around long term, but he'd go along with her suggestion. "I'll agree to that," he said, pulling his hands from his pockets. "Now, I'll get your dinner."

"Alright, and please let Leslie know I'd like to see her. I need to tell her of my decision."

He headed for the door. Before reaching it, he turned around and said, "Thanks, Carmen. You won't regret it."

When the door closed behind Redford, Carmen stared at it for a long moment. Although she might not have any regrets, there was a chance he might. For her, this connection between them had never been about lust but love. She shook her head at his assumption that he could research almost every single thing. Did he not know there were some things that couldn't be analyzed?

Then for him to admit that he hadn't had the desire to sleep with another woman was hard to believe, but she had seen the look in his eyes and knew he had been telling the truth. He hadn't seemed happy about it either.

And he was right that the sexual attraction between them was still hot, even in her less than attractive condition. That was proven wrong when he'd been holding her hand. And when their gazes had met, she had seen it. Intense desire. She had felt it. A longing she shouldn't be feeling.

A longing like the one they'd shared that night at the cottage in Westmoreland Country. The night that had produced the baby she was carrying.

Knowing Redford would be returning soon with dinner, she moved to sit on the love seat where the mobile table was still in place. She couldn't help but be amazed at all the stuff Redford had said, and couldn't wait to see if all his research would pay off.

She had accepted that she was not his soulmate. Yet, frustration was building inside of her because there was a part of her that refused to move on. Namely, her heart. As much as she wished otherwise, she was still very much in love with Redford St. James. However, he would be the last person to know that.

Maybe it was time she did her own research. Specifically, on how to stop loving a man who would never love her back.

Chapter Fifteen

Redford knocked on Carmen's bedroom door and then took a deep breath before slowly exhaling.

"Come in."

He entered and his gaze immediately went to her. Instead of being in bed, she was sitting on the love seat with her laptop and studying whatever was on the screen. She didn't even glance up at him.

The brightness from the light in the ceiling seemed to highlight her radiant features. He could imagine having a daughter who looked just like her.

She was wearing a different gown from the one she'd had on earlier. This one had a matching robe. He recalled she had mentioned when he'd brought her dinner that she would shower and go to bed early. Obviously, she had changed her mind about sleep and was on her laptop.

"I just wanted to see if you need anything else before I retire for the night."

She glanced over at him and smiled. "No, but you might want to key your phone number into my phone. That's how Leslie and I communicated with each other. It's over there on the nightstand. The passcode is my birthday."

He looked at her when he picked up the cell phone. "When is your birthday?"

"August the twenty-first."

"That's next month."

"Yes, and I'm hoping my health improves since Chandra and her family will be back from South Africa by then."

"Have you told your sister or parents that you're pregnant?" he asked, glancing over at her while adding his phone number to her contacts.

"No. My parents will be happy to have another grandchild, and my sister would love a niece or nephew."

He nodded. "Any reason you've put off telling them?" He happened to notice on her phone, when the call list popped up, that she talked to them daily.

She crinkled her nose and her brow furrowed before she said, "Yes, there is definitely a reason. There's no way I could tell them about my pregnancy without mentioning how sick I am. Chandra would shorten her trip and come home immediately if she knew. And my parents would come, too. The last thing I need is to have all of them here making me feel helpless. I'm hoping by the time I tell them I'll be back to my old self. Have you told your parents?" she asked him.

He placed her phone back down on the nightstand and eased into the chair beside her bed. He saw she had closed her laptop so he figured she was finished with it for tonight. "No, I haven't told them for basically the same reason you haven't told yours. This will be their first grandchild. A grandchild they never thought they would have."

He shook his head and chuckled. "It would not have mattered if your pregnancy had been smooth sailing the entire nine months. My mother would have shown up on your doorstep anyway. Just to get to know you, the future mother of her grandchild. Trust me, you would never have gotten rid of Lorelei St. James."

He watched her smile spread and couldn't help thinking for the umpteenth time just how kissable her lips looked. "What about your father?"

He chuckled again. "Dad would have waited for an official invitation. But not Mom."

"I have a feeling I'm really going to like her."

He had a feeling his mother would like Carmen as well. Already he knew there would be problems. He didn't know about her parents but he knew his would expect them to marry, which wouldn't be happening. "How will your parents handle the fact that we won't be getting married, Carmen?"

"They will handle it just fine. They stopped meddling in my and Chandra's lives when we left home for college. That's the one thing I've always appreciated about them. Besides, I will assure them I will be married when I have my second child."

Why was tension suddenly building in his body? There was no way he could be jealous of the thought of her marrying one day. Any man would appreciate a woman like her. Even him, if he was the marrying kind. But he wasn't. He figured the tension was the result of thinking that the man she would marry might assume that his child would be more important in their family dynamics than hers and Redford's.

All it took was for him to recall David Lattimer, a guy who went to college with him, Sloan and Tyler. David lived across the hall in their dorm and when they noticed he never went home during the holidays or school breaks, they'd inquired why. That's when he'd told them all the horror stories of the torment he'd endured with a stepfather while growing up.

Redford refused to let his child go through such a thing. He would demand custody of him or her before anything like that happened. There was no need to get Carmen upset by telling her that now. Besides, for all he knew, the guy she eventually married might be swell. If Redford thought that, then why was even more tension building inside of him?

"Can I get you anything before I leave, Carmen?"

Hadn't he asked her that already? Why was he asking again? And why had he suddenly become aware of her outfit when she stood? Because she'd been sitting down, he hadn't realized just how short the nightgown and robe were. The hem fell halfway down her thighs. The yellow silk robe seemed to hug every curve on her body and the color seemed to make her skin glow.

He wanted to call himself all kinds of names when lust invaded his thoughts. His gaze roamed all over her, and it took every ounce of willpower he could muster to hold back the desire permeating his body. Why did her legs look so sleek? The fit of the top of the gown did a good job exposing the shape of her breasts. She definitely looked too sexy for his peace of mind.

"No, there's nothing else I need," she said, padding over to the bed. He watched as she threw back the covers, and then, ignoring his presence, untied her robe and shrugged it off her shoulders to place at the foot of her bed. Then she eased into the bed. It suddenly occurred to him that this was the first time he'd seen a woman get into a bed without him.

When she was beneath the covers, she shifted to what he knew was her favorite position. Then she raised her head from the pillow to glance over at him. "Is something wrong?"

"What makes you think that?"

She gave him one of those "duh" looks before saying, "You're just standing there staring at me."

"Oh, sorry. I guess I was thinking that you don't look pregnant." That hadn't been what he'd been thinking; however, at the moment, that was the best answer he could come up with.

A smile touched her lips. She wouldn't smile so often if she knew what it did to him. "It's early yet. The baby is still small. No larger than a lemon at this point."

He chuckled. "Hard to believe something that small could cause so much trouble."

She chuckled as well. "Like I told you, I'm going to have a lot to tell our child when he or she gets older."

He nodded. "I'll let you get some rest now. Good night, Carmen."

He was headed toward the door when she called out to him. "Redford?"

He turned around. "Yes?"

"Could you close the curtains? I prefer not looking at the stars."

He paused to consider what she'd just said. He couldn't help but recall the night she'd not only looked at the stars but had also made a wish upon them. So had he. He also remembered her telling him how much she enjoyed staring at them while in bed. Was what happened the night they spent together the reason she preferred not looking at the stars now?

"Why not? It's a beautiful night," he decided to say.

She glanced out the window and then looked back at him. That's when he saw the pain in her eyes thanks to the moonlight peeking through that same window. Her voice was almost a whisper, "Like I said, I prefer not looking at them."

In a way, he had his answer. Crossing the room, he closed the curtains, bringing the room into total darkness. He moved to leave the room again as she said, "Thanks."

He didn't deserve her thanks because he now knew that, although not intentionally, he had hurt her. Both Sloan and Leslie had told him he had. Now he saw it for himself and his heart ached.

"Honestly, Leslie, you've only been gone two days and you're not giving me a moment's rest," Carmen said with a chuckle in her voice.

Yesterday her best friend had called around five times and from the look of it, she would beat that number today. "If you keep it up, Redford will assume you don't trust him to take care of me."

"Is he taking care of you?"

She paused in nibbling on the dry cereal she liked eating as a snack during the day. For some reason, it was a good feeling knowing she was being cared for by the father of her child. He might not love her, but he was doing his best to take care of them.

He prepared a delicious breakfast for her every

morning, fixed a tasty sandwich for her at lunch, and
then at dinner he always surprised her with some nutri-
tious meal. She still loved his soups the best, but he'd
even taken a shot at baking and prepared brownies for
her last night when she'd said she had a sweet tooth.

She knew letting him stay here could result in emotional pain, but she liked knowing he was sleeping in
the guest room beneath hers. Last night, he'd listened
to her complain that she would be missing her pedicure
appointment, so he'd seen her vain side. However, he
hadn't seemed to mind. While she ate dinner, he'd been
on his laptop. She figured he was researching something
but hadn't bothered to ask what.

"Carmen, if you have to think about an answer, then
that concerns me."

She had not intended to stay quiet for so long. A concerned Leslie could become a worrywart, and that's the
last thing she wanted. "No reason for concern, Leslie.
Yes, Redford is taking good care of me and our little
bun."

However, what she wouldn't tell Leslie was that sickness or no sickness, her hormones were kicking whenever he was around, which was all the time. The only
reason he wasn't in the room with her now was because
he'd wanted to give her and Leslie privacy.

He had come in after her lunch and nap to make sure
she was on schedule with her medication. Then he had
remained to watch a movie with her. Not once had he
complained that it was a chick flick.

She thrown up three times today and no longer felt
embarrassed that he saw her in such a way, and afterward he was always ready to assist her. The last time,
she had finished brushing her teeth while standing at the

vanity and happened to glance at the mirror while rinsing out her mouth. He'd been watching her. His brow had been furrowed in deep concentration and worry. When their gazes connected, she had felt hot all over. She'd broken eye contact with him to soak a face cloth in cool water for her face. He had come to her, covered her hand with his and said in a husky voice, "Here, let me do that."

She should not have been surprised at how painstakingly gentle he was. And when he had pulled her tenderly against him, she sighed into his chest while he held her close, telling her everything would be alright. Then, as if it had been the most natural thing for him to do, he had kissed her on the forehead. She was convinced she could still feel the warmth of that kiss on her skin.

"Well, if you're sure you are in good hands, Carmen…"

She of all people knew just how good Redford's hands were. "I'm sure," she said, bringing her thoughts back to the present. "Letting him stay here with me was a good decision. He's been telling me a lot about his family's history. That's good to know so I can pass it on to our child."

She and Leslie talked a little while longer before they ended their call. Whatever Redford was cooking smelled good. The aroma seeped into her bedroom without upsetting her stomach. She was glad of that. The visiting nurse had assured her that although she still threw up a lot, her condition hadn't gotten worse.

Carmen eased up in bed when she heard the knock on the door. "Come in."

The bedroom door opened and there he stood. Handsome as ever. Bigger than life. Sexier than any man should be. And then her heart pounded when the corners of Redford's mouth lifted in a smile. If she wasn't careful, that same smile would be her undoing.

"How do you feel, Carmen?"

There was something about how he said her name. He had an accent, sort of Midwestern. However, there was a noticeable difference whenever he or any of the Outlaws spoke. She thought their speech articulation was rather unique and she loved the sound of it.

"I feel fine."

He came into the room and slid into the chair by her bed. "Do you think that maybe your appointment with the doctor should be at her office instead of one of those laptop visits?"

She heard the concern in his voice and knew why. Yesterday hadn't been a good day for her. She'd been sick so many times. "I'll tell her about yesterday. If she wants to see me then I'll go in."

"And I'll take you."

"Thanks." She appreciated his offer. "The nurse said I'm holding my weight. I haven't lost any, thank goodness. In fact, I've gained a couple of pounds."

"I can't tell. Your stomach is still flat."

She wondered how he figured that. When had he seen her stomach? She then remembered that while throwing up profusely yesterday, he'd been on the bathroom floor beside her not only stroking her back but also gently rubbing her stomach.

"Whatever you're cooking smells good."

"It's a lemon pasta dish I came across."

"In your research," she asked, unable to fight back a smile.

He chuckled. "Yes, in my research. Are you ready for dinner?"

"Yes, I'm ready."

"I'll be back in a minute."

When he left, she released a deep sigh, wishing there was some way to avoid such a potent attraction to him whenever they were in the same room.

Easing out of bed, she moved to the love seat and the table. Although she had researched it, there wasn't much advice on how to stop loving a man who didn't love you. At this point she didn't care. She loved Redford, and maybe one day he would realize she was a woman who could heal his broken heart.

Chapter Sixteen

"You've gained weight and that's good, but after telling me about what happened earlier in the week, I want to see you. How about on Tuesday?"

Redford saw the worried look on Carmen's features. She must have felt his gaze because she looked at him with a forced smile before turning back to the doctor's face on her laptop screen. "Yes. What time do you want to see me?"

"I'd like to review your lab reports first. That means I'll need you to go to the lab before I see you here. They are in the same building as my office. I will make the appointment there for around eleven and will see you around one."

"Alright."

"And don't eat anything that morning," the doctor instructed.

Redford and Carmen sat side by side on the loveseat. When the virtual doctor visit ended, he tightened his arms around her. He could feel her tension. What stood out more than anything was the doctor saying she was concerned about the number of times Carmen had thrown up recently. Honestly, so was he, although he tried hard not to show it.

Things hadn't gone well for Carmen that morning. He had awakened to the sound of her feet rushing to the bathroom. By the time he had slipped into his pajama bottoms and rushed up the stairs, she'd been in her usual spot on the floor over the commode.

There she had stayed, longer than she had ever before. He had been so concerned at one point that he'd thought about calling 9-1-1. When she'd finally finished, he had picked her up in his arms to help her over to the vanity, certain she was too weak to walk. He had wiped her face with a cool cloth before handing her a toothbrush and cup of mouthwash.

He had then carried her over to the love seat and eased down to sit with her in his lap. Once cuddled in his arms, she had drifted off to sleep. After a while, so had he. The sound of the phone ringing had awakened them. It had been Leslie checking to see how she was doing. Following Carmen's request, he hadn't mentioned anything to Leslie about her severe episode of morning sickness earlier.

"How do you feel now?" he asked.

"Okay, after such a rough morning. It's not even noon yet."

He nodded. "Hungry?"

She smiled. "Yes, a little."

As far as he was concerned, that was a good sign. The doctor had reiterated she should eat light meals but more of them. "What do you have a taste for?"

Her smiled widened a little and she said, "I might pay greatly for it later, but I have a taste for ice cream."

"What flavor?"

"My favorite is vanilla."

He chuckled. "So is mine."

Several minutes passed in silence while he cradled her in his arms, then he said, "Everything is going to be okay, Carmen. I know I have a lot of nerve saying such a thing when I'm not the one throwing up their guts every day, but I believe it."

She pulled slightly away to look at him. "She didn't deserve you, you know."

He lifted a brow. "Who?"

"Candy."

He wondered what had made her say that. As if she read his thoughts, she said, "You're such a nice guy."

"Thanks." He then asked, "You still want ice cream?"

"Sure," she said, snuggling back into his body. "But right now, I just want you to hold me, Redford. Whenever you do, I don't feel afraid about the baby. You help me believe it will be alright. That I will be alright."

"You both will. I'm going to make sure of it, Carmen."

"I believe you."

He doubted she knew how much her words meant. He'd never been a sound sleeper so even the littlest movement in her bedroom would get his attention. He knew whenever she got up to use the bathroom or was restless. Those nights when he knew she was getting a good night's sleep were the ones when his own mind would be calm. That's when he would lie in bed and remember his one night with her. Even now he could still say, without a doubt, it was the best lovemaking of his life, and he was still in awe as to what they had shared. The memories made his body simmer inside. Like what was happening now.

Without thinking about what he was doing, merely acting on instinct, he took her face in his hands to study it. Even while under the weather, she was beautiful. "I want a daughter who looks just like you, Carmen."

He could tell by the look in her eyes that his words had surprised her. Redford searched her eyes. Obviously, what he'd said had meant something to her, and he was glad. He couldn't lose track of the fact that she'd been through a lot, not only today but other days as well. Just for their baby.

"Thank you."

He was about to tell her she didn't have to thank him when something welled up inside of him. It was a longing he'd been fighting since seeing her again. A longing he'd convinced himself he had power to deny. However, he didn't want to deny it now. He wanted to act on it.

Unable to control his emotions any longer, he lowered his mouth to hers.

The moment Carmen felt the taste of Redford's tongue, memories consumed her and broke down every defense she had against him. Not only was she moaning, but she was returning his kiss with a greed that astounded her. The way he devoured her mouth bordered on scandalous, and she was right there with him.

Carmen recalled how, after their night together, she would have endless dreams about him. She still did, and in those dreams, he would always kiss her this way. With a greed and hunger that set every cell in her body on fire. Finally, he released her mouth and they both drew in a deep breath as he rested his forehead against hers.

He murmured against her lips. "I should not have done that, Carmen."

She didn't hesitate in responding. "I'm glad you did, Redford."

He seemed surprised by her response. "Why?"

She knew what he was asking. There was no reason not to be honest. "Because I enjoyed it, and after feeling lousy over the past weeks it was nice to engage in something I enjoy."

"And you enjoy kissing me?"

"Just as much as you enjoy kissing me." There was no point in him denying he enjoyed the kiss they'd just shared. She could tell he had.

He smiled at her. "You're right, Carmen, I enjoy kissing you. Probably, too much."

"I guess everyone has a weakness, Redford."

There was no doubt in her mind he would furiously deny he had a weakness of any kind, especially one pertaining to a woman. However, instead of denying it, he swiftly changed the subject. "Are you ready to see the doctor next week?"

His question forced her to think about what the visit meant. "Yes and no. Yes, because I'm hoping she will tell me that everything with the baby is fine. And no, because the vain side of me wishes I was more presentable."

His brow lifted as if taken aback by what she'd said. "More presentable how?"

She couldn't help but roll her eyes. "Look at me, Redford."

For a minute she wished she hadn't asked him to do

that. The heat of his gaze seemed to touch every inch of her body. He then met her eyes. "I don't see anything that makes you not presentable."

Carmen figured she should take his words as a compliment but couldn't. Holding her hands in front of her, she said, "Although my nails are passable, my toes are a different matter. I missed my last two pedicure appointments."

"Oh, I see."

She figured he did see since she remembered having mentioned the issue before. He probably figured she was vain. Now it was her turn to change the subject. "Tell me about the resort you're thinking about building in Skagway." He had mentioned something about it yesterday, saying the city had finally decided to sell him all the land he needed.

"Now that the land deal is finalized, it will be full steam ahead."

They discussed the resort plans for a long while. Then, it wasn't long before she began feeling sleepy. Obviously, Redford had detected it. He stood with her in his arms, walked over to the bed and placed her in it. "Will you be alright for a while? I need to run out."

She felt herself nodding and then he leaned in and placed a kiss across her lips. "Be good while I'm gone."

Before sleep took over her mind, Carmen mumbled, "I will be good. But our baby might misbehave."

She dozed off with pleasant memories of Redford's kiss floating through her mind.

Chapter Seventeen

A few hours later Redford returned and knocked on Carmen's bedroom door.

"Come in."

Opening the door, he saw she was sitting up in bed wearing a gown he'd never seen before. That meant she'd had another bout of nausea while he was away. "Are you okay?"

She nodded and smiled. "I am now."

He couldn't help but smile back. "Does that mean our child acted up while I was gone?"

She chuckled. "Afraid so."

"Well, hopefully, this will cheer you up," he said, producing the bag he'd been holding behind his back. He handed it to her.

When she glanced in the bag and back at him, her face lit up. "Ice cream!"

He grinned at the excitement in her voice. "Yes, and your favorite flavor."

She eyed him suspiciously. "Does that mean we have to share?"

He laughed. "Not at all. Besides, I'll be busy while you're eating the ice cream."

"Busy doing what?" she asked, not wasting any time digging the spoon out of the bag along with the pint of ice cream.

"I will be performing my first pedicure."

"Pedicure? Are you serious?"

"Yes." He saw the concern on her face and smiled. "Relax. I did some research. I'll be back with everything."

He left and returned within a few minutes with a box labeled "At Home Pedicure." She had gotten out of bed and was sitting on the love seat. He went into her bathroom to get a towel and a few cotton balls he'd seen in a container on her vanity.

In no time at all, he had removed everything from the box and filled the basin with water. He then added everything needed, including the oil Leslie had shared was Carmen's favorite fragrance. Kneeling in front of her, he lifted her feet and placed them in the water. The sweet scent of the oil wafted between them and filled him with a sense of pride that he was doing this for her. It was the first pedicure he'd ever done for a woman. But then, Carmen was becoming his first for a number of things.

Redford thought she had pretty feet; and honestly, he didn't see anything wrong with her toes. However, if she thought there was, he wasn't about to argue. He wanted to take care of her.

And he did.

Taking his time, he went through the process, step-by-step, as outlined in his research. He appreciated that

Carmen trusted him to do this. She calmly ate her ice cream while listening to the music he had turned on: Beethoven. He grinned when he noticed her toes moving to the music.

An hour or so later, he leaned back on his haunches pleased with what he'd done. The polish matched her nails; again, thanks to Leslie who knew her favorite color.

He looked at her. She had finished her ice cream. "So, what do you think, Carmen Golan?"

Carmen glanced down at her toes, and a huge smile curved her lips. She seemed happy. He knew, at that moment, that if given the chance, he would keep that smile on her face forever.

"You did a great job, Redford. I'm beginning to think you might be in the wrong line of work."

He chuckled. "Thanks, but I'd rather stick to resort development." He stood. "There's a casserole dish that's ready for the oven." He glanced back down at her feet. "Let your toes dry before moving around."

"Alright and thanks."

"You're welcome."

Redford was halfway down the stairs when his cell phone rang. Recognizing the ring tone, he pulled it out of his back pocket. "Yes, Sloan?"

"What's this I hear about you giving a woman a pedicure?"

He grinned as he thought about the past hour or so. But he hadn't given just any woman a pedicure. He'd given one to the woman who would be the mother of his child. He'd felt like pampering her, and he had. She deserved it, and he intended to see that she had plenty more pampering while he was here.

"What of it?"

"Nothing, I guess."

Upon reaching the living room, he leaned against the bookcase. "Out with it, Sloan."

"Out with what?"

"The reason you called. I'm sure Leslie told you."

"Yes, she told me of your plans. Doing something like that just doesn't sound like you."

Redford rubbed his hand down his face. "In case you've missed it, a number of things I've been doing lately that involve Carmen don't sound like me. The main one is getting her pregnant."

"Mistakes happen to the best of us."

The last thing he wanted to tell Sloan was that he honestly didn't think Carmen getting pregnant was a mistake. Although it certainly hadn't been intentional, why was he beginning to think it was meant to happen? Like fate, which was something he normally didn't believe in. Therefore, he decided not to respond.

Wisely, he chose to change the subject. "How's my goddaughter?" He smiled knowing that question would work each and every time. Sloan loved giving Cassidy updates.

As Sloan went on about his daughter's latest escapades, Redford's mind drifted back to Carmen's smile. Since she wasn't someone who could easily mask her feelings, he knew she was genuinely appreciative of the pedicure and pleased with what he'd done.

Sloan's voice trailed off and Redford knew it was time to end the call before his best friend chimed back in on the pedicure. "Time for me to prepare dinner, Sloan. I'll talk with you later."

Redford clicked off the phone and headed into the kitchen.

* * *

Carmen couldn't help staring down at her toes yet again. Just the thought of Redford giving her a pedicure still had her in awe, and he'd done a good job. His hands on her legs had kept sensual sensations flowing within her. She was certain he'd been aware of them, which was probably why he'd spent such a long time massaging her legs.

Each time he'd touched her feet, ankles or legs, her heart beat wildly. One time, even her breathing became erratic. When that happened, he'd looked up at her and their gazes locked, and she could see the heat, need and hunger reflected in his eyes.

Using her hands, she fanned herself. Honestly? How could her body even think of sex while in this condition? Easily, when she had a drop-dead gorgeous man living under her roof. A man who had no problem touching her and kissing her.

Carmen dragged in a deep breath. The last thing she needed were reckless impulses.

Less than an hour later, Redford was back with dinner that he shared with her while they watched a movie. They ended up watching two. It was during the second movie that she felt nauseated again, but the moment quickly passed. She hoped that was a good sign and shared those hopes with Redford.

"I hope so, too. I can't wait to hear what your doctor says next week," he said.

Carmen was nervous about the doctor's visit but refused to share those anxieties with him. She had to believe everything would be alright, especially since the morning sickness seemed less severe than it had been even a few days before.

Yet that seemed to pose another sort of challenge.

With less bouts of nausea, she noticed Redford more and more. Not only did she notice him, but she also desired him. And when he did all those nice things for her, she fell deeper in love.

Later that night, after telling her goodnight, Redford brushed a kiss across her lips. A short while later, she was tossing and turning, unable to sleep. She slid out of bed, went to the window and pushed back the curtains to look at the stars. She didn't want to remember the night she'd made a wish upon them, but she did.

She turned when she heard a knock at her door. "Come in."

Redford strode in with his pj's riding low on his hips and concern etched on his face. "Are you okay, Carmen? I heard you moving around."

She recalled him saying how sleeping below her bedroom meant he could hear all the sounds above him. "I'm fine. I just couldn't sleep."

"Feeling nauseated again?"

"No. Just restless."

"Oh."

He came to stand beside her at the window. Her attention was no longer on the stars but on him. He was shirtless, and she recalled another time when she'd seen him wearing nothing at all.

That had been the first time she'd seen a man strip off his clothes. She'd watched him from the bed, wide-eyed, as he removed every single stitch. When she'd seen his naked body, she couldn't get over just how well-endowed he was. There hadn't been an inch she hadn't found impressive. Why was she remembering that now, and why could she feel heat radiating from his body to hers?

"The stars are pretty tonight, aren't they?"

Stars were the last thing she wanted to discuss. That's how that night had started. Her believing in the stars. "Yes, they're pretty."

She made a move to turn from the window when he touched her arm. The connection was so hot, she almost jerked away.

"I was restless tonight too," he said.

"You were? Why?"

"I was thinking about you and the kiss we shared earlier."

There was no way she would admit the reason she'd been restless was because she had been thinking not only of him and that kiss, but that night when their child had been conceived. "What about me and the kiss?"

"I was thinking how good it was and how delicious you tasted."

She nibbled on her bottom lip. Did he have to be so direct with his answers? His words stimulated her hormones. Something she didn't need. "Why would you be thinking about that at this hour?"

He smiled at her. "I will admit that since our night together, I think of you at all hours of the night."

This was the first time they had talked about that night. They had only discussed the results, namely her pregnancy. He'd even told her how that night had left him unable to desire another woman. But as of yet, they hadn't talked about how making love with her had done that to him. Something so unprecedented. She doubted he would bring it up, so maybe she should force him to do so.

"Tell me about that night, Redford."

He didn't respond immediately, and she thought

maybe he hadn't heard her request. He proved her wrong when he asked, "What do you want to know about that night?"

"Everything. I'm sure you're aware that was my first time with a man."

He looked out at the stars and then back at her. "I know. At least it didn't take me long to find out. You're in your thirties. What had you been waiting on?"

Deciding to be honest, she said, "I thought I was waiting on you."

"Sorry I disappointed you."

"You didn't. As far as the lovemaking went, you were worth the wait." She allowed a shy smile to touch her lips when she added, "It was definitely better than anything I'd read in my romance novels."

"Is that a fact?" he asked. She didn't miss the arrogant smile that quirked the corners of his lips. Typical man.

At the risk of stroking his ego anymore, she said, "Yes, that's a fact. But then there was nothing I had to compare it to other than those novels. For all I know, multiple orgasms might be common."

He wrapped his arms around her shoulders and looked at the stars again before saying, "They aren't."

"Oh."

He didn't say anything for a minute. "There was a lot I could have compared it to, Carmen, considering my reputation with women. However, I must say, you rocked my world that night. I hadn't expected…"

When he didn't finish, she refused to let him stop now. "You hadn't expected what?"

He turned slightly and stared down at her. "So much passion from someone so inexperienced."

She honestly didn't know what to say to that, so she said nothing. Instead, her body reacted to the way he was looking at her. It was as if he wanted to deliberately stir that passion he was talking about. It didn't help matters that he had what she thought was a beautiful chest.

He lowered his head toward her, and she lifted hers to him. When their lips touched, like before, heat flared into flame. And when he captured her tongue with his, she didn't think it was possible for more passion to be generated than before. Yet it was, when he deepened the kiss and sucked on her tongue.

That prompted salacious thoughts to enter her mind. She loved all the feelings his tongue invoked. His warm chest against her robe offered no barrier to the heat, and when she felt the hardness of him pressed against her middle, it took everything she had to keep her knees from buckling. He must have sensed it; he swooped her up into his arms and carried her over to the bed.

She was tempted to ask him to join her there but couldn't. If they ever made love again, he had to be willing. When and if that day came, she would be willing, as well. There was no way she could not be with all the love flowing in her heart for him.

After placing her on the middle of the bed, he leaned down and brushed a kiss across her lips again before whispering, "Good night, Carmen."

"Good night, Redford."

She then watched him leave her bedroom.

Chapter Eighteen

"I'm ready, Redford."

He turned at the sound of Carmen's voice. "Wow," he mumbled, studying her. He'd only seen her in night-gowns lately and now seeing her dressed in a pair of slacks and a fashionable blouse made him even more aware of why he'd been attracted to her from the first.

Redford fought back the urge to cross the room and take her into his arms. Instead, he stood there and al-lowed the scent and beauty of her to ram through his senses. He noticed her braid was gone. In its place were thick brown tresses flowing around her shoulders.

"Well, how do I look?" she asked, probably because of the way he was staring at her.

"Beautiful." And he meant it. Finally crossing the room to her, he leaned in and lightly brushed his lips against hers. Their kisses were one area where he fought to maintain control. He enjoyed kissing her, and from her own admission she enjoyed kissing him. However, he knew kissing could lead to other things if they weren't careful.

She smiled. "And I think you look handsome."

He chuckled. "Thanks."

He'd decided to wear a pair of dark slacks and a light blue button-down shirt. He'd never accompanied a woman to a doctor's appointment before and didn't know what to expect. However, what he did know was that he wanted to be there for Carmen and their baby. Like he'd told her a number of times over the past few days, her pregnancy was something he wanted them to share together.

Moments later, he ushered her out to the private car he'd ordered. Once they got into the backseat and the driver closed the door, Redford placed his arm around Carmen's shoulder. "All things considered, this is a nice town."

She smiled. "I take it you don't visit here often."

"No. The only other times I've been here were with Sloan whenever he visited Jess."

It didn't take long to reach the medical complex where both the lab and doctor's office were located. The staff was friendly and efficient, and he appreciated they didn't wait long to be seen. In trying to keep Carmen relaxed, he fought hard to keep himself calm as well. He refused to think something wasn't right with the baby; it was normal procedure for her doctor to order lab work before seeing her.

His anxiety grew, though, when the doctor was an hour late. Of course, he didn't voice his concerns to Carmen. Had the doctor found something wrong with her lab work? He was glad when a medical assistant finally entered the examination room and said the doctor had gotten delayed because she'd been called away to deliver a baby.

When the doctor finally arrived, she went straight to discussing Carmen's lab reports. Redford was relieved to find there was nothing concerning in the labs, and he could tell Carmen was relieved too. It seemed that even with the nausea, everything was in the expected range. She stressed that Carmen wasn't out of the woods yet, but that her condition was definitely improving. Hopefully, over the next few weeks the nausea would be less severe. That was good news to hear.

"In the meantime," the doctor said, closing Carmen's chart, "I want you out of the house more, even if you have to carry a barf bag around with you. I suggest you take walks in the morning and afternoon, breathe in some fresh air. You can even go bicycling. The only thing I would not suggest yet is horseback riding." The doctor then gave them a cheeky grin when she added, "And in case you had stopped engaging in sexual activities, there's no harm in resuming them now."

Redford refused to look at Carmen but figured she was blushing. So was he. When had the subject of sex ever made him blush? Obviously, the doctor assumed that because they were here together they were in a solid relationship. Neither he nor Carmen corrected her assumption.

The doctor then told them something Redford hadn't been prepared for. "I want to listen to the baby's heartbeat."

While listening, he held tight to Carmen's hand and wiped tears from her eyes. He knew this moment was just as special to her as it was to him. He would never forget the experience. The gentle, steady, strong beats made him realize the significance of the life he and Carmen had created. He was convinced he had fallen in love with their child the moment he'd learned of her pregnancy. But listening to the heartbeats made him fall in love with their baby even more. It was a moment he'd honestly thought he would never share with a woman. Together they would one day tell their little bun about it.

"It's too early for me to reveal the sex of the baby today, but I'll be able to do so during your next visit if either of you are interested," the doctor said, smiling.

Redford met Carmen's eyes, and as if he could read her thoughts, he said, "We'd rather it be a surprise."

The doctor nodded and entered their request into her records. Moments later, after Carmen had dressed, she wrapped her arms around him and they held each other. A profound feeling of happiness washed over him, and he touched his lips to her forehead. She snuggled closer to him. When she buried her face in his chest, he knew she was crying. He felt his composure slipping.

Leaning in, he whispered words he hoped comforted her. He told her that he knew she would be a great mother to their child, and he couldn't think of any other woman he would want to share parenthood with.

She raised her tear-stained face and thanked him and then she leaned up on tiptoes to place a kiss on his lips. Everything about that moment felt right. She was the center of his thoughts and his feelings as he deepened the kiss. When he finally released her mouth, he continued to hold her close. He needed to share this moment with her.

He needed her.

When had he ever needed a woman other than sexually? Emotions he'd never felt before seeped into him, and he wasn't sure how to handle them.

He decided right then that he *wouldn't* handle them. He would just let things take their course. The most important thing was that he had heard his child's heartbeat. For a moment, the sound had seemed perfectly in sync with his own.

Carmen leaned back to look up at him and gave him a bright smile. He doubted she had any idea what that smile did to him. How it made him feel. "Ready to go, Dad-to-be?" she asked.

A huge grin spread across his face. He liked the sound of that. "Yes, Mom-to-be. I'm ready."

He took her hand in his and they left the examination room.

"Wow! You actually heard the baby's heartbeat. That's wonderful, Carmen," Leslie said in an excited voice.

"Redford and I thought so, too." She then told Leslie everything else the doctor had said, including the part about encouraging her to engage in more outside activities. "I'm glad I'm able to do more than be confined to a bed now. I'm more than ready to start going on those walks."

"Just don't overdo it."

She chuckled. "I won't. I doubt Redford will let me. Even now, he's downstairs in the kitchen trying out another new recipe for dinner."

"You like having him there, don't you?"

Carmen thought hard about Leslie's question before answering. "Yes. I really didn't think I would. I appreciate that at no time does he try to exert dominance. He lets me handle things, and when I can't, I know he's here for me and the baby. That's a good feeling."

"I know it can be. Sloan and I are surprised at how he's stepped into his role as your caretaker. Never in a thousand years would we have pictured him giving a woman a pedicure."

"And he did an awesome job."

"I know. I got the photos you sent over. Redford might be in the wrong business."

Carmen chuckled. "That's what I told him." She then got serious for a second as she told Leslie of the doctor's other suggestion. The one about them resuming sexual activities. "I wonder why she would think we would be in that kind of relationship."

"Honestly, Carmen, why wouldn't she think it? Redford was there with you today, and I'm sure the doctor noted how attentive he was to you. And I bet the two of you were transmitting strong sexual vibes. I doubt you and Redford realize how easy it is for others to pick up on it."

"You think that was it?"

"I'm sure it was." Leslie paused and then asked, "So are you and Redford going to take the doctor's advice and resume things?"

Carmen rolled her eyes. "We only slept together that one time, Leslie. There's nothing to resume."

"Are those your thoughts or Redford's?"

"They're both of ours."

"Does that mean you and Redford aren't sharing any more hot kisses? Like the ones you've been telling me about?"

Leslie's question made Carmen recall the scorcher of

a kiss they had shared at the doctor's office. "I wouldn't say that."

"Then I wouldn't say making love is off the table. Kisses are known to lead to other things, so be prepared if they do."

"That's not possible. Redford won't let things get out of hand."

"He's a man. And according to him, he hasn't desired a woman since making love to you. He's probably all but climbing the walls about now."

Carmen arched a brow. "You think so?"

"Yes, and there's a way to find out for certain, if you're interested."

Was she? She sighed deeply when curiosity got the best of her. "Okay, tell me."

"It's simple. Seduce him."

Chapter Nineteen

Redford felt himself slipping into the deep throes of ecstasy. He was about to make love to Carmen, and he refused to accept that this was only a dream, one he staunchly refused to wake from. He eased into position above her, ready to slide in, anticipating...

Suddenly, he was awakened by movement in the room above his. Carmen was awake and pacing. Why? Was she restless again tonight? Was something medically wrong? The thought had him bolting out of bed, rushing from the guest room and up the stairs. Forcing his overstretched nerves under control, he knocked on her bedroom door.

"Come in."

He opened the door then stopped short. She stood in the middle of the room and, unlike last night, she wasn't wearing a robe. She wore a nightgown that looked even shorter than the one from last night.

He swallowed the deep lump in his throat before asking, "What's wrong, Carmen?"

She lifted a brow. "What makes you think something is wrong?"

He frowned. "I heard you moving around. Why aren't you in bed asleep? Are you restless again tonight?"

She shook her head. "No, I'm not restless."

He nodded and came farther into the room. The way the light from the hallway shone into her bedroom highlighted not only how short her gown was, but also the lack of undergarments beneath it. Why were there so many tempting curves on her body? Her hair flowed loosely around her shoulders. He recalled that when he'd left her tonight she had bound it back in a ponytail. The wild mass gave her an even sexier look. He'd offered to help her wash it and re-braid it tomorrow.

"If you're not restless tonight, then what's wrong?" he asked, coming to a stop in front of her. Was he imagining things or was she emitting heat? Why? Was she running a fever? Instinctively, he checked her forehead.

"What are you doing?" she asked.

"Checking your temperature. You feel a little hot."

"I'm not running a fever, Redford. At least not exactly."

He dropped his hands from her face to his side. Her words confused him. "Then what exactly?"

She began nibbling on her bottom lip, and he detected she was nervous. "What's wrong, Carmen? What's bothering you at this hour? You can tell me anything. Remember, we're in this together."

He watched her draw in a deep breath, and then as if she'd made up her mind about something, she said,

"I've never been into game-playing and want to be completely honest with you about something."

This sounded serious. "Okay. What?"

She paused. "I knew if you heard me moving around up here that you would come check on me. I apologize for that."

"You don't have to apologize."

She looked at him with a very serious expression in those beautiful, almond-shaped, light brown eyes. "But I do."

He tilted his head to look at her. "Why do you feel that way?"

Instead of answering, she nibbled on her bottom lip again. He doubted she knew how much of a turn-on that was. Reaching out, he took her hand and brought it to his lips to kiss her palm. He tried convincing himself he'd done it to calm her nervousness more than to placate his raging testosterone.

"Tell me, Carmen, why you feel that way," he said, releasing her hand.

He watched her draw in another deep breath before saying in a low voice, "I wanted you to come up here so I could seduce you."

He blinked, thinking he'd heard her wrong. "Seduce me?"

Now she was nervously wringing her hands together. "Yes."

Desire surged through him at the thought that she'd wanted to seduce him. "Why?"

She looked up at him. "Why what?"

"Why do you want to seduce me?"

She released what sounded to him like a disgusted

sigh. "The doctor planted the seed in my head by thinking we're intimate."

He nodded. "A logical conclusion since you're having my baby."

She shrugged. "That's what Leslie said when I gave her a recap of my doctor's visit."

"I gather you changed your mind about this plan of seduction, then?" he asked, and thought his voice sounded husky, even to him.

"Pretty much. I can't be that manipulating, especially since I know how you feel."

He took her hand in his. She seemed to be a mass of nervous energy, flustered and apprehensive. "And how do I feel?" he asked.

"You said that we would never be intimate again. That you needed the willpower to make sure such a thing didn't happen. Knowing that, it wouldn't be right for me to try to seduce you."

He was convinced Carmen was way too honest for her own good. She had more integrity in her little pedicured toe than some people had in their entire body. In a way, he had known from the beginning that she was different, but initially, he had refused to let that mean anything. Like all the others, he had put up his "do-them-before-they-do-you" defense.

"So, you can go back to bed, Redford. I'm sorry to have disturbed you," she said, breaking into his thoughts.

Was she actually dismissing him now? Did she think he could walk away after everything she'd told him? He released her hand and tenderly caressed her cheek, loving the feel of her soft skin. And the degree of desire he saw in her eyes was something she couldn't hide, and he was so glad that she couldn't.

"What if I told you that I have no problem with you seducing me, Carmen?"

"Why? Because you know that I can't?"

"No, because I know that you can. And as far as my willpower, I've discovered over the past week, it's a lost cause where you are concerned."

Her eyes widened like saucers. "Why?"

"Because of the magnitude of what we shared that night. A night I still have strong memories of. Now I understand why our lovemaking made such a lasting impression on me."

"You do?" At his nod, she asked, "Why?"

"Because something that wonderful and magnificent was never meant to be a one and done."

Without giving her a chance to say anything, he leaned in and brushed a kiss across her lips and whispered, "So go ahead, Carmen. I give you permission to seduce the hell out of me."

A lump formed in Carmen's throat when she repeated Redford's words in her mind. Staring deeply into his eyes, she saw a longing in their dark depths and couldn't ignore the sense of satisfaction that fueled her own desire. When a smile spread across his lips, she felt emboldened to seduce him, although she'd never done any such thing before in her life.

"I wouldn't know where to start," she admitted.

"Start anywhere you like and do anything you want," was his response. The deep sound of his voice did things to her. Made her feel things that only he could make her feel. Suddenly, she felt very warm. The sliver of the moon through an opening in the curtain highlighted his features. His very handsome features.

His words floated back through her mind once again. They motivated her, made her want to do just what he'd suggested, to start anywhere and do anything. Just the thought sent a sensuous tremor through her.

So what was she waiting for?

Leaning up on tiptoes, she pressed her mouth to his. He returned the kiss but in no way did he try to dominate it, even though he was holding her solidly against him. Yet this kiss stirred something deep within her. Although he let her control every aspect of it, at the same time, in his own way, he assured her that he was all in.

In no time at all, the kiss ignited a craving within her, one she'd tried to contain since his arrival a week ago. There was a greediness unleashed within her that made every part of her ache with an urgency that was overtaking her senses.

If someone had told her after her last encounter with Redford that she would be allowing such a thing to occur again, she would have laughed. But here she was, back in his arms again and anticipating what she knew would happen next.

Nothing she and Redford shared had anything to do with love. At least not on his part. The chemistry between them was strong, unrelenting and nearly burning out of control.

She broke off the kiss to take a deep breath, filling her nostrils with his masculine scent and her eyes with all that was him. The last time they'd been together, he had undressed her. Tonight, she wanted to experience how it would be to undress him. He was already shirtless and his jeans hung low on his hips with the fastener unsnapped. Evidently, he had slipped into them quickly when he'd heard her move around up here.

"Need my help with anything?"

She met his gaze and saw the heat of desire in his eyes. Knowing he wanted this as much as she did had her melting inside. "No, I got this."

To prove her point, she took a step closer and immediately felt the hard throb of his erection against her middle. She tried not to react to it but couldn't help doing so. There was no way he didn't see genuine female appreciation in her eyes.

Reaching down, she began easing down his zipper. Then kneeling down in front of him, she tugged on his jeans. After a few tries, she finally eased them down his legs. Since he wasn't wearing any briefs, she could only assume he slept in the nude. The thought of such a thing was a total turn-on for her.

When he kicked the jeans aside, she stood back up to let her gaze roam over his naked body. She thought the same thing now that she had their one night together. He was a perfect specimen of a man. She couldn't help leaning in to brush a kiss across his lips and whispering, "We're halfway there."

As she took a step back, his dark eyes stared at her as she eased the nightgown from her shoulders to drop at her feet. Now it was his gaze roaming over her nakedness.

There was something hot about his look that made her move toward him. She reached up to wrap her arms around his neck and recaptured his mouth with hers. Kissing him in ways she'd spent several nights dreaming about.

Evidently, she was doing something right, she

thought, when she felt his hands stroke her back. In no time at all she became lost in the sensuality that was the epitome of Redford St. James. Although he let her dominate the kiss, there was something about the way he was doing so that had her senses reeling. Not only was she trying to light his fire, he was also lighting hers.

She pulled away from the kiss and unwrapped her hands from around his neck. Then she began doing something she'd wanted to do the last time but hadn't been bold enough to try. Mainly to touch him. All over.

Her hands trailed over his chest and shoulders before moving lower to his hips and thighs. Feeling bolder still, she cupped that ultra-male, large part of him in her hand, amazed at the hardness of it. Just thinking how this particular part had been instrumental in making a baby with her elicited a sensual moan from deep within her throat.

His voice was husky, his breathing choppy and erratic, when he murmured, "I love the feel of you touching me, Carmen."

Carmen had news for him. She found this part of him fascinating and loved touching him, too. The more she did so, the more she wanted him. From the sounds he was making, he wanted her, too.

"Not sure how much more I can handle of you doing that," he said in a throaty voice while framing her face in his palms. She had no choice but to look at him instead of looking down at what her hands were doing.

He released her face when her fingertips began making circular motions around the tip of his manhood. She looked into his eyes when he inhaled sharply, as if his breath had been snatched from him. "What's wrong?" she asked, concerned, but not enough to stop what she was doing to him with her hands. The eyes staring back at her were so filled with heat, they nearly snatched her own breath away.

"You have no idea what you're doing to me, Carmen," he said through gritted teeth.

He was right, she didn't know, but she had a good idea. Feeling naughty, she leaned in and licked the side of his face and whispered, "What I want to know is whether I've seduced the hell out of you yet, Redford."

Reaching down, he gently cradled her face in his hand. "Yes, sweetheart. You have done that and more. Now it's my turn to seduce you, Carmen."

He swept her off her feet and into his arms.

Chapter Twenty

Redford placed Carmen on the bed. The air around him seemed inflamed with the scent of her. Why did she have to smell so good and taste so delicious?

He stared at the naked woman who'd seduced the hell out of him, like he'd suggested. He was a pro at seducing women and never had one seduce him. Until tonight he hadn't thought such a thing was possible. In the past, he'd not only called the shots but was also the one who decided when and where his game of seduction would be played out. However, tonight Carmen had taken that decision out of his hands and placed it into hers. Literally.

He tried fighting back his body's demands. If just her touch could do that to him, he didn't want to remember what being inside her body would do. He tried breaking eye contact with her but couldn't. Now he recalled his earlier assertion to Sloan that she had p-whipped him.

However, he was beginning to think it was more than that. What? He wasn't sure.

Every muscle in his body desired her to the point where emotions he'd never had to deal with before crowded in on him, taking over his mind the same way they'd taken over his body. Could nearly three months of forced celibacy do that to him? Or…had he finally met his match? He didn't want to think that such a thing was possible, but at that moment his mind was too messed up, and he was filled with so much need for her that he couldn't think straight.

"Are you sure you're up to this?" he asked her, indicating his huge erection.

She gave a somewhat shy smile and said, "Just as long as I know it's *up* for me."

He couldn't help but grin at her play on words. "Trust me. It is. Only for you." Even more desire surged through him, yet in consideration of her health, he had to make sure he wasn't being an insensitive ass. "And you're sure you're okay, healthwise?"

She eased up on her haunches and his gaze followed the movement. "I am, so don't try to back out now, Redford."

"The only thing that can stop me at this point is you telling me to do so."

"And I won't do that. I want you too much."

Her words slipped him into the sensual world that was Carmen Golan. A world he had been part of once and hadn't been the same since. More than anything, he wanted to see if all those orgasms were a fluke or common for them.

He moved toward the bed and she leaned in to meet him. Drawing her against him, he captured her mouth with a need he felt not only in his erection but in his entire body. His hands began stroking her all over, her bare skin felt hot beneath his fingertips. He specifically liked tracing a path over the smoothness of her shoulders. From the sounds she made, he knew she was enjoying his touch…just like he'd enjoyed hers earlier.

His tongue greedily explored her mouth. When he finally got a mind to end the kiss, he pressed her back against the pillows. She stretched out her arms to him and that was an invitation he intended to accept. Before moving to her, his gaze roamed over every inch of her delectable curves, a pair of beautiful breasts with hardened nipples and a flat stomach. She'd told him the other day that she could detect a little protruding stomach, but as of yet, he could not. Then his gaze lowered still to the very essence of her—namely, her feminine folds. Just the sight of her made his erection throb and her scent made his tongue thicken in his mouth.

"What's taking you so long, Redford?" she asked in a voice filled with need. He switched his gaze to her face and smiled. A thick mass of hair was fanned out against the pillow.

"I just want to savor the moment. You are very beautiful, Carmen," he said, truthfully. "And, lying here like that makes you look delicious, too."

"Delicious?"

His smile widened. "Yes, delicious. Let me prove what I mean."

Moving closer, he pulled her forward and let his hands rest on a pair of firm breasts. Cupping them, he used the pads of his thumbs to gently finger the hardened nipples.

She moaned deeply in her throat. "You're driving me to madness, Redford."

"You haven't experienced anything yet, sweetheart." Then he leaned in and began devouring her breasts.

Seeing them and touching them had done something to him. He believed it had to do with knowing that one day these twin globes would be the source of his child's nourishment. Whatever the reason, at that moment he couldn't help but greedily feast on them himself. The more he tasted of her, the more he wanted.

Knowing he couldn't make love to her breasts forever, no matter how good they tasted, he finally pulled his mouth away and then lowered her to the pillows. He was a man who appreciated beauty, and he was convinced his gaze was taking in the most beautiful creature ever created.

"Now to taste another part of you," he said, reaching down to stroke her inner thigh. From her expression, he knew the same sensations stirring within him were also stirring within her. When his fingers slowly stroked her feminine folds, the skin there felt soft. He glanced up and saw heat lodged in her eyes and understood. She had confessed to having her dreams like he'd had his.

Knowing he couldn't delay tasting her any longer, he lifted her legs over his shoulders and put his mouth on her center. His tongue eased inside and found her hot and wet, like he'd remembered. Just the way he liked. First using the tip of his tongue to lap her up and then easing his tongue farther inside, he delved deeper, then retreated to capture her clit. He actually heard himself moan at the same exact time that she did.

Then he locked his mouth down and held tight to her thighs. He had almost three months to make up for, and he intended to do just that. His tongue thrust deeper and he felt the slight pain when her fingers grabbed hold of his shoulders, then the side of his face as if to keep him in place right there. She definitely didn't have to worry about him going anywhere. He was enjoying the delicious taste of her way too much.

He knew the exact moment her body was about to explode, and he was more than ready for the decadent appetizer he knew awaited him.

Carmen screamed as a multitude of spasms rushed through her body. She was convinced that never had an orgasm been as needed as this one. Her world spun out of control as every nerve ending inside her came alive and shattered her to a million pieces.

Through dazed eyes she saw the moment Redford pulled his mouth from her and lowered her legs from his shoulders. He then eased back to stare down at her while licking his lips. "You taste good, baby. Simply incredible."

He then leaned in and captured her lips. He kissed her with the same intensity he'd used just moments ago between her legs. Within seconds he had stirred her hunger again to the point where she felt hot blood racing through her veins.

Obviously, the chemistry flowing between them hadn't lessened any. If anything, it had heightened. The very thought of them making love again caused sensual stirrings to erupt in the pit of her stomach. As if he felt it, too, he moved in place over her.

He continued to stare down at her and she was captured by the beauty, as well as the heat, she saw in the depths of his dark eyes. Moments later, while he still held her gaze, she felt him ease inside of her and fill her completely. Was she imagining things or was his erection actually getting bigger, longer and harder inside of her?

Before she could dwell on that possibility, he began moving. Going in deep and then pulling out. Advancing and then retreating, over and over again, deliberately establishing a sensuous rhythm that had her groaning and moaning. He'd started out slowly, and then, as if he was seized by an overabundance of desire, he began thrusting harder and faster.

She released a series of moans, and he placed his mouth over hers. That's when their mouths picked up the same mating rhythm as the lower parts of their bodies. She gripped his shoulders as their tongues moved in a frenzy that had them moaning even more.

Regardless of what this was for him, for her it was displaying what she felt for him in a physical way because she would never speak it aloud. This wasn't just sex for her, it was love.

At the first sign of her orgasm, he pulled his mouth away and she released a scream. She hoped her neighbors couldn't hear her but a part of her didn't care if they did. When she opened her eyes to stare up at Redford, his gaze was both hot and predatory. That's when another orgasm hit and she saw it had hit him as well. Then another, and she sensed a need within them both that was taking over their bodies.

She widened her legs for him, wanting it all, and watched in hot fascination as he threw his head back and the cords in his neck tightened while the solid hardness of him continued to stretch her. The thought of him embedded so deeply within her had her moaning. She felt him all the way to the hilt.

When she screamed his name again, he screamed hers, detonating a barrage of passion that spread through them, seeming to ignite every cell in their bodies. When one orgasm ended and before one scream stopped, another orgasm was beginning to capture them in its clutches.

She could recognize his orgasm from the way he would slow his thrusts, only to start up again in a fast pace, then groaning her name. They kept coming, nearly nonstop. Then finally, as if he refused to collapse on top of her, he quickly shifted his body off her for them to face each other.

He kissed her with a tenderness she felt all through her body while cuddling her in his arms. Before dozing off, she recalled each and every time she felt the essence of him explode inside of her. The hot, molten liquid felt right. Like it belonged only to her, and from what he'd told her, she was the only woman with whom he'd shared himself to that degree. The last time hadn't been intentional. Tonight, it was as if he hadn't cared. Probably because she was already pregnant.

Regardless of the reason, it made her smile knowing she had again shared something with him no other woman had. Considering his history with women, that said a lot. But then that wasn't all. His baby was growing inside of her. Their baby. She cuddled closer to Redford and breathed her happiness into his chest.

She might not have his love, but she would always have a part of him they would share forever.

The sound of Carmen in the bathroom brought Redford awake. He was lying flat on his back in her bed.

And it was morning. Memories of their night together rushed through him, lighting his body with a fire that only Carmen could ignite. That had been proven over and over during the night.

He'd been concerned about exhausting her in her delicate condition, but she dismissed his worry and proceeded to show him that the depth of her need for him was just as great as his had been for her. After pleasuring each other time and time again, they had finally succumbed to a peaceful sleep.

He glanced at the clock and saw it was a little past seven in the morning. The sound of her in the bathroom immediately caught his attention again. That's when he realized she was enduring a bout of morning sickness.

Rushing from the bed, he opened the bathroom door and immediately found her on the floor in front of the commode. Crouching down beside her, he pulled her hair back from her face and then began gently stroking her back, whispering calming and what he hoped were comforting words to her. When she finished, he lifted her to stand in front of the vanity while she brushed her teeth, rinsed her mouth and wiped her face with a cool cloth.

"I didn't want to wake you," she said, turning to ease into his arms.

"You should have," he said, softly, placing a kiss across her lips. "We're in this together, remember."

She nodded. "I need to take a shower."

"Okay."

Moving away from her, he started the water. She removed her robe to reveal her nakedness, and he was glad she wasn't showing any signs of morning-after shyness or regret. Before stepping into the shower, she glanced over her shoulder, smiled and asked, "Would you like to join me, Redford?"

It was early, yet it seemed the desire in her gaze was just as potent as what she probably saw in his. "Most definitely, sweetheart."

Typically, he didn't use terms of endearment with women. However, he'd used a number of them with her last night. For some reason, doing so had come naturally for him. "Besides, I promised to wash your hair today," he added.

They showered together, tenderly washing each other's bodies before he began washing her hair. Then they made love in the shower, a novelty for both of them.

After their shower ended, he and Carmen toweled each other dry before he re-braided her hair the way he'd watched Leslie do for her one day and thought he'd done a decent job. He then suggested they go for a walk after breakfast. It was a beautiful day. Instead of walking the neighborhood again, he ordered a car to take them to the National Harbor. They walked at a steady pace along the Potomac River and even visited several shops along the way. Afterward, they returned to her home in time for him to prepare lunch.

Carmen got sick later that day. Considering that was a reduction in the number of times, he thought it was a good sign. She thought so, too. Instead of going upstairs and taking a nap when they returned, she hung out down in the kitchen and kept him company while he prepared dinner. He enjoyed hearing about the classes she taught and how the current bill in the senate was vital for the country's economy.

Neither said anything about the night before. However, the sharing of smiles, less than innocent touches and stolen kisses whenever they felt like it, spoke of a heightened level of intimacy between them.

Nothing was said about sleeping arrangements but that night they took another shower together. When he joined her in bed, it seemed like the most natural place to be. All he'd intended to do was hold her in his arms; however, she had other ideas.

"What do you think you're doing?" he asked when she slid from his arms and placed her body over his.

She smiled down at him. "Feeling naughty."

He chuckled. "Weren't you naughty enough last night?"

"No."

And after that single word, she lowered her mouth to his. He didn't hesitate returning her kiss.

Chapter Twenty-One

The following weeks seemed to fly by. Carmen's morning sickness wasn't as severe as it had been. During her most recent doctor's visit, she was told her body was showing increased signs of improvement and there was a chance the nausea would be gone altogether in another week or two.

It was.

Carmen knew that meant it was only a matter of time until Redford would be leaving. Her next appointment with the doctor was on Friday, and she saw no reason why the doctor would not give her a clean bill of health and tell them her pregnancy was no longer at risk.

She figured Redford thought the same thing. Just that morning she had overheard him communicating with his management team that chances were, he would be returning to the office within a week. She wanted to believe he hadn't sounded all that excited about leaving, but a part of her knew she'd probably just imagined it.

They still shared a bed every night and woke up in each other's arms every morning. She'd tried not to get used to having him there, but he had become a monumental part of her life. There was no doubt in her mind she would miss him something fierce when he was gone. The time she had spent with Redford, and the way he had taken such good care of her, was something she would forever appreciate and something she would never forget.

She had gotten to know him as someone other than the father of her baby. He was a person she could talk to about anything, and he was someone who was full of information on any given topic. For those topics he wasn't sure about, he wasted no time in doing the research. In addition to enjoying their conversations, she looked forward to the times they lay cuddled up together watching movies.

Over the past month they had formed a special relationship, and the thought that it would soon end made her heart ache. She knew the only way to prepare for his departure was to start withdrawing. That way the pain of him leaving wouldn't cut so deep.

That resolution was on her mind later that night while she lay in his arms after they'd made love. Having him in bed with her whenever the sexual need struck definitely had its benefits. There was never a time he didn't pleasure her immensely. He'd been her first, and she was certain he had ruined her for any other man. In a way, that wasn't good.

But still, she couldn't regret the time they had spent together. Her only regret was in knowing their days together were numbered and it was time to start protecting her heart. Redford didn't love her; he would never love her. That was a reality it was time for her to accept, no matter how good things were between them now.

Redford awoke with a start. Glancing over at Carmen, he saw she was still sleeping snugly in his arms with their limbs entwined. Recently, he'd begun noticing changes in her, and it was more than the little pudge he saw in her stomach or how her nipples had gotten darker. He'd also noticed she had begun withdrawing from him.

He had detected it a few nights ago. Although they still made love with abandon, with a yearning and intensity that took his breath away, he could tell their relationship was changing. He couldn't help wondering if now that she felt better that meant she was ready for him to leave.

Honestly, there wasn't a reason to hang around any longer since her doctor had stated during her last visit that she was out of danger. From here on out, all signs indicated she should have a rather normal pregnancy. Of course, they'd been glad to hear that, but he'd gotten used to taking care of her, of being here with her.

He'd contacted his office one morning to tell them he would be back in a week and before that day had ended he'd called them back and told them to disregard his earlier call. He wasn't sure exactly when he'd be back, mainly because he wasn't ready to leave.

If anyone had told him weeks ago that he would have this frame of mind, he would not have believed them. The past weeks with Carmen had meant everything to him, and thanks to her he'd been able to face a lot about himself. He now realized that episode with Candy had affected him more than he'd known.

It had taken Carmen to show him that there were

women who could be trusted completely. Women who didn't have any deceitful bones in their bodies. Women worth risking his heart for.

So many had tried convincing him of that—Sloan, Tyler, his parents and others—but he had refused to believe them. It had taken Carmen's pregnancy to show him another side of a relationship, other than a purely sexual one.

He now knew he had fallen in love with her. Although he wasn't sure exactly when it happened, it had happened. However, thanks to his earlier actions of treating her like all those other women he'd been involved with, she would never love him again. He felt a painful ache in the pit of his stomach in accepting that.

At least he had his memories of the days they would wake up together, shower together, go walking together, prepare meals together and go to bed together. The one thing they hadn't talked about was raising their child together as a unified family. Where they lived in the same house in a loving and committed relationship. Namely, marriage.

Maybe it was time they talked about that possibility, because he knew without a shadow of a doubt that he adored her. Every part of her that she had shared with him over the past month or so. He had fallen in love with her and had fallen hard.

She had been right from the beginning. They were soulmates, and it had taken her getting pregnant for him to accept that. He couldn't imagine any other woman in his life. Carmen was the one woman he refused to live without. However, the big challenge would be convincing her of that.

He would make his first attempt to do so tonight when they made love.

* * *

Carmen glanced up when Redford entered her bedroom. Tonight, he had surprised her with a candlelight dinner. It had been beautiful and romantic; however, she would have appreciated his efforts a lot more if she hadn't known it was his way of letting her know he was leaving. She could barely enjoy the delicious dinner he had prepared because she was waiting for him to tell her he was going back to Alaska. But he hadn't told her at dinner, so she could only assume he had decided to tell her later...which was now.

She watched him lean against the closed door staring at her. Her heart began pounding when he pulled off his shirt and tossed it in the chair and then proceeded to slip out of his jeans and briefs.

Carmen wondered if he intended to make love to her first before breaking the news he was leaving. There was no reason to think he would not return every once in a while to check on her and the baby, but still. She had gotten used to the time they'd spent together and had hoped...

What? That a man who'd stated more times than she could count that he would never fall in love with a woman would miraculously change his mind and do so? Why had she been kidding herself when she had vowed not to? Her only excuse was that things had been so good between them lately, and he'd honestly seemed to enjoy being here. But then, in the end, she had to face the fact that it had only been about the baby and the sex.

He strolled across the room to her. "I don't know why you bothered to put this on," he said, clasping the hem of her short night gown, removing it and tossing it across the room to join his clothes in the chair.

She no longer wore her hair braided and he glided his hands through it. "You're beautiful, do you know that?"

Forcing a smile to her lips, she said, "Only because you tell me." And he did so, often.

He smiled and then captured her mouth with his. She wanted this kiss; she needed this kiss. She would add it to all the other memories stored in her brain of the kisses and lovemaking they'd shared.

When he began walking her toward the bed, she decided to be the one in control tonight. When he tried easing her down on the bed, she shifted her body and eased him down on his back instead. His features showed his surprise seconds before she positioned her body over his. Widening her legs, she lowered her body to his erection, moaning when he assisted by lifting his hips off the bed for deeper penetration.

He was so powerfully male, and the feel of him embedded deep inside made her body begin to shiver. He gripped her hips when she began moving up and down, while he lifted his body to make each thrust even deeper.

"More, Carmen. More."

His guttural plea got to her, made her give him just what he wanted. More. Clutching his sides with her knees, she began riding him the way she'd learned to ride a horse years ago. She established a rhythm and he fell right in sync.

Over and over, she thrust down and he thrust up, and when she began flexing her inner muscles as if to drain everything out of him, he pulled her mouth down to his and took it with a hunger that made her moan again. Breaking off the kiss, she threw her head back as she continued to ride him to her heart's content. Making memories she would need when he left.

Suddenly, everything inside her exploded, seeming to rip her in two, and she noticed the same thing happening to him. They always came together and never knew when to stop.

"Carmen!"

"Redford!"

They screamed each other's names as orgasms ripped through them. Seemingly nonstop. And she knew that no matter what tomorrow brought for them, she would always have memories of tonight.

Chapter Twenty-Two

A short while later, Carmen was slumped down on Redford, unable to move after what he knew had been one hell of a lovemaking session. Somehow, he managed to raise his hand to stroke her back. He knew at that moment just what she meant to him.

"Carmen?"

She slowly raised her head to look down at him. "Yes?"

"There's something I need to tell you."

"There's something I need to tell you, too, Redford."

Deciding to let her go first, he asked, "What is it?"

"Since I'm doing better, there's no need for you to hang around here any longer."

Redford tried not to flinch at her words. "There's not?"

"No. I'm sure you want to get back to work, and I need to start writing that book. I got an extension on the deadline and figured if I get started on it right away, I'll be finished with it by the end of the year."

She shifted her body to lay beside him and added, "Besides, Chandra will be returning in a couple of weeks, and since she hasn't seen me most of the summer, I have a feeling she'll be paying me a visit."

He nodded. "Do you think she suspects something?"

"I doubt it. My family assumes I've been busy working on my book, which is why they haven't been calling a lot lately."

"I see." He really did. She wanted him gone before her family arrived. Why did the thought of that bother him?

"What did you have to tell me, Redford?"

There was no way he would say what he'd intended to say. Especially now that she'd made it clear she wanted him gone. In that case, he had no reason to stay any longer. "I was basically going to say the same thing," he lied. "Since you're doing a lot better now, my services are no longer needed here. It's time I go back to work. I've got that resort in Skagway to build, and you have that book to write."

"Right."

"I'll make arrangements with my pilot to come tomorrow."

"Okay." She leaned over and placed a kiss on his lips. "Thanks for everything, Redford. You were a big help, and I appreciate it."

"Don't mention it."

"At least we accomplished what we set out to do," she said, looking at him.

"What's that?"

"Bond. Although we don't love each other, we used

the time together to bond for our baby's sake. That's what we wanted, right?"

He stared into her eyes, thinking yes, that's what they wanted, but in the end, he'd also gotten something he hadn't thought he wanted. A woman he would love for the rest of his life. "Yes, that's what we wanted."

"Time to go to sleep now," she suggested, resting her head in the cradle of his shoulder. He had gotten used to her sleeping that way beside him and knew in the coming nights he would miss it. He would miss her.

Redford was still awake, long after he'd detected from Carmen's even breathing that she had fallen asleep. Sleep might have come easy for her tonight, but it hadn't for him. He had a feeling during the coming nights, after he returned to Anchorage, he would lie awake and think of her. However, he'd never been a man who stayed where he wasn't wanted. Nor would he remain with a woman who didn't want him, no matter how much he might want her. Or love her.

He exhaled a long breath knowing that he'd taken a chance on love for the second time in his life. This time he had truly learned his lesson.

"I think I got everything, but if you find something I'm leaving behind, let me know," Redford said.

"I will."

Carmen thought he wasn't wasting any time leaving. He had called for his jet that morning, prepared breakfast for her one last time and talked her into going for a walk around the neighborhood. When they'd returned, it hadn't taken him long to pack after receiving word a private car would be picking him up at one o'clock.

"Will it be okay if I call and check on you and our baby sometimes?"

"Yes, of course."

"Good."

Taking a step closer to her, he brushed her chin with the pad of his thumb. "Take care of yourself, Carmen, and our son or daughter," he said in that throaty voice. The one that could turn her on in an instant.

She forced a smile, fighting back the urge to tell him she didn't want him to go. "I will."

He leaned in and feathered kisses along her jaw. "I'm going to miss you."

Would he really? Didn't he understand she had to send him away? She couldn't go through life loving a man who would never love her. The longer he was here, the more she was bound to get attached to him, and she would be setting herself up for heartbreak of the worst kind. But still, she couldn't stop herself from saying, "I'm going to miss you, too."

Suddenly, he kissed her fully on the mouth, capturing her tongue in his as he stroked a need within her she didn't want to deny but knew that she must. It would be for the best. When their paths crossed again, hopefully by then she would be better equipped to deal with the only kind of relationship she and Redford would share.

Pulling her mouth away, she said, "If you don't get going your driver will wonder what the holdup is in here." She knew her words sounded unemotional, but she couldn't wane on her resolution. Nodding, he took a step back before turning and walking out the door.

Carmen moved to the window and fought tears as she watched Redford get into the private car. Not once did he look back, and that made the pain in her heart worse. Knowing she needed to leave, get out of the house for a while, she decided to go walking around the neighborhood.

She needed time to think and come to terms with what she'd done to protect her heart. She had sent away the man she loved.

"I just got word from air traffic control that takeoff is being delayed for about thirty minutes due to foreign dignitaries arriving in this air space, Mr. St. James," the pilot said over the intercom.

"Thanks, Todd." Unfastening his seatbelt, Redford stood and stretched his body before heading for the minibar. His phone rang and the special ringtone indicated it was Sloan.

He clicked it on. "Yes, Sloan?"

"I heard that you're returning to Alaska."

Redford selected a bottle of bourbon from the rack. "Any reason I shouldn't? Carmen is better now."

"Unless you lied to me yesterday when you admitted to being in love with her, I can think of a number of reasons why you shouldn't be leaving. Did you tell her how you felt about her?"

A part of him wished he hadn't confessed his feelings about Carmen to Sloan. "No, I didn't tell her. She didn't give me the chance. She said there was no reason for me to stay, and she asked me to leave."

"I still think you should have let her know how you feel, Redford."

"Evidently, you didn't hear what I said, Sloan. She all but asked me to leave."

"Did she ask you to leave or suggest that you leave?"

Redford rolled his eyes. "What difference does it makes?"

"A big difference since the two are not the same. Do I need to remind you that Carmen thought she was your soulmate and you broke her heart when she discovered that she wasn't? I suspect she's trying to protect herself from further heartbreak since you haven't told her that you have fallen in love with her. All I'm saying is that miscommunication can destroy a relationship. Trust me, I know. You remember what happened to me and Leslie for those ten years."

Yes, Redford thought. He remembered. He and Tyler had tried a number of times to get Sloan to go to Leslie and straighten things out, but he had refused to do so. "I don't think confessing how I feel to her is a good thing now."

"Would it ever have been a good time for you?"

Redford frowned. "What does that mean?"

"You've been protecting your heart for years. Maybe it's time to let go."

Redford released a deep breath. "I had let go. In fact, I had intended to tell Carmen last night. But she suggested I leave before I had a chance to do so."

"You should have done so anyway. I think you're making a mistake by not sharing your true feelings with her. And knowing Carmen like I do, I suspect she's doing something else, too."

"Something else like what?" he asked.

"Giving you an out. Maybe the reason she said you should leave was so you wouldn't feel bad about leaving her when you did so."

Redford hadn't thought of that possibility. "I hadn't

given Carmen any reason to think I was leaving or that I wanted to leave." Had he?

"Well, I still think you're making a mistake. Safe travels back to Alaska, Redford."

"Thanks."

After disconnecting the call, he again racked his brain. Had he given Carmen any reason to think he had wanted to leave? He then recalled the phone conversation with his vice president yesterday morning while Carmen had been in the shower. Had she overheard it and assumed those were his plans? He'd discovered showers had ears. Leslie had assumed Sloan had been in the shower when he'd overheard her conversation with Carmen about her pregnancy.

"Mr. St. James, I just got notification from the tower," his pilot broke into his thoughts to say. "We'll be ready to takeoff in ten minutes."

Redford placed down the bottle of bourbon he was about to pour into a glass. He pushed the button to the intercom on the wall. "I've changed my mind about leaving, Todd."

Carmen adjusted the earbuds while walking and talking to her sister. "We miss having you spend the summer here with us, Carmen. I hope you got a lot of writing done."

Releasing a deep breath, she wanted to let her sister know she had something to tell her, but she decided to wait until Chandra returned to the States. Instead of responding to what her sister had said, she asked, "Will Mom and Dad be coming back with you guys for a short visit?"

"Yes. They plan to take a cruise out of Florida before returning to Cape Town in September. We should be back in Atlanta in two weeks."

"I plan to come visit. I miss you guys."

"And we miss you, too. It wasn't the same without you."

Carmen rounded the corner to where her townhouse was located and slowed her pace when she saw Redford getting out of the same private car he'd left in a few hours ago. "Chandra, I'll call you back later," she said quickly, clicking off the phone.

She increased her steps when she saw him heading toward her front door. He no longer had a key since he'd returned it before leaving. "Redford?" she called out to him. "What happened? Did you forget something?" she asked, joining him on the porch and then opening the door.

"Yes, I forgot something."

"Oh." She figured it must have been important for him to come back for it when she'd agreed to send him anything he had left behind.

When they entered her townhouse, he closed the door behind him. "You went walking. That's good," he said.

She nodded. "Trying to follow doctor's orders." She glanced around, not wanting to stare at him. "So what did you forget?"

He slowly moved away from the door to walk over to where she was standing. "It's nothing I forgot per se, Carmen. I didn't do something that I should have done before I left."

She lifted her head to look up at him. "Oh. And what didn't you do?"

He shoved his hands into the pockets of his slacks. "Tell you how I feel about you. That I have fallen in love with you and that I want you and our baby as a permanent part of my life."

She knew her features showed her shock. "But you said you would never fall in love again. That you weren't capable of loving anyone."

"And I meant it when I said it. However, that was before I spent time with you here. Quality time. Meaningful time. You showed me that you aren't like Candy. You're different. You're unique. You're you. And you are who I fell in love with, Carmen. I was going to tell you last night after we made love, but before I could, you asked me to leave."

"You were planning to leave anyway. I overheard you giving your employees notice that you were returning."

"I only did that because I noticed you withdrawing from me over the past few days."

Yes, she had been. "I was withdrawing because I was trying to spare my heart, Redford. I had fallen in love with you before and erroneously assumed you had fallen in love with me, too. I'd learned my lesson and didn't want to make the same mistake again."

He took a step closer. "I love you, Carmen, and you were right all along. You truly are my soulmate. I never knew such a thing was possible, but you've proved me wrong." He wrapped his arms around her waist. "My question to you is, do you still love me?"

That was an easy answer to give. "Yes."

"Then will you marry me? Not for the baby's sake but for my sake? I realize how much I need and want you in my life. The thought of me, you and the baby as a family is what I want more than anything."

"Oh, Redford," she said, burying her face in his chest, loving his scent as usual. "Yes, I will marry you."

Lowering his mouth to hers, he captured it and then swept her off her feet. When he carried her over to the sofa, he broke off the kiss and sat down with her in his lap. "I know you hate cold weather so we can live here if you like."

"I want our baby to grow up loving his or her father's homeland. I'm willing to try Alaska for a while. I've gotten used to the weather somewhat whenever I visit Leslie and Sloan."

He gathered her close. "Tomorrow, we go looking for your engagement ring. I want to make it official before we bring our families into the thick of things."

"Good idea," she said, looking forward to meeting his family and him meeting hers.

She wrapped her arms around his neck, knowing for them the best was yet to come. They loved each other and they loved their baby. Life was good and they would be sharing it together.

"And now to celebrate our engagement." Redford stood with her in his arms and headed for the guest bedroom. "It's closer and we've never shared that particular bed."

He placed her on the bed and then joined her. "And just so you know, Carmen," he whispered close to her ear in that throaty voice she loved. "You and I never had sex. From the first, our experience was different. I didn't understand why. Now I do. Every time we shared a bed, we made love. I love you."

"I'm inclined to agree with you. And I love you, too, Redford."

Then he kissed her with all the longing and hunger she was happy to return to him. They had a wedding to plan, but first things first.

Epilogue

Redford glanced into Carmen's eyes as he slid the ring on her finger. Moments earlier in the presence of their families and wedding guests, he had vowed to love her, cherish her and honor her, forever, and he'd meant everything he said.

They had decided on a small wedding in DC with family and close friends. Sloan and Tyler were his two best men, and Leslie and Chandra were Carmen's matrons of honor.

He would never forget the happiness he felt watching Carmen walk down the aisle to him on her father's arm. The degree of love he saw shining in her eyes matched his own. Today, he was marrying the woman who'd truly captured his heart.

After the reception they would fly to spend two weeks in Bora Bora for their honeymoon. He was happy with the decision they'd made to set up residence in Skagway since he would be spending a lot of time there during the construction of the resort. And his parents were close by whenever he needed to travel.

Just like he'd known they would, his parents fell in love with Carmen and were excited to learn they would be grandparents in six months. The same thing with Carmen's family. They were happy about the baby, and he got along great with them.

"I now present Redford and Carmen St. James," the minister said, breaking into his thoughts. "You may kiss your bride, Redford."

Smiling down at Carmen, he kissed his wife with all the love he felt and knew that he'd been well and truly tamed.

* * * * *

A Q&A with Brenda Jackson

What or who inspired you to write?

At the time I started writing, I was doing a lot of business traveling while in management for my company. I'm not what I consider an adventurous person so instead of exploring the cities I visited, after my daily meetings, I would go back to my hotel room and let my imagination flow by writing short stories. Then the stories became longer in length. So, I guess you can say I was inspired by boredom.

What is your daily writing routine?

My daily routine is to get up by nine and begin writing. I break for lunch around one, and then start writing again around three. I take another short break around six. Then depending on how much writing I was able to do that day, I write three more hours from eight to eleven. I usually write at least ten hours a day. I write less on the weekends.

Who are your favorite authors?

Because of my writing schedule I usually don't have time to read other authors unless it's at bedtime via audiobooks. I enjoy historical romance novels by Beverly Jenkins, and contemporary romance novels by Iris Bolling, Delaney Diamond, Lori Foster and Nora Roberts, especially her J. D. Robb series.

Where do your story ideas come from?

My story ideas come from listening to songs, reading articles in newspapers and people sharing with me how they met or became engaged.

Do you have a favorite travel destination?

I have a beach house on Amelia Island, and I consider it my get-away place. I also love taking cruises to various countries and usually take one every six months.

What is your most treasured possession?

The promise ring my husband gave to me when I was fifteen years old. I still wear it and for me it represents the beginning of our love that lasted forty-seven years before he passed away.

When did you read your first Harlequin romance? Do you remember its title?

My first Harlequin Romance was *Corporate Affair* by Stephanie James (aka Jayne Ann Krentz). I read it in 1982, and I still have my original copy, which was published under Harlequin's Silhouette Desire line.

How did you meet your current love?

Gerald and I grew up together; attended the same

schools until middle school. His parents lived within a block of my grandmother's house. He was two years older and was the playmate of my older cousins.

What characteristic do you most value in your friends?

Honesty.

How did you celebrate or treat yourself when you got your first book deal?

It was in 1994 and my husband, kids and I took our first cruise to the Bahamas.

Will you share your favorite reader response?

I enjoy receiving letters from readers telling me how my books help them through a divorce, sickness or the loss of a loved one. It's a good feeling to know the words I write bring comfort to others.

What are your favorite character names?

Bane (short for Brisbane)—I felt that name suited him. Thorn—his name matched his surly disposition. Justin—the first hero I wrote about.

Other than author, what job would you like to have?

Before becoming a full-time author, I worked in corporate America and loved it. I supervised the training department for a while and on occasion I taught in corporate classrooms. I would love to be a professor who taught writing at a university.

Also by Synithia Williams

Counterfeit Courtship
The Spirit of Second Chances
Summoning Up Love

Visit the Author Profile page
at Harlequin.com for more titles!

A LITTLE BIT OF LOVE

Synithia Williams

Chapter One

Sheri "Lil Bit" Thomas squinted at the back door of her restaurant. She couldn't be seeing what she thought she was seeing. The dim lights in the back parking area and the waning 4:00 a.m. moonlight had to be playing tricks with her eyes. She shuffled around in the canvas bag she carried instead of a purse, pushing aside her wallet, multiple lipsticks, old receipts and other random items until her hand finally settled around her cell phone. Pulling it out, she turned on the flashlight and beamed the bright light on the back door.

"Well, damn," she muttered to herself.

Her eyes weren't playing tricks on her. There were scratches around the lock. Scratches and a dent in the metal door as if someone had taken a crowbar to it and tried to pry their way in. Sheri glanced up and down the alley that separated the back doors of the row of businesses on the south end of the strip in Sunshine Beach and the chain-link fence of a parking lot behind another row of buildings. No one and nothing was there. Whoever had tried to break into her restaurant was long gone.

Cursing to herself, she cut off the flashlight and dialed her mom's number. She balanced the phone between her ear and shoulder, while she reached into her bag and felt around for the keys to the building.

"Lil Bit, what's wrong?" Dorothy Jean's voice was scratchy, as if she'd just woken up, and filled with concern.

"Why does something have to be wrong?"

"Because you only call me this early when there's a problem. What's wrong?"

Her mom was right. Sheri didn't call this early unless something was going on. Her mom helped in the restaurant, but she didn't come in until right before they opened at seven. Sheri knew her mom was not about to get out of bed before 5:00 a.m. so she tried to reserve her calls for help at the restaurant before opening for when she was desperate.

"I think someone tried to break into the restaurant."

A heartbeat passed as if the words had to sink in before her mom shrieked, "What? Are you sure? Are they still there?"

Sheri shook her head even though her mom couldn't see. "I don't think they got inside. Scratches on the door. That's why I'm calling. Did you see scratches yesterday?"

"Scratches? There weren't any scratches. Did you call the police?"

"Not yet. Like I said, I don't think they got past the dead bolt, but still."

"Girl, if you don't get your narrow behind off this

phone with me and call the police, I'm getting dressed and coming." Her mom's voice was breathless and a little muffled. She'd probably jumped out of bed and was scrambling around her room. "Is JD there?" JD was their main line cook.

"Not yet, but he should be here soon," Sheri answered. "He's usually right after me." She looked down the alley again as if he might magically materialize.

"Goodness, you're there alone. Call the cops. Now. I'm on my way."

"Yes, ma'am." Sheri hung up and then dialed 911.

JD arrived right before the cops did. Tall and stout with golden brown skin, JD had an ever-present scowl on his face, unless he was listening to old-school jams. Then he grinned and crooned out the hits with a surprisingly mellow voice.

When Sheri left her job waiting tables at the Waffle House to open her own restaurant, JD was the first person she'd thought of asking to help her. He'd been the best line cook at Waffle House. She hadn't wasted any time calling and begging JD to come work for her when she'd received a grant from the town of Sunshine Beach for small business owners willing to open in south end—an area the town was desperate to revitalize. To her surprise and excitement, he'd immediately said yes.

"What happened to the door?" he asked. His yellow T-shirt had The Breakfast Nook, the restaurant's name, across the front and he'd matched it with a pair of gray sweats and a pair of white New Balance sneakers.

Sheri was in the kitchen waiting for the cops to arrive. She'd already pulled out the ingredients needed for the buttermilk biscuits and pancake mix and slipped a red apron over her own yellow The Breakfast Nook T-shirt and jeans. The person hadn't succeeded in breaking in, so she'd had no good reason to at least get started pulling together what they'd need to start breakfast.

"I think someone tried to break in," she said.

JD's scowl deepened. He crossed his arms and looked around the room as if wishing the would-be robber would pop out so he could jump them. "When?"

Sheri shrugged. "Last night. I didn't notice scratches on the door when I left yesterday. Did you?"

He shook his head. "I would have noticed scratches. Who would break in here?"

"I don't know, but I don't like it," she muttered.

The reflection of blue lights flashing in the dining area caught her attention. "The cops are here."

JD recoiled. "You called the cops?"

"That is what you do when someone tries to break into your place of business."

JD waved a hand. "You don't need a cop to tell you what happened."

"What happened?" Sheri headed to the front door.

He wagged a finger toward the front of the restaurant toward the street. "Probably one of those kids hanging around on the corner. They see you doing well and think there's money up in here."

"It might not be the kids," Sheri replied, but JD only grunted.

Sheri didn't want to immediately blame the teens who hung out along the strip. She used to be one of those kids. The south end of the beach was where most teenagers hung out. When she was younger, the south end was the area with the record and video game stores, an arcade and restaurants with the kind of cheap, delicious foods a teenager could afford on a budget. Many of those same hangout spots had closed over the past fifteen or so years, but the few remaining places were enough to still make the south end a popular hangout spot.

The town wanted to revitalize not just because of empty storefronts bringing down the property value at the beach but also because of the number of young people who loitered in the area. Sheri, who'd grown up loving that part of the beach, had jumped at the chance to open her breakfast and brunch spot in the area where she'd spent so much time in her youth. She wanted the area to get back to the thriving center it had once been but wasn't convinced revitalization had to come at the cost of kicking out all the teens. Sunshine Beach wasn't as lively as Myrtle Beach and didn't lean into the Southern charm like Charleston. The town was trying to find a way to get more tourists to visit.

"Probably one of those kids hanging out on the corner," Officer Duncan said after looking at her back door and checking to make sure nothing else was damaged or taken. "We've had a string of break-ins and vandalism. Most coming from a young group that's calling themselves a gang."

JD snorted. "Gangs, in Sunshine Beach? What are they representing? Whose subdivision is harder than the other?"

Officer Duncan gave a half smile. "You'd think we wouldn't have that problem here, but unfortunately, we do. Even for a small town we've got young people who think being in a gang is cool."

Sheri crossed her arms. "Well, what is the town doing to give these kids other alternatives? Most of the places that kept them busy on this end of the beach are shut down. The town cut the budget for the after-school programs at the community center. They have nowhere to turn to."

Officer Duncan tore a sheet of paper from his note-book and held it out toward her. "Talk about the town's budget is above my pay grade," he said. "This is a copy of the report I'm going to file. I recommend you keep that dead bolt on the back door, but also put in some cameras in the back just in case they come back. We'll increase patrols over the next few days."

"Increased patrols won't make the kids hanging out feel more comfortable." If anything, increased patrols might cause anxiety for the kids.

Officer Duncan winked. "Exactly."

Sheri pulled back and frowned. "Look, I don't want my business broken into or anything, but I don't think scaring the kids is the answer. There has to be some-thing else we can do."

He looked exasperated with her plea but thank-fully, no signs of frustration came through in his voice. "Look, if you want to get involved, the man who owns the burger shop asked us to start a neighborhood watch after his place was broken into the other week."

"There's a neighborhood watch?" That was the first she'd heard, and she'd been open for just over a year.

Officer Duncan nodded while adjusting the belt around his hips. "The next meeting is in the old Kings Clothing store building on Wednesday evening. Maybe come and learn more about the problems these kids are causing before you start worrying about police presence making them uncomfortable."

Sheri lifted her chin. "I will."

Her mom rushed in just as Officer Duncan was leaving. Like a hurricane, Dorothy Jean Thomas flew through the back door and surveyed everything. Seeing her mom move with such efficiency through the building was something Sheri wouldn't have thought she'd see when she'd come home years ago to help her recover from a stroke. Seeing her mom up and thriving, something she couldn't have imagined even three years ago, made giving up the job in Charlotte and starting over worth it.

"Oh my word, what happened?" Dorothy Jean said, examining Sheri from head to toe. She'd put her short, pixie-cut-style wig on crooked and her yellow The Breakfast Nook T-shirt was on backward. "Are you okay? Did they take anything? Who broke in here? I'm going take a switch to their behind."

JD waved off her mom's words. "Just some kids, Dorothy Jean. They didn't even get in here."

Her mom pressed a hand to her ample chest. Sheri and her mom had the same shape, top-heavy with not much to brag about in the hip and thighs department. "Thank goodness. You sure nothing is taken?"

Sheri reached out and straightened her mom's wig. "Nothing was taken. They didn't even get in the back door."

Her mom raised a hand. "Praise Jesus." She slapped Sheri's hand away. "Are you okay?"

Satisfied that her mom's wig was correct, she stepped back to avoid being swatted at again. She'd deal with the backward shirt later. "Other than being annoyed that the police want to scare the teenagers away and being aggravated that we didn't get the chance to start on the biscuits yet, I'm good."

"You don't worry about those kids. Especially if they're trying to break in. If they are trying to break in it's only because they've got nothing to do. An idle mind is the devil's playground." She pointed at Sheri. "As for the biscuits, I can help you and JD get them started."

JD grunted and nodded in agreement with her mom. He turned away from them and started grabbing the ingredients needed for the biscuits.

"I can't help but care about the kids in the area," Sheri said. "I used to hang out down here. Every kid who's down here isn't a juvenile delinquent. There just isn't much to do in Sunshine Beach for teenagers."

"That's not your problem to solve." Dorothy Jean glanced at the clock on the wall and threw up her hands. "Goodness, look at the time. JD, when do your helpers get here? We got to get the biscuits made and someone needs to start getting the chicken battered and ready for the fryer for the chicken and waffles."

"They'll be here in a second," JD grumbled. Typically, he'd already be complaining about the kitchen crew not being there by now, but as much as he complained he also was protective of the people he worked with. Because her mom asked, he wasn't going to throw them under the bus.

"I'll start the chicken if you help with the biscuits," Sheri said.

They split up and began preparations for their breakfast offerings. The rest of the kitchen staff arrived a few minutes later. Despite being busy with the prep work, Sheri couldn't get her mind off the way JD, her mom and Officer Duncan were so eager to accuse the teens in the area of the break-in. Just another reason to push the kids off the strip like they'd tried to do when she was younger. A curfew and increased police patrols had resulted in what they wanted. Sheri and her friends found other places to hang out and the south end of the beach had lost a lot of business. By the time they'd lifted the curfew and put the police in other areas, the south end businesses had declined. Now, they wanted revitalization without considering every part of the population who used the area.

Not if she had anything to do with it. She was going to the neighborhood watch meeting and instead of complaining, she was going to demand that the Sunshine Beach Police Department do something to help the teenagers in the area instead of just trying to scare them off.

Chapter Two

Sheri stood outside the old storefront that used to be a popular clothing store. Now the vacant building was being used as the location for the neighborhood watch meeting, the place where she would make her case that the new businesses and the teens who hung out in the area could find a way to coincide. She'd never really gotten involved with community issues, but that didn't mean she couldn't start now. Everyone had to start somewhere. She took a fortifying breath and nodded firmly.

A folding table stood inside the door. Multiple papers and flyers covered the tabletop. A young white woman Sheri didn't recognize sat behind the table and greeted Sheri just as she entered. She wore a dark blue shirt with the Sunshine Beach PD seal on the chest.

"Hi, I'm Rebecca. I'm a community liaison with the Sunshine Beach Police Department," she said cheerfully. "Sign in here, please."

Sheri returned Rebecca's smile before scribbling her

name, business and contact information on the sign in sheet. "I own The Breakfast Nook. This is my first meeting."

"That's great and welcome!" Rebecca said shaking Sheri's hand. "The neighborhood watch only recently started as part of the department's efforts to become more involved in the community. This is just the second time we've pulled the group together. Thank you for coming by tonight." Rebecca handed Sheri a few sheets of paper. "Here's your agenda and information on the latest crime report."

"The latest crime report? Why do I need that?" Sheri quickly scanned the paper and saw the attempted break-in at her restaurant listed near the top.

"We go over what's been happening in the neighborhood. This keeps everyone in the loop so they know what to be on the lookout for."

Sheri nodded, even though seeing the list of recent crimes in the area made her stomach twist. Sheri folded the paper in half as she went farther into the building. Metal chairs were set up in neat rows facing the back wall. A podium with a microphone attached to it stood in front of the chairs. Several people already mingled around the refreshment table set up in the left corner or sat in the chairs reviewing the same information Sheri had been given.

She recognized a few of the other shop owners. When she'd been setting up her restaurant, she'd made a point to go by and introduce herself to the other owners on the block. There was Ivy, who owned the tattoo and piercing parlor. She was curvy, with honey gold skin, a wide afro of reddish-brown curls and beautiful tattoos of flowers and the African goddess Oshun on her right arm. Then she saw Jared, the owner of the

CDB oil shop. She remembered the tall, lanky white guy with curly brown hair from high school. He'd been cool back when they were in school and he'd been just as laid-back and welcoming when she'd reintroduced herself after opening her restaurant. She also recognized Mr. Lee and his wife, a sweet Korean couple who'd run the souvenir shop for as long as Sheri could remember.

Some of the newer owners who'd taken advantage of the grants from the town were also in attendance. She'd met Kelly, a mahogany-skinned self-proclaimed geek taking her chance on her love of comics by opening her own comic book shop, at the orientation meeting for people interested in the revitalization grants. Her eyes met with Belinda, someone else Sheri remembered from high school, though they'd run in opposite groups. While Sheri hung out in the south end of Sunshine Beach, Belinda had attended ballet lessons and cotillions. Sheri hadn't believed her eyes when she'd visited the new yoga studio and discovered Belinda was the owner. In high school Belinda belittled the kids hanging out at the south end of the beach.

Sheri tried not to hold Belinda's attitude in high school against her. People could change. Lord knew she'd gone through a rough patch that some people still judged her for. One that she couldn't even blame on youth. She'd vandalized the car of her ex, Tyrone Livingston, thanks to too much tequila, her cousin's bad influence and a bruised ego. So, she would not judge Belinda because the woman had come across as stuck-up when they were teens.

Sheri went around and spoke to everyone she knew and introduced herself to a few people she didn't. Surprisingly, many of the residents in the surrounding neighborhoods were also in attendance. She'd assumed the meeting was focused on the commercial area, but the crime watch zone extended into the residential district.

A few minutes after she'd made her way around the room and gotten a plate of cookies and a cup of lemonade, the door opened and the officer who'd responded to her attempted break-in entered, followed by another man. Sheri's brows rose as she took in the tall, handsome Black man behind Officer Duncan. He wasn't in uniform like Officer Duncan, but his commanding presence and quick, efficient scan of the room gave her a "he's in law enforcement" vibe. He looked familiar, but she couldn't place where she knew him from. His chin was free of a beard, and his dark hair was cut in a neat fade. His broad shoulders filled the dark blue T-shirt he wore, and his tan slacks fitted just enough to show off strong legs.

Sheri quickly made her way to one of the seats near the front of the room next to Ivy. She leaned over and asked, "Who's the guy with Officer Duncan?"

Ivy glanced over her shoulder. Her curly red hair made a halo around her face and a nose ring stud was the only visible piercing outside of the three in both ears.

"Oh, that's Lieutenant King. He's the head of the community outreach team at the Sunshine Beach Police Department and the one who started up the crime watch for our neighborhood."

The cookie in Sheri's hand dropped into her lap and her heart slapped against her rib cage. "Lieutenant King?"

Ivy raised a brow and nodded. "Yeah, why?"

Sheri closed her eyes and cursed. Recognition slammed into her hard and fast. He was the same officer who'd arrested her when she'd decided to channel Jasmine Sullivan and bust the windows out of Tyrone Livingston's car.

Lieutenant King and Officer Duncan moved from speaking to Rebecca to join the rest of the group. He seemed to know everyone there and asked about their business. When his eyes scanned the front row, they skimmed over her before jerking back. Sheri stopped chewing the cookie. She waited for recognition to brighten his eyes. For a frown to cross his handsome face before he lectured her again on how *"a guy isn't worth catching a charge"* as he'd done the night Tyrone's neighbors called the cops.

He didn't do either. A heart-stopping second after his eyes met hers, he gave a brief nod of acknowledgment before glancing away and continuing his conversation with Mr. Lee. Sheri let out a sigh of relief. Then she frowned. Did he recognize her, or was he pretending he didn't to be polite? Not like he had a reason to be polite and act like he didn't remember. Unlike her family, who loved to remind her of her moment of stupidity.

His conversation with Mr. Lee wound down and then Lieutenant King's deep, rumbling voice called out to get everyone's attention before he started the meeting. He was quick and efficient as he went over the crime report: three break-ins, five attempted break-ins, two reports of stolen items from unlocked vehicles, numerous calls of loitering and one public drunkenness.

Even though she had a copy of the crime report, hearing the listing of all the activity in the area was surprising. She knew that end of Sunshine Beach had its challenges, but she'd considered them limited to the lack of investment in the shops over the years and the need for renovations. She had not considered that crime was truly a problem.

"With the increase in activity lately, the Sunshine Beach Community Outreach Unit would like to host an outreach event in the area," Lieutenant King said after completing the report. "This will also give us an opportunity to learn more about what's happening in the area and help you come up with solutions to improve the situation."

"Please do," Belinda said in an exasperated voice one row behind Sheri. "These kids in the neighborhood and their antics are scaring away my clients. No one wants to finish a yoga class only to go out and find a bunch of delinquents hanging out around their car." The slightly fake, welcoming tone Belinda had used when Sheri had greeted her was gone, replaced with one of disdain and irritation. So much for not judging too early.

Sheri spun around in her seat and scowled at Belinda. "They aren't delinquents."

Belinda raised a brow. "Then what do you call them? I didn't want to go so far as to say *thugs*, but if the shoe fits…" Belinda waved a hand.

Sheri stood up and placed a hand on her hip. "They aren't thugs, either. They're just kids."

"Kids who like to break into cars and take whatever they see," Belinda continued. A few other people in the room made sounds of agreement. "As far as I'm concerned, if the city really wants to revitalize this part of town they'd do something about these delinquents."

Sheri opened her mouth to shoot back, but Lieutenant King spoke before she could go off. "The city *is* doing something. It's engaging with you all who are invested in the community like we're doing tonight and finding ways to reduce crime while also not displacing the kids who just want to come out and enjoy the beach."

Sheri spun toward him, pleasantly surprised he hadn't immediately agreed with Belinda. "Thank you. Just because some kids are making trouble doesn't mean they all need to be treated like criminals."

"I agree," he said evenly.

"I used to be one of those kids," Sheri said. "I loved hanging out on the south end because this was the end that had stuff for teenagers to do. I chose to open a restaurant at this end because of those memories. I want to achieve my dream here but also keep some of the things that made the south end special."

Lieutenant King nodded and smiled. "I couldn't agree with you more."

His smile was like sunshine on a cold day, warming Sheri's insides in a way that she wasn't quite prepared for. Her cheeks prickled with embarrassment from her reaction, and she nodded. "Thank you." She looked away quickly before he noticed she wanted to grin back at him and gave Belinda a triumphant look.

"Which is why I think you'll make the perfect head of our neighborhood outreach committee."

Sheri blinked and she looked back at him. "Say what now?"

Lieutenant King placed his hands on his hips and stared at her with confidence and authority. "Congratulations on being appointed as the head of the South End Community Outreach Committee."

Chapter Three

Deandre King stared at the front door of The Breakfast Nook. The words were painted in a gold script across the door and a sign emblazoned with the same words hung above the door. He remembered when the restaurant opened. Once he'd taken over as the head of the department's Community Outreach Division he'd kept up with the people using the grants given out by the city to support new businesses along the south end of the beach. In the year since The Breakfast Nook opened there'd been a steady stream of people coming in and out, but this was his first visit. Breakfast might be the most important meal of the day, but Deandre didn't make breakfast a priority. He wasn't a big fan of what was considered breakfast food, so he hadn't thought of visiting a restaurant focused on breakfast and brunch.

Maybe that's why he hadn't realized that the Sheri Thomas who opened the place was the same woman he'd arrested when he'd first moved to Sunshine Beach and taken the job with the police department. He'd forgotten all about her after she'd been bailed out and the charges dropped. Well, mostly forgotten. The guy she'd been so angry with that she'd thought taking a bat to his car was worth it had gone on to get a television show investigating ghosts with his brothers and was engaged to someone else now. Deandre had thought about Sheri when he heard that bit of news. He'd wondered what happened to her and if she'd moved on.

Now he knew. She had moved on. Started a business. And, apparently, was going to be working with him to plan a community outreach event in the area. A community event he'd championed to have so he could prove the area could be restored without the heavy hand of law enforcement. The way she'd championed for the area the night before had made him quickly pick her to help, but was she really the right person to help him, or had he been blinded by her enthusiasm and made a knee-jerk decision?

"One way to find out," he muttered before opening the door.

The smell of food and coffee greeted him. Despite forcing himself to eat a banana that morning with his coffee to get something in his stomach and avoid not eating anything until lunch, his stomach rumbled, and his mouth watered. He might not be a fan of breakfast, but whatever they were cooking sure as hell smelled good.

A young girl at the front greeted him. She looked to be in her early twenties, had dark brown skin and long braids that fell past her waist. "Welcome to The Breakfast Nook. Did you place a carryout order?"

He shook his head. "No, I'd like to speak with Sheri Thomas if she's available."

The girl frowned. "Sheri is in the back and helping wait tables. I can sit you in her section if you'd like."

"That's fine."

She nodded, grabbed a set of silverware rolled up in a napkin and took him to one of the empty seats near the back of the restaurant. Once he sat down, she pointed to a QR code on the table. "You can scan that for the menu."

"I'll just have some coffee," he said.

She raised a brow. "You sure? We have great chicken and waffles. Plus, our pancakes are delicious."

He shook his head. "Just coffee. Pancakes aren't my thing."

"That's because you haven't had my pancakes," a woman's husky voice came from his side.

He turned away from the hostess and met Sheri's big, brown eyes. She was attractive; he'd noticed that the night he'd arrested her. Slim, but curvy enough to make his eyes want to linger on her full breasts and pert ass. He'd wondered why a woman as good-looking as her would even bother with vandalizing some guy's car. She could easily find someone else who'd appreciate her…unless she made busting taillights a habit.

She sashayed over to stand next to the hostess. *Sashay* was the only word that came to his mind watching her walk. "Go back to the front, D'asa, I've got him."

D'asa walked away and Sheri focused back on him. The lights in the restaurant glowed off her dark brown skin, and she'd pulled her thick, black hair into a ponytail that stopped just past her shoulders. All hers or a weave? he wondered. Didn't matter. Either way she looked good.

The wariness that had been on Sheri's face when she'd first seen him at the neighborhood watch meeting was gone. At first, he'd chalked up her hesitancy to unease from meeting a cop. He understood caution and mistrust was some people's initial reaction. Later, when she'd stood up and confronted Belinda from the yoga studio, he'd recognized her voice and realized who she was. Her hesitancy made even more sense then.

"You sure you don't want any pancakes with the coffee?" She leaned a hip against the chair across from him.

"I don't like pancakes."

Her eyes widened as if he'd declared that he hated sunshine. "Who doesn't like pancakes?"

He lifted a shoulder. "A person who prefers waffles when he does decide to eat breakfast."

She chuckled, and her laugh was like her voice, husky, throaty, and both brushed over him like an unexpected caress. Heat flared in his midsection along with a spark of arousal. He shifted in his seat. It had taken two years after losing his wife to accept that his heart might be broken but his body still had sexual urges. He'd needed another year to be open to the idea of possibly dating again. But this was the first time in the six years since she'd passed that he'd had a strong reaction to someone. He frowned, not liking the idea of Sheri causing the reaction. He'd arrested her before, for goodness' sake.

Sheri cocked her head to the side. "No need to get upset. I can make waffles if you want. Though, after working at the Waffle House for years I'm kind of tired of them."

He relaxed his features, not wanting to explain that his frown was caused by his body's reaction to her and not because of his aversion to pancakes over waffles. "Coffee is fine. I actually came by to talk to you about the community outreach event."

"I figured as much." She glanced around the room as if judging the level of activity before looking back at him. "I can talk for a few minutes. I'll get you some coffee and be right back."

A few minutes later, she came back and set a cup of coffee in front of him along with a plate with a biscuit on it and a selection of jams and honey.

He raised a brow as he watched her settle across from him. "I didn't need a biscuit."

"You look like you need something in your stomach. Go ahead, try it."

"This wasn't necessary."

She slid the plate closer to him. "I know, but I can't help it. My mom likes to feed people and I do, too."

"I guess that's why you opened a restaurant." He sliced the biscuit in half and reached for the grape jelly. Not because he wanted it, but because it would be rude to continue to reject her offering.

"One of the reasons. I worked at an expensive steak house when I lived in Charlotte after graduating from the University of South Carolina with a degree in hospitality. I was the business manager there but came back home when my mom got sick. I took the first job I could find, which was at the Waffle House."

"That's a lot different than a steak house." The biscuit smelled delicious and when he took a bite, it nearly melted in his mouth. "Damn, this is good."

Her full lips spread in a triumphant smile. "I knew you'd like it. And, yeah, Waffle House is a lot different, but they pay decent, the tips are good and I needed the flexibility to work early in the morning or late at night so I could take Mom to her appointments during the day. That taught me how to be quick on the go. When Mom got better, and I heard about the city wanting to revitalize what used to be my favorite hangout in town, I decided to give opening my own place a try."

He looked around the restaurant and back at her. "Looks like you're doing pretty good."

She shrugged. "I'm doing okay. I survived my first year, so that's worth celebrating. My customers are mostly locals, but I'm trying to get those people visiting the bougie north end of the beach to come on down to the south side and give my place a try."

"But you don't want to kick out the teenagers like some of the other shop owners."

She shook her head, the smile on her face disappearing. "I don't. I used to be one of those kids. I loved hanging out down here. We don't have to displace the people who live in Sunshine Beach just to draw in the visitors looking for a quaint beach experience. We can make it work."

"How?"

Her bright eyes widened, and she threw up her hands in a "Who knows?" fashion. "I don't know, but that's what we're figuring out together, right?"

He took another bite of the biscuit and nodded slowly while he considered her words. After he washed it down with the coffee, he studied her. "You don't have a problem working with me?"

She hesitated a second before shaking her head. Her eyes narrowed slightly as she asked hesitantly, "Why would I? Because you're a cop?"

He chuckled softly. She was willing to play dumb if he was. But playing dumb wasn't his style. "Because I'm the cop that arrested you a few years back."

She flinched, closed her eyes and let out a heavy breath. "Damn, I thought you didn't recognize me."

"I didn't at first."

She opened her eyes. "What gave me away?"

"I thought you'd take a baseball bat to Belinda's head like you did that car." He softened his words with a smile.

She laughed and waved a hand. "My baseball bat days are over. Belinda is bougie as hell, but not worth catching a charge over."

"Neither was Tyrone Livingston."

She sighed and crossed her arms on the table. She sat forward and met his eye. "Neither was he, but that's over and done with now. No, I don't mind working with you. If you don't mind working with me."

He wanted to know more about why she'd done what she did. Had she and Tyrone been serious? Was she still interested in Tyrone? He cut those thoughts short. Her baseball bat days may be over, but her fiery personality was still there. He needed her fire to bring the community together, but not in any other way. He'd always told his son to stay away from women with drama. Sheri was drama.

He lifted his coffee mug and saluted her. "I don't mind working with you at all."

She uncrossed her arms and slapped her hand on the table. "Good. Glad that's out of the way. So what do we do next?"

He looked up as another person entered. "How about we meet up tomorrow afternoon, when you're not working, and talk about some things."

"Works for me. Your place or mine?" She cocked a brow.

Deandre choked on his coffee. Sheri's eyes widened and she handed him a napkin. He took it and wiped his mouth. Did she have to sound so sexy saying that? "Excuse me?"

"Where do you want to meet and plan?" She spoke slowly as if he were having a hard time comprehending.

Considering where his mind had gone, he was having a hard time. Too much time had passed since he'd had sex. Now his brain was finding innuendos where there were none. "My bad. I can come back here after you close. Or we can use the Kings store again. It's become the spot for the Community Outreach Division's work on the south end. The city is thinking of setting it up as a visitor center later."

She sat up straight. "I like that idea. Yes, let's meet at Kings. We close at two and it takes some time to clean up. How about three? That work for you?"

He thought about his day. DJ, his son, had wrestling practice until six. He'd still have time to get home and get dinner together before he got home. "That works."

Sheri beamed. "Good. Enjoy your biscuit. It's on the house, partner." She winked and he sucked in a breath. "It's about time for the late morning rush. Let me finish helping out but stay as long as you need."

Just like that she got up and walked away, oblivious

to the way he'd reacted to her. He watched her greet the guy who'd sat down at the table next to him. Deandre tried not to focus on Sheri as he finished his biscuit and coffee. His efforts were in vain. He was aware of her movements. Her husky laugh with customers, the friendly greeting she gave them all, the way her hand touched the shoulders of some regulars when she chatted them up. He quickly downed his coffee, dropped a ten-dollar bill on the table despite her saying not to pay and got out of there before he became even more rattled than he already was.

Chapter Four

Sheri went out the front of the restaurant to bring in the sign with the specials handwritten in chalk from the walkway. It had been a busy day. Her shoulders ached and her feet were tired, but she wouldn't trade the feeling for anything else. She loved that the restaurant was doing well. She'd worried so much and prayed so hard that stepping away from a steady paycheck to open her own place would be worth the fear and uncertainty. So far, it had been. So, she would accept every ache, pain and fatigue that came after a busy day.

The sound of a catcall whistle from her left caught her attention. She looked up and sighed after spotting the group of boys standing a few doors down from her restaurant. She'd seen the boys before. Teenagers, who roamed up and down the strip after school and on weekends. She'd never witnessed them doing anything wrong, but she knew their hanging around outside the businesses was part of the reason some other shop owners wanted something done to keep the kids out of the area.

One of the boys stood in the middle. His mouth spread in a wide grin as he eyed her from head to toe. He rubbed his hands together and tried, she assumed, to look interesting.

"Hey lady, can I get your number?"

Sheri couldn't help herself, she laughed. Did this little boy really think she was about to give him her number? "Young man, you don't want my number. I've got shoes older than you."

He lifted a thin shoulder. "I like my women seasoned."

"Seasoned? Lord, child, get out of here with that nonsense. Go try that mess with a girl your own age."

His friends laughed. Sheri shook her head and picked up her sign. She headed back inside. But she heard him grumble, "I didn't like her old ass anyway," before the door closed.

Sheri scowled. "Old?" she mumbled to herself. She was older than him, but she wasn't old. She locked the door with a flip of her wrist before heading to the back of the restaurant.

The "old ass" comment irritated her all the way from the restaurant to her mom's house. It was the first time she'd been referred to as *old*, within earshot at least. She knew the kid was just trying to save face after she'd shot him down, but the words had hit a mark. Sheri was, indeed, getting older. She would be forty in a couple of years. While her life was good, she still wasn't where she'd thought she'd be at this age. She'd expected to still be living in Charlotte, or maybe to have moved to Atlanta or even New York. She'd be working for a high-end restaurant, married to, or at least dating, the perfect man and on the road to having the two beautiful kids she'd always wanted. She never would have imagined she'd be back home in Sunshine Beach, living in a house next to her mom's, still single with no prospects.

She pulled into her mom's driveway and let out a sigh. Even though she wasn't where she thought she would be, she wasn't in a bad place, either. She constantly focused on that. She owned her own business, and her restaurant was successful. She'd inherited her grandmother's home next to her mom's, so she didn't have to worry about a mortgage, and she'd finally shaken off the stigma of taking a baseball bat to her former lover's car. All in all, her life could be worse. She wouldn't let a kid calling her an "old ass" make her start to doubt herself.

Internal pep talk complete, she went inside to check on her mom. It was part of her daily routine. Leave the restaurant, check in at her mom's house to make sure she was still feeling good, taking her meds, and maybe grab a meal if her mom had cooked. She knocked on the screen door before opening.

"Ma, it's me," she called out.

"In the kitchen," her mom called back.

Sure enough, the house smelled divine. The familiar smell of her mom's fried chicken filled the air. Sheri's stomach grumbled. She'd been so busy today she barely had time to eat. She wondered if Lieutenant Deandre King had eaten later in the day. The thought made her frown. She did not need to worry about whether or not he ate. The man was grown and could find his own meals. She blamed her mom. Her mom couldn't stand to see people not eating when there was plenty of food around. It was why Sheri had brought him the biscuit with his coffee. She'd caught the way his eyes had lingered on some of the plates on the tables. She hadn't been able to help herself. Her need to feed people kicked in, and she'd brought him food.

Her mom stood in front of the fridge, and pulled out two cans of Pepsi in her hands as she headed toward the door that led to the back patio. "I'm sitting out back with your aunt."

"Aunt Gwen's here?"

"Yeah, she stopped by after she got off work. Come on out back."

Sheri quickly moved to the back door and opened it for her mom. Her mom's sister Gwen sat under the umbrella connected to her mom's patio table. It was a warm and humid afternoon, so an oscillating fan was plugged up to speed along the intermittent breeze. Despite the heat, her mom and aunt loved sitting on the back porch.

"Hey, Auntie." Sheri went over and gave her aunt a hug.

"Hey, Sheri, your mom said you would be here in a little bit." She was still in the dark blue uniform she wore as part of the custodial crew for the city of Sunshine Beach. She wore wire-framed glasses and her salt-and-pepper hair was pulled back into a ponytail.

Sheri pulled out a chair and sat around the round, glass patio table. "Did you need to see me?"

Her aunt took the Pepsi from her sister with one hand and pointed at Sheri with the other. "Why didn't you tell me someone tried to break into the restaurant?"

Sheri gave her mom a look. But her mom just shrugged. "What? You thought I wasn't going to tell her?"

"It wasn't that big of a deal. They didn't get in. I went

to the neighborhood watch meeting, and they're already working on plans to try and help the south end."

Her aunt nodded. "They need to do something. The south end of the strip used to be a nice, safe place to go. Now, it's full of kids doing God knows what."

Sheri shifted her chair to try and get in the direct aim of the fan when it turned her way. "The kids are doing the same thing I did as a kid. Hanging out and looking for something to do."

"Well, I don't like it," Gwen said with a frown.

Her mom nodded. "Me, either. I'm glad the city is trying to make the south end better, but I need them to do something about the crime. How can your business stay successful if they're breaking in all the time?"

Sheri held up a finger. "First of all, it was one attempted break-in." She lifted another finger. "Second, we're looking at solutions."

Her mom's eyes narrowed. "That's why you were talking to that cop earlier today."

Sheri didn't bother to ask how her mom knew even though she hadn't come in this morning. JD probably called and told her mom the second Sheri had sat down at the table.

"Yes, that's why he was there. He's in charge of the new community outreach division. They want to create a better relationship between the department and the citizens. He wants to get my ideas."

Her aunt grunted and shook her head. "I don't trust cops."

Her mom nodded. "Me, either."

Sheri understood where they were coming from. She remembered the way her family and neighbors hadn't trusted law enforcement in and around Sunshine Beach when she was a kid. The delayed response to calls, the lack of engagement in their community, the harassment by the less-than-stellar cops. The mistrust ran deep and over generations.

"I get it," Sheri said. "And I'm not saying I'm going to marry him, I'm saying he wants to help the community, so I'll work with him and see if he's for real."

Gwen leaned forward with a skeptical look in her dark eyes. "What if he's not?"

Sheri shrugged. "Then, I'll find another way to help the community. I want the south end to be like it used to be. Working with the police is just one way to get there, but not the only way."

Her mom nodded. "Well, I hope he turns out to be okay. I would hate for a man that fine to be dirty."

Gwen sat up straight. "How do you know he's fine?"

"D'asa told me," her mom said. She looked at Sheri with a raised brow. "Is he?"

Fine wasn't enough to describe that man. Intense, good-looking, sexy, commanding. All of that and she still didn't think she'd accurately captured everything appealing about Deandre King.

Sheri waved a hand. "I mean, he's alright. I don't care about that. I'm just trying to help the neighborhood."

Her aunt waved a finger at Sheri. "Well, don't think about that. Even if he is fine. It's hard enough to trust a man, but if he's a cop." She sucked her teeth and shook her head. "No telling what he'll do."

"What's he gonna do, Gwen?" her mom asked laughing.

"I don't know, but I don't trust men and I don't trust cops, so obviously, you can't trust a man cop."

If Sheri were honest, she didn't trust herself more

than she didn't trust men in general. Her judgment and track record when it came to guys wasn't great. She didn't have a hard time finding a guy. It was just that the type of guys she was typically attracted to turned out to be the worst kind of guy for her. Men like Deandre wouldn't usually cross her radar. Sure, he was good-looking, but he was a "nice" guy. Sheri had to admit she always went for a hint of bad boy with her good looks.

But bad boys, playboys and wanna-be thugs had given her nothing but a world of disappointment and embarrassment. Maybe she needed a nice guy like Deandre in her life. It wasn't as if he would give her a chance. He'd arrested her when she was at her worst. Nope, no need to focus on how sexy Deandre King was. That ship wasn't sailing.

Sheri sighed and patted her aunt's hand. "Don't worry. I'm not trying to do anything with Lieutenant King but help the community. No matter how cute he may be."

Deandre did everything he could to leave work on time. He rushed to the grocery store to pick up ground beef, hamburger buns, frozen fries and sloppy joe sauce for his son DJ's favorite meal. DJ's birthday was that weekend. Deandre had to work, but he'd set a personal objective to try and make every other day of the week special for his kid.

They'd moved to Sunshine Beach right after DJ's mom, Jamila, passed away suddenly. The aneurysm took her from them quickly when no one was at home to deliver first aid or call the hospital in enough time to possibly save her. As much as it had pained him to find his wife like that, he was thankful that he'd gotten home before DJ. She'd passed away a few days before his son's birthday, which was why Deandre tried his best to make DJ's birthday special.

He made it home in enough time to get the sloppy joes created and was just taking the first batch of fries out of the fryer when the back door opened. He turned off the deep fryer and spun toward his son.

"Hey! You're just in time. I've got dinner ready," Deandre said cheerfully.

DJ gave him a look that said the cheerfulness wasn't needed or very much appreciated. Not surprising. DJ was a good kid, but he was filled with teenage attitude. Deandre spent a lot of time trying to figure out when he'd gone from being his son's best friend to the person he wanted to spend the least amount of time with. They'd been close before his wife passed and had grown closer in the years after they'd lost her. But, sometime in the past year and a half, his relationship with DJ had shifted. His son's answers were short, his eye contact brief to nonexistent, and the time they'd spend hanging out together only happened when Deandre forced it.

"Yeah, I'm here," DJ said in a flat tone.

DJ reminded him a lot of his mother, with the same wide-set brown eyes, flat nose and dimpled chin. His height, broad shoulders and growing muscles all came from Deandre. His son wore a pair of dark blue joggers and a white hoodie. He'd let his hair grow out. The curls at the top were thick and wild enough to make Deandre want to cut them, but he was trying to let his son express himself. That's what Jamila would have wanted.

"I made dinner." Deandre pointed toward the plate of hot fries and the pan with the sloppy joe mixture on the stove.

DJ glanced at the food and shrugged. "I'm not hungry." He turned to leave the kitchen.

"Hold up," Deandre called.

DJ didn't sigh out loud. He wasn't outright disrespectful, just mildly disdainful with receiving attention from his dad. Still, Deandre *felt* the sigh and eye roll as he watched his son's shoulders lift and lower.

DJ turned around. "Yeah?"

Deandre raised a brow. "Yeah?"

"Yes, sir?" DJ replied in the same flat tone of voice he'd used before.

Deandre wrestled back his growing annoyance with considerable effort. "You've been in school all day and then you had wrestling practice afterward. I don't believe you're not hungry."

"I already ate."

"Ate? When and where?"

"My boy Jay wanted to get some pizza so we stopped by the place down on the strip and got something to eat."

Deandre looked at his watch. DJ wouldn't have had time to eat if he was coming home straight from wrestling practice. "When did you have time to do that?"

"After school."

"What about wrestling practice?"

DJ shifted his stance. He glanced away quickly before meeting Deandre's eyes and lifting his chin. "Oh, I quit."

"You quit?" Deandre asked, narrowing his eyes. He braced his hands on his hips and stared at his son. DJ had loved wrestling. He'd won a medal the year before. "Why would you quit?"

DJ shrugged. "The coach started changing stuff up. I didn't like it, so I quit."

"Change things up how? And, why didn't you tell me?"

"Just new rules and stuff. This is why I didn't tell you. I knew you'd have a bunch of questions."

"I'm going to ask questions because you liked wrestling. If the coach was acting weird, then you tell me and I can talk to him."

DJ waved a hand. "See, that's why I didn't tell you. I knew you'd go all *cop* on me and want to make it a big deal. I was just tired of wrestling. It took up too much time and I want to hang with my boys. So, I quit when he started changing the rules. That's all."

Deandre's argument deflated. He didn't want to *go all cop* on his son. Deandre set rules and insisted on order in his house, but he never wanted his son to feel like he was being treated as a suspect. It was one of the things he'd promised Jamila when they'd gotten married. She'd said if they were going to build a family they had to treat each other like family. Meaning Deandre couldn't come in setting law and order as if they were the people he arrested every day.

Deandre dialed back the steel in his voice and tried to sound more like a father and less like a cop. "I still think you should have talked to me about it."

"I'm talking to you about it now."

Deandre took a deep breath. He would not get frustrated with his son and let this spiral into an argument. "Before you make big decisions like that I need to know."

"Okay," DJ said in a flat tone.

"Okay what?"

"I'll tell you before I make big decisions."

The quick agreement wasn't a win. It was a deflection tactic. Something DJ had also started in the last year. Instead of talking about anything Deandre tried to discuss, he said "okay" or agreed to whatever Deandre said. It had taken Deandre a few weeks to catch on that his son was using the quick agreement to end the conversation faster.

"And you need to call me if you're going somewhere after school. Anything could happen and I wouldn't know where you were."

"Okay."

Deandre waited for more, but the wait was a waste of time. DJ wanted the conversation to end and, honestly, he wanted to move on and try to salvage the rest of the night. "Let's eat and we can talk some more."

DJ rubbed his stomach. "I'm full from pizza and I've got homework."

He tried a different approach. "Did you want to do anything for your birthday?"

"You're working, so no. I'll just hang with my boys."

There wasn't any accusation in his son's voice, but the reminder still sent a knife through Deandre's heart. He'd tried to find a way out of working, but the police chief was scheduled to speak at a community event with several politicians on Saturday, and she wanted him, as the new head of the Community Outreach Division, to also be there.

"But we could still do something. I'll be done by three or four."

DJ lifted a shoulder. "Okay. You just tell me where you want me to be."

"I want you to tell me what you'd like to do. We

could go to dinner with your grandparents. Or check out a movie."

"Grandma and Grandpa said they'd take me to breakfast. I'm going to a movie with my friends. I'm good."

The guilt wrapped around Deandre's heart tightened its grip. DJ already had plans for his birthday. Plans that didn't include or require him. "Squeeze in some time for me. Let's grab something to eat before you go to dinner with your friends. That work?"

"Okay. Now, can I go do my homework?" DJ asked.

Deandre bit back suggesting DJ to do his homework downstairs so they could talk while he ate. He already knew what the answer would be. Instead, he nodded. "That's fine."

DJ turned and walked out without another word. Deandre watched his son go, then looked at the sloppy joes and French fries he'd made. He didn't know how they'd gotten to this point, and what scared him even more was that he didn't know how to change things, either.

Chapter Five

Sheri went inside the Kings store, now the home of the south end's neighborhood watch, for her meeting with Deandre. She'd spent most of the day making sure everything was settled at the restaurant so she could leave in enough time to meet him that afternoon. She didn't like to leave the rest of the workers by themselves at closing time. Not because she didn't think they could close up without her, but because she didn't want to give the impression that she wasn't just as willing to work late and hard with them. After the attempted break-in, they were all more than willing for her to leave early and meet with Deandre. They'd practically pushed her out of the door.

Inside was dark compared with the bright sunshine outside the building. Only half of the overhead fluorescent lights were on. Deandre sat at a desk in the back corner of the open space. He'd been looking at his phone when she'd walked in but gave her his full attention when the doors opened. He put his phone down and stood.

"Come on in." He pointed to a seat in front of his desk, one of the folding chairs they'd set up in rows for the neighborhood watch meeting. "Have a seat."

"Is this your office?" she asked, raising a brow. She looked around the wide, empty space as she crossed over to him. During the neighborhood meeting, she'd been so caught up in what was happening that she hadn't paid attention to what the inside of the building looked like.

Without all the people inside, it was dark and dreary. There wasn't anything in the space except for the desk in the corner. She supposed the tables and chairs put out for the meeting were stored away behind one of the doors along the back wall.

Deandre shook his head. "No, I have an office down at headquarters. But since I started working in the Community Outreach Division, I try to meet people in their neighborhoods. When I'm in the south end, this is where I meet people. Coming down to the police station isn't always comfortable for everyone."

Sheri hung her purse on the back of the folding chair before sitting down. "Can you blame them for not being comfortable?"

He shrugged and his broad shoulders stretched the material of the dark blue polo shirt he wore. "Not really. I understand why they would feel leery about being down there. Our conference rooms look a lot like interrogation rooms. I'm trying to build bridges, not intimidate."

"That's good to hear."

"Why is that?"

"Some cops like to intimidate people."

She waited for him to deny it. Or get defensive. Instead, he nodded. "Some do. I don't."

She watched him, impressed and surprised by his answer. She lifted a brow and studied his shoulders. "Come on, a big strong man like you. You've never intimidated anyone?"

The corner of his mouth quirked. "I learned long before I became a cop that my size and voice intimidates some people. Just my presence can heighten the tension in a situation. Instead of leaning into that, I chose to figure out the best way to diffuse the situation versus making it worse."

Dang, she was even more impressed. He was self-aware. She thought back to when he had arrested her. She could tell he'd been irritated with the situation, but he hadn't tried to tower over her, talk over her or try to make her feel afraid. She'd been pissed off, angry and afraid of what would happen that night, but she hadn't been afraid when he was around.

"I think I'm going to be okay working with you." She stretched her legs out in front of her.

Deandre leaned forward and rested his forearms on the desk. They were muscled and toned, just like the rest of him. "You didn't think you'd be able to work with me before?"

Sheri jerked her eyes away from his arms and back to meet his direct gaze. "I wasn't sure. You're the cop who arrested me. But the more I talk to you, the more I think you're okay."

This time the lip twitch turned into a half smile. "I appreciate that."

He continued to hold her gaze as he smiled. The air electrified. Sheri's pulse increased and sparks shot across her skin. The man was handsome but when he smiled, he was devastating.

His cell phone chimed. He looked away, breaking the spell and allowing Sheri to breathe. She rubbed the back of her neck. She had to get a hold of herself. Yeah, it had been a while since she'd had sex, but she wasn't so hard up that she would risk embarrassment by trying to hook up with the cop that arrested her. Besides, he was cool with her and everything, but he did not seem like the type of cop who also tried to slide his phone number on the traffic ticket he wrote you. She'd bet money he was not interested in her in any kind of way outside of helping him reach out to the south end community.

"Dammit, DJ," he muttered. His fingers tapped against the screen as he frowned down.

"Anything wrong?" she asked.

He looked up and then looked embarrassed. "I'm sorry. I didn't mean to curse."

Sheri chuckled. "*Dammit* is far from being one of the worst words I've ever heard. Any trouble?"

He shook his head. "No, it's my son. He was supposed to be going back to wrestling practice but instead he's gone home."

"You have a son?" Which meant there was a mother. Which meant he might be married or in a relationship. Further proof why she did not need to be salivating over the man in this meeting.

He nodded. "Yeah, he's sixteen. A sophomore in high school. He suddenly decided to quit wrestling but won't give me a good reason."

"Oh. Well, I'm sure he has a good one."

"I wish he'd tell me." He gave her a curious look. "Do you have kids?"

She shook her head. "No. Wanted one or two one day, but just haven't met the right person to impregnate me."

He blinked. "Oh."

Sheri laughed at his stunned expression. "You don't have to look so… I don't know, surprised. Having a kid is a big deal. I can't be having one with just anybody."

His shoulders relaxed and he held up a hand. "I'm sorry. I just never heard it phrased that way. But I understand what you mean."

"What about your son's mom? Is she your wife?"

He nodded. "She was. She died, six years ago."

Sheri put a hand to her chest. "I'm so sorry. I didn't mean…"

"I know. It's a little easier to say it now. That's why we moved to Sunshine Beach. Her family lives here. I wanted my son to grow up with family around. My family is…not as reliable."

"In what way?" she asked, then flinched. "Sorry, I'm being nosy."

He shrugged. "And I'm dumping personal stuff on you. My bad."

She kind of liked that he was talking to her. It made him seem a little less off-limits. Not that she was going to cross those limits. But seeing a personal side of him took away some of the space she'd expected to be between them.

"It's okay. I've been told I'm easy to talk to. You'd be surprised the personal things my customers say to me when I bring them their food. I guess I've got that kind of face."

"It is a nice face," he said.

Heat flooded Sheri's cheeks. She pressed a hand to one. "Oh, well, thank you."

He glanced away and then shifted in his chair. "I

mean, you seem trustworthy. I get a sense about people. You're a good person."

"I try to be." She got a vision of the disappointment in his face when he'd taken the baseball bat from her the night of her arrest. Her cheeks burned even more. "At least, I've been trying harder to be a better person."

He cleared his throat. "So, about the community outreach."

She snapped her finger. "Yes, about that. I was thinking a fair or something. We invite people over to talk about what's happening in the area and what we'd like to see."

"People like who?"

"I don't know. Like folks who work for Sunshine Beach. We haven't heard from council members. Or the ones making plans for the area. Then there are the people in law enforcement."

"People don't just come out for a panel discussion from politicians and bureaucrats." His words held a hint of humor that surprised Sheri. He could also tease. She liked that.

Sheri slid forward in the chair. "Then let's make it more than that. Let's make it fun. Draw them in and then teach them something while they're here."

"That could work."

"I know it can. We can bring it up at the next neighborhood watch meeting. Get some ideas and form a committee to help plan."

"You came with all the ideas already, huh?"

She grinned. "I mean, it is why you asked me to help. You could tell I'm a good person and that I can get things done."

"That is true. Okay, Sheri, let's plan a fair."

Chapter Six

Deandre sat at his desk in headquarters working on paperwork when there was a knock on the door. Looking up, he spotted LaTisha Fuller. They'd worked together when he was on patrol, and he'd become friends with her and her husband, Omar. Their son was about the same age as his and he'd quickly latched on to other people he could connect with and give his son a community when he'd moved to Sunshine Beach.

"What's up, Tisha?"

LaTisha pointed over her shoulder. "Chief wants to see you. What did you do now?"

Deandre thought about everything he'd worked on this past week and couldn't think of anything. Not that he made a habit of messing up and being called to meet with the chief. He played by the book and followed the rules. "Nothing that I know of."

LaTisha laughed. She was a little under six feet tall, with golden brown skin and a halo of curly hair she wore slicked back in a tight ponytail. When he'd left patrol and accepted the offer to head up the Community Outreach Division, he'd hoped she would've accepted the role of heading up the section with him. But she hadn't wanted to be strapped to a desk. He couldn't blame her, and, thankfully, their friendship remained intact.

"Well, she's itching to see you, so you've probably done something."

Deandre scooped up a notepad and pen and headed out the door. "If I did something, then I'll deal with it."

Latisha shook her head. "You're always acting like stuff doesn't bother you."

"It bothers me, but I put things in perspective. I realize what's worth the effort and what isn't. Chief wanting to see me, that's not worth any anxiety until I get there and find out why. No need to borrow trouble. She may have something good to say."

Latisha shrugged. "I hope so. Lunch later?"

He checked his watch. "Nah, I'll be taking a late lunch. Maybe tomorrow."

"Sounds good." She held out her fist.

He bumped his fist with hers before turning the corner to head to the chief's office. The police chief was still considered new, since the previous chief had worked for the department for twenty years. She'd been hired to take over the Sunshine Beach Police Department six months after he'd moved to the town and taken a job with the force. Higher-ups had brought her in because the previous chief had been caught up in one too many scandals with his subordinates. The final affair was with a married woman in Dispatch. Her husband had blown the whistle, sending text messages, pictures and emails to the local news. Once his bad deeds could no longer be hidden, the department went under scrutiny and everything wrong about the way he ran things came to light. The previous chief had created a lack of trust in the community, a high turnover rate of officers and a toxic environment that didn't offer any benefit for doing the right thing. Chief Montgomery had been hired and given the task of fixing all of that. And she'd taken her job seriously.

Suddenly, people were held accountable for their actions. Transparency and integrity were valued over sweeping things under the rug and an unwritten policy of talking through smoke and mirrors. She'd slowly made changes and they were finally starting to see the benefit of her efforts.

He knocked on the door and entered after hearing a terse "come in." Chief Montgomery gave him a quick glance before looking back at her computer. Her fingers flew furiously over the keyboard as she typed.

"Lieutenant King, come on in and have a seat."

Deandre entered and sat down in the chair across from her desk. "I heard you wanted to see me."

"I do. Let me finish my thoughts on this." She was short but had enough confidence and attitude to make up for her stature. She wore her brown hair in a short style. Her cheeks were slightly flushed beneath her pale skin and her eyes narrowed as she typed. Whoever was on the other side of her email had obviously pissed her off.

"Go right ahead."

Her chin lifted and lowered before her brows knitted and she went back to typing. Chief Montgomery had spent the past fifteen years in law enforcement after an eight-year stint in the army. She was straightforward, no nonsense and one of the few people he knew who truly believed in always doing the right thing. She was a stickler for following the rules but was also empathetic enough to try and understand why decisions were made. He liked that about her and believed that was the reason why she'd been able to make the department better.

She finished with a few hard taps on the keyboard before her lips moved as she read over the email. Then she hit the enter key hard. "There, that's done."

"Who's getting eviscerated now?" Deandre teased.

She looked at him and raised a brow. "The town manager. I swear that guy likes to push my buttons."

"What's the problem now?" On the one hand, the town manager respected the way Chief Montgomery had improved the police department. On the other hand, the popularity she received for doing so and the love of the community meant her power with the elected officials and the public was higher than his. The battle of egos commenced whenever the two were together.

"That's why I want to see you," she said. "What's happening in the south end?"

"I met the with community liaison. We're looking at dates to have an outreach event in the neighborhood. Why?"

Chief Montgomery pointed at her computer and frowned. "He's once again griping about crime in the area. Mostly because business owners are griping to him. He doesn't want to hear about the community outreach team. Instead, he wants to hear about the number of arrests we've had."

Deandre scoffed. "Why, so he can turn around and

blame us for ruining the town's reputation with the residents?"

"The Community Outreach Division wasn't his idea, and he doesn't like it. The man hired me to make things better, but he fights me on everything I'm trying to do."

"Your work proves him wrong all the time. That's what matters." Deandre had seen that for himself several times over the past six years. The chief and town manager would argue about one of her ideas, but things would turn out great and her approval ratings in the community went up several more points.

"Yeah, well this time he's got at least two council members on his side. They want to see arrests for the break-ins, and they want more patrols to handle the hoodlums in the area." She held up a hand. "Their words, not mine."

Deandre nodded but his shoulders tensed. "There aren't any hoodlums. Just teenagers with nothing to do."

"Well, I need to give them something. Maybe your outreach event will work out. I can ask them to come and speak. Elected officials love a chance to speak."

"If they're willing to come, we'll have them. We were even thinking about asking the public defender and solicitor's office to show up. We'll take a few council members."

She nodded. "Good. Let me know when you finalize a date and I'll get it on their calendar. This has to work out. I don't need him to give me any more crap about the community outreach division. If we can show that having a presence in the neighborhoods that's positive and not just to scare people but still get results, then I can shut him up."

"I'll get on it. I'm meeting with Sheri later today to go over possible dates and locations."

Chief Montgomery stopped in the middle of turning back to her computer to give him a sharp glance. "Who's Sheri?"

"She's the community liaison. She agreed to help after the last neighborhood watch meeting. She wants the area to get better, but not at the expense of kicking out the kids who rely on the area as a place to hang out."

The line between Chief Montgomery's eyes lifted before she nodded. "Good. Let me know what you'll need. I'll see if I can get it for you."

"I will." He stood and turned toward the door.

"And Lieutenant,"

Deandre faced her. "Yes, ma'am."

She clasped her hands on her desk and met his eyes with an intense stare. "We've got to make this good. I don't know if he means it, but he threw out dissolving the Community Outreach Division to focus more on a tactical team that focuses on crime. I can't let that happen."

Deandre understood exactly what that would mean. An increased police presence and a heavier hand from law enforcement. A stronger push to not only remove the teenagers from the area, but revitalization efforts that also pushed out the current businesses for ones that were higher-end like the north side of the beach. Gentrification in the name of community improvements.

The Community Outreach Division had been Chief Montgomery's idea—an idea Deandre had supported and been more than willing to support after seeing how well the similar division had worked back in his hometown. He'd accepted the offer to head the division because he'd wanted to be part of the solution to rebuild trust in the police force. He'd become a cop because he wanted to make a difference, not because he wanted to be in control or scare people. The Community Outreach Division could make a difference not just by reducing crime in the area, but also by building a much-needed bridge between the force and citizens that hadn't trusted in the town's willingness to meet their needs.

He gave her a thumbs-up. "We won't let that happen."

Sheri held her breath and leaned forward as she watched and waited for Deandre to take a bite of the fried chicken she'd brought him. They'd agreed to meet up at the neighborhood center to talk about plans for the "Connecting the Community" outreach event—a name she'd come up with that morning while making biscuits. Her kitchen was good at making sure they didn't have too much leftover food by the time they closed, but today she'd asked them to try and have a few extra pieces of chicken available. She'd also packed some of the biscuits he'd liked and a side of her special collard greens. He'd already mentioned not eating breakfast, and when she'd visited him the other day to discuss plans, she'd seen the protein bar and sandwich that looked like it had come from a gas station on his desk.

She didn't need to feed the man. He wasn't her responsibility, but there she was. Arriving with a basket packed and insisting that he eat.

"Mmm." Deandre's eyes closed. He licked his full lips and nodded. "This is good."

Sheri's lips parted as she sucked in a shallow breath. She wasn't sure if it was the compliment or the way her eyes followed the movement of his tongue on his lips, but either way she clapped her hands. "I'm glad you like it."

His eyes opened and he raised a brow. "You *knew* I would like it."

She shrugged and tried not to look too smug. From the way he'd enjoyed the biscuit the other morning, she'd been confident he would love her fried chicken. Her chicken and waffles was the most popular item on the menu. "I assumed you would, but it's always good to get confirmation."

"You didn't have to bring food."

Sheri reached down in the bag she brought and pulled out a bottle of water. "I had some left over. We're meeting and I figured we needed to eat. It should be enough for you to take home." She twisted off the top and set the bottle on his desk.

"How much do I owe you for this?" He took a sip of water from the bottle.

"You don't owe me anything. Consider it a bonus for working with me to put together the community event."

"You don't have to feed me because of that. I'd help regardless."

"Yeah, but hopefully the food will really put your heart into it." She winked.

He chuckled and quickly looked down at the food. "Believe me, my heart is already into this. I want to make this event just as successful as you do."

"Oh really? Why?" She sat back and crossed her legs.

She was still in her jeans and The Breakfast Nook T-shirt, which was stained after a busy day. Whereas he looked neat and put together in his wrinkle-free police station collared shirt and khakis. She wished she'd thought to bring a change of clothes before they'd met.

"The Community Outreach Division is still new. Although our chief wants it to be successful, some of the higher-ups aren't convinced that this is the fastest way to clean up the South End."

Sheri sat up straight and pointed a finger at the sky. "The south end doesn't need to be cleaned up. We're not dirty."

Deandre held up a hand as if to surrender. "I didn't mean it like that."

"I know what you're trying to say, but words matter. Saying the area needs to be cleaned up makes it sound like something is wrong with the south end. We just need more help for the businesses, investment from the town and meaningful things for the kids in the area to do. That's not cleaning up, that's just providing support."

"I hear what you're saying. I won't use those words anymore."

Sheri studied his features and didn't see any signs that he was just agreeing to make her be quiet or move along. His gaze remained steady and his voice was sincere.

She nodded and returned to leaning back in the chair. "Thank you. You're the officer most of the people in the area will deal with. Think about what you're saying so that you don't push them away."

"Point taken." His voice remained even. He didn't seem upset or irritated by her correction.

"What kind of support do the higher-ups think the area needs?"

"Not the community outreach kind. The town manager wants to create a tactical team to focus on crime.

There are concerns about gangs and the access to opioids in the community."

"That doesn't sound like support." In fact, it sounded like a scare tactic.

"For the people that are complaining about the break-ins and drug trafficking, it sounds like the perfect answer."

Sheri let out an annoyed breath and shook her head. "I remember what it was like dealing with the police in Sunshine Beach when I was a teenager."

His head tilted to the side. "What was it like?"

She considered trying to find a nice way to say what was on her mind. But the interest in his eyes made her want to speak the truth. If they were going to work together on bringing the community together, then he would need to know how some people still felt about the police department.

"Don't trust them. Don't call them. Don't say anything because they're always looking for trouble. I was terrified when I found out one of Tyrone's neighbors called the cops on me."

"You didn't think someone would call the cops when you went over with a baseball bat?" A spark of amusement lit his eye.

Sheri shrugged and looked to the ceiling. "I was listening to my cousin and blasting angry, love-gone-wrong songs. I wasn't thinking clearly." She focused back on him and patted her chest. "But when the blue lights pulled up, it hit me just how bad things could go."

"I didn't want to terrify you."

"I'm glad it was you and not someone else. I was surprised by how...calm you were." She thought back to that night and the way he'd quickly diffused the situation. He'd been direct and to the point and taken charge without throwing his ego around. "I could tell you were disappointed maybe, but you weren't belittling, and you didn't treat me like I was nobody. I don't ever want to get arrested again, but if I have to, then I'd prefer it be like that."

"Going in guns blazing only makes a situation worse. I'm not that kind of person or cop. Our chief is the same. She spent her first year or two weeding out the bad apples in the bunch. We're not perfect, but we're on the right path."

"That's good to hear. Honestly, my family warned me about working with you."

"Because of our past connection?"

She shook her head. "Nooo! I did not tell them you were the cop who arrested me. I try not to bring up that part of my life with my family."

"Then why didn't they want you to work with me?"

"Just because you're a cop. They remember the old days even more than I do. They're worried you'll take the hammer approach to helping out the neighborhood."

"The hammer isn't my first approach."

She narrowed her eyes and grinned "But you will use it?"

The corner of his mouth quirked before he lifted one broad shoulder. "Only when necessary. My late wife talked about how she used to love hanging out on the beaches when she grew up here. She loved this place and always talked about us moving back here one day."

"She was from here? I know you said you moved after she passed because your in-laws were close, but we have a lot of people who move to Sunshine Beach later in life."

"She was. Grew up here and then moved to Greensboro after graduating from North Carolina A&T."

"Hold up? Was your wife Jamila Davis?"

Deandre blinked and froze for a second before nodding. "You knew her?"

"I mean, I knew who she was. She was what…two years behind me in high school. Her family goes to my aunt's church, so I'd see her around. I heard she went to A&T and that she passed away a few years back."

Sadness filled his eyes and a bittersweet smile hovered around his lips. "Yeah, that was her."

The sorrow in his eyes made her want to get up and give him a hug. Which was completely inappropriate, so she asked a question that would hopefully remove some of the pain. "How did you two hook up?"

The sadness left his eyes and he let out a soft laugh. "We met at a protest."

"Wait, what? Don't tell me you arrested her?"

He grinned and shook his head. "I didn't arrest her. It was a peaceful protest. I was there to protest, too. Against a new ordinance the city was passing. We caught each other's eye in the crowd. She came up and said hi and… That was it."

The way he spoke the words, as if some magic spell had come over him that granted him everything he ever wanted, made her want to believe fairy tales existed. She leaned forward and rested her elbow on his desk. "How long were you married?"

"Eleven years," he said slowly. His eyes still focused on the past.

She nodded but didn't know what to say. That was a long time to be with one person only to lose them so permanently. She didn't have the right words and instead of saying something wrong she decided to stay quiet.

"It was a good eleven. I wouldn't trade them. Even if I knew how they'd end."

"Sounds like you really loved her."

"I did. Maybe one day..." He looked at her and their gazes connected.

He didn't have to finish his words; the wistful look in his gaze told her the rest. Maybe one day he'd fall in love again. What would it be like to be loved by this man? To be loved so much that even knowing the ending would be tragic, he still wouldn't walk away?

Sheri's breath caught in her throat. She was fantasizing about falling in love with him while he talked about his late wife. To make matters worse, she'd leaned on his desk and was right in his face. He looked away quickly and she pushed back to sit fully in her chair.

"I hope that one day, if you're ready, that you can find someone who makes you happy."

He glanced back at her. She couldn't read his expression or what he was thinking. That didn't stop her heart from racing faster or for the air to feel thin and hot around her.

The door opened. And a voice called out. "Hey, Dad, you here?"

Deandre blinked and stood. "Yeah, I'm here. Meeting with Ms. Thomas to talk about the community event. Come and say hi." His words were rushed, almost guilty.

Or maybe Sheri was projecting. Thank goodness for the interruption. His heart had been given away a long time ago and wasn't going to be given away anytime soon, much less to her. Plus, he had a teenage son. She was far from ready to be anyone's stepmom. Her attraction to Deandre wasn't going to go away, but she would have the decency to be professional while they worked together and keep all fantasies to herself.

She stood as well and turned to meet his son. When she spotted the kid, she had to blink twice. His son froze in place, his eyes wide.

"It's you," Sheri said.

Deandre frowned. He looked from Sheri to his son. "You've met."

"The other day," Sheri said. "He offered to help me with my sign." Right before trying to hit on her and calling her an "old ass."

Deandre's frown cleared up and he smiled. "Oh, good. I'm glad to see that DJ was being helpful."

"Yeah, real helpful," Sheri said dryly.

"You know me, Dad. I'm always trying to help my elders." DJ looked at Sheri and gave an innocent smile.

Sheri's eyes narrowed. Was he was calling her old? Again! Sheri pulled back the attraction she felt for Deandre and shoved it to the darkest corner of her mind, slammed the imaginary door with a kick and locked it. Being interested in a man who had no interest in her was one thing. Being interested in a man with a sly teenager who liked to play games was 100 percent out of the question.

Chapter Seven

Sheri was flipping through the rack of shirts in TJ Maxx with her cousin Cora by her side talking endlessly about the last date she'd gone on, when the sound of a familiar voice caught her attention. She stopped searching and lifted her head. Sure enough, walking across the store to the men's section was Deandre, a cell phone pressed to his ear.

"Deandre!" she called before she could think.

He stopped walking and glanced around. Her cousin stopped flipping through the clothes and followed Sheri's gaze toward him. Deandre caught her eye, lifted a hand and smiled.

Cora leaned over and whispered. "Lil Bit, who is that?"

"The cop I'm planning the community event with."

"Oh? Then why are you calling him like he's your man?" Cora cocked her head to the side and narrowed her eyes.

Sheri elbowed her cousin. "Shut up. I'm not calling him like he's my man."

"Mmm-hmm," was Cora's unconvinced reply.

Deandre spoke into the phone before pulling it away and sliding it in his back pocket. He walked over to talk to her from the other side of the aisle. He was dressed in regular clothes, a basic black T-shirt that fitted his muscled arms and broad shoulders perfectly and a pair of blue basketball shorts that stopped right above the knee.

"Everything good?" His gaze scanned the area before gliding across her face as if checking to make sure everything was okay around her. Or, maybe she was projecting. The guy probably always scanned the perimeter.

"Yeah, everything is good. I recognized your voice when you were walking by. You didn't have to get off the phone. I just wanted to say hey."

He nodded. "I was looking for a reason to end that call. My friend LaTisha can sometimes get on a roll."

Sheri's heart dimmed. Based on the name, she assumed his friend was a woman. Did he mean friend as in, they were cool, or friend as in *girlfriend*? Why did she care? She'd already decided she was not going to do anything about the attraction she felt for Deandre.

"This is my cousin." She pointed to Cora watching intently next to her.

Cora shoved her hand over the rack. "Nice to meet you." She leaned forward, nearly spilling her cleavage out of the tank top she wore, and poked her tongue out of the corner of her mouth. Sheri rolled her eyes at her cousin's familiar flirty move.

Deandre shook her hand. "Deandre. Nice to meet

you, as well." When he tried to pull back, she didn't let go.

Cora tilted her head to the side and eyed him. "You look familiar. Have we met before?"

Deandre shrugged. "I'm not sure. I'm around town a lot. You might have seen me. I'm in the Community Outreach Division of the Sunshine Beach Police Department."

Cora finally let go of his hand. "Maybe that's it."

Sheri was glad Cora didn't immediately recognize him. She'd been with Sheri the night Deandre arrested them for acting like some broken-hearted vigilantes. No telling what Cora would say when she put two and two together.

"Well, it was good seeing you," Sheri said quickly. "I'll see you Wednesday at the neighborhood watch meeting, right?"

"You will. I hope the rest of the neighborhood is as excited about your idea for the event as I am."

"I hope so, too."

Cora tapped her chin. "I swear we've met before."

Time for them to go. She looked at Cora. "We better check out if we want to get to the grocery store and pick up the stuff your mom needs for the potato salad."

Cora's attention immediately snapped back to that. "Girl, you're right. We've been in here way too long. Nice meeting you." She waved and headed to the register.

"Same here." Deandre looked back to Sheri. "See you on Wednesday."

"If you need anything before then just give me a call." She should be following her cousin instead of prolonging the conversation, but she didn't always make the best choices when she talked with a guy she was feeling.

"I think we're good. Even though I have been thinking about the chicken you dropped off the other day."

Pride ballooned in her chest. He'd been thinking about her. Well, her chicken, but she'd take that. Maybe he'd told someone about her food who would check out the restaurant. "If you've been thinking about it, then I'll have to bring some over."

"No need to do that."

"I don't mind feeding you." Honestly, she'd like to do a lot more than feed him, but she kept that thought to herself.

Her thoughts must have shown on her face because his smile faltered and he glanced away. Her mom always said everything she thought came through on her face.

Deandre pointed to the men's section. "I'd better go. I was looking for some shirts for my son."

Yes, the son who called her old. A good reminder of why she needed to keep her thoughts in her head instead of showing up in her expressions or words. "I'll let you go. See you around."

Sheri turned away and followed her cousin to the checkout. They'd put their purchases in the back of the car and were driving to the grocery store when Cora slapped the steering wheel.

She pointed at Sheri. "He's the cop that arrested us!"

Sheri closed her eyes and groaned. "Damn. I'd hoped you wouldn't remember."

"I remember everything. Why didn't you tell me?"

"Because I didn't want to make a big deal out of it."

"Does he know who you are?"

"He does. He remembered me almost immediately."

"And he doesn't mind working with you?"

"No, and I don't mind working with him. We talked about it, and for the sake of supporting the businesses in the south end, we agreed to work together."

Cora glanced at Sheri from the corner of her eye. "But you like him."

Heat spread across Sheri's face. She focused extra hard on keeping her expression neutral. Cora could always read her like a book. "Yeah, he's nice."

Cora pursed her lip. "Don't play with me. I mean you want to sleep with him."

Sheri scoffed and looked out the window. "No I don't."

"Girl, if you don't quit lying to me. I've known you all my life and I can tell when you like a guy. You get that horny look in your eye."

Sheri spun back toward Cora. "I don't have a horny look."

"Yes you do, it's like this." Her cousin batted her eyes, pursed her lips and lifted her shoulders with exaggerated breathing.

Sheri crossed her arms. "You ought to stop! I am not that bad."

Cora laughed and fixed her face. "You're bad enough. So, are you going to sleep with him?"

"Hell no! We're working together."

Cora sucked her teeth. "You're working together on a community event. That's not the same. And my man is sexy." Cora's voice dipped with the last sentence, and she licked her lips.

"He's a widower with a teenage son who called me an old ass the other day."

"Wait, what?"

Sheri recounted the story and running into him later. "I didn't want to tell Deandre what happened."

"Why not? He should know if his kid is acting up."

"It's not my place." Sheri didn't have kids and therefore tried not to get into the business of parents. She didn't know his parenting style or how he'd handle her saying anything negative about his son.

"We knew that everything we did as a kid in Sunshine Beach would get back to our moms. That's why we didn't act the fool too much. These kids don't think we will say anything. Besides, if he's hanging with the kids who the other business owners are saying are the problem, it'll get back to him sooner or later. You might as well give him a heads-up."

Cora had a point. Deandre's eyes lit up when he talked about his son. He'd be embarrassed if he found out his son was causing problems. "You really think I should tell him?"

"Yep. And then, you can sleep with him."

Sheri laughed. "I'm not sleeping with anyone. I'm not signing up to be a stepmom."

"Who said anything about being a stepmom to his kid? I said sleep with him." Cora shook her head. "There you go being all romantic and delusional again. Girl, just get yours and move on."

The words put Sheri on the defensive. Cora loved pointing out that Sheri was too quick to get caught up in a fairy tale when dealing with guys. Cora was only about getting what she could and moving on when the guy no longer served a purpose. Sheri had tried to be detached with her hookups and that had gotten her arrested. Proof that she could not separate feelings from sex.

"I'm not set up to just sleep with someone. Call me old-fashioned if you want to, but I'm ready to settle down. I don't want to get caught up in a guy who is only looking to have a good time."

"I told you not to get attached just because the sex is banging," Cora said in a lecturing tone.

"You did and I thought I could be okay. Well, I wasn't. Every time I try, I catch feelings. Let's face it. I'm not built for the hookup lifestyle."

Something Sheri had finally accepted about herself. Since high school she'd tried to be like Cora. When Cora said she needed to date multiple people, Sheri had done that. When Cora said never like a guy more than he liked you, she'd pretended as if she wasn't waiting by the phone for a guy to call. She'd spent so much time trying to be the independent, *I don't need a man*, love-and-leave-'em type that her friends and the single women in her family said she should be because she'd been too afraid to admit that she wanted what her mom and aunt hadn't had—a long-term committed relationship with a man. Marriage, a house and kids. All that jazz. But she was almost forty with no prospects in front of her and a police record because she spent too much time lying about what she really wanted in a relationship. No more.

Her cousin sighed and patted her shoulder. "You know what. You're right. I've accepted that."

Sheri brushed off Cora's hand. "I'm not about to sleep with Deandre only to find out I don't like his kid and he's not looking to settle with a woman he once put in handcuffs. Not in the good way. We'll just be friends."

"What if I sleep with him?"

Sheri cut her eyes at her cousin. "Don't even go there."

Cora sighed as if Sheri was asking for her right ovary. "Fine. Gotta ask. I won't go there."

"Thank you."

After the Tyrone situation, she and Cora had a "Come to Jesus" talk. Her cousin had been interested in Tyrone and admitted she was jealous when Sheri started seeing him. That's why she encouraged her to damage his car and started rumors online about his dating habits to try and sabotage his career. Sheri didn't agree with what her cousin had done, but she was family, and Sheri's mom always instilled in her that she couldn't turn her back on family. They'd made a truce with a strict rule. If one liked a guy, even a little bit, the other didn't mess with him. They didn't need any more messy situations.

She glanced at Sheri again as she started singing along to the song on the radio. She just hoped her cousin would stick to her side of the bargain.

"I don't see how this is going to help us," Belinda spoke up in the middle of Sheri's presentation.

Sheri stopped talking midsentence and raised a brow. *Oh, we're interrupting people now?* Sheri thought to herself. She'd barely started talking about why they wanted to have the Connecting the Community event and how it would benefit the area when Belinda started shifting in her seat. Sheri could feel the heat of her hard stare. Now she wasn't even going to let Sheri finish making her case?

"I see you're eager to jump in," Sheri said. "Since you won't let me finish my presentation, why don't you give us your thoughts."

Belinda had the decency to look halfway chastised. "I'm just saying, I don't see how a community event is going to stop the crime or the kids hanging out in the area."

"First of all, the goal isn't to stop the kids from hanging out. This is their town, too, and they deserve to have access to the beach just as much as your yoga clients. So, let's get that clear. The goal of the community event is to give residents and business owners information about what's happening in the area, give them a chance to hear from more than just the police department, and bring people together."

Belinda crossed her arms and raised her nose in the air. "Well, it sounds like more of a warm-and-fuzzy approach to our problem."

"Are you saying you want a cold-and-hard approach? For the police to come through and treat the teens and residents like criminals and not form any type of connection with the community?"

Belinda glanced at Deandre before looking back at Sheri. "That's not what I'm saying."

Sheri put a hand on her hip. "Then what are you saying?"

Belinda sputtered, "You're trying to make me sound horrible."

"You're doing a good job yourself."

Mumbles went through the group. Belinda's eyes narrowed. Sheri raised a brow and dared her to clap back.

Deandre stepped forward. "No one is trying to make anyone look bad." He spoke in an even, "everybody calm down" tone of voice. "We know that there are a lot of challenges in the south end. We hope this event will allow us to reach the people in the area who may not be coming to the neighborhood watch meeting. Not all business owners are here or all residents, but they have concerns. We don't want to leave them out of this conversation. We also don't want to increase the police presence just to scare the people who live and work in the south end. If we increase patrols, we want people to know we're here as a community partner as well as to keep them safe. Not to hurt anyone or make them feel unwelcome." He smiled at the end, the dimple in his cheek peeking out.

The fight in Belinda's eyes melted and she grinned back, her head tilted to the side. "I think that's a great idea."

Sheri blinked. "Seriously?" Belinda wouldn't let Sheri get through her presentation, but Deandre flashes a dimple and she's cheesing and agreeing with the event?

"Thank you, Belinda," Deandre said. "I hope this means you'll help us plan for the event."

Belinda nodded so fast she looked like a bobblehead doll. "I'd love to help."

"That's great." He looked at Sheri and nodded.

Sheri rolled her eyes. "I guess so."

Deandre gave her a look. Sheri shrugged. She could read the "play nice" in his eyes. She didn't want to play nice. She wanted to call out Belinda for being a hypocrite, but now wasn't the time. They were trying to convince people to be excited about this event. If Deandre's dimples made Belinda shut up and go along with her idea, then that would have to work.

The rest of the meeting was spent going over ideas for the community event. They even agreed on keeping Connecting the Community as a name after Belinda said it wasn't "the most clever" name she'd ever heard. Sheri stuck around after the meeting to talk with some of the other business owners and residents. Despite Belinda's original negativity, most of the others were excited about trying to do something that wasn't going to scare people away from the area.

"I mean, I moved over here because I want to see the area revitalized," Kelly, the owner of the comic book shop, said after the meeting. She wore a superhero T-shirt and jeans. "I'm glad that the city is willing to invest in this area and not just write us off as a bad part of town."

Sheri was vindicated hearing other people didn't feel the same way as Belinda. "It's on us to remind them that we're just as relevant as the north end of the beach."

Kelly's eyes lit up and she snapped her fingers. "Exactly. Hey, I'm having a drop-in at my comic book store this weekend. If you're not busy, you should come on through."

Sheri lifted a brow. "Really?"

"Yeah. I invited some other business owners, too. It's another way for us to get to know each other. And, with me being fairly new in town, it's a good way to meet up with new people."

She wasn't a big comic book fan, but she liked Kelly. She only hung out with family members, and if she was going to be staying in Sunshine Beach and wanted to make new friends, she'd need to make an effort to get out of her comfort zone. "Sounds like fun. I'll come through."

Kelley grinned and gave her a thumbs-up. "Great!" She looked over Sheri's shoulder.

"What about you, Lieutenant King? Will you be able to come by?"

Sheri turned as Deandre walked up beside her. "If I'm invited. Is it okay if my son comes with me?"

"Sure, the more the merrier," Kelley said with enthusiasm.

"Then I'll try to come through," Deandre said.

"Awesome! I'll see you both later." Kelly smiled and waved before leaving.

Sheri turned to look up at Deandre. He didn't try to tower over her, but when he stood close she was reminded of how tall he was. Tall, strong and tempting. Heat flooded her midsection and spread through her body. Sheri took a step back before her thoughts started playing out on her face again. "The meeting went okay."

He nodded. "It did. I'm hoping that means we'll have a good turnout."

"I think we will. If every business promotes it and the residents tell their neighbors, then we'll have a lot of people show up."

"I'll borrow some of your enthusiasm," he said with a half smile.

Sheri's stomach flipped. She understood why Belinda had changed her mind so quickly just because he smiled. The man was good-looking and seemed to be a decent human being. Basically, he was perfect.

"Belinda seems to like you," she blurted out.

He frowned. "I knew you were going to say that."

Sheri grinned and pointed. "So you know she likes you."

He waved a hand and shook his head. "I don't know that. I said I knew you were going to say that."

"Why, because she looked like she wanted to throw her panties when you popped that dimple on her?"

Deandre laughed. "Like she wanted to do what?"

Sheri waved her finger toward his face. "That dimple. You have to know the effect it has on women."

He rubbed his cheek. "It has an effect, huh? Well, then, I'll make sure I use my power for good instead of evil."

Sheri rolled her eyes and grinned. Good-looking, decent and has a sense of humor. He was everything she wanted. *If* there was a chance they could be anything more than temporary lovers.

"Be sure you do that." She looked around the now empty space. "Where are all the helpers who stayed behind last time to help you lock up?"

"I only have one or two, and they had to leave early. I'm good. It doesn't take much to clean up. I'll leave the tables and chairs out until tomorrow and get my son to help."

"Why doesn't he come to these meetings?"

Deandre walked toward the front of the room and she followed. "Even though I enjoy working in the community, these meetings are technically work. I don't bring him to work with me." He stopped at the front door.

"You seem to be out in the community a lot. He isn't interested in getting involved?"

"I'd love for him to take an interest, but he's at the age where dad being a cop isn't as cool as it was. When he was younger, I could show up in my car and turn on the lights and he'd think I was the best dad in the world."

Sheri smiled, imagining a younger version of his son being excited to see the lights on his dad's car. Then she thought about the way he'd called her "old ass" and couldn't imagine him being thrilled about blue lights. "Teens are like that."

He crossed his arms and leaned against the wall. Sheri was glad to see that he didn't seem to be in a hurry to leave, but instead appeared to be enjoying talking to her. "I know, but it's still taking me some getting used to. We were close before his mom passed and got closer after. It's hard watching him pull away. I wish I knew what was going on with him, but I don't."

She opened her mouth, ready to tell him about running into his son that day, but then closed it back. Now wasn't the best time. Not when he was already feeling bad about his kid growing further away from him.

Deandre's brows drew together. "What?"

She shook her head. "Nothing."

He straightened and gave her a no-nonsense stare. "No, it's something. What did you want to say?"

"It's not that big of a deal."

"Obviously it is, or you wouldn't hesitate to tell me. Is something wrong?"

"Not exactly." When he continued to watch her with concern, she decided to take Cora's advice and be honest with him. "I just… Well, I ran into your son. Before you introduced me to him."

"When?"

"Outside of my restaurant when I was closing up. He was with a group of teens. Some of the same kids that the other business owners have complained about. He was kind of rude."

Deandre's stance shifted and his gaze sharpened. "Rude how?"

Sheri held up a hand and shook her head. "Damn, see, I wasn't trying to get him in trouble."

He reached over and wrapped his hand around hers. He gently lowered her arm before letting her go. The touch was firm, but surprisingly gentle, and way too brief. "If he's acting out in the community, I need to know. What happened?"

Sheri forced herself not to rub her wrist. Not because he'd hurt her, but because she still felt the heat of his quick touch and she wanted to savor the feeling. To rub it in so she could melt in it later.

She told him the entire story. "It was just kids being kids," she said. "I wasn't hurt or anything, but I just thought you should know since you're trying to connect with the people in this area."

He frowned and ran a hand over his face. "I'm sorry, Sheri."

"For what? You didn't do anything. Please, if you talk to him, don't be too hard on him. It really wasn't that bad."

He raised a brow. "I'll talk with him and get him to apologize."

Sheri closed her eyes and groaned. "Now he really is going to think I'm a mean old woman."

"He'll know that if he acts up in this area that it'll get back to me and that actions have consequences."

She opened her eyes and met his gaze. He seemed concerned, but not upset with her for telling him about what happened. She'd been right in her assumption that he wouldn't go off on her for pointing out flaws in his kid.

"Fair enough," she said. "But I still feel like a snitch. And you know snitches get stitches."

His lips quirked and he laughed again. "No one in my family will be giving you stitches. Seriously, thank you for being honest with me. It's good to know. I want my son to grow up into a responsible person. If he's being rude to adults in the area, then I need to know."

"Hopefully, this won't come up again. And we can only talk about fun stuff when we're together."

"Fun stuff?"

He pushed away from the door. He didn't come closer, but with him standing straight and giving her his complete attention, it made her mind think of all the fun but inappropriate stuff they could do. Like the two of them wrapped in each other's arms. His body between her legs.

She blinked and pushed that thought out of her head. "You know, like the community event, the chicken I bring you, stuff like that."

"In between the fun stuff, can you let me know a little bit more about you?"

She pressed a hand to her chest. Her heart beat frantically beneath her rib cage. "Me?" Thank goodness her voice didn't tremble like her insides.

He nodded. "Yes. I'd like to know more about my partner."

"Your partner?" Her cheeks heated. Damn, she liked the sound of that.

"Yeah, my partner on planning. Plus, I'll be in the area a lot. We can be friends."

Friends. He wanted to be…friends.

Sheri's stomach plummeted. Even if she were able to be a hit-it-and-quit-it girl, she still didn't have a chance with him. She was holding back from salivating over him, while he'd, very easily, put her in the friend zone.

She grinned but the movement felt stiff. Embarrassment churned her stomach, but thankfully, he didn't seem to have any idea about the fantasies going through her mind. She would be a professional and work with him on this project without making a fool of herself.

She took a step forward and opened the door. "We sure can. Friends it is."

Chapter Eight

Deandre drove home with the weight of what Sheri told him pressing down on him, urging him to speed the few miles to their house, but the reminder from his late wife that he should always get the full story before going into "cop mode" with the family held him to the speed limit. He would get to the bottom of things and find out if what Sheri said was the truth. And if it were, why would DJ do that?

Deandre knew his son wasn't perfect, but he'd always believed he was a good kid. Good kids didn't go around trying to hit on women old enough to be their mother or call them names when they were rejected. As much as he didn't want to believe what Sheri said, he'd also dealt with enough delusional parents in his career to hesitate before saying "my kid would never do that."

His in-laws' car was in the driveway when he pulled up. He'd forgotten they'd mentioned coming over to check on DJ while Deandre worked late at the neighborhood watch meeting. They often stepped in to spend time with DJ when Deandre had to work. Their support for him and DJ after Jamila's death was invaluable. His parents currently lived in a rental house in Denver. Since retirement, his parents embraced the "live it up" lifestyle and spent most of their time traveling to places they'd always wanted to visit. He didn't blame them; they'd raised him and his three brothers and wanted to enjoy their life. A part of him wished they'd spend more time with DJ, but he was forever thankful for Jamila's parents for providing a level of consistency even Deandre couldn't handle on his own.

He went inside and found Cliff and Rose sitting on the couch with DJ. The three of them watched a sitcom on television. His in-laws laughed at something on screen while DJ looked unamused. Which was his typical look lately. At least he didn't have his phone in his hand. Rose and Cliff had a strict rule that DJ couldn't scroll when he was with them. A rule DJ followed with minimal complaint.

Rose spotted him first. "Hey, Deandre, how was work?" He'd liked Rose from the start.

She'd treated him like family from the moment Jamila had introduced him to her. They got along well, and, with his own mother so far away, he'd easily accepted and absorbed the love she'd given him when he'd married her daughter.

"It was pretty good. The area seems excited about the event. So that's a good thing. I didn't think you would still be here."

Cliff pointed to the television. "We were going to go, but then I remembered my show was coming on. DJ was okay with watching it with us."

He glanced at DJ. "Well, that was nice of him."

DJ shrugged. "I'm a nice kid."

"When you want to be," Deandre countered.

Rose reached over and patted DJ's shoulder. "He always is."

Deandre sat in the chair next to the couch. "I want to believe the same thing, but I've been hearing some things."

"Things like what?" DJ asked.

"Things like you're going around saying inappropriate things to some of the shop owners on the south end."

Deandre didn't mind having the conversation in front of Cliff and Rose. If anything, DJ would be more likely to tell the truth in front of them. The glacier-cold wall DJ had built in the past year didn't extend to the relationship with his grandparents. He was more patient and accepting of their questions and prodding into his life. Deandre wished he'd get the same treatment, but, thankfully, Cliff and Rose and Deandre were a team in parenting DJ. If he came to them with any problems, they wouldn't hesitate to bring the situation to Deandre for them to work together on a solution.

DJ rolled his eyes. "She's lying. I didn't say anything to her."

Rose turned to DJ. "Her who?"

Deandre leaned forward. Disappointment tightened into a knot in his stomach. "Yes, DJ, her who, because I didn't say anything about where I heard it."

"I don't have to guess," DJ said with an irritated sigh. "I already know. I was just joking with her. That's all."

Deandre cocked his head to the side. "Joking? Do you joke with me or your grandparents like that?"

DJ huffed but shook his head. "No, sir."

"Then what makes you think it's okay to joke around with any other adults that way? Come on, DJ, what's going on with you? You quit wrestling and now you're hanging around, insulting adults you don't know."

Cliff sat up straighter. "You quit wrestling?" He sounded just as shocked at Deandre had.

DJ shrugged. "It's no big deal. Nothing is going on. I just didn't want to wrestle anymore, and I really was just joking. I'm not going through something."

Deandre pointed at his son. "You're going with me on Saturday to apologize."

DJ threw up his hands. "Come on, Dad."

"You're coming. You understand me? I'm working hard to build trust with the people in that area and I can't have you going behind my back undermining the trust and proving to them that the kids in the area are part of the problem. There are some business owners who think you and your friends are the reason for the break-ins and increased crime. They want us to come through arresting you all and scaring you away. If you're running round with a group of kids who think it's funny to hit on older women and call them *old ass* when they tell you no, then you're not helping. You understand?"

Rose pressed a hand to her chest. "Old what? DJ, did you say that?"

DJ closed his eyes and let out a heavy breath. He hesitated a beat before opening them back and nodding. "Okay. I get it. Don't embarrass you."

"It's not about embarrassing me. It's about also protecting you. Look at me, DJ."

His son slowly turned and met his eye.

"There are people who want to take my job and weaponize it against you and your friends. Don't give them a reason to do that. That's what this is about. Do you understand that?"

Some of the defiance left DJ's eyes. "I get it."

"Good."

"Can I go to my room now?"

Rose reached over and patted his leg. "You want to leave us now that we know what you did? Don't do something if you'll be embarrassed for us to find out about it later."

"Yes, ma'am. I've got homework," DJ said in that same, unconvincing voice that irritated Deandre.

Rose sighed but nodded. "We'll see you another day."

"Okay, Love you." DJ hugged her and then Cliff before disappearing down the hall to his room.

"Teenagers," Cliff said shaking his head.

"Tell me about it," Deandre replied. "He's still a good kid, but he's pushing boundaries."

"They'll do that. I remember when Jamila would fight us on everything," Rose said.

"Hold up," Cliff cut in. "She fought you on everything? She never argued with me."

Rose rolled her eyes and grinned. "That's because she was a daddy's girl through and through."

Deandre lifted his lips in a wistful smile. "DJ's personality is so much like hers. I wonder if he'd still be doing this if she were around."

"He would," Cliff said matter-of-factly. "Teenagers like to spread their wings and see how far they can go."

"Maybe, but boys are different with their mommas," Rose said. "He'd still be butting heads with you, Deandre, but he'd have a softer side in the house to calm him down."

Deandre leaned back in his chair. "I'll work on developing my softer side."

"Or, you can find a nice woman to settle down with," she said with wide, hopeful eyes.

Deandre closed his eyes and smiled. In the past year, Rose had gotten it into her head that Deandre needed a wife. At first, he'd been surprised. Not because he expected his in-laws to want him to remain alone for the rest of his life after losing Jamila, but he just hadn't expected them to actively try and push him into the arms of another woman, either. But they both were strongly on the side of him getting back in the dating pool.

"If I find the right person I'll consider that. But not because DJ needs a new mom. We're doing okay."

"Have you been looking for the right person?" Cliff asked curiously.

A vision of Sheri drifted into his mind. Her bright eyes, wide smile and sexy figure. She wasn't as dramatic as he'd assumed she would be, but she did have a fiery spark to her personality. One she'd wanted to let out on Belinda today.

He sat up straight and his eyes popped back open. What was that? Yeah, he found her attractive, and yes, she'd awakened his sex drive, but why would he think of her when he thought of a potential future wife? She wasn't even in the running.

"Hmm." Rose narrowed her eyes on him. "I think there may be someone."

Deandre shook his head. "Nah, there isn't. It's not like that."

Rose and Cliff shared a look and grinned. "What's not like that? Who is she?"

Deandre held up a hand. "There is no she and there

is no situation to update you on. Right now, I'm focused on keeping DJ out of trouble and making sure the town sticks behind their promise to support the revitalization of the south side of the beach."

"There's always time for a little romance," Cliff said with a wink.

"He's right," Rose agreed. "We want to see you happy, too, Deandre. And, you know Jamila would have wanted you to be happy, as well."

Deandre nodded. "I know. I'm not trying to rush into anything. But I hear you and I appreciate that you want good things for me."

They exchanged another look, communicating silently in a way that Deandre had once hoped he and Jamila would get to. But they never would get to that point, and while the pain of her loss would never go away, he was no longer too gutted to poke at the scar.

He did have a quick moment with Sheri earlier. When their eyes met, and she'd wanted to keep arguing with Belinda but he'd pleaded with her to be nice. She'd understood him. He'd imagined her voice saying *"Fine, this time for you,"* before she'd let the conversation drop. Maybe that's why he was imagining her as more than just a partner in this project. But deep down, he knew it could be more if he let it. The instant attraction, the connection, the way he just *liked* her. He hadn't felt that since…

"Anyone want something to drink? I'm going to get some tea." He cut off his own thoughts before they could take hold.

"I'll take some. We'll leave after the show is over," Cliff said.

Deandre nodded and looked at Rose, who shook her

head and said she was good. He went to the kitchen and prepared the drinks. He'd deal with getting through today, helping his son and the community event. That's it. He wasn't quite ready to deal with the weird message his libido, or maybe his heart, was trying to deliver to his brain.

Chapter Nine

DJ sighed for what had to be the hundredth time since Deandre told him to get in the car so they could go to the gathering at Kelly's comic book store. Deandre hadn't expected DJ to jump up and down with excitement to apologize to Sheri, but he had hoped his son wouldn't act as if he were being dragged to the guillotine. Comic books were one of the few things DJ still enjoyed reading.

"Come on, DJ, what's the sigh for?"

DJ looked at him as if he should know exactly what the sigh was about. "I didn't have to come here tonight."

"You're here to apologize."

"I can do that anytime. Why tonight in front of everyone?"

"I won't make you apologize in front of the group. You like comic books. I thought you'd enjoy coming to the store."

"Manga."

Deandre frowned. "Say what?"

DJ rubbed a hand over his face and gave Deandre a "you're clueless" expression. "I read mangas. Not comics."

"Aren't they the same thing?"

DJ closed his eyes and shook his head. "Bruh…" he sighed. "They are completely different things."

"Well, *bruh*, maybe there are mangas in here."

"There aren't."

"How do you know?"

"I've been in that shop before. It's all comics, maybe a few mangas, but not what I'm reading."

"Well, check out the comic books anyway. Maybe you'll find something you like."

"Yeah, maybe," he said just a tad shy of sarcastically.

Deandre accepted that he wasn't going to get anything more positive out of his son, and parallel parked the car in a spot a few storefronts down from the comic book store. They got out of the car and went inside. Several other business owners and some residents mingled inside the store. Deandre's eyes searched the crowd until they landed on Sheri standing in the back talking with Kelly. Sheri threw her head back and laughed at something Kelly said and Deandre's breath hitched in his throat. Damn, she was fine.

"Can I go after I apologize?" DJ's voice cut into Deandre's thoughts.

He blinked and looked over at his son. "I may not be ready to leave."

"My boy Julian is at the pizza place. He said he'll pick me up."

Deandre shook his head. "You came with me, and you'll leave with me. End of discussion."

"Oh, man," DJ muttered.

"Come on. Let's go say hello."

"And get this over with," DJ mumbled.

They were stopped by several people who recognized him as they made their way across the room. Even though DJ didn't want to be there and was more than happy to show his irritation to Deandre, the kid had enough home training to not act out or say anything rude while they spoke with the people in the store. DJ was all yes ma'am and no sir with eye contact and a pleasant expression when he spoke. Pride swelled in his chest. DJ was "pushing boundaries" as Cliff said, but he was still a good kid.

They got to Kelly and Sheri just as soon as it looked like Sheri was about to walk away. She caught his eye and smiled. It was so bright, he wondered if she'd been waiting for him to arrive. No, he was reading too much into that. She always smiled like that.

"Lieutenant, how are you?" Kelly asked.

"I'm good, Kelly. How are you?"

"I'm great. Is this your son?" Kelly asked, grinning at DJ.

"It is. This is Deandre Jr., or DJ for short."

DJ nodded to them both. "It's nice meeting you."

"Likewise. Do you read comics?" Kelly asked.

DJ shook his head. "Not really. Mostly mangas."

Kelly pointed to a section across the room. "Ah, I've got a few but not many. I hope to expand the section one day. Maybe you can tell me some of the series you're reading, and I can get them in stock."

DJ's brows lifted. "You'd do that?"

"Of course. I like mangas, but comics are my true love. But I would like to bring in all types of customers.

Just let me know." She nodded at someone who called her name from across the room. "Let me check on this. Thanks for coming, Lieutenant. Nice to meet you, DJ." She left the three of them.

"I'm going to check out the mangas," DJ said, turning away.

Deandre cleared his throat and placed a hand on his son's shoulder. DJ sighed and turned back. "Yes, sir."

"Aren't you forgetting something?" Deandre tilted his head toward Sheri.

DJ looked like he wanted to roll his eyes, but his son was also a smart kid and knew better. He turned to Sheri. "I'm sorry for what I said the other day. It was rude and it won't happen again."

Sheri's eyes widened. She looked at Deandre, then back at DJ. "Oh, well, thank you for apologizing. It's accepted."

DJ nodded then looked at Deandre. "Now can I check out the mangas?"

"Fine, go ahead." DJ quickly ran off.

Sheri chuckled. "How much did it hurt him to have to apologize to me?"

"Enough to warrant about fifty million sighs on the car ride over and a request to leave immediately afterward."

Sheri crinkled her nose. "That much, huh? You didn't have to get him to do that, but I do appreciate it."

She wasn't dressed in her usual The Breakfast Nook T-shirt and jeans. Instead, she wore a sleeveless tan-colored shirt that fitted her breasts perfectly and a pair of distressed jeans that hugged her curves. A gold chain with her nickname, Lil Bit, hung just above the swell of her breast. He forced himself to keep eye contact and not let his gaze wander over the smooth brown skin of her neck, chest and shoulders.

"I did have to get him apologize. I let him know that kind of behavior is what's making some people want him and his friends banned from the south end of the beach. I think he understood."

"Well, for what it's worth, that was the only thing I've seen happen with him and his group of friends. They don't really cause any trouble as far as I know. I don't think he's running around with a really bad crowd."

"That's good to know. He doesn't know how much I worry about him. I get it, he's sixteen and able to be out in the world on his own to an extent, but it's still hard for me to not want to protect him like he's still six years old."

Sheri placed a hand on his arm. "I think I get what you're saying, but don't let him hear that. I don't know any sixteen-year-old who wants to still be viewed like they're six." Her eyes sparkled with humor.

She gently squeezed his bicep before her hand fell away. He didn't know if the movement was meant to be reassuring, or a way for her to feel the muscle, but either way, his arm seemed to sizzle from where she'd touched it.

"I'll try and remember that," he said.

She glanced away and nodded as she caught some-one else's eye. Was she about to walk away? He wasn't ready for their conversation to end. "How long have you been here?" he asked quickly.

She looked back at him. "Not too long. It's a nice thing to get to mingle with the other shop owners and learn more about Kelly's store. I think I may host something at the restaurant later for everyone."

"That would be a good idea."

"Yeah, keep the vibe going and help us all get to know each other as we build up the area." Her eyes darted to the side again. Whoever she'd noticed before must have gotten her attention.

Deandre shifted his stance a little to the left. Sheri's dark brown eyes lifted back up to meet his. "I hope I get an invite."

Sheri's tongue darted out and touched the edge of her mouth. "You'd come?"

He would, but the hope in her voice and the way her lips lifted in the sexiest of smiles triggered something in his brain. He'd rearrange his entire schedule to make it to anything she ever put on. "For you? Of course I'd come."

Her hand lifted to toy with the chain around her neck. His eyes followed the movement of her slim fingers above her breasts and there was a stirring in his groin. He quickly lifted his eyes back to hers.

Sheri sucked in a breath, then pointed to his left. "I'm going to go say hello to Ivy and see if she wants to host something at her tattoo parlor. I'll talk with you later."

Deandre wanted to find another reason to keep her talking to him, but he was also blurring the line between their working together and flirting. Sheri solved his problem by dashing across the room before he could think of something else to say. Which was probably for the best. What was wrong with him? A few weeks ago he wasn't even entertaining the idea of doing anything about his attraction to her. Now he was searching for ways to keep her nearby? He'd better get this under control because she was obviously not interested in him that way. He wanted this project to succeed and hitting on his project partner was a surefire way of ruining everything.

Sheri spent most of the night trying to avoid being alone with Lieutenant King again. Not because she didn't enjoy his company. That was the problem. She enjoyed his company *too* much. The man was handsome, thoughtful, kind and funny. He was all the checkboxes she made for herself after realizing that one-night stands and friends-with-benefits type situations weren't going to work for her anymore. Which meant her attraction for him was about to have her make a dumb decision. A potentially embarrassing decision when he rejected her if she hit on him.

Sure, there had been that one time when he'd checked out her cleavage. She had to admit, her cleavage was amazing in her shirt. She'd worn it partially because she'd wanted him to see her. But, like a gentleman, he'd lifted his eyes quickly and looked apologetic. The man was a man, but he obviously was not a man coming to her for anything other than the community event.

Despite her growing attraction for Deandre and her efforts to avoid him, Sheri had a good time at the comic book shop. It was the first time she'd had a chance to mingle with some of the other business owners and not focus on crime in the area or ways to get support from the city. Outside of her cousin Cora, Sheri didn't have a lot of friends. When she'd moved home, family was her support system. They were whom she spent time with when she wasn't working. The friends she'd had while she'd grown up had either moved away or were married with their own kids and things to deal with. So hanging out with Kelly and Ivy from the tattoo parlor made her want to branch out and expand her social circle.

"Let's do this again," Sheri said when she was saying goodbye to Kelly later that evening.

"Have a get-together at the comic book store? Sure."

Sheri shook her head. "No, I mean let's hang out sometime. I'm just going to be straight up. I mostly hang out with my cousin, and even though I love her, I wouldn't mind expanding my social circle. If you're cool with it, let's hang out sometime."

Kelly grinned and nodded. "I'm cool with it. I need to get out more." She looked to Ivy. "What about you?"

"I work late hours at the shop, but if you give me enough heads-up, then I can make it work. I'm down."

"Cool. I'll send out some dates and we'll see what works." Sheri kept her voice calm and collected even though she wanted to bounce with excitement.

She was finally making some new friends. She wanted new friends. Not because she didn't like hanging out with Cora, but she also needed different viewpoints. Cora was cool and all, but she didn't always encourage Sheri to make the best decisions.

Speaking of her cousin. Sheri pulled out her cell phone and texted her. She'd let Cora borrow her car while her car was in the shop, and she'd dropped Sheri off and promised to be here by nine to pick her up. Sheri had texted her to make sure she was still coming, but the return texts had stopped.

R U on the way?

Can u catch a ride?

Sheri cursed and looked up at Ivy and Kelly. "My bad. I need to make a call. We'll catch up soon."

They waved as she walked outside. She was going to have to curse out her cousin and she didn't want to do that in front of everyone in the room.

Once outside, she dialed her cousin's number. Cora answered on the fourth ring. "What do you mean *catch a ride*?" Sheri said immediately.

"Look, I thought I'd be done, but Tim needed a ride." Cora didn't sound the least bit apologetic for leaving Sheri stranded while she gave someone else a ride.

"Who the hell is Tim?" Sheri put a hand on her hip.

"You know, the guy I've been trying to hook up with?"

"You said you needed my car to run an errand while yours was in the shop. Not because you were taking some guy for a ride."

"He's not just some guy. Do you ever listen?" Cora had the nerve to sound exasperated with Sheri.

"I'm listening now while you tell me you're giving someone a ride in my car."

"I said it was an errand. I didn't say what kind."

Sheri pinched the bridge of her nose. She took a deep breath before asking. "When will you come and get me?"

"See, what had happened was—"

"Cora!" Nothing good ever started with those words.

Cora plowed ahead. "I told Tim I would take him to pick up some money from his boy's house."

"I don't give a damn about his boy."

"But he owes me the money," her cousin said as if that were explanation enough. "So, I said I'd take him to get the money."

Sheri tapped her foot. She wanted to shake Cora. "Still not my problem."

"Well, his boy lives in Myrtle Beach."

"Myrtle Beach! You're an hour away."

"And his friend is having this party, so, can you catch a ride? I promise I'll be back as soon as I can."

"You're gone with my damn car! How am I supposed to get home?"

"Uber? Lyft? Call your momma?" Again, Cora didn't sound apologetic. She had the nerve to sound as if Sheri should already have the answer for how to get home.

"I'm not calling my mom. You said you'd be here to get me by nine."

"My bad. Look, I'll pay for the Uber."

"You know what. Forget you and Tim. You owe me and when I see you, I'm going to cuss your—"

"I know you will. Send me the cost for the Uber and I'll send you the money. Bye!" She ended the call.

Sheri stomped her feet and cursed again. "I don't want to call a damn Uber!"

"I'll give you a ride home." Deandre's voice came from behind her.

Sheri spun around. Deandre watched her with a concerned expression. His son watched her as if she were as pitiful as she felt. Stranded at the beach while her cousin ran off with her car.

Sheri shook her head. Her cheeks burned with embarrassment. "You don't have to do that."

"I couldn't help but hear some of your conversation. I wouldn't want you waiting out here for some stranger to take you home. Let me give you a ride."

"But…" She glanced at his son. "I live kind of far out."

"I'll drop off DJ and then take you. I live about five minutes from here."

She could order an Uber and go back inside to wait. She was sure she'd have fun talking to Ivy and Kelly some more. But it was embarrassing enough to be stranded. And he was there, and he was offering to give her a ride. And, even though she'd tried to stay away from him most of the night, the reckless side of her brain couldn't resist a man who was willing to step in and help when the opportunity presented itself.

"If you don't mind, then sure," she said before she could second-guess or remind herself how this was not going to help her get over her attraction to him.

Deandre looked as if he'd been hoping that would be her answer. "Good, let's go."

Deandre was parked a few cars down from the store. DJ got in the back seat and Sheri took the passenger side. When they were in the car, Sheri tried to think of something cool or interesting to say but her mind drew a blank. Not that it mattered. Other than showing mild irritation when his dad offered to give her a ride home, DJ had shown more interest in his phone than he had in Sheri, or his dad, for that matter.

"Thanks for this," she finally said once they'd dropped DJ off and were heading to her place. She'd given him the address and he'd known the area.

"You don't have to keep thanking me. It really is no problem."

"I know, but you could be doing anything other than dragging me out to my house. I swear I'm never letting my cousin borrow my car again."

"Does she usually leave you hanging like this?"

"It depends. I don't usually have to go so far as to let

her use my car. Hers is in the shop, and she swore this would just be a quick trip. But when it comes to Cora and a man, then, yes, she will drop me like a balled-up receipt."

Deandre shook his head, then chuckled. "Damn, not like that."

"Exactly like that. She's my cousin, and I love her, but she doesn't always make the best choices. Or support me making the best choices."

"Is she the friend that encourages bad behavior?" His voice was light, not judging.

She nodded. "Most definitely. To be honest, she's part of the reason you got called out to arrest me that night."

He turned to look at her quickly before glancing back at the road. They were farther away from the town now. The streetlights were now nonexistent, and the sliver of a moon barely lit up the road. "How?"

"I don't throw all the blame on her. I mean, it was me holding the bat. But she did encourage me to use it." Sheri shook her head and groaned. "I still can't believe I did that. It took me way too long to live that down."

He was silent for a second before asking hesitantly, "Were you and he…very serious?"

"We weren't. I knew it, but when you get caught up in something, reason doesn't always make sense. So, when my feelings got hurt, and Cora and I were watching *Waiting to Exhale*, that's how we ended up there. It wasn't until later that I realized Cora also liked Tyrone. That may have played into her encouragement."

"For real?"

"For real."

He was quiet again. Sheri looked out the window,

wondering what he was thinking but also hesitant to ask. She didn't like to play the mind-reading game, but she couldn't help but worry that he was thinking she was immature and overly dramatic.

"The event tonight was cool," she blurted out. Anything to keep him from thinking about her bashing the car of a guy she was no longer interested in.

"It was," he said evenly.

"We're thinking of having more. It'll be a good way to bring the community together."

"I like that idea. I don't get out much, so it'll give me a reason to socialize."

"Why don't you go out much?"

Did that mean he wasn't dating? They'd been planning the event for a few weeks, and he hadn't mentioned a girlfriend. Not that she'd asked. There also hadn't been phone calls, texts or anything that gave the appearance of him having someone in his life.

"Between the job and raising DJ, I didn't worry about a social life. Now that he's getting older, it's time for me to try to figure out how to interact with people again."

"I think you interact pretty well."

He nodded. "Most of my interactions aren't in a social setting. My former partner and friend LaTisha, along with my in-laws, keep asking me to get out there and start living my life again. In fact, if they don't drag me out of the house, I don't do much of anything."

"I love going out and doing stuff. I had a side job as event staff at the convention center in Myrtle Beach. It was a great way to get out, meet people and see interesting events. But once I opened the restaurant, I gave it up. Now, I'm kind of like you. Looking for excuses to get out and do stuff."

"Do you hang with your cousin a lot?"

"We hang a little, but we haven't as much since I opened the restaurant. She's got her thing and I've got mine. We catch up when we can, but lately it's been a lot of her dropping me for other interests."

"Hmm."

She raised her brow and looked at him. "Hmm, what?"

"Nothing, just looks like we're in the same boat. Need a reason to go out and socialize."

"Well, if you ever see something you're interested in and want a partner, let me know. I'll go with you."

Damn, why had she said that? Did it sound like she was asking him on a date? Because she wasn't. Not really. She said the words before she could think about them and talk herself out of making the suggestion.

"We're friends, you know," she said quickly. "Friends hang out."

He nodded slowly. "They do."

That wasn't much of a reply. Her cheeks burned and she wanted to get out of the car and walk the rest of the way home. What in the world was wrong with her? She was Sheri "Lil Bit" Thomas. She wasn't afraid to talk to anyone or try something new. She knew her own mind and was confident in herself and her abilities. So why did conversations with this man make her wonder if she was somehow lacking? Sure, he'd seen her at her worst, but that wasn't all of her. She had to get herself together. They were friends and working together on this project. That was it. She was not going to act like a schoolgirl with a crush on the popular boy that was so hard she couldn't even speak to him.

"So it's settled, then, friend," she said. "We'll hang

out if we see something interesting." She infused her voice with confidence, and an "I will not be hurt if you say no" string of steel. The string was micrometers thick and could be bent, but it was still steel.

He glanced at her again. "Settled."

They were silent for the next few minutes. The radio played soul music thanks to the local station's *Saturday Night Juke Joint* playlist. She sang along to some of the songs and was pleasantly surprised when Deandre did the same. She glanced his way and their eyes caught. They both grinned and continued to sing along with the lyrics. The rest of the trip went by fast but was the most fun she'd had all night.

She wished it would last longer, this impromptu sing-along with Deandre that didn't make her feel immature or overly flustered.

"Thanks for dropping me off."

He put the car in Park. "I'll walk you to the door."

"You don't—"

"I know I don't have to," he cut in. "But blame it on my upbringing and being a cop. Your house is dark, you live away from town and I'd feel better walking you to the door."

She pointed to the house next door. Her family owned most of the property on the road. Two years ago, before her grandmother passed, she'd split two acres so her daughter could build a home and given the quarter acre where she'd built her home to Sheri.

"My mom's light is on, so I'm sure she's watching from behind her curtains."

"Even more reason for me to walk you to the door. I don't want her to think I don't have any manners."

Sheri couldn't help but laugh as she opened the door. "You're worried about what my mom thinks?"

"You never know when I'll need to make a good impression."

Her heart rate tripled. She shook her head as she got out of the car. He was just being nice. He walked her the short distance from the gravel drive to her front door. She hadn't left the porch light on, and with the limited moonlight, the only illumination came from the tall light on a pole along the border of her property and her mom's they'd installed to light up the side yard where they had cookouts long into the night with family.

She unlocked her door, then turned back toward Deandre. "Thanks again, for the ride and bringing me home."

"You're welcome." He shifted his weight.

Sheri got the impression he had something to say. "Anything wrong?"

"That guy… Tyrone. Do you still have feelings for him?"

The question was so out of the blue that she took a step back. "What? No. Why would you ask?"

"If we're going to hang out, I just wanted to know if there was someone you had feelings for."

"Definitely not him. You know he's getting married, right? We made our peace with each other, and I wish him well."

He slowly lifted and lowered his head as if letting her words settle in. "No other guys in the picture?"

"Not right now." She cocked her head to the side. Her pulse pounded as a wild thought entered her mind. "Are you asking for a reason?"

"Just curious."

"No, you don't ask that kind of stuff just because you're curious. Is there a reason?" She had to know. Otherwise she'd be up all night wondering why he asked and what he meant. She wasn't about to put herself through that kind of torture.

He straightened his shoulders, and even in the darkness of the porch she could feel the intensity of his gaze. "Because I want to know for personal reasons. If you're available."

Her breathing hitched. Okay, so maybe he was interested. "I'm available," she said quickly.

He nodded, a short, succinct movement of his head. "That's good to know."

"Why?" She shifted closer.

"I'd like to get to know you. Not just for the community event and not just as a friend."

Sheri's knees felt like Jell-O. She wanted to jump up and down and twerk, but instead, she held in her excitement and nodded. "Oh…well… I like that idea."

God how she wished there was more light for her to see. She could swear his body stilled, but she couldn't see his face. The humid night air felt electric and ten times hotter, thicker. Was that just her? Did he feel it, too?

"Good. Then it's official."

She blinked. "What's official?"

"You and me. We're…officially getting to know each other."

She smiled, loving his direct manner. "We are."

"I'll call you tomorrow, then."

"I like that."

He nodded and took a step backward. Sheri was excited, but she wasn't ready to let him go. Not just yet. "But you can kiss me tonight."

There was just enough light for her to see the way heat flared in his gaze. He glanced at her mom's house. Then back at her. Time seemed to slow down before he stepped forward and pulled her into his embrace. The kiss was soft, and sweet. He explored her mouth with the same direct confidence he'd used to confirm that they would officially get to know each other. She wanted him to kiss her deeper, harder. If she were honest, she wanted him to back her against the wall, and kiss every part of her body. She pressed forward, but he pulled back.

"I'll call you tomorrow," he said in a deep, rumbling voice.

"But…"

He silenced her with another kiss. When he pulled away, he smiled. "Tomorrow."

Chapter Ten

Sundays were the busiest day in the restaurant, and Sheri typically didn't have time to have any thoughts in her head other than prepping food, serving customers and making sure everything was happening on schedule. But this Sunday, she had an extra bounce in her step and nothing but personal thoughts filled her head.

He'd said they were officially "getting to know each other," so did that mean she was officially dating Lieutenant Deandre King? Did that mean she could refer to him as her man, or was "getting to know each other" not an automatic step into official relationship status? Was she being silly for overthinking this? Shouldn't she just go with the flow and let whatever happened happen? No. Going with the flow meant not knowing where she stood and misunderstandings. Clarity was important.

"Lil Bit, if you don't quit daydreaming and get your food off the counter, then I'm going to throw an egg at you." JD's gruff voice broke into her thoughts.

Sheri blinked and shook her head. "I'm not day-dreaming." She was preoccupied. There was a difference.

Cora came up to her side. Her cousin sometimes helped on the weekends. She hadn't agreed to come in today, but Sheri assumed she'd shown up in an attempt to make up for ditching Sheri the night before.

"Yes, you are," Cora said. "This got anything to do with whatever man dropped you off last night?"

Sheri's head whipped to the side so she could eye her cousin. "Who said a man dropped me off?"

Her mom sidled up next to JD in the kitchen and peered at Sheri with a hand propped on her hip. "I said it because I saw it. It was dark last night, but I recognize a man's shoulders."

JD slapped his spatula on the griddle. "I don't care who dropped her off. I made those waffles and eggs and they're gonna get cold if y'all keep clucking like chickens. Take the food and worry about the man later."

Sighing, Sheri grabbed the plates off the serving station and hurried from the kitchen before she could be further questioned. She wasn't ashamed to tell her family about her and Deandre, but she wasn't ready to get their input, either. A part of her was dying to talk to someone, but she could guess her mom's and Cora's opinions. Her mom would warn her not to trust or date a cop and Cora would find something negative about Deandre to put a damper on Sheri's excitement. She wanted to enjoy this moment, before she let family come in and cast their shadows of doubt.

She took the food to the table for her customers. "Here you go. Can I get you anything else?"

The two women glanced over their food, eyes brightening the way she liked to see. "No, I think we're good for now."

"Extra napkins, please," the other lady said at the same time.

"I've got you." Sheri got the napkins and then went to serve the next table that had just been seated.

They were busy, as usual. They even had a wait-list started. She glanced at the people lined up outside through the window and nearly stumbled. Was that? She squinted and leaned forward. Her heart jumped. Yes, that was Deandre standing outside. He was with a woman she didn't recognize, another man and had DJ with him. He'd said he'd call her today, but she hadn't expected him to show up.

"What are you smiling at?" Cora scooted up next to Sheri. She looked out the window, too. "Isn't that the cop you saw at TJ Maxx the other day?"

Sheri turned and hurried away to fill the drink order for the table she'd just visited. She hoped Cora would move on to her own tables, but no, her cousin just followed her to the back where they prepared the drinks.

"Is he the one who dropped you off?" Cora's voice dripped with judgment. For what reason, Sheri didn't know. Cora tended to go straight to judging Sheri's relationship decisions from the start.

"Why are you worrying about who dropped me off?" Sheri grabbed the sparkling wine out of the cooler to make mimosas. "No one would have had to drop me off if you hadn't left me hanging."

Cora held up a hand. "Didn't I say I'm sorry? Besides, I'm here now helping out."

"You're not helping. You're over here bothering me. You know we're busy. We can talk about it later."

"He did drop you off, didn't he?" Cora's eyes lit up with the excitement of new gossip. "Girl, wait till I tell your mom."

Sheri reached out and grabbed Cora's shirt before she could head in the direction of where her mom worked with JD making the food.

"What, are you a snitch now? Why are you going to tell her?"

"Because she was worried about you. I'm just looking out." Cora tried, and failed, to look and sound innocent.

Sheri didn't believe that for a second. Cora was eager to tell Sheri's mom to start drama in the middle of the busiest shift. "No, you're being messy. I don't want messy right now. Not with him, okay."

Cora raised her brow. "What's that supposed to mean?"

"It means what I just said. He's a nice guy. He wants us to get to know each other. So that's what we're doing."

Cora scrunched up her nose. "Get to know each other? Sounds like a simple way to say he just wants to sleep with you."

"He's not trying to sleep with me. He's taking it slow."

"For what? You're both grown. Girl, something is probably wrong with him."

Sheri rolled her eyes and groaned. Why had she even bothered to give an explanation? Cora didn't believe in taking things slow. She got hers and moved on and dealt with guys who wanted the same. "Nothing is wrong with him. He's just a nice guy. Can I be with a nice guy for once?"

Cora threw up her arms. "If you say so. Let me go help at the front." She turned and walked out of the kitchen.

Sheri closed her eyes and groaned. Damn, Cora, and her negative attitude. She would immediately jump to saying something was wrong with Deandre instead of seeing what he'd done as something decent.

Sheri left the kitchen to deliver the mimosas. Cora was at the front talking to the hostess, their younger cousin D'asa. D'asa looked outside, grinned, then nodded. Sheri had to take her customer's order, so she couldn't run up and find out what Cora had said. The next few minutes were harried as she put in the order, delivered more food and greeted another set of customers. When she was able to check on Deandre's progress again, he and his party were seated, but they were across the room. Not in her section but in Cora's.

Double damn! So that's what Cora was up to. And her cousin wasted no time rushing up to Deandre's table to take their order. Sheri took a step in that direction to intervene. She did not need Cora's messiness this early in whatever kind of relationship she was starting with Deandre.

"Excuse me, Sheri, can I get a refill?" the customer at the table next to her asked.

As much as she wanted to curse for being interrupted, she remembered customer service was something she prided herself in and overcame her need to snatch Cora by her ponytail and pull her away from the table with her man. She turned and smiled.

"Sure, I've got you." She took the cup and went back to refill it and prayed Cora wasn't going to do something to sabotage this relationship before it started.

* * *

Deandre hoped he would be seated in Sheri's section but felt he did a decent job hiding his disappointment when the hostess put them across the room from where she worked. He hadn't intended to come here for breakfast, but when LaTisha and her husband, Rob, called to see if he was up so they could drop off the chain saw they'd borrowed before going to breakfast, and then mentioned they were checking out Sheri's place, he'd found himself inviting him and DJ along before the thought could finish forming in his mind.

"Now I know why you wanted to come eat here," DJ said with a smirk.

LaTisha raised a brow and gave DJ a curious look. "Why?"

His son looked across the room at Sheri talking to a couple at another table. "For her."

LaTisha and Rob both turned in that direction. "The waitress?"

"She owns the place," Deandre said quickly.

DJ sat forward in his chair, a frown on his face. "Is this why you made me apologize? Because you like her?"

"Wait? You like her?" LaTisha asked with a big smile as she pointed over her shoulder.

Rob chuckled and shook his head. He was shorter than Deandre, with a bald head, golden brown skin and well-defined muscles gained from hours in the gym. He was a paramedic who'd met LaTisha when they'd both responded to an emergency. Twelve years later, they were still together. "I knew you had a reason for coming," Rob said.

Deandre focused on DJ instead of the teasing looks

in his friends' eyes. "I had you apologize because it was the right thing to do. Not just because I like her."

DJ shook his head and glared down at the menu. Deandre didn't get a chance to respond to his son's mumbled "whatever" because LaTisha was tapping his arm.

"Hold on. You like her for real?" LaTisha's voice rose in pitch with her excitement.

"Can you not announce it to the entire restaurant?" Deandre said, looking around at the other tables. Who, thankfully, seemed to be preoccupied with their own conversations.

LaTisha lowered her voice, but her enthusiasm was still visible in her eyes. "When did this happen? How did you meet her?"

"She's helping me with the community event."

The waitress walked up to their table, immediately blocking Deandre's view of Sheri across the room. He looked up and recognized her as Sheri's cousin Cora. Cora studied him through squinted eyes. She was sizing him up. For what he didn't know. Had Sheri already told her about what happened the night before?

"Well, hello, Officer." Cora's voice was syrupy sweet. "It's good to see you again."

"Good seeing you, too."

She looked at LaTisha. "This your girlfriend?"

Deandre coughed. "What? Nah?"

LaTisha returned Cora's smile with a fake one of her own before slipping her arm through Rob's. "I'm with him. And I'd like coffee and orange juice, please."

"Water and coffee for me," Rob replied.

"I'll take an apple juice," DJ ordered.

"Coffee and water," Deandre finished with a nod.

Cora looked at the four of them. He could see the irritation in her eyes. He'd bet she wanted to linger and get more information out of him, but thankfully LaTisha peeped her game as well and cut it short.

"I'll be right back with those drinks." She turned and walked away.

"What's up with her?" LaTisha asked as soon as Cora was out of earshot.

Rob shrugged and picked up his menu. "It's not the first time someone asked if you were with Deandre."

"Yeah, but she said that with intention." LaTisha cut her eyes in the direction Cora had gone.

LaTisha had been his partner and they hung out after work, so people had assumed they were together before. Nothing ever happened between them, and Rob was just as much his friend as hers. Most of the time the assumption wasn't made when the three of them were together.

"That's Sheri's cousin Cora," Deandre said. "I think she's a bit of a troublemaker."

DJ lowered his menu. "Didn't you warn me to stay away from girls with drama?" he said. "I'd think you'd do the same."

"Cora is not Sheri, and we're just…getting to know each other."

DJ rolled his eyes. "Sure."

"Leave your dad alone." LaTisha waved her hand at DJ. "It's good that you're testing the waters."

"And Sheri is not her cousin."

Cora returned with their drinks. "Have you been here before?"

LaTisha answered, "It's our first time."

"I can tell you the specials."

"No need," LaTisha said with an unwavering smile. "I want the chicken and waffles."

Rob ordered, then DJ and finally Deandre. Which didn't leave Cora much time to chat. She hurried away. Sheri came out of the back as Cora was heading into the kitchen. Sheri stopped her cousin, who said something that made Sheri cringe and glance their way. Cora continued to the kitchen and Sheri made a beeline their way.

"Is everything good over here?" she asked.

Deandre shifted forward and smiled. A sheen of sweat beaded her brow, her ponytail was tousled and what looked like syrup stained her yellow The Breakfast Nook T-shirt, but she still managed to look sexy as all get-out. She was obviously busy, with many more things to focus on besides him and his friends. He shouldn't have come to distract her, but when he'd been faced with the chance to see her, he hadn't been able to stop himself from coming.

"We're great. Busy morning?"

She nodded. "Yes, Sunday is our busiest day." She looked to LaTisha and Rob and held out her hand. "Hey, I'm Sheri Thomas."

Latisha took Sheri's hand. "LaTisha and Rob Fuller. I've been wanting to try this place for a long time."

"Well, I'm glad you decided to give us a try." She looked at DJ. "Good to see you again, DJ."

DJ barely glanced up from his phone. "Yeah, same."

Sheri's smile stiffened at the edges. Deandre nudged his son's foot under the table. DJ gave him a "What's the matter?" look before sitting up and giving Sheri a plastic smile. "Good seeing you, too, ma'am."

Deandre placed a hand on her forearm. "We dragged him out early."

"It's no problem. I'm just glad to see you." Her eyes

met his and he knew that despite the rush of people, her nosy cousin and his rude kid, she meant the words.

"Likewise."

"You all enjoy your meal. Give me a call later, okay?" She squeezed his shoulder before going back to her tables across the room.

LaTisha and Rob both beamed at him. "She likes you, too."

"I'd hope so," he said, trying not to let it show how much those words made his morning.

DJ sucked his teeth but kept looking at his phone. Deandre decided to let it go for now. No need to make a scene in the restaurant and ruin breakfast. DJ was more than likely still upset about having to apologize. He'd eventually come around.

The conversation drifted to the neighborhood and the latest renovations to LaTisha and Rob's house. The food came and Cora realized they didn't want to chat with her and went on about her business. At the end of the meal, she came back and gave him a smug look with her hand on her hip.

"Looks like your food was comped today," she said.

"What?" Deandre looked around the room. Sheri met his eyes and winked. "No, I can't let her do that."

"She's the owner and can do what she wants. You better not hurt her, that's all I've got to say."

Deandre frowned. "I don't plan to hurt anyone."

Cora snorted. "That's what they all say. Have a good rest of your day." She turned and sauntered off.

"Ignore her," LaTisha said. "Your girl really likes you."

"Free food is cool," DJ agreed.

"I really shouldn't," Deandre said.

"Dad, why you arguing? She's *your girl* now, right? Just take the W and move on. I'll meet y'all at the car." He got up and walked out.

He looked at Rob and LaTisha. "It's too much."

"It's her restaurant, don't make a scene. Just make it up to her later in a nice way," LaTisha said.

"How?"

Rob winked at him. "You'll think of a way." They got up and headed to the door.

Deandre stood as well, but instead of going to the door he crossed the room to where Sheri was turning away from a table. She grinned at him, and he had a funny sensation in his chest that he hadn't felt in years. Something that told him that if he wasn't careful, he could fall hard for Sheri. It was part of the reason why he wanted to take things slow. He'd tried quick hook-ups and casual flings after his wife passed, but that life wasn't for him. He was open to a long-term relationship, maybe even getting married again one day. He wasn't sure if Sheri was the person he'd do that with, but he didn't want to rush into sex with her and create an awkward situation.

"Did you enjoy the food?"

She had the same hopeful look in her eye that she always had when she brought him food. She looked so cute he couldn't help himself. He placed his hand on her hip, pulled her forward and kissed her quickly.

"I enjoyed seeing you more. I owe you."

She leaned into him. The light press of her breasts against his chest caused a stirring in his midsection that made him want to pull her closer and kiss her deeper. He definitely needed to take things slow with Sheri or else he'd lose himself.

"You don't owe me anything."

"I do." He'd figure out something nice to do for her. "Call me when you're done. Okay?"

She bit the corner of her lip and nodded. "Okay."

He needed to pull away but couldn't help himself. He kissed her again before letting her go and walking out. He could feel the eyes of the entire restaurant on him as he left. He didn't care. Sheri had agreed to be with him, and with the way he was feeling, he didn't care if the entire world knew.

Chapter Eleven

Sheri jumped in the shower and changed clothes as soon as she got home from work. As promised, she'd called Deandre when she was leaving work. He'd asked her to go out on their first official date. Bonus point, he'd already planned what they were doing that evening. They were going to the movie at the park downtown, and he was bringing a picnic basket of treats. She'd nearly swooned when he'd told her the plans. He'd put some thought into their first date. She couldn't remember the last guy who'd taken the time to plan a date. Most of the guys she'd dated asked her out and then put all the effort of planning on her shoulders. Deandre was a take-charge kind of person and she liked that.

The thoughts that bothered her at the start of the day no longer took up as much room in her brain. When he'd kissed her, no matter how quick and sweet the kiss was, it had been a definite show of them being together. At least, that's how she was taking it. She would still tell him what she wanted out of a relationship. She was too old to play games or be dishonest with herself. If they were dating, she wanted it to be exclusive and she'd tell him she was looking for something that could be serious. If that scared him away, then she'd be better off in the long run. Having her feelings bruised now was better than being heartbroken later.

She'd agreed to meet him at the park, even though he'd offered to pick her up. She did not want her family to see him coming by. If they knew she had a date with him, they'd immediately find a reason to come to her house just so they could see and talk to him. She'd barely been able to get out of the restaurant on time after he'd kissed her. Her mom hadn't seen, but Cora had, and she'd made a point to make sure everyone in the kitchen knew what happened.

She'd seen the look her mom had given her, but they'd been too busy for her to pull Sheri to the side and talk. That, and JD had already said he wasn't in the mood to have his kitchen slowed down by gossip. So, her mom had let things slide. She'd had to leave before closing to run an errand with her aunt Gwen, and Sheri had thanked her lucky stars when she didn't see her mom's car in the yard when she'd pulled up.

She wasn't meeting Deandre for another hour, but she was going to get out of the house before her mom had time to come and question her. She was showered, dressed and heading to her front door in no time. She'd opted for a light blue jumpsuit with spaghetti straps. The soft material was thin enough to keep her cool and her shoulders and décolletage looked amazing when she wore it. She'd taken her hair out of its usual ponytail so it hung thick and loose around her shoulders. She slid her "Lil Bit" necklace around her neck and paired it with large, silver hoop earrings. She hoped she looked casual but sexy at the same time.

She opened the front door and froze immediately. Her mom and Aunt Gwen both stood on the front porch. Her mom's finger hovered just above the doorbell.

"Where you going?" her mom asked.

Sheri barely stopped herself from stomping her foot with frustration. She tried not to show her irritation on her face, but something must have crept through because her mom crossed her arms and gave her *the look*.

Sheri fixed her face and smiled. "Just got to run some errands. I may hang with Cora later."

Her aunt Gwen shook her head. "I know you're not going out with Cora because she's running behind that man in Myrtle Beach tonight. So what man are you running behind?"

Sheri sighed and walked out onto the porch. If she let them in the house, she was trapped for at least an hour. "I'm not running behind anyone. Just going out real quick."

"It's that cop, ain't it?" her mom asked. "Cora told me he kissed you today."

No need lying to her mom about what happened with Deandre. "He did."

"Why's he kissing you all in the middle of your job?" Aunt Gwen asked, sounding affronted.

"Because we're dating."

That was met with silence as the sisters exchanged looks. Sheri couldn't decipher the look, but she could imagine the things in their head. *There Sheri goes again. What's going to happen with this guy? Is she going to embarrass the family one more time?*

Ever since the Tyrone fiasco, her mom had questioned Sheri's dating decisions. She was afraid Sheri would get caught up with another guy who would have her acting out and doing foolish things like damaging a car. Her mom was a firm believer in not playing the fool for any man. Something she'd preached to Sheri, which meant when Sheri had done just that over Tyrone Livingston, a known playboy at that time, she'd been so disappointed to have her daughter acting "desperate and dumb" over a man. Sheri swore her mom viewed her actions as a personal failure on her mothering abilities.

"Dating, huh?" her mom said.

"Yes. Dating. He asked me and I said yes. Anything wrong with that?" She would not feel bad about wanting to be with a guy instead of pretending as if she were good with keeping things casual or claim she didn't need or want a man. Sheri didn't need one to provide for her, but she did enjoy having a guy in her life.

Her mom threw up a hand. "Nah, nothing wrong. I'm just saying…"

"That you're happy for me and hope things work out," Sheri insisted.

Her mom's eyes narrowed. "You know he's got a kid. You ready to play step momma?"

Sheri wasn't sure if she was ready to play stepmom. She wasn't even sure what was going to happen with this. She doubted DJ liked her, but she wanted to at least see what it was like to date a nice guy. She'd only focus on her relationship with Deandre and worry about how things would play out with her and his son if things progressed that far.

"I'm ready to see what happens. No one is playing step momma."

"You be careful," Aunt Gwen said. "I'm not hating or anything. I just don't want you to get hurt."

Her mom grunted and studied her nails. "Or act out like you did last time."

Sheri was used to them bringing up her past dating mistakes, but her defenses rose. She'd messed up, but she'd learned from her mess-ups. No matter how much she tried to prove that, she was getting tired of her family's inability to focus on anything else.

"I'm not going to act out. That was a one-time thing. Can we not bring it up again?"

Her mom stared longer but nodded. "I guess you're not letting us in so you can run and meet him?"

"I just have stuff to do before I catch up with him later."

"Bring him to the house so we can meet him," her mom said.

"Why? You don't need to meet him yet."

Gwen nodded. "Dorothy Jean is right. We need to make sure he's good people. I think I know his in-laws."

"He's not married."

"Well, his late wife was from around here and I know Cliff and Rose. They go to your cousin's church, and they are really involved with their son-in-law. So, he may not be married but he has in-laws."

"And a kid," her mom chimed in. "Think about that while you out having fun with him tonight."

Sheri hadn't considered the rest of his family despite his mentioning he'd moved to Sunshine Beach because his late wife's family was from here. Sheri had known who his late wife was, but she didn't know her parents like that. If her aunt knew them, then she could get all the information she wanted on Deandre, DJ and his family. Which also meant his family could get any information they wanted on her, too. So many people in town knew she'd been arrested after damaging Tyrone's car. The gossip had died down until the brothers got the television deal and then it came back up thanks to internet trolls. Trolls stirred up thanks to her cousin Cora's digging into his past. Would his in-laws be okay with him dating her? Did he listen to them?

She shook the thought out of her head. She wanted to learn about him from him. Not from what people thought of him. Deandre seemed like the type of guy who would feel the same. The good thing was, he already knew her shady relationship past better than anyone and they'd talked it out. She wouldn't worry about his in-laws unless they became serious.

"I've really got to go."

"Go on, have a good time. But be careful, Lil Bit." Her mom's voice was serious in the end.

She and her mom had different views when it came to relationships, but she knew her mom cared about her. She'd been hurt by Sheri's dad when he'd left her and she shielded her heart. She didn't want Sheri to have the same heartbreak.

She gave her mom a hug. "Ma, don't worry. I know what I'm doing this time."

The date was even better than Sheri hoped it would be. Deandre had ordered sandwiches along with a meat, fruit and cheese tray from a local restaurant that he already had spread out on a blanket. He'd paired it with a blackberry lemonade that was delicious. When she'd asked about wine, he let her know that he didn't drink due to the job. When he was a patrol deputy, he'd stopped drinking alcohol and the habit stuck even when he was no longer on patrol.

The movie was *Grease*, and he hadn't believed her when she said she'd never seen the entire movie before.

"I'm not really a musical person, plus, I didn't even know what it was about."

"I was in chorus in high school, and they made us watch it because we sang all the songs from the movie for our end-of-year performance," he'd told her as they sipped lemonade and waited for the movie to start.

Sheri's eyes widened. "You were in chorus?" That explained the impromptu sing-along in his car when he'd driven her home. He liked singing.

"I was."

"Did you play any sports?"

"I played football and ran track. I sang in the choir at my grandmother's church growing up, so I liked music. I wasn't really interested in the band, but chorus was fun. Plus, they had the best field trips. What about you? What activities did you do in high school?"

"I was a cheerleader, but that was about it. I wasn't in any other clubs or anything else. I couldn't wait to graduate and get out of Sunshine Beach."

"What brought you back?"

"My mom got sick. I thought I'd stay in Charlotte working at that steak house until I got a job at another high-end restaurant. But I moved back to help take care of my mom after her stroke. My aunts and cousins were around, but I didn't want to leave her in their care."

"She seems to be doing a lot better now."

"She is. Sometimes I can't believe she recovered. Thankfully, my aunt had just watched something on the news about recognizing the signs of a stroke. She saw my mom was dizzy and numb so she called 911. She got to the hospital in time, but she still had to go through rehabilitation. When she started physical therapy, she asked if I planned to move back to Charlotte, but by then I knew I couldn't leave her. I started working at Waffle House for the flexible hours and decent pay and then got the wild idea to open my own restaurant."

"Are you happy here in Sunshine Beach?"

She thought about it, then nodded. "I am. Growing up I just wanted to experience a new place. But when I came back I realized how much I love this town. I might have been able to open a restaurant in Charlotte, but opening my restaurant here was so much better. I had people I could call on and help me like Aunt Gwen, my cousin D'asa and even Cora. Then there's JD. He left Waffle House to come and work with me. My family is here and can help me fill in while I work to build up my staffing levels. Then there are the people who knew me growing up and want me to succeed. It's just a different sense of community that I didn't have in Charlotte."

"Did you have friends up there?"

"Yeah, some work friends and a few from college. We keep in touch. When I get a chance, I go up and visit every once in a while. What about you? Do you still keep up with friends and family back in Florida?"

He shook his head. "Not so much. DJ was ten when my wife died. We moved to Sunshine Beach a year after. At first it was too hard to keep in touch with the people and the life I left behind. It was easier to start over here."

"I'm surprised you moved closer to your in-laws instead of your own parents."

"Her parents are the ones who stepped in and helped me with DJ when I needed them. I love my parents, but they're off living their own life. They felt bad for me when I lost Jamila, but they'd already moved to Destin. Just last year they moved to Denver. They're enjoying their retirement, and I can't blame them. They come down and visit us, but they weren't ready to move closer and help me raise DJ. When Rose asked me to move to Sunshine Beach so they could help with DJ, I didn't hesitate. I turned in my resignation, packed our stuff and moved."

"It's good that you're close with your in-laws. Even after…"

"I love them just as much as I love my parents. I'm forever grateful for them and the way they helped out."

"My aunt Gwen says they go to my cousin's church."

"Mount Olive AME?" he asked.

She nodded. "That's the one. My cousin Faith and her husband, Gary, go there."

"I'll ask them if they know them."

She shook her head. "No need. My cousin Faith is cool, but she's messy. They probably know all my business and the trouble I've gotten into. They may tell you to stay away from me if they know who she is."

She tried to keep her voice light, but a part of her worried that was the case. Even before Tyrone, back when she was a teenager, she would sometimes get into trouble. She wasn't ashamed of her past or the mistakes she'd made, but she was tired of defending herself. She liked Deandre, but she didn't want to have to defend herself to him or his family.

Deandre leaned forward and met her eyes. "They can tell me, but it doesn't mean I'll listen."

A flutter when through her chest. "Why not?"

"Because what they think about you, or your cousin,

doesn't matter to me. All I care about is how *I* feel about you."

The words settled over her and wrapped her in a comforting embrace. She eased closer to him and warmth spread through her chest. "How do you feel about me?"

"I'm still figuring it out, but so far, I'm feeling pretty good about you."

"Pretty good, huh? What does *pretty good* mean?"

He reached for her hand and threaded his fingers with hers. "It means that I want to get to know you. I don't want to see anyone else while I do that. That I'd like for us to take our time to see where this goes. Is that cool with you?"

More than cool. In fact, it was perfect. Sheri squeezed his hand. "Cool with me."

They didn't talk as much during the show. She watched as many people sang along to the songs in the movie. Deandre didn't sing along with as much enthusiasm, but he did hum and nod his head a few times like a true chorus kid. After the movie, they packed up their items and he'd walked her to her car before suggesting they walk to the ice cream place downtown.

"I've got ice cream at home," she said.

He frowned. "Oh, are you ready to get back?"

She lifted a brow. "That's my not-so-subtle way of inviting you back to my place."

His eyes darkened. She'd parked on a side street about a block away from the park. The streetlights kept the roadway well lit, and there were several other people who'd watched the movie who'd also parked in the area, but the look in his eye made her feel as if they were the only two people on the street.

"I don't know if that's a good idea."

She poked out her lip. Not the least bit embarrassed to show her disappointment. "Why not? It's just ice cream."

Deandre raised a brow. "It's more than ice cream. Or, at least, I'm going to be thinking about more than ice cream."

"No rush or no other expectations. I just don't want the date to end just yet." Which was true, but she wouldn't pretend as if she didn't want to kiss him again. The brief kisses he'd given her before only made her crave more.

"Neither do I."

She stepped forward until their bodies almost touched and lowered her voice. "Then come by. Just for ice cream. Nothing else. We'll both be good." Though the way he looked at her, with so much heat and longing she felt like her skin would catch fire, made her want to be anything but good. She wanted to be naughty.

The question flashed in his eyes for another second before he nodded. "Just for a few minutes. I need to get home and check on DJ."

She grinned. "A few minutes works for me."

Chapter Twelve

Deandre watched Sheri get into her car before walking around the corner. His stomach churned as if he were about to go on the most important job interview of his life while his heart pounded as if he'd just won an Olympic gold medal. He was just going to her place for ice cream. He wasn't trying to push for anything more. This was their first date, and he'd never been the type of guy who expected something on the first date. But that didn't stop his imagination from going to all kinds of places. Places where he had Sheri in his arms again. Felt her lips on his and got to spend endless amounts of time kissing and caressing her skin.

"Deandre? I thought that was you."

The sound of Chief Montgomery's voice stopped him in his tracks. He turned, caught her eye and smiled. "Chief, how are you doing?"

Deandre kept his voice pleasant, even though he wanted to just wave and hurry to his car. Most days he wouldn't mind stopping to talk to the chief, but the memory of how Sheri looked at him before she'd gotten in the car, as if she was thinking the same thoughts as him, had Deandre ready to be rude and on his way.

"I was here for the movie in the park. The family just went to the car." She pointed over her shoulder where her husband and two daughters were chatting next to her large SUV.

Deandre waved at her husband before focusing back on her. "Tell everyone I said hello. I was just about to leave."

"I know, I saw you here earlier." She took a few steps forward. "With Lil Bit Thomas."

Deandre blinked, surprised to hear the chief use Sheri's nickname. "You know Sheri?"

She crossed her arms and watched Deandre with an assessing gaze. "Not very well. I know who she is. She's the one you arrested back when you were on patrol." The words weren't a question.

Deandre's defenses went up. "She was."

"And now you're dating her?" That was a question, and the chief's tone said she hoped the answer was no.

"She's also working with me on the community event for the south end of the beach."

"Are you telling me that you're just working together?"

Deandre respected Chief Montgomery, but he didn't like the questioning or the judgment in her eye. "Can I know why you're asking?"

Chief Montgomery stepped closer. "Look, I don't like to step in and make comments on my employees' personal lives. But I want you to also know that the work we're doing in the south end is important. They already think I'm going too soft on the crime in the area. If the higher-ups find out that the officer I put in charge of the area is also, I'll just be frank, sleeping around with one of the business owners down there, it won't look good."

"I'm not sleeping around with anyone. And even if I were, it doesn't matter."

"Look, I'm not telling you this to be mean. I'm telling you this because I need you to understand the situation we're in. Everything we do is going to be scrutinized."

"Look, I understand what you're trying to say, but I don't plan to stop seeing her because the higher-ups are going to scrutinize my motives. She cares about the neighborhood as much as the rest of the community and she's the one who stepped up to help. If they have a problem with me seeing her, then they can come tell me to my face."

"I'm just trying to look out for you."

Deandre held up a hand. "I appreciate the thought, but I don't need you to look out for me when it comes to my personal life."

She looked like she wanted to say something else, but instead she pressed her lips together and nodded. "Fine. I'll stay out of it."

"Thank you." He turned to walk toward his car.

"But…"

Sighing, Deandre faced her again and raised a brow.

"If this becomes a problem, then you deal with the fallout. Understand?"

"I understand, but there won't be any fallout."

His irritation at the intrusion grew with each step he took toward his car. He wished he could ignore her worries and warning as foolishness, but he'd worked in the department long enough to know that if Montgomery thought it was necessary to say something to him, then her concerns had some validity. People may look at any relationship he formed with Sheri and their past together and try to use that to undermine any work he did in the area. It was messed up and unfair but knowing Chief Montgomery had pressure on her to use a stick approach versus a carrot to reduce crime in the area meant that those in favor of the stick weren't afraid to pull out their own.

The thoughts bothered him on the ride to Sheri's place. He arrived at her home several minutes later and tried to push them to the back of his mind. He didn't want to ruin the night with talks about what Chief Montgomery had said.

Sheri greeted him at the door with a smile and a bowl of ice cream. "What took you so long?"

He took the bowl of ice cream and grinned. "Ran into the chief on the way to my car."

"Oh really?" She took his free hand and pulled him farther into the house. "Is everything okay?"

"Yeah, she was there with her family. She stopped me to talk about something."

Sheri's house was cute and decorated with comfortable-looking furniture. Pictures of her family lined the walls. They stopped in her living area that was separated from the kitchen by a small island.

"Nothing too bad, I hope." She grabbed another bowl of ice cream off the counter.

"Nothing bad, but she was...concerned." When Sheri raised a brow, he decided to be honest. Otherwise, she'd notice he was distracted and that would ruin the night. "About us."

He recounted what she said and his response for her to stay out of his personal business. By the time he finished, Sheri had put down her bowl of ice cream and paced in front of her couch.

"Are you serious? No one will ever let me live down one mistake."

He put his ice cream on the coffee table and placed his hands on her shoulders. "This isn't about your past mistake. This is squarely on me."

"Yeah, but if I was Belinda or some other Goody Two-shoes in the town they wouldn't care so much. They'd probably applaud you."

"Did you hear what I said? I told her to stay out of my personal business. I don't care what they think. I mean it, Sheri. I haven't been this interested in someone in a very long time. I'm not going to stop getting to know you because of something like this."

The corner of her mouth lifted. "You're so straightforward and honest."

"Is that a bad thing?"

"No." She raised her arms and wrapped them around his neck. "It's actually very, very sexy."

Fire flooded his veins and stirred in his groin. If she kept looking at him like that, he was going to be hard as a rock. "You know I only came for ice cream?"

"I know, but that doesn't mean you can't have a little sugar." She lifted on her toes and kissed him.

Thoughts of ice cream fled as her tongue glided across his lower lip. Deandre opened his mouth and let her deepen the kiss. She was just as straightforward with her kiss as she'd said he was with his words, and he loved it. She tasted like strawberry ice cream and he loved strawberries.

His cell phone rang. He wanted to ignore it, but not many people called his cell. "Sorry." He pulled back and reached to get his phone out. To his surprise, his son was calling. "It's DJ."

She stepped back and pushed her hair behind her ear. "Handle that. It could be important."

She licked her full lips and he bit back a groan. He had to clear his throat before he answered. "DJ, what's up?"

"You still at the movie?"

Sheri played with the Lil Bit necklace around her neck, drawing his eyes to the swell of her breasts just below the neckline of her jumpsuit. "Huh…ah, nah, it just ended."

"I've got a problem."

Deandre's focus immediately went to his son. "Problem, what's wrong?"

"I'm kind of embarrassed to say, but I locked myself out of the house. Can you come home and let me in? I didn't want to call because I thought you were still on your date."

Guilt twisted his insides. He never wanted his son to feel as if he couldn't call him. If he'd gone straight home like he'd planned, DJ wouldn't be locked out. "Nah, don't ever feel like you can't call. I'll be home in a few minutes."

"Cool, thanks, Dad." The relief in DJ's voice made Deandre feel like his son's superhero. He hadn't felt like his son's hero in a long time.

"I'm on my way." He ended the call and looked at Sheri. "DJ's got a problem. I need to check on him."

"I get it. Please, go check on him." Even though he could see the disappointment in her eyes, her voice was understanding. He could relate to the disappointment. Now that he knew DJ wasn't in any immediate danger, the passion he'd felt in her arms came rushing back.

He took her hand and pulled her closer to him. "Rain check on dessert?"

She grinned before lifting up to kiss him again. "Rain check." Her lips pressed his once more before she lightly bit his lower lip.

He thought his erection would burst out of his pants. He wanted to linger over the kiss. To trail his lips across her chin to her chest just in the spot where her necklace sat. But the sound of DJ's voice pulled him back. His son was locked out of the house. Sure, he could call Rose and Cliff, but DJ had called and asked him for help. He wouldn't pawn him off on someone else. He'd have time to kiss Sheri later. "I'll call you tomorrow," he said before leaving.

Chapter Thirteen

Sheri entered the storefront that was starting to feel like a second home to her. They were a few days away from the Connecting the Community event. Which meant this was the last planning meeting before the big day. Most of the business owners and residents were excited. Everyone had come together to think of ways to encourage people from outside the South End to attend. Ivy had created a social media campaign to drum up interest. Deandre and the police chief had encouraged the city to promote the event on its social media pages. The city of Sunshine Beach even sent out a press release to local media, which Sheri had also forwarded to her childhood friend Vanessa Steele-Livingston. Vanessa lived in Charlotte, but she was a news anchor and had roots in Sunshine Beach. She'd reached out to her connections at the local affiliate to get them interested in following the story.

The event started as a forum for community members to learn about what the city was doing to address crime in the town and ways the community could participate. As interest grew, they'd expanded the day to include several vendors from the area who didn't have a storefront but lived nearby selling their goods along the sidewalk. All the shops would be open during the event and Sheri had extended her hours so that the restaurant wouldn't close until two hours after the event ended.

The team of people they'd pulled together to help were all at the last planning session. Sheri's eyes narrowed when she spotted Belinda giggling next to Deandre. She and Deandre hadn't hidden their relationship from the group, but they also hadn't made a big deal about it. Most had guessed there was something going on, because he offered to take her home or they talked openly about getting together later in the week. But Belinda still flirted as if Deandre were single.

Sheri was mostly amused by Belinda's attempts. Deandre was clearly not interested and hadn't followed up on of her blatant hints about them getting together to discuss "the neighborhood." But, when Belinda put her hand on Deandre's shoulder, Sheri's eyes narrowed. She barely got to touch him the way she wanted. She wasn't about to stand by and watch Belinda grope him.

"Hey, everyone, sorry I'm late," Sheri announced herself a little too loudly.

Deandre looked her way and the light in his eyes when he saw her that hadn't been there when he looked at Belinda cleared away the storm clouds of jealousy swirling over Sheri's head. "We were just getting started."

He left Belinda behind and met Sheri halfway across the room. Sheri rose up on her toes and pressed her lips against his. The kiss wasn't long enough. Not for her, but it was good enough for her to make her point. Deandre was spoken for.

Deandre's eyes widened. "What was that for?"

"Just because," she said loud enough for anyone listening to hear. She lowered her voice. "And because we didn't get to finish what we started last night."

The light in his eyes quickly flared into a fire. They'd made a point to try and see each other whenever they had time. But every time they went on a date, DJ seemed to have some type of crisis. Locking himself out of the door was just the first of many times. Since that night three weeks prior he'd run out of gas, lost something he needed help finding, or needed his dad to help him get something last minute for school. All of the calls were legitimate, but Sheri was starting to suspect DJ was interrupting them on purpose. She just didn't know how to say that to Deandre without sounding paranoid.

"I do plan to finish what I started," he said in just as low a tone.

"When? I'm growing anxious." She tried to keep her voice light, but some of her frustration crept in. She appreciated that he liked taking things slow, but she was tired of having to handle her own needs when she was dating a deliciously sexy man.

Some of the heat left his gaze and was replaced with an apology. "Soon."

His eyes were filled with the same frustration, making her want to jump him in a crowded room. He wasn't just teasing her or playing hard to get. Deandre felt some, if not all, of what she felt, which made her not want to make him feel guilty for having to cut things short because he was being a good parent.

She patted his chest. "It's no problem. I was just teasing."

"You sure?"

She nodded. "I'm sure."

"Good, because DJ is hanging with his grandparents tonight, and I was thinking that maybe…"

"You can come over for ice cream?" She grinned so hard her cheeks hurt.

"Most definitely."

She did a hip shimmy to celebrate, then looked back to Belinda. She didn't bother to hide her smug "he's mine" smirk. She'd been patient enough with Belinda. Now it was time to clearly put up her boundaries.

Deandre lightly tapped her hip. "Let's get started." He called the meeting to order. Sheri grabbed a seat next to Kelly.

Kelly leaned over and lightly elbowed Sheri. "Finally giving Belinda the hint to back off, huh?"

Sheri smirked and winked. "She's lucky I didn't snatch her hand off him."

Kelly held out her hand palm up and Sheri rubbed her palm over hers. They both giggled; the modified high five was something they'd started when they'd hung out after the first neighborhood get-together. Sheri didn't want to jinx anything, but she was pretty sure she and Kelly were on the way to becoming good friends.

The door to the center opened. DJ walked in followed by two older adults who looked familiar. A second later, everything clicked. They were Jamila's parents. Deandre's in-laws.

Deandre gave them a puzzled look. "What are you doing here?"

Rose led the three of them farther into the room.

"Well, DJ was telling us about all the work you put into planning the community event, and we decided to come and see if we can help in any way."

Deandre seemed surprised, but pleased. "Sure, I'd love for you to help out. Everyone, this is Rose and Cliff, DJ's grandparents."

Several excited exclamations came around the room as everyone welcomed them. Sheri joined in the welcomes and watched as Belinda quickly ushered them over to the empty seats next to her. Sheri tried, and failed, not to feel some type of way about that. Instead of acting jealous, she focused on what she was there for. Rallying the community to support revitalizing the south end.

The meeting went by quickly. Everyone knew their assigned tasks and was ready to see everything come together that weekend. After things wrapped up, Sheri chatted with Kelly and some of the others before approaching Deandre. He was talking with his in-laws, DJ and Belinda. She wasn't sure if Cliff and Rose knew about her, and she didn't want to make a bad impression. She took a reassuring breath. All that mattered was how Deandre felt.

"Deandre, we were taking DJ to get some tacos. You should come eat with us," Rose was saying as Sheri walked up.

Deandre glanced Sheri's way. "Uh… I already—"

"We're going to the place you like," DJ cut in. "Come on, let's all have dinner together."

Deandre caught Sheri's eye. "I was going out with Sheri."

Sheri stepped next to Deandre. "Hi, nice to meet you all."

Rose's brows rose and she looked at Sheri with interest. "Oh, so you're Sheri."

Cliff snapped his fingers. "You're Dorothy Jean's daughter." He spoke as if he'd just figured out the answer to a riddle.

"I am. I think one of my cousins goes to your church."

"They sure do," he said. "How's your aunt Gwen doing? Me and her were close back in high school."

"She's doing good."

Rose's eyes narrowed on her husband. "You still asking about her? All these years later." Rose sounded more exasperated than upset.

Cliff shrugged. "It was just a question."

Sheri looked from them to Deandre. Deandre raised his brows and looked just as confused as she felt.

Rose looked back at Sheri. "Your aunt Gwen was his high school sweetheart."

"Oh... Well, I didn't know that." She wasn't sure what she was supposed to do with that information.

"Dad," DJ cut in. "Come with us to get tacos. I'm thinking of joining wrestling again."

"I thought it was too late?" Deandre asked.

DJ shook his head. "Coach said I could still join. But I'm not sure. I wanted to talk to you about that."

Deandre glanced from DJ to Sheri and back. She wasn't a detective, but she could deduce what was going on. He wanted to be with her, but also wanted to find out about DJ rejoining the wrestling team. He'd mentioned his frustration with DJ quitting suddenly. As much as she wanted them to finish what they'd started numerous times, she wouldn't pull him away from his kid.

She shrugged. "Go on with them. We'll catch up later."

"Sheri you can come with us," Cliff offered.

Sheri quickly shook her head. Rose didn't seem seriously upset about him asking after her Aunt Gwen, but Sheri was not about to potentially put herself in a situation where she'd have to answer questions about his high school sweetheart all night. "Nah, you all got it. I've got stuff to do. I just wanted to say hi and meet you."

"Maybe next time. A friend of Deandre is a friend of ours," Rose said, sounding friendly enough.

"She's more than—"

"Good, let's go," DJ cut Deandre off. "I'm hungry."

"Me, too," Rose agreed. "Nice to meet you, Sheri. Let's go."

Sheri walked out with them. She caught DJ's gaze as Deandre locked the door. The smug satisfaction as he looked at her proved she wasn't being paranoid. Deandre's son was purposely trying to keep them apart.

"You ready to tell me what you're doing?" Deandre asked DJ when they walked into the house after dinner. DJ had decided that he no longer wanted to spend the night with his grandparents and was going home since Deandre was done with work and was also going home.

DJ looked up from his phone. "Checking my phone."

Deandre shook his head. "That's not what I'm talking about. You wanted me to come to dinner so we could talk about you joining wrestling again, but you never brought it up."

DJ shrugged. "We talked about other stuff."

"And you came to the meeting tonight."

"*You* said I need to be more involved so that people

won't treat me like I'm some thug. I thought you'd be happy I showed up."

Deandre took a long breath and gathered his thoughts. "You know what I mean."

"I don't know what you're talking about." DJ turned to go toward his room.

"You're always calling when I'm with Sheri."

DJ faced him again with a raised brow. "I can't call you when you're with her?"

"That's not what I'm saying. But I've noticed the pattern. You went from barely wanting to spend time with me to suddenly needing my help whenever I'm with her."

"I can't help it that things mess up when you're around her. If you don't want me to bother you when you're with her I won't." DJ tried to sound pitiful, but Deandre didn't miss the dare in his son's eye. He hadn't wanted to believe that DJ was intentionally trying to keep him away from Sheri, but tonight proved something he'd tried to pretend wasn't happening.

"Don't twist my words."

"I'm not twisting your words. I'm just saying what you're telling me."

"What's your problem with her? Is it because I made you apologize?"

"I don't have a problem with her. I don't see why you're interested in her in the first place, but I don't have a problem."

"You don't have to see why I'm interested in her. You just have to understand that she and I are together right now."

DJ looked away and shook his head as if he couldn't believe what he was hearing. "Did you arrest her?"

Deandre's head snapped back. How in the world did DJ know about that? He didn't come home and talk about the stuff he'd see when on patrol. He also hadn't talked about Sheri's past with him.

"Who told you that?"

He shrugged. "I overheard it somewhere. That she was acting all ghetto and you had to arrest her. You always told me to avoid girls with drama, but you're with someone like that."

The judgment in DJ's voice made Deandre's neck tighten. He took a second to take a breath and count to five before responding. If he reacted negatively, DJ would lash back and they'd get nowhere. "First of all, what you heard and what happened are not the same. Second, Sheri isn't dramatic or ghetto. So, mind what you say."

DJ threw up a hand. "Fine. Are we done now?"

"No, we aren't done."

"You want me to like her, fine, I can like her. But she better not come in here trying to act like she's my momma, 'cause she ain't."

Deandre shook his head, confused by how the conversation had just gone left. He and Sheri had just started dating. DJ had known he'd gone on dates before. He'd even joined in with Rose and Cliff when they'd started pushing him to date again. So, why was DJ suddenly against it? Or was it just he was against Sheri?

"She wouldn't do that." DJ snorted and Deandre narrowed his eyes. "Listen, you're going to be nice to her and you're going to stop playing these games when I'm with her. I'm always here to help you. Don't doubt that, but I know what you're doing. I don't know why, but I don't like it. So, if you've got something to say, now's the time to say it."

"I don't have anything to say." DJ closed his mouth and stared at the ceiling as if suddenly bored with the entire conversation.

Deandre wanted to shake him. DJ was shutting down again. He didn't know what to do or how to make his son open up to him. He wanted to make DJ sit down and not move until he told Deandre what was going on in his brain. Deandre couldn't ever remember struggling with his own dad like this, but then again, he also hadn't spent a lot of time having heart-to-heart conversations with his dad. To this day, other than the weekly call to check in on his parents, he didn't talk to his dad much. He wanted more than that for him and DJ. In a few years he'd be going to college and become even more distant. But he didn't know how to bridge this gap.

"Fine, DJ, but when you're ready to talk, I'm ready to listen."

DJ nodded and turned. "Uh-huh," he said before going down the hall to his room.

Chapter Fourteen

Sheri took a deep breath and then glanced at the crowd. The committee agreed that holding the question-and-answer session with town leaders at the Connecting the Community event outside instead of crowding everyone inside the store used for the neighborhood watch meetings was the best way to get more participation. The town agreed to set up a stage in the vacant lot between the old record store and the pizza parlor. They'd also supplied the chairs for people to sit, and a microphone.

The amount of people who were picking their seat for the question-and-answer session surprised Sheri. The entire turnout for the event had surprised her. Sure, she'd hoped they would have a lot of people come through, but Sheri was a realist. She hadn't had much hope that a huge crowd would show up for what was essentially a public meeting. But they had. The amount of participation in the event had blown everyone away. The shops along the strip had several new visitors. The vendors stayed busy, and the weather was perfect enough for the beachgoers who'd come just to enjoy the water to also wander up to see what was happening.

Someone stepped to Sheri's right. Sheri turned and met the eyes of the police chief. She liked Chief Montgomery well enough. The woman seemed to be interested in turning around the police department and doing what was right for the town and the residents. But, after what Deandre said about the chief's concerns with their relationship, she wasn't sure if the woman liked her.

"You ready?" Chief Montgomery asked, nodding toward the crowd.

Sheri shrugged. "Ready as I'm going to be."

"How did you get picked to moderate the panel discussion?"

"Since I'm the de facto chair of the planning committee, I was *encouraged* to do it."

She kept her voice light, but her stomach was a jumble of nerves. Sheri could talk to almost anyone, but public speaking wasn't her thing. She'd wanted to help from the background, but when the rest of the group had urged her to serve as moderator for this panel, she'd agreed. The discussion had been her idea. She'd been up half the night practicing what she was going to say so she wouldn't screw anything up.

Montgomery stared at her quietly for a second before nodding as if the answer were acceptable. Sheri just stopped herself from rolling her eyes. She didn't like being assessed by the police chief.

"I'm not here because Lieutenant King wants to show off his new girlfriend," Sheri said. "You don't have to worry about that."

Montgomery's shoulders stiffened before her eyes

narrowed. "I wasn't worried about that. Lieutenant King knows how important this event is. For all of us."

"I do, too. I care about this area because I'm from Sunshine Beach and I hung out here as a kid. I don't want to see the town turn it into a carbon copy of the bougie, touristy north end, and I don't want them to ignore us and treat it like a crime-riddled problem. We're on the same side."

Again, Chief Montgomery stared at Sheri for a long moment before lifting and lowering her head. "He said you cared."

Sheri lifted a brow. "Believe him now?"

"I do."

She wouldn't dare show it, but relief rushed through her. Instead, she gave Chief Montgomery the same stiff nod that she'd given Sheri. She believed Deandre when he said he didn't care what people thought about their relationship. That didn't mean she wanted his boss to think she was somehow going to ruin his career or reputation.

"The rest of the group is here. Let's get started."

Chief Montgomery took her seat. They'd pulled together an impressive panel—the town manager, solicitor, county sheriff, mayor and district attorney. Sheri hoped everyone's participation was a good thing and meant they took reinvestment in the south end seriously.

Sheri looked back at the crowd. Deandre stood at the back with several other officers. He gave her a smile and thumbs-up. She lifted her hand in a quick wave, before bringing the microphone to her face.

"We'll get started now. Thank you all for coming out to the south end neighborhood's Connecting the Community event. The growth and success of the south end equals growth and success for all of Sunshine Beach. Which is why we have many of the leaders from the town and the county here today to talk about their plans to continue to reinvest and keep the south end safe for everyone."

There was a round of applause and cheers from Kelly and Ivy. Sheri grinned and relaxed. Having the rest of the business owners here helped calm some of her nerves. She wanted this event to go off perfectly, so everyone would see the great things the south end had to offer.

"Administrator, I'll start with you. The town has invested heavily in retrofitting the vacant buildings here and partnering with small businesses like mine as part of their revitalization efforts. Can you tell us what led to that decision?"

The panel discussion went smoothly. As a business owner, Sheri was glad to hear from everyone on the panel about the ways they wanted to see the community continue to thrive—from more investment by the town to help businesses grow, to the connection of law enforcement to connect people to mental health and substance abuse assistance as a way to help address crime. By the time they opened the discussion to questions from the audience, Sheri was leaning back in the chair relaxed and happy about how great things had turned out.

Kelly gave the sign that there were five minutes left. Sheri sat forward and spoke in the mic. "We've got time for one last question." She looked at the woman standing at the microphone they'd set up in the crowd for questions. "Go ahead."

"This question is for you," she said with a raised brow and pursed lips.

Sheri sat up straight and returned the woman's direct stare. She looked kinda familiar, but Sheri couldn't immediately place her. "Okay, what's your question?"

"I think it's great that you pulled this together, considering you also have a criminal record. Was that part of the reason why you chose to have this event?"

Sheri sucked in a breath. Had she misheard? She must have misheard, because that question had nothing to do with the event and was a shot aimed right for Sheri.

She focused on her again and realized she was someone from her aunt's church. One of the people who always had something negative to say. Sheri didn't want to sit here and accept being disrespected. She also couldn't curse the woman out like she wanted to with so many law enforcement officers on the stage. No, Sheri had to be the bigger person. She had to prove she wasn't the same hotheaded person this woman was trying to prove her to be.

"Ma'am, I have no criminal record." Mostly true. She was never convicted for the damage to Tyrone's car. "I'm a business owner who cares about the community. I also know the importance of second chances. I don't shy away from any mistake I may have made. I got the chance to be a part of the city's program to bring life back to a part of town I care about. I want to do my part. I don't participate in idle gossip or spend energy trying to tear other people down. I suggest that anyone who wants to see things get better do the same."

There was applause from the crowd. Kelly was already next to the woman and took the microphone before she could answer. The lady glared at Sheri. Sheri stared back with a fake smile on her face. She was not going to give this woman the benefit of getting a rise out of her.

Sheri stood, and the rest of the panel thanked her for doing a great job. She smiled and nodded patiently, but she wanted to get off that stage, find the woman and ask just what the hell did she think she was doing. But that would only embarrass Sheri and make a scene.

Despite the negative last question, several people came up to Sheri when she left the stage and thanked her for doing a great job pulling everything together. By the time she escaped them, the crowd had dispersed, she didn't see her hater anywhere and the only ones around were family and friends.

Her mom and Cora came over. "You did a great job!" her mom said, pride in her eyes.

"Don't worry about that woman," Cora said. "We'll deal with her later."

A hand rested on Sheri's shoulder. Deandre. "No need to deal with anyone. Sheri already dealt with her."

Sheri grinned at him. "Did I?"

"She ran out of here with her tail tucked between her legs." He squeezed her shoulder. "Great job."

That was true. Sheri had long moved on from the mistakes of her past. The life and relationships she had now was more important than having it out with someone whose opinion didn't really matter.

"Everything did turn out pretty good, didn't it?" she said. "Hopefully it'll help. And we'll get more people to join the neighborhood watch." She looked at her mom. "How's the restaurant?"

Her mom had managed things for Sheri earlier in the

day, but said she would leave to see the panel. "Good. Don't worry. We know how to close things out. I told the family to come to my house later this evening to celebrate you showing the town who's boss."

"I didn't do all that," Sheri said, grinning.

"Girl, you know your mom don't need much of a reason to have a cookout," Cora said.

"True." She looked at Deandre. "Want to come eat with us tonight?"

"You won't be tired after all this?" Concern filled his dark eyes and he squeezed her shoulder again.

The last of Sheri's irritation melted away. She was tired, but she'd drink ten cups of coffee if she needed to stay up and spend more time with him. "I'll be good. Besides, it's just a small family thing. Bring DJ with you."

Maybe if his son was with him, he wouldn't have a good reason to pull Deandre away.

"You sure?"

She nodded. "I am." She had a feeling DJ didn't like her, but she was going to at least try.

"Cool. We'll swing through."

Chapter Fifteen

Deandre had a different definition of "a small thing" compared with Sheri. That's what he thought as Sheri introduced him and DJ to her aunts, uncles and several cousins. He was pretty good at remembering names, but he doubted every name would stick. There were at least three Willies and four Ericas.

DJ had not been excited about coming. Not that he'd said anything, but his lack of words and excess sighs expressed his lack of interest more than if he'd complained. Thankfully, some of Sheri's younger cousins knew DJ from school and pulled him in with the group of other teenagers.

Sheri took him over to a table with her uncles and a few male cousins. "Sit tight while I fix you a plate."

Deandre shook his head. "I can fix my own plate."

She grinned and patted his shoulder. "I know. It's my rule. First time you're here, I'll fix your plate. After that, you're on your own."

Her uncle, the first Willie if he remembered correctly, chimed in. "You better let her go on and fix you a plate." The other guys at the table agreed.

"You all be nice to Deandre until I get back." Sheri pointed at each of the men at the table.

Willie waved her away. "We got him. And make sure you bring him the big piece of chicken."

Sheri rolled her eyes before walking away. Deandre sat in one of the black plastic chairs set around the fold out table.

"Lil Bit must really like you," Willie said, grinning. "I ain't never seen her fix any man a plate."

The guy next to him, her cousin Kenny, he thought, nodded. "She sure doesn't. Not even before that mess with Tyrone."

Willie elbowed Kenny. "Don't be telling all of Lil Bit's business."

Kenny pointed to Deandre. "Hell, he knows. He's the one who arrested her."

Willie's eyes widened before narrowing. "You a cop?"

Deandre nodded. "I am. Hope you don't hold it against me."

"Depends. You a good one or a bad one?"

"I try real hard to be a good one. And I don't put up with the bad ones."

That seemed to satisfy her uncle because he nodded. "Well, if Lil Bit likes you, then you might be alright. But, for real, you arrested her?"

He wasn't about to dig up that situation today. "So, Willie, I heard that red sixty-seven Chevy out front is yours," Deandre said. "You remodeled that yourself?"

Willie laughed and wagged a finger at Deandre. "I

see what you're doing. Cool, cool. You must like Lil Bit, too. Good. She's a good woman. Treat her right."

"That's my plan."

"That is my Chevy out front. Man, I had to drive all the way to New Jersey to get that engine."

Willie spent the next thirty minutes talking about the work he'd done to remodel the truck. He followed that up by taking Deandre to look under the hood and then for a test drive to see how well it ran. Deandre took it all in stride. He had a feeling Willie was partially checking him out. He found out through their conversation that he was Sheri's mother's brother. He'd been the father figure in her house after, per Willie, Sheri's dad hadn't bothered to live up to his responsibilities.

Sheri rushed up to him as soon as he and her uncle pulled back onto the side of the road. The driveway and front yard were filled with cars.

"Uncle Willie, where did you take him?"

"Just for a ride. What? Your man can't spend some time with your uncle?"

"He's here to spend some time with me," she said with a sly grin.

Deandre walked over and wrapped his arm around her shoulder. "I had fun with your uncle. The truck runs like a dream."

"Told you it would," Willie said as if Deandre shouldn't have expected anything less. "You two go on and get your time in. I'm going to get me a piece of pound cake."

"You better hurry," Sheri said. "They cut it ten minutes ago. I made it, so you know it's going to go fast."

"Damn, let me hurry up. Come around again, Deandre." Willie threw up a hand before power walking toward the backyard where the food was set up.

Sheri laughed and turned to him. Deandre kept his hands on her hips. "Sorry about that. Uncle Willie loves that truck, and if you show a hint of interest, he'll take up all your time."

She'd changed into a loose, dark blue sundress that skimmed over her curves and constantly drew his eyes to the sway of her hips. The Lil Bit necklace sparkled in the late afternoon sunlight just above her cleavage.

Deandre tried to pull his mind away from how good her hips felt beneath his hands. And how much he wanted to pull her closer kiss the spot above her necklace. "I really didn't mind. He's a cool guy. Loves you, a lot."

"I know. He's like a dad. He helped mom a lot when I was growing up. I think he still tries to look out for me. He likes you if he told you to come around again."

"That's a good thing. I'd like to come around some more." He glanced toward the backyard. "How's DJ?"

"Good, actually. He's still hanging out with my cousins. They were playing Uno a little while ago."

Deandre pulled out his phone with one hand and texted. You okay? To DJ. He quickly texted back. I'm good.

Deandre smiled and slid his phone back into his pocket. "I'm glad he's having fun."

"I was going to my place to grab the other pound cake I made. I didn't lie when I said the first one was going to go fast. I always keep an extra hidden so that I can have a slice. Want a piece before everyone else gets it?"

"You had the energy to make a pound cake after the event today?"

She gave a sly wink. "Me and my momma made them yesterday. She planned this cookout weeks ago to celebrate me becoming a community activist."

She walked toward her house, and he followed from behind. He put his hands on her bared shoulders and gently massaged. He couldn't help but touch her. "You know you're amazing, right?"

She grinned over her shoulder. "I know."

The quiet inside her house was welcome after the noise of the music and conversation from everyone outside. Even though Uncle Willie was cool, he'd talked nonstop for the past hour. The few minutes inside her place were the first moments they'd had the chance to be alone for a long time.

Deandre took Sheri's hand to stop her from picking up the cake. She faced him and raised her brow. "What's up?"

"Nothing. I'm finally alone with you. I can't help but want to do this." He pulled her into his arms. She came willingly. Her arms wrapped around his neck, and she lifted on her toes to kiss him.

He felt like he hadn't kissed her in years. Had it only been a few days since he held her in his arms? Why did a few days without her feel like he'd gone nearly a lifetime? Why did every moment he spent with her still not feel like enough time? He knew why, but he wasn't ready to say it out loud. But damn, if holding her like this didn't make his feelings impossible to ignore.

She pulled back and smiled at him. Emotion tightened around his heart. He was so close to losing himself when it came to this woman.

"If you keep kissing me like this I'm going to forget about that cake and take advantage of us having a few minutes alone." The devilish spark in her eye combined with the huskiness of her tone made him instantly hard.

He knew exactly how he wanted her to take advantage of their time alone. "Will anyone come looking for you?"

The teasing light left her eye and desire flashed instead. "No. What about…"

"He's good and distracted."

They stared at each other, contemplating how long they had before they'd be missed or people would start wondering what was taking so long. He wanted their first time together to be special. Drawn out. Where he had the chance to savor every part of her body. But the look in her eye and the way her hips pressed forward against him said there would be enough time for drawn out and savor later. He hadn't been spontaneous or felt this rush of excitement in years. The responsible cop and parent in him knew they should get the cake and go back to the cookout. The man who'd had the time with her in his arms interrupted too much said take everything he could get now.

Sheri saw the moment he made the decision and she wanted to jump for joy. There was no time for jumping. Not when they only had a few minutes together. She lifted on her toes, wrapped her arms around his neck and kissed him with all the restrained desire pulsing through her body. The second he'd gotten out of his car wearing a beige T-shirt that clung to his chest and shoulders and those shorts that showed off his strong legs she'd wanted to climb him like a tree.

Deandre's kiss was just as hot and urgent as hers. Did he feel the same way she did? As if she would explode into a thousand pieces if she didn't get the chance to touch him? To feel his body against hers? The way his hands gripped her breasts and behind said he had to. She wished they had more time, but that would wait until another day. The weeks of interruptions and broken dates were the longest foreplay she'd ever had.

They moved frantically, knowing each second could be interrupted like so many precious seconds before. She slid her fingers beneath his shirt, marveled at the warm softness of his skin over the hard muscles beneath. Deandre moaned, low and deep, before his large hand palmed her breast through the thin material of her dress. His fingers rubbed over, then toyed with the hardened tip until she whimpered and pushed forward for more.

He wrapped an arm around her waist and lifted her up. Sheri grinned and wrapped her legs around his waist. Yes, he most definitely felt the way she felt.

Deandre moved and set her on the kitchen table. The table wobbled, nearly toppling Sheri to the floor.

"In the chair," she said laughing. "If this ends because you drop me I'm going to strangle you."

Deandre grinned as he kicked out the chair and sat with her straddling his waist. "I'll strangle my damn self."

She rolled her hips to push his erection against the juncture of her thighs. Pleasure exploded through her body. She reached down and pulled at the button of his shorts. Deandre stopped her movement by tugging on the straps of her sundress and bra. Pinning her arms against her side, she wiggled and he tugged until her arms were free and she reached around to unhook the bra until her breasts spilled out.

Deandre moaned. "You don't know how much I think about your breasts."

The raw desire in his voice nearly pushed her over the edge. "How much?"

"Every damn time you wear this necklace." He leaned forward and kissed her chest right above her Lil Bit necklace. "You play with it and usually when you're wearing a low-cut shirt. Then all I can think about is your chest, your breasts and what I want to do to them."

Sheri's breathing hitched and she arched her back. "Show me what you want to do."

"Yes, ma'am." His warm hands cupped her breasts, lifting them before he sucked the hard tips between his lips. Sheri twisted her hips. Her hands grasped the sides of his head. Wanting more and never wanting this moment to end.

She reached for his waistband again. Deandre dropped one hand to quickly unfasten the button while his other hand and mouth remained on her breast. They shifted and shoved until his pants and underwear were out of the way and he sprang free.

"Do you have a condom?" she asked.

"My wallet." He reached down into the back pocket of his shorts and pulled out the wallet and then the condom.

"You're always this ready?"

"Since we started dating? Hell yes."

Sheri grinned, loving the need and urgency in his voice. He quickly opened the foil package and covered himself. Then he placed his hand on her back and pulled her forward. "Come back here."

"Yes, sir," she said, her voice thick with need.

She took his solid length in her hand. He was thick and hard and felt so damn wonderful as she slid down on him. They both groaned with pleasure before their lips came together in a hard kiss. She rocked back and forth. Taking him deeper. Moaning with each movement because every touch and slide was better than the one before.

Deandre's hands gripped her waist. His strong arms guided her up and down first in slow, deep strokes that grew fast, more frantic and urgent. She gripped his shoulders, her head thrown back as her world constricted to nothing else but the feel of him inside her, his strong hand on her hip, his lips on her breasts and the pleasure rushing through her body. He pulled the tip of her breast deep into his mouth and she was lost. She shattered into a million stars as her body squeezed around him. He cried out with his own release, his fingers digging hard into her hip as his body jerked.

Sheri collapsed against his chest. Their breathing was choppy as they both came down. She lifted her head. He watched her through slitted lids, contentment and another emotion she couldn't quite name on his face. Because she believed in fairy tales and perfect endings, she wanted to believe that was love on his face. But it was too soon for that, right?

Deandre cupped the back of her head and pulled her forward to kiss her slowly. As if they had all the time in the world and didn't need to rush back before people came looking for them. Her heart fluttered. Maybe it was too soon, but it was too late for Sheri. She was falling hard and fast in love again.

Chapter Sixteen

"Another good day," Sheri said to her mom and Cora as she put the bank deposit for the next morning in the safe.

"Sure was," her mom said. She leaned against the doorframe of the office. "I think more people came out after seeing you at the event on Saturday."

"Well, I'll take it." Sheri closed the safe and double-checked the lock. "We were doing good already, but I'll never turn down more business."

Cora pointed at Sheri and grinned. "Ain't that right."

Sheri and her mom both laughed. Sheri's phone chimed. She picked it up and checked the text message.

I've got an hour alone.

Sheri grinned as she quickly replied. Where?

My place? DJ just left to see his grandparents.

OMW!

"Sheri!" Cora's voice snapped. "Girl, why are you grinning at your phone like that?"

Sheri shrugged and stood. "I've got to go."

Her mom shook her head. "It's Deandre. That man has her acting brand-new."

Sheri let out an incredulous laugh. "No he doesn't."

"Yes he does. Normally, I'd tell you to be careful, but I like Deandre. Even if he is a cop. Willie said he's a nice guy."

And that's all it had taken for her mom to warm up to Deandre. She didn't trust most men, but if her brother gave a guy the stamp of approval, then she was willing to give him a chance. Sheri didn't care if her uncle's cosign was what it took for her mom to be okay with her dating Deandre. She was just glad that their relationship wouldn't be a problem.

"That's because he *is* a nice guy," Sheri said. "I guess it's true that there are a few of them left out there."

Cora smirked. "Are you sure he's nice or are you just blinded by the sex?"

"What?"

"You heard me. We all know it don't take that long to get a cake from your house."

Sheri's cheeks burned. Really? Cora had to call her out right now in front of her mom. Her mom knew she wasn't a virgin, but that didn't mean she wanted to be called out for getting a quickie at a family cookout.

"Mind your business, Cora," Sheri warned. "Let's get out of here." She left the office and went toward the back door.

"I'm just saying," Cora said, following her.

"No, you're just doing too much."

Her mom spoke from behind them. "It's okay, Lil Bit. He is a nice guy. Don't be embarrassed for enjoying each other."

"Thanks, Ma." Sheri wanted the entire conversation to end.

Cora, unfortunately, wasn't ready to let it end. "You don't have to be embarrassed, but you do need to be careful."

"Careful for what? Deandre is cool. He's respectful and isn't about playing games. It's all good."

They went out the back door and Sheri pulled out the key to lock it behind them.

"Yeah, well, you better watch that son of his."

Sheri frowned. "DJ? Why?"

"Emory said that he was bragging about being in a gang," Cora said, referring to one of their younger, teenage cousins.

Sheri nearly dropped her keys. "What? He's not in a gang."

"Well, that's what he said," Cora spoke as if she were repeating the God's honest truth. "He said him and his boys control this end of the beach and that everyone knows not to go messing with their group."

"Emory must have misheard. DJ wouldn't be in a gang. His dad is a cop."

"Yeah," her mom agreed. "Let's be honest. I love Emory, but the girl likes to exaggerate. Besides, there aren't any gangs in Sunshine Beach."

Not exactly true, but DJ and his friends hardly qualified as a gang. "I've seen DJ with his friends, and they don't look like a gang. They look like regular teenagers who hang around the area."

Cora waved off Sheri's words. She gave Sheri a look that was both pitying and disbelieving. "You're just being delusional because you're all into Deandre."

Sheri stopped walking and faced her cousin. "I'm not being delusional. I'm also not going to start spreading rumors about gangs in the south end. Especially rumors that Deandre's son is part of one."

Cora put a hand on her hip. "It's not a rumor when the boy said it himself."

"Did you hear him say that?"

Cora glanced away before lifting her chin defiantly. "I'm telling you what Emory said."

"We all love Emory, but Mom is right. She can exaggerate. I think you just want to try and find something wrong with Deandre."

Cora's jaw dropped. "Ain't nobody trying to find something wrong with Deandre."

"Really, Cora? Don't even play like that. It's what you do. You always hate on whatever guy I'm dating. I'm not following you down the yellow brick road this time." Sheri turned to stalk away from her cousin.

"I don't know what you're talking about. I don't lead you down any roads."

Sheri spun back. "Yes you do. You always try to find something wrong and push me into doing something dumb."

"You make your own decisions. Don't blame me because you pick the wrong guys."

"No, Cora, you pick the wrong guys. And then you want to find something wrong with every guy that I try to spend time with. It's not going to work this time. I'm not going to let you bad-mouth Deandre or his son."

Her mom stepped between them. "Both of ya'll stop

right now. You are not about to fall out in this parking lot over a man. You're family. You understand me?"

Her mom's intervention did nothing to calm Sheri's irritation. "I understand, Ma, but it has to be said. Cora is going too far."

Cora rolled her eyes. "You know what, I don't know why I'm even talking to you. When you figure out that his son is some wanna-be thug, then I'll be the first to tell you I told you so." Cora turned and stomped off.

"You won't be telling me anything," Sheri called after her.

Her mom put her hand on Sheri's arm. "Lil Bit, stop. Why are you being like that with your cousin?"

"Because, Ma, you know how she is. She makes everything worse and always looks for the negative."

"But she doesn't mean you any harm."

"Yes she does. She did it before and she'll do it again."

Her mom pointed. "Don't go blaming Cora for the decisions you made. Did she egg you on? Yes, but at the end of the day you took the bat to that man's car."

"Ma." Sheri wanted to argue. Her mom was supposed to take her side. Dorothy Jean didn't give her a chance to continue.

"Don't 'Ma' me. It's the truth. Cora isn't perfect, and she was wrong for encouraging you, but you can't go putting all your activities on account of her."

"But she made things worse." Not just that night, but by spreading rumors when she was jealous. Not to mention the way she constantly ditched Sheri whenever some new guy came around. Cora was family, but she didn't always act like a good friend.

"Then be mad at her for the things *she* did. Not for

the things you did. And I don't know if Emory is right or not, but where there's smoke there's usually fire."

"You think DJ is in a gang? Seriously?"

"I don't know enough about the boy to say anything about him. But if Deandre really is your man, then how about you tell him what was said at the party. Let him figure it out before you get lost in love. Because if he is in a gang, then honey, you're signing up for a lot more than what you bargained for."

Deandre bit the corner of his lip as he watched Sheri stretch as she sat on the edge of his bed. She raised her arms high over her head with her back arched and her breasts pushed forward. Even though they'd just made love, he wanted to pull her back into the bed and get lost in her body all over again.

"I needed that." Sheri grinned at him over her shoulder.

"Did you?" He shifted on the bed until his legs straddled her and his feet rested next to hers on the floor. He wrapped his arms around her waist and brought her back to his chest.

She nodded and leaned into him. "I did. It was a busy day at the restaurant."

Deandre kissed her shoulder and breathed in the sweet scent of her skin. "There are a lot more people on the south end of the beach since the event. Which is a good thing."

"Do you think things will get better?"

"I think it showed the town leaders that the people in the area are serious about making things even better. Montgomery also told me they heard loud and clear that the business owners and residents don't want us coming through with a heavy hand. I think they finally understand and are good with us becoming a part of the community."

Her eyes widened and she squeezed his arms still around her waist. "That's great. I'm telling you things aren't that bad."

"I know they aren't."

She moved to get up, but he held on to her. "You sure you don't want to stick around for dinner? DJ will be home soon and can join us."

Her body stiffened. Deandre let her go. She didn't pull away but she shifted so that she could look at him. "I don't know. I'm trying not to come on too strong around him. I think we need to ease into the time together."

"I know what he's been doing."

She glanced away. "What do you mean?"

"You know what I mean. We both know he's been trying to keep us separated. I talked to him about it."

Her body relaxed and relief filled her gaze. "What did he say?"

"He said he wasn't trying to do that. Then made me feel guilty for saying that he was calling just to interrupt us."

She cringed. "Dang."

"Yeah. I don't want him to think I don't want him around or calling when we're together. That's why I asked you to stay. I'm thinking you and I are going to be together for a while. I want him to get used to you being a part of our life."

"You want me to be a part of your life?"

The hopeful smile on her face made his lips turn up. "Yeah. I told you I'm not about sleeping around. I like you. We're good together. I'd like to see where this goes."

The seconds she took to study him while chewing on

the corner of her lip were the longest, sexiest seconds in his life. "So would I."

"I'm not asking you to step in and be DJ's mom or anything. But I would like for the two of you to start getting along."

"I would like to get along with him."

"So will you stay?" She glanced away again. Deandre frowned. "What's wrong?"

She shifted until she could face him better, her hand resting on his thigh. "I need to tell you something. It's part of the reason I was so wound up when I got here."

Dread tightened his shoulders. Things were going so well, he hoped she wasn't having any concerns about their relationship. "What is it?"

"Something my cousin Cora said. Which, I don't believe because she's always stirring up trouble."

"What did she say?"

She sighed and looked like she didn't want to say it. He gently squeezed her hand. She met his eyes. "She says that at the cookout the other day, DJ was bragging about being in a gang."

Deandre jerked back. "A what?"

"I know. It's the dumbest thing. There's no way he would be in a gang when his dad is a cop. Then she started talking about how I shouldn't get involved with you because of DJ and that you weren't as great as I thought. That's why I don't believe her. I think she's just trying to start problems."

Deandre swung his leg from around her and sat on the edge of the bed. He shook his head. "He couldn't."

"I don't believe it."

Deandre thought about the last few months. The withdrawal from the things DJ usually liked. The new set of friends that he didn't want to bring around. The way he was cagey with his answers about whom he'd been with and what they were doing. "He wouldn't."

Sheri placed a hand on his knee. "I know. Cora is just being messy."

"But if he's saying things like that, then I need to talk to him about it."

"I'm not trying to get him into trouble."

"I know you're not, but I'm glad you told me." All kinds of thoughts and concerns spiraled through his brain. Had he missed something so big with DJ?

"Look, I can't prove he really said that. It's what I got from Cora, who said our younger cousin Emory heard him say this. This is literally hearsay."

"Even if it's hearsay, I still need to let him know. If he said it, then I need to know why. If he didn't say it, then I need to find out what he said that could have made them think that."

Maybe it was just a mix-up. Confusion over a turn of phrase. He could make sure DJ was aware that words held power and could cause big problems if he wasn't clear.

"Wait, do you think there's something to this?"

The concern in her eyes mirrored his own. He was glad that she cared. Glad that she'd told him and was still willing to stick with him in this relationship after hearing something so negative about his kid. Something he prayed was not true.

"I don't know. But he has changed in the last few months. I don't know what's going on with him. I'd rather rule this out than pretend as if he never would get involved with the wrong crowd and be wrong."

Chapter Seventeen

Deandre sat up on the couch when the sound of the key in the front door's lock echoed through the quiet. Sheri had left two hours ago when it was obvious that DJ wasn't coming home anytime soon. When he'd called his in-laws to see if they were still with DJ, he'd been shocked to learn that DJ had never made it to their place.

Deandre had been disappointed and confused. DJ's lie wasn't one that he would be able to get away with. Which meant he didn't care about being caught. Deandre wasn't sure what was going on with his son, but he was going to get to the bottom of everything tonight. He'd tried to respect DJ's space and give him the room he needed to go through whatever teenage transition he was having. But lying to him was something he was not going to accept.

The front door opened, and Deandre waited. There was no need to rush forward. DJ would see him as soon as he crossed the threshold. His son walked in slowly, his brow furled and shoulders slumped. He quietly closed the door and locked it behind him. When he turned and entered the living area, his gaze collided with Deandre's. He paused for a second, eyes wide as if for a split second he was surprised to find his dad there. Maybe a part of him had hoped he wouldn't get caught. But the second of surprise quickly faded, and DJ straightened his shoulders and lifted his chin.

Deandre clenched his hands into fists. This was what they were doing? His son was really going to flex on him? After he'd done wrong? The level of audacity made Deandre's stomach churn and his blood boil. He took a long breath and calmed himself. They were going to have a showdown, but he was the adult. This wasn't going to go anywhere if he let anger rule him.

"Where have you been?" Deandre asked.

DJ glanced away and rubbed his chin before looking back. "With some friends."

"You were supposed to be going to your grandparents' house."

DJ lifted a shoulder. "My plans changed."

"You didn't think to tell me about your change of plans?"

"I didn't think you'd care."

Deandre frowned so hard his forehead hurt. He slowly stood and crossed his arms. "Why wouldn't I care? When I called your grandparents, and they said you never came by, they were worried. They thought something happened to you."

Guilt flashed in DJ's dark eyes before he blinked it away and lifted his chin again. "I didn't tell them I was coming. There wasn't any reason for them to worry."

"But you told me that. I expected you to be with them. They weren't the only ones worrying. I worried."

"Well, I'm fine now." DJ patted the front of his hoodie and joggers as if to support the statement.

"Fine now?" Deandre paused, breathed, then continued. "Boy, have you lost your damn mind? You don't change your plans and tell me you're going one place and then go somewhere else. That's not how this works. You're supposed to call me."

"You told me not to call when you're with *Sheri*." DJ rolled his eyes and said Sheri's name as if it were some kind of disease.

Deandre uncrossed his arms and planted his hands on his hips. "You know good and damn well that isn't what I said or what I meant. Now, if you have a problem with Sheri, then you tell me that straight up. What you won't do is try to use that as a reason to lie to me. Now give me your phone."

DJ scowled. "For what?"

"You know what for. You're on punishment. You aren't allowed to leave this house except to go to school, to be with me or with your grandparents. You can't use your phone, laptop or any other electronic device in this house for anything other than homework. I'm disabling the internet on everything in here."

DJ scoffed. "Whatever." He pulled out his cell phone.

Deandre crossed the room and snatched it from his son. Then he froze. He sniffed the air and leaned in closer. His eyes narrowed as he realized what he smelled. "Were you smoking weed?"

DJ's eyes widened. "What? Nah! I swear!"

"You've already lied to me once. Don't lie to me

again. I know what weed smells like and I smell it on you. Is it true? Are you in a gang?"

"Dad, I wasn't smoking weed. Some guy I knew had it—"

"Some guy you knew? Are these the so-called friends you're hanging with? No, we're not doing that. I didn't want to believe Sheri but—"

"Sheri? So, she's snitching on me again?" Disbelief filled DJ's voice.

"She's not snitching. If there's something going on with my son, then I need to know. Gangs and drugs? DJ, how could you?"

"I'm not—"

"You're getting tested."

"What?" DJ's eyes bugged with disbelief. He threw up his hands.

"Right now." He grabbed his son's arm and pulled him down the hall to Deandre's room. Deandre went into the bathroom and pulled out the at-home drug test he kept. Something he never thought he'd have to use.

"Do this. Right now."

"Dad, you're really going to drug-test me?"

Deandre tossed the box and DJ caught it. He crossed his arms and glared. "Yes. I really am."

Sheri didn't see Deandre again until later in the week. He'd given her an update via text and phone calls of what DJ had been up to. She was glad that he'd made his way home safely, while also hating the fact that Deandre had worried about him. She'd even called her mom to apologize for some of the antics she'd done as a kid.

"I didn't realize how much kids could make their

parents worry," she'd said as she'd sat on the porch with her mom and aunt the night before.

"You never stop worrying. You and Cora would get into some things, but thankfully you were never too bad. At least I didn't have to worry about you being in a gang or anything."

Sheri had nothing to say to that. Deandre hadn't confirmed the rumor about DJ being in a gang. But that hadn't stopped Cora from making sure everyone in the family knew. Sheri was so done with her cousin and her antics. But she'd deal with that later.

When Deandre texted her at work and asked if he could come by after she got off, she'd quickly agreed. She missed him. And even though DJ wasn't her son, she wanted him to be okay. She worried that she was the reason for his acting out. She was falling hard for Deandre, but she didn't want to be the reason he and his son grew further apart.

Deandre looked tired when he got to her place. She cut him a huge slice of the lemon pound cake she'd baked and set it in front of him at the table. Despite the weariness in his eyes, his face lit up at the sight of the cake.

"When did you have time to bake this?"

"Don't worry about all that." She'd baked the cake during the day at work. "Just eat. You probably skipped lunch again today."

"I ate lunch. It just wasn't as good as your fried chicken."

"You should have come by the restaurant."

He shook his head. "Busy day. We're looking into the suspected gang activity in the south end."

She sat next to him. "There really is a gang problem?"

"Some kids are grouping up. It started with two separate groups fighting during the football season and the problem's escalating. We're figuring out a plan with the school district to see if we can curb it before things turn violent."

"Is DJ...?"

He sighed and shrugged. "I can't prove anything. I drug-tested him. It came back negative. Thankfully. But he's hanging with some kids that I do think are a part of the problem."

"What can we do?"

He looked up from the cake and raised a brow. "We?"

"If I can help in any way, I want to. I know I'm not family, but I care about you. Which means I care about DJ."

He took her hand in his. "You don't know how much I appreciate that. I wish DJ would give you a chance."

The words iced her heart. She pulled on her hand. "He doesn't like me."

Deandre didn't let her go. "He doesn't know you."

"But he doesn't want to try and know me. If I'm the problem..."

"You're not." He squeezed her hand.

"I'm part of the problem. Or you dating me is making it worse. Do you think we should—"

"No," he said firmly. "Let's give it some time."

"We've given it time. I don't want to end things, but maybe we do need to take a step back. Let you focus on DJ and whatever is going on with the kids he's hanging around. I know it's not ideal, but it's probably the right thing for now."

He sat up straight. "You want to break up?"

She shook her head and her hands. "No, hell no!

We're just chilling for a while. If you're not available or have family and work stuff, I understand. Right now, DJ is your priority and I respect that."

Deandre put down the fork. He placed his hand on the back of her head and pulled her forward for a kiss. It was quick and hard and made Sheri want to climb on his lap and take him deep. When he pulled back, she was breathless.

"Thank you for being great," he said.

Sheri's cheeks tingled as she grinned. "You just like my pound cake."

"No. I like you. And hopefully, we'll get through this."

Chapter Eighteen

Sheri walked into the alley behind her restaurant and froze. The space was darker than usual. The overhead lights that illuminated the back doors of the businesses were out. It wasn't unusual for one or two to go out. They weren't the LED lights that lasted forever, but for them all to be out wasn't normal. She'd decided to go into the restaurant early to work on the schedule for the following week before everyone else came in and things got busy. She hadn't seen Deandre in two weeks, and when he'd texted her last night asking if they could meet up when she got off, she'd immediately said yes.

She missed him. Way more than she'd thought she would. So, getting up earlier than usual so she could get out of there as soon as possible after closing was an easy decision. They hadn't had problems with break-ins since the Connecting the Community event, so she also hadn't worried that whoever had tried to rob the place weeks ago would be back.

What little light came from the streetlights and waning glow from the moon glinted off broken glass on the ground behind the building. The lights weren't out because the bulbs were old. They were out because someone had vandalized the building.

She pulled out her cell phone and turned on the flashlight. The light from her phone seemed bright as the sun when she used it at home, but in the dark alley it felt inadequate. She studied the area but there weren't any signs that anyone was still there. She just needed to unlock the door, get in and then she'd call the police. The business owners had gone in together to purchase cameras to monitor the alley as part of the recommendations to have better surveillance in the area. The police could pull the footage and they'd quickly find out who'd done it. Probably just some bored kids, and no one who meant any real harm.

She pulled her keys out of her purse and then quickly walked to the back door. The hairs on the back of her neck stood up as soon as she put the key into the lock and turned. A second later, the sound of footsteps hurrying down the alley echoed off the building.

Sheri turned to see two figures approaching her fast. She didn't wait to find out what was going on. She opened the door and rushed inside, her heart pounding. She tried to turn and slam the door, but the people behind her were already there. One of them slammed into the door. The impact was so sudden and unexpected that Sheri stumbled back.

The person came inside, followed by another figure. They wore masks over their faces and were dressed in all black. She guessed based on their size that they were male, but from what she could see of the first one, she immediately assumed teenager or young adult.

"What do you want?" She tried not to sound intimidated despite her racing heart and the cold sweat breaking out over her body.

"The money in the safe. All of it," the guy said. Definitely a teenager.

Sheri frowned. "I don't have money in a safe."

"You've got money in here. I know you do. Now get it."

Sheri held up her hand and shook her head. "Look, I don't keep cash in here like that. I'm not a bank or a convenience store. If you're looking for money, you came to the wrong place."

She did have money in the safe in the office, but there was no way she'd let on that there was anything there. She needed them to leave as soon as possible. And preferably without damage to her or the restaurant.

"That's a lie. Now give me the money." He reached into his pocket and pulled out a gun.

Sheri's heart dropped to her stomach. The room spun and she took a step back, arms raised. "I swear I don't have anything."

The other kid stepped forward. "Hey, J, you said you were just going to scare her."

The first one looked at the second. "And if she doesn't give us the money, I'm really going to scare her."

Sheri blinked. She had to be hearing this wrong. "DJ?"

The second kid's eyes swung to her. Her stomach twisted into a tight knot. She shook her head. No, not DJ. Why in the world would he be robbing her?

The first kid, J, stepped into her line of sight. Gun

still pointed straight at Sheri. "To hell with that. I'm not playing. Give me the money or I'm going to shoot your ass."

"Yo, J, hold up," DJ said, his voice panicked and tight. "That's not what we talked about."

"I don't care what we talked about. This place is always busy. I know there's money up in here."

"Nah, I'm not down for this," DJ said, taking a step back.

"You want to be a part of us, then you have to be down." J looked back at Sheri. "And if she knows who you are, then she'll snitch." He focused on DJ. "So we can't leave her to tell."

"What? Nah, man! No." DJ moved back toward the door.

J turned his back to Sheri. That was all she needed. She grabbed a bowl off the counter and tossed it straight for J's head. She missed and hit his hand instead. The gun went off. The sound of the shot was like a crack of thunder in the small space.

J cursed as the gun fell from his hand. Sheri grabbed a rolling pin and ran toward J. Kid or not, she was going to clock him. He was going to shoot her! Which meant she felt no guilt about trying to defend herself. She swung, but he was fast. He ducked out of the way. Then his hand shot out as he punched the side of her face. Pain exploded through her head. Sheri stumbled and fell to the floor.

"The cops!" DJ yelled.

"Shit!" J ran toward the back door, shoving DJ out of the way as he hurried out.

Sheri placed a hand to the side of her head. Pain throbbed with every heartbeat and her vision was blurry. She'd never been punched in the face. The experience was new—and horrible. DJ rushed over. Sheri flinched when he reached for her.

"Sheri, damn, I'm sorry. It wasn't supposed to go down like this. I was just trying to…"

She scowled. "Scare me! Well, it worked!"

"Lil Bit!" JD's voice echoed as he burst in the back door. His frantic eyes searched the room, landed on DJ standing above her and fury filled his face. "You little punk." He rushed forward and grabbed DJ by the back of the neck.

Sheri jumped up, the room spun and she shook her head to clear the fog. Not a good idea. That just made everything hurt worse. "Hold up. It wasn't him."

DJ struggled against JD's hold, but he didn't let go. "Then why's he struggling? I'm holding his behind right there until the cops come."

Sheri stared at DJ. He didn't struggle against JD's grip. If anything, the fear in his eyes said he knew he'd messed up. Sheri wished she didn't have to make the call, but what he'd done? What his friend had done? It couldn't be ignored. She nodded slowly to not make the pain in her head worse.

"You call the cops, and I'll call his dad."

"I told you to stay away from him."

Sheri sighed before dropping the ice pack pressed to the side of her face. She glared at Cora standing at the base of the stairs leading up to the porch. Sheri had wanted to spend a few minutes alone to process everything that happened that day. The day felt like a blur. The police coming. DJ getting arrested. Her mom insisting Sheri go to the hospital to get checked out, and Sheri compromising with a trip to urgent care instead. Followed by going to the police station to give a statement.

In all of that she'd only seen Deandre in passing. He'd been dealing with the fallout with DJ. Their eyes met as they crossed paths in the station. He'd taken one look at her face, scowled and stalked away. She wasn't sure if she should call him or leave well enough alone.

She had enough to deal with and wasn't in the mood to deal with Cora's smug attitude. She narrowed her eyes at Cora. "Did you come here to gloat?"

Cora held up her hands in surrender before coming up the stairs. "I came to check on you."

"And to say I told you so."

Cora leaned against the porch rail. She sucked her teeth and shook her head. "Your eye is swollen."

"I already knew that. If you came to point out the obvious, you can go." Sheri picked up the ice pack and put it back on her face.

Cora sighed and crossed her arms. They sat there in silence for several minutes. Sheri refused to break the silence. She was mad. Mad that DJ would go so far to scare her. Mad that Deandre could barely look at her. Mad that she'd had to shut the restaurant down for the day because of this foolishness. And, especially mad that Cora had been right about DJ all along.

"Look," Cora finally said. "I didn't come to say I told you so. I was worried about you."

"I'm fine. You've checked on me. Now you can go."

"Lil Bit, don't be like that. I didn't want things to turn out like this. Deandre *is* a nice guy."

She looked at her cousin. "You're ready to finally admit that."

Cora huffed out a breath before flicking her bang out

of her face. "I never said he wasn't. I just knew his son was a problem, and you got all mad at me."

"I got all mad because you seemed to love telling me how things weren't going to work out with him. You know how hard it's been for me to move on since that mess with Tyrone. Why couldn't you at least be supportive?"

"Because I was jealous."

Sheri blinked. "What?" That was not what she expected.

Cora rolled her eyes. "Don't act like you didn't know. Why do you always end up with the good ones and I get the bustas?"

"Good ones?" Sheri dropped the ice pack to point at her chest. "Since when do I get the good ones?"

"You do okay. The nice guys like you and the sorry ones come my way. So, yes, I was jealous. But I wouldn't try to intentionally hurt you. Not after you got in trouble back then."

"Did you intentionally try to hurt me then?"

Cora met her gaze. "No."

Sheri believed her. Plus, her mom was right. Cora had egged her on, but ultimately, the decision to take her revenge on Tyrone for hurting her was her own. "Were you glad to see my heart broken?"

Cora's shoulders straightened. "No! I knew he was going to hurt you. That's why I was down when you wanted to mess up his car after he did. Not because I was happy about how it went down. Just like I'm not happy about what happened today. You really think I want to see you robbed and beat?"

Sheri slumped back in her chair. "No. And I didn't get beat. I got hit once." Despite everything, she knew

Cora wouldn't wish bad on her. Her cousin was messy, and gossipy, and an instigator, but when push came to shove, she'd always been there for Sheri. Even when she was doing dumb things or making foolish decisions.

"I told you about DJ because you thought Deandre was perfect. Well, girl, he's not. When I heard his son might be in a gang, then I knew that was going to be trouble. I was just trying to give you a heads-up. That's all."

Sheri closed her eyes and dropped her head back. "I wanted this to work out."

"I don't see how it can. Not when this happened. DJ doesn't like you and I'm not going to be cool with watching him try to hurt you."

"I know. But…" She looked at her cousin. "Cora, I really like Deandre. Like, I think I love him."

Cora's eyes widened. She quickly moved and sat in the chair next to Sheri. "Lil Bit? You serious?"

She nodded, tears welling in her eyes as the anger from the day turned into pain. "I do. But if his son hates me enough to do this…"

"Then how can you make it work?"

"I don't know. Even if I want to try, Deandre might not. He barely looked at me today."

"Because his son tried to rob you and you almost got shot. If he did look you in the eye without a problem, then I'd say that's a problem. Don't you take on any responsibility for this one. This is on Deandre and his son. Not you."

"I know." Sheri sat up and swiped at her eyes. "I just really hate that when I finally find a guy that I can love, it has to end like this."

Cora sighed. "You know what?"

Sheri put the ice pack back on her face. "What?"

She waited for Cora to tell her to move on. That she didn't need to waste tears for a man. That she was better off without him.

"Maybe things will work out."

Sheri swung her head toward Cora so fast that her headache throbbed. "Come again?"

Cora shrugged. "I'm just saying. You've been through a lot. Deandre is a good guy. Maybe, and that's a big *maybe*, he feels the same and ya'll can make this work."

Sheri grinned before reaching over to lightly push her cousin's shoulder. "That's the nicest thing you've ever said to me."

Cora rolled her eyes and pushed Sheri's hand away. "I've been around you too long. Got me hoping in fairy tales. But who knows. Maybe the little bit of love you're feeling for him will work out."

Sheri grinned even though in her heart she wasn't sure how they would make it all work. She looked at the sky and sent up a silent prayer. "Maybe so."

Chapter Nineteen

DJ knocked on Deandre's door after midnight. Deandre stared at his closed bedroom door. He was angry,
frustrated and disappointed. But mostly, he was tired.
It had taken calling in every favor he had and pulling his position with the police department to keep DJ
from spending the night in jail. At first his plan was
to let his son spend the night in jail. Maybe two. If he
wanted to be a damn thug, then he'd see what life was
like for one. But Rose had cried and Cliff had begged,
so Deandre had pleaded with the judge and the chief
and pulled money out of his savings account to get his
son out on bail.

He hated that he had to do that. Hated that he was
using an advantage that so many other people didn't
have in this situation. Hated that DJ had put him in this
situation in the first place. That he'd *missed* it. That
missing this had damn near cost Sheri everything.

DJ knocked again. "Dad, you up?"

Deandre wanted to ignore him. Wanted to turn off his light, pull the covers over his head and forget this horrible day. But he couldn't. When he signed up for parenthood it hadn't been just for birthdays, holidays and special occasions at school.

"Come on in, DJ," he called back.

A second passed, then another before his son opened the bedroom door. He'd showered and changed into pajamas, a pair of basketball shorts and a T-shirt. His shoulders were slumped, and he looked wary as he entered Deandre's bedroom.

"I just want to say I'm sorry. About today."

Deandre narrowed his eyes. "You're sorry? Do you even realize how much of a privilege it is for you to even be here, in my room, saying you're sorry? You should still be in jail right now with your friend J. But I had to pull strings to get you here to even tell me you're sorry."

DJ flinched and crossed his arms in front of his chest. For the first time in months, he looked like a kid. No defiance and frustration in his eyes. Just sadness and fear.

"I know. I messed up. Things got out of hand. It wasn't supposed to go down like that."

"Then how was it supposed to go down? What did you want to happen?"

"Just to scare her a little," he said in a small voice.

"For what? Do you hate her that much? Is the idea of me dating her so bad that you want to scare her off? Scare her so bad that you get a kid who's trying to recruit you into his gang to come at her with a gun? You hate her enough to risk this armed robbery charge?"

That part had come out in the aftermath. DJ wasn't officially in J's gang, but he'd started hanging with them and showing interest. Deandre had been shocked, hurt, but mostly he'd been disappointed in himself. He hadn't been there for his son. He hadn't noticed what was going on. He should have pushed for more information. He should have made DJ tell him what was going on. Instead, he'd gotten lost in work and missed all the signs.

"No, I mean…" DJ paused, then sighed and held out his hands helplessly. "I don't know. I just… She was getting all your attention."

"What?"

"You've been busy. With the switch in your job and you're always worried about fixing the south end of the beach. You're never around. And then, all of a sudden, she was there. You already weren't paying attention to me and then you had her. It was like you didn't care about me anymore."

Deandre frowned. He got up from the bed and crossed the room. "DJ, I will always care about you. You're my son. I love you. No matter what's going on."

"I didn't mean to join them. It was just hanging around. I was losing on the wrestling team and the other guys started teasing me. But when I started hanging with J, they left me alone. It got out of hand. I didn't know how to get out." His voice cracked. "They wouldn't let me out."

Deandre put his hands on his son's shoulders. "That's when you come to me." He moved his face until DJ finally met his eyes. "There is always a way out, understand? I'll fight this entire damn world to help you. No one is going to take advantage of my son. You hear me?"

DJ nodded. He hastily wiped his face and looked away. Deandre's own eyes burned. "But, DJ, even if you felt that way, you should have told me. I asked you over and over to talk to me. Why didn't you?"

"I thought you'd be upset."

"Yeah, I would have been, but I would have helped you figure a way out."

"Then she told you what I said that day when I was with J."

"She told me because she cared about you. She didn't want you to get in trouble."

He used *cared* because he wasn't sure how Sheri felt now. He hadn't had the chance to talk to her. He didn't even know what he would say. How could he approach her after what DJ had done? He couldn't blame her if she never wanted to see either of them again.

"I know, but… You told me that you'd always love Mom."

The softly spoken words tore a hole in Deandre's heart. He squeezed DJ's shoulder. "I will always love your mom. The way I feel about Sheri is different. It won't replace that love or make me forget your mom."

"I don't want you to forget her."

"I won't. Just like I won't stop trying to be there for you. If you need me to be around more, or to be more available, I will. We'll start over. We'll get through this and figure out the best way forward. Even if it means without Sheri in my life."

The last words burned like acid as he spoke them. He didn't want to give her up, but this crisis showed him one thing. His son needed him, and he'd missed the signs. He wouldn't blame it on his relationship with Sheri. DJ had started acting differently before they'd come together. But he wouldn't put her in harm's way again.

"For real?" DJ asked.

Deandre nodded slowly. "If that's what it takes to make things right with us, then I will."

DJ looked at the floor. "I didn't think you'd do that for me."

Deandre gently shook DJ's shoulder until he looked back up. "Son, I love you. You're the most important thing in my life. You're in a world of trouble for this. But that doesn't take away that I want to help you."

DJ's eyes glistened. He quickly wiped them and Deandre pulled him into his arms. For the first time in months, DJ hugged him back.

"I love you, too, Dad."

Chapter Twenty

Sheri was in the back going over the sales receipts for the day when her mom came into the office.

"Lil Bit, that boy is out there to see you."

Sheri looked up from her calculator and frowned at her mom. "What boy?"

Her mom crossed her arms and twisted her lips. "Deandre's son."

Sheri's jaw dropped. She never expected DJ to come see her. "What for? I said everything I needed to say in court earlier."

Sheri had gone to his bond hearing and told the judge she was not pressing charges against DJ. His friend J, on the other hand, was not getting his charges dropped. Though she hadn't forgiven DJ for agreeing to go along with this, he at least hadn't come with the intention of trying to shoot her. He also didn't have to stick around and help her even though he was going to be arrested. J hadn't bothered to show any signs of remorse, where DJ

had apologized to her. Something she was sure Deandre
had a hand in, but knowing he wasn't a bad kid, she'd
given him a second chance just like she'd been given.

"He says he wants to say something to you. You want
me to kick him out?" her mom asked a little too eagerly.

"Is his dad with him?"

"Nope. Just him."

Intrigued, Sheri stood. She wasn't afraid that he'd
hurt her. Not after what happened and not with the
workers in the restaurant still there. "I'll go see what
he wants."

She left the office and went out into the dining area.
The restaurant had closed an hour earlier and most of
the waitstaff had finished up cleaning their areas and
were finalizing end-of-the-day prep in the kitchen. DJ
stood by the hostess's stand, his head bent as he kicked
at the floor. He was still dressed in the suit and tie he'd
worn for court earlier that day, but now the tie was
loose.

"You wanted to see me?"

DJ's head jerked up. He glanced around nervously, as
if he wasn't sure why he'd come, before finally meeting
her eye. "Um…yeah. I mean, yes, ma'am."

Sheri pointed to one of the tables. "Want something
to eat?" She couldn't help it, food always made difficult talks a little easier.

He shook his head. "Nah, I'm good." He pulled out
a chair and sat.

Sheri sat opposite him. He scratched at the table for
several seconds before Sheri asked, "What's up?"

"Why did you drop the charges?" he blurted out.

Sheri took a long breath before crossing her arms and

sitting back in her chair. "Because you stuck around to help me."

His brows drew together. "That's it?"

"That, and you're not a bad kid. Everyone deserves a second chance. I got one."

"When you messed up that guy's car?" he asked.

She let out a dry chuckle before shaking her head. She would never live that down. "No, before that. When I was your age. Hanging out down here on the south end of the beach. Me and my friends thought it would be cool to steal key chains from the gift shop. We would try to see who could get the most. Well, one day I had the most and I was the one the security guard caught."

DJ sat forward in his chair. "You were stealing key chains? Why?" he asked as if that were the most asinine thing he'd ever heard.

She shook her head and laughed. Looking back, it was an asinine decision. "No good reason other than the key chains had dirty phrases and we wanted them."

He nodded as if that made sense, then leaned forward and asked, "What happened?"

"The security guard called the police, but the store owner, Mr. Lee, got there at the same time. He told the cops he'd given me permission to take them. Later, he told me that I was a good kid and didn't need to mess up my life trying to steal his key chains. He gave me a second chance when he didn't have to. All because he saw potential in me even when I wanted to be dumb with my friends. I don't know why you decided to run with J and his crew, or why you decided that scaring me was what you needed to do, but I've seen you with your dad, your grandparents and around other adults.

You're not bad. So, this is my second chance for you. What you do with it is up to you."

DJ chewed on his lower lip. His eyes studied the table for several seconds before he sat up and met her eye. "I didn't want you with my dad."

Sheri shrugged. "I figured that much."

"I thought you'd be drama. That you'd get mad at him and mess up his car. That's what I heard anyway."

"Rumors aren't always the truth. But I will give you that. I made some bad decisions before."

"And you and my dad, y'all broke up…because of me?"

"He wants to focus on being there for you because he loves you. I want to make sure your dad is okay because I care about him. And, believe it or not, I care about you, too."

DJ nodded slowly. "I meant what I said earlier today. About being sorry. My dad didn't make me say that. I just wanted to play a prank. I didn't think J would…" He trailed off and drummed his fingers on the table.

Sheri reached over and placed her hand over his. "Thankfully, nothing bad happened. But, DJ, if this happens again, things may not turn out okay. For your dad's sake, try not to run with that crowd."

She pulled her hand back. DJ looked down at his hand before focusing on her again. "If I said I never wanted you with my dad, would you walk away?"

She sucked in a breath. Stepping back from Deandre had already been difficult to do. She loved him and missed him. The realization that she loved him made her chest ache. She wanted to see him smile, bring him lunch so she knew he would eat on a busy day, and listen to him talk. But she knew how much he loved his son. If being with her would damage his relationship with DJ, then, yes, he might still choose to be with her, but at what cost? She didn't want to put him in that situation and find out.

"I don't want to come between you and your dad," she said honestly.

"I don't want to come between you and my dad," DJ said. "Not anymore."

Sheri sat up straight, surprised by his words. "What?"

"Look, I don't know how this works. My dad didn't really date like that after Mom passed. I don't want him alone forever, I just didn't want him with…excuse me for what I'm about to say, someone I thought was kind of rachet."

Sheri blinked, then laughed. She wasn't offended. It wasn't the first time someone had tried to label her, and it wouldn't be the last time. "I don't think your dad would be into me if I was."

He smiled. It was the first time he'd smiled at her. "True."

She raised a brow. "So… You're good with me and him together?"

He nodded. "Yeah. If you'll give him a second chance. And, if you're cool with me."

Sheri's mom came from the back into the dining area. "Sheri, his dad is here to see you."

Sheri and DJ swung toward her mom. "Deandre's here?"

Her mom nodded. "He came to the back door and knocked. He's lucky JD didn't hit him with a rolling pin. He scared us knocking on the door like the damn police. You want to see him?"

Sheri and DJ exchanged a look. Deandre was, in fact, the police. But they wouldn't point that out.

"Yes, send him in here." Her mom went back toward the kitchen and Sheri turned to DJ. "Does he know you're here?"

DJ shook his head. "Nah. He left me at home while he went out. I came here on my own."

"Are you going to get in trouble for being here?"

DJ shrugged. "I don't know. Maybe."

Sheri rolled her eyes and sighed. Teenagers. She and Deandre would have a time with him.

Deandre came from the back. He looked at Sheri, then DJ and back at her. Her heart ached with the need to cross the room and wrap her arms around him. She missed being with him so much.

His focus finally settled on his son. "DJ, what are you doing here?"

DJ stood. "I came to thank Ms. Thomas for not pressing charges."

Deandre's worried expression morphed to one of surprise. He clearly hadn't expected that answer. "Oh."

"And, to tell her that I'm good with you two being together." He walked to his dad. "I'll let ya'll talk." DJ placed a hand on his dad's shoulder. He looked back at Sheri, smiled, then went toward the kitchen.

Deandre watched with a slack jaw as his son disappeared into the kitchen. He swung back to Sheri several seconds after DJ disappeared "What did I miss?"

Sheri stood. "I don't think he thought I would give him a second chance. He wanted to know why."

"And when you told him why?"

"Then he understood that I wasn't doing it just because I love you, but because I was given a second chance. I didn't expect him to give us his blessing."

Deandre held up a finger. "Hold up, go back. What did you say?"

"I said I was given a second chance."

He shook his head. "Nah, before that. That you weren't doing it because why?"

Sheri's heart jumped and her palms turned slick. She'd said she loved him. Just blurted it out as if they'd been saying it to each other for years. When she may have jumped the gun. She could brush over it. Take the words back or pretend as if she hadn't said them. But she wasn't the type of person to back down from what she said or lie.

"I said, I didn't just do it because I love you."

Deandre was across the room with his arms around her in two steps. His mouth covered hers and he kissed her as if he'd learned the secret to everlasting happiness and that secret was in her arms. Sheri didn't hesitate. Her arms wrapped around his neck, and she lifted to her toes, pressing her body against his as she kissed him just as desperately. When he broke off the kiss, their breathing was ragged.

"I love you so much," he said in a tight voice. "I missed you. I thought you wouldn't want to be with me after what happened. That's why I came here."

She pulled back and frowned. "You came here to break up with me?"

"No. I came here to convince you that somehow, we'll make this work. That I believed DJ had learned his lesson and, if you were willing, we could start over."

"How did you know DJ would be good with us?"

"He was floored when you dropped the charges. His

grandparents got on him about how wrong he'd been when you'd been nothing but nice to him. He admitted he messed up. I didn't know he would come here."

"I'm glad he came. We needed to talk and air things out. I want to start over with you, too, but I gotta admit, knowing that DJ is okay makes this even better."

"Does that mean you agree? That we'll give this another shot? Even though I once arrested you and my son made a horrible decision that nearly ruined your life?"

Sheri considered everything. What she was agreeing to. To try and heal the rift between her and DJ. To try and make a relationship work with Deandre. To, maybe not be a stepmom right away, but be there for both Deandre and DJ as they figured everything out. All things she never thought she'd want to do. Things she wouldn't have considered if she hadn't met and fallen for the last guy on earth she ever thought she'd be with.

She met his eyes and said with her entire heart, "Yes. Let's give this a shot and see if we've got enough love to make this work."

Deandre grinned and placed his forehead on her. "Lil Bit, we've got more than enough."

* * * * *

A Q&A with Synithia Williams

What or who inspired you to write?

I've always wanted to write, but I remember my grand-mother calling me one day when I was in college or my early twenties. She asked if I was still writing and told me not to give up on my dream. That inspired me to keep writing even when my focus was on school and starting my career.

What is your daily writing routine?

I typically write at night around 9:00 p.m. I work full time, so during the day on my lunch break I try to plot out the scene that I'll write that night. On weekends I work until around 2:00 p.m. and then the rest of the day is free. I don't like writing in silence, so I usually have background music with no words or the sounds of a coffee shop playing.

Where do your story ideas come from?

My ideas come from everywhere. I'll be sitting in a meeting and something will spark an idea. A lot of times they'll come when I'm watching television. Both scripted, documentary and true crime stories can spark an idea. Several ideas will come just from having conversations with people. One sentence will make me wonder "what if?" and then, there it is.

Do you have a favorite travel destination?

I love going to the beach. I've visited Wrightsville Beach, North Carolina; Jacksonville Beach, Florida; and St. Simons Island, Georgia, multiple times.

When did you read your first Harlequin romance? Do you remember its title?

I can't remember what my first one was, but I know I got it from the library when I was around thirteen and it was a Presents. After that, I filled out the form in the middle to get books mailed to me (I really wanted to get mail) and have been reading Harlequin romances ever since.

How did you meet your current love?

I met him at work. We both were in a customer service job. I didn't think he liked me, but I guess he did. Over eighteen years later, we're still together.

What characteristic do you most value in your friends?

I value that they want to get out and enjoy life as much as I do. I love that my friends are open to traveling or just hanging out. My friends will text me the most random things to do (i.e. play tennis or do a mud run) and I'm always down.

How did you celebrate or treat yourself when you got your first book deal?

I was at work when I learned about my first Harlequin deal. A coworker created a certificate for me and gave it to me on her break. I kept that certificate, and it makes me smile every time I look at it. That little celebration is what I remember most. I think I also bought a new laptop.

Will you share your favorite reader response?

I don't have just one response but love it when readers email me. I save each email and when I need a pick-me-up or the writing is hard, I go back and read them. They make me smile and remind me that writing *is* hard because I want readers to laugh, cry and relate to my characters.

Other than author, what job would you like to have?

I want to be a librarian, the person who calls out the lottery numbers or open a bookstore/coffee shop.